OVERWORLD ASCENSION

OVERWORLD CHRONICLES BOOK 20

JOHN CORWIN

RAVEN HOUSE

TO KILL A GOD

Elohim thumbed his nose at Eve's creation and started the countdown to annihilation.

With the relics of Juranthemon reassembled, the realms are collapsing in on themselves. When they hit ground zero, Earth will be recreated in a violent collision, destroying most life in the realms. If Elohim has his way, all life will be extinguished, paving the way for him to recreate things just the way he wants it.

Justin and gang have only one option to save the realms. A primal seed of creation, a crystalis, might provide enough power for their resident demigoddess, Emily, to stop the collapse. Failing that, they might be able to recruit Eve, provided she doesn't go insane and kill them all.

But there are major obstacles. Olivia muted Justin's powers and Emily's powers were corrupted during her last altercation with Eve. Any attempt to use her powers causes an equal and opposite malaether explosion. If she tries to stop the collapse with a crystalis, she'll probably blow up half the universe instead. She can't even reactivate Justin's powers without risking his life.

With only days left until the realms are bulldozed into oblivion, Justin and gang must fix Emily, recruit a mad goddess, and kill Elohim or all life in the Earth realms will be gone forever.

BOOKS BY JOHN CORWIN

CHRONICLES OF CAIN

To Kill a Unicorn

Enter Oblivion

Throne of Lies

THE OVERWORLD CHRONICLES

Sweet Blood of Mine

Dark Light of Mine

Fallen Angel of Mine

Dread Nemesis of Mine

Twisted Sister of Mine

Dearest Mother of Mine

Infernal Father of Mine

Sinister Seraphim of Mine

Wicked War of Mine

Dire Destiny of Ours

Aetherial Annihilation

Baleful Betrayal

Ominous Odyssey

Insidious Insurrection

Utopia Undone

Overworld Apocalypse

Apocryphan Rising

Soul Storm

Devil's Due

Overworld Ascension

<u>Assignment Zero (An Elyssa Short Story)</u>

OVERWORLD UNDERGROUND

Soul Seer

Demonicus

<u>Infernal Blade</u>

OVERWORLD ARCANUM

Conrad Edison and the Living Curse

Conrad Edison and the Anchored World

Conrad Edison and the Broken Relic

<u>Conrad Edison and the Infernal Design</u>

<u>Conrad Edison and the First Power</u>

STAND ALONE NOVELS

Mars Rising

No Darker Fate

The Next Thing I Knew

Outsourced

For the latest on new releases, free ebooks, and more, join John Corwin's Newsletter at www.johncorwin.net!

1

The world ended in the blink of an eye.

It had not been the outcome Xanos expected. Long had she waited with bated breath for the final showdown. Long had she sown the seeds of distrust among her siblings, spread rumors around the land to draw them to Juranthemon. To attract Elohim, she'd sent word far and wide that Eve had achieved a perfect creation, a new demigod no other god could create.

To attract the Apocryphan, she'd leaked rumors that Elohim planned to destroy Eve's work and wrest control of the world from her children. Kathazal and his lackeys had grown too drunk with power to let even one of the original gods get in their way.

The plan had worked perfectly to a point, but this was not what she had intended. Had creation itself been utterly destroyed? Where the world had once been there was now nothing but a white void. Eve's grand design had been wiped clean leaving a blank canvas.

Xanos wondered how she alone had been spared from the destruction. True, she had shielded herself so she might watch the battle royal from the comfort of her position, but even her shield could not have withstood destruction on such a grand scale.

She propelled herself through the emptiness, unable to tell if she was actually moving without a point of reference. A slight ripple against the white drew her attention to the general area where Saila and Elohim stood only moments ago. By channeling gray mist she was able to highlight dozens more of the rippling anomalies. Hesitantly, she reached out and touched one.

Pleasant warmth greeted her fingers, so she thrust her arm deeper inside where it vanished from view. A gentle breeze coursed against her skin. Xanos put her head into the ripple. A rocky plain appear. Ocean waves crashed against a distant shore. Ocean birds soared on the horizon.

What is this? she wondered.

Xanos stepped into the ripple and once again found herself in the sun. Ocean water sparkled beneath blue skies. The wind bent scrubby bushes along the rocky shores. But the perfect day was marred by evidence that the world had not ended without cost.

Bodies were strewn across the rocky ground, some burned, others torn to pieces, while more than a few looked perfectly whole. Among them walked the living, moaning, crying, and confused. A quick look told Xanos they were all humans.

Some saw her and ran screaming at the sight of an Apocryphan. The others looked toward the disturbance, and those that could run followed the others, a flock of sheep fleeing the wolf. Xanos didn't care. She had no questions to ask of them because they knew even less than she did about what had happened.

She returned to the anomaly and stepped back into the white void. She chose another ripple and went through, this time finding herself in a desert. Xanos took to the air but found no signs of life. Once again, she returned to the void and selected another ripple, repeating the process to see what lay on the other side of each.

There were worlds of endless forests, one of nothing but water, another covered by blubbery flesh that tried to eat her the moment she stepped on it. There was no explanation for what had happened. Xanos knew of the multiverse, having spent time battling outsiders, but this was something else entirely.

These new worlds resembled far off lands such as the Azure

Forest of the Seraphim lands, or the Crimson Desert of the Nazdal territory. She recognized the carnivorous lands of Hell, Dragons Mount, and the flying cats of the fae forest.

It was as if Earth had been split into multiple dimensions—independent realms with characteristics carried over from their origins. After visiting hundreds of different worlds, Xanos rested on the world with the beach, giving herself time to process what had happened. When she woke, the gateway had grown noticeably smaller.

"My time is limited," she said to herself. It was evident she'd have to find the ideal world and make it her home until she understood the scope of what had happened.

Back in the void, she chose another gateway. This one resisted her flesh, pushing back as if it meant to admit only her soul. Xanos closed her eyes and projected her consciousness into the gateway. What she found on the other side shocked her to her core.

Juranthemon stood before her, whole and unharmed. Beings of pure energy wailed in the streets, many of them still bearing semblance to the physical forms they'd held not so long ago. There in the center of Unity Plaza stood a man in a striped robe turning in circles, casting his gaze about as if unable to believe his eyes.

It was Elohim, or what was left of him.

"This is not the afterlife," Xanos murmured. "What is this place?"

The spirit of a Siren cried out. "Where am I?" She shimmered like a mirage, red energy sparkling beneath her surface.

Elohim snarled and gripped her throat. "Quiet!" He held her off the ground. "Silence!"

She flailed uselessly in his grasp. Energy poured from her mouth and into his, sparks flying whenever she tried to wrench herself free. Within seconds, only Elohim remained, his body now glowing with the essence of the stolen spirit.

His gaze settled on Xanos. "You, Apocryphan!" Elohim crossed the distance in an instant, hand grasping for her throat.

Xanos gasped and withdrew the projection. Panting with fear, she stared at the gateway, hoping Elohim didn't come after her. Her frightened mind finally calmed. It seemed Elohim was no longer in physical form and could not come through the gateway after her. He seemed to be trapped in a realm similar to the afterlife, and yet was not.

Xanos grinned. Perhaps her siblings had suffered the same fate. Surely, they had to be in one of the nearby realms. She flooded the area with gray mist to highlight any portals she might have missed. As she glided among them, something caught her eye. It was small and transparent, nearly invisible if not for the mist.

She plucked it from the nothingness and examined it. It was a crystal no larger than a human hand, roughly hewn but clear. It looked familiar, but Xanos couldn't remember where she'd seen it. And what was it doing here?

Only one person could answer her questions right now and that was Mother. The only question was whether Xanos could locate Eve before the portals vanished. It was also possible Eve wouldn't be in any of the new worlds. She was known to create her own hidden worlds and hide for centuries at a time.

Xanos located a portal she hadn't marked and entered it. An endless expanse of water was on the other side. Countless bodies drifted in the waves below. Their blood stained the ocean deep red as far as the eye could see.

A massive seashell floating above the water caught her eye. Dozens of water dragons perched on the topmost spines. Humanoid figures stood in the hollow below. The coral shades of their hair told Xanos they were Sirens.

She flew to them, landing lightly on the edge of their refuge.

"Xanos?" One with a regal bearing strode up to her. "Where did you come from?"

"I awoke moments ago and found myself here," Xanos lied. "What happened?"

The Siren shook her head. "We have filled the world with a song of seeking. Earth is no more, but we sense multiple worlds in its place, all occupying the same space but across multiple quantum realms."

The Sirens were perhaps the most intelligent beings Eve had

created. Their analytical nature made them Kathazal's favorites. Zon, on the other hand, preferred the raw power of the Seraphim and the warlike nature of the Nazdal.

Xanos identified with the cunning nature of the fae, but respected the logic of the Sirens. Abiding among them might be the best choice if she wished to understand what happened.

"Kathazal has gone to explore this world," the Siren said. "Perhaps he will be pleased to learn you survived the destruction." Her tone of voice indicated the opposite. It was no secret that Xanos was an outcast.

Xanos grinned. "Do not patronize me, Siren. I know I am unwelcome among my kin."

The Siren nodded. "Then do not lie about having been here, Outcast. Our song would have found you earlier."

"You must be Vitania."

The Siren nodded. "I am the first of my people."

"Such intelligence." Xanos shrugged and held up the crystal. "Perhaps you can tell me what this is."

Another Siren gasped. "That is what caused the refractions in our song."

Vitania backed away from Xanos. "Where did you get that?"

"The void where Earth once was." Xanos enjoyed the confusion that flickered across their faces.

Vitania shook her head. "That is a crystalis, an extremely rare seed of creation formed where the infernal and primal founts intersect. It must have been in the vicinity when the Apocryphan struck down Saila."

Xanos examined it. "I sense no power in this thing."

"Because its energy has been spent." Vitania shook her head. "That must be what created this new existence."

"So, it is useless?"

"I cannot say." Vitania held out a hand. "May I see it?"

Xanos reluctantly handed it over.

The Siren sang softly to the crystalis, taking her time divining what she could while Xanos kept a wary lookout on the horizon. She did not want to be here when Kathazal returned. He would know or at least suspect that Xanos had a hand in the events that shattered Earth and would torture her relentlessly.

Vitania grew quiet and gave the crystal back to Xanos. "It is no longer what it once was. Somehow it has transmuted into something indestructible."

"A crystalis can be destroyed?" Xanos asked

Vitania nodded. "It is extremely hard to do, but it can be done. The magical properties of this object have entered a state of immutability. I have never seen it before, but this object cannot be destroyed unless it is somehow transmuted back to its original state."

A group of Sirens approached them. The lead one bowed slightly at Vitania but ignored Xanos entirely. "The council has come to a decision after a careful analysis."

Vitania nodded. "I am pleased to hear that, Dactia."

"This event shall henceforth be known as the Sundering," the council leader said. "Earth is shattered into realms and ours will be named after our homeland, Aquilis."

"The council's decision is wise," Vitania said. "There is much work to be done. We must determine if travel is possible between these realms and how to achieve that."

Xanos nearly told them about the portals but there seemed no point since they would soon be gone. "Thank you for your help. I will take my leave."

Vitania reached out for Xanos. Her hands looked tiny in comparison to those of an Apocryphan, but the Siren took no note of that. "I will make no mention of your part in this Xanos. We knew of your plan to lure your Apocryphan brethren into a battle. We supported your efforts in the hopes it might free the world from tyranny. I am sad that your plan failed spectacularly."

Xanos scowled. "Goodbye."

"Xanos." Vitania held out a hand. "The crystalis is at the core of the event. Perhaps if you left it with us, we could undo the Sundering."

"No, I have other plans." Xanos launched into the air and flew back to the portal. She had no other plans and was, in fact, at a total loss of what to do next. The portal was too small for her natural size to fit, so she shrank her form to the size of a human and squeezed through.

She quickly explored other unmarked portals. One was too tropical. The next was an arid desert and the one after that a frigid wasteland. The portals were dwindling too quickly for her to explore them all. She considered returning to the one with the humans but couldn't bring herself to be trapped for an eternity with the dreadful creatures.

Then again, anything would be preferable to existing in this nothingness. She peered into another new portal and was heartened at what she found. Fae and animal corpses were scattered as far as the eye could see. The earth was saturated with blood, burned, and looked as if it had been hammered with meteors.

It was perfect.

Xanos felt an affinity for the fae that few of the other Apocryphan shared. In fact, her siblings often ignored the fae because they were such difficult creatures to control. Their ruthless cunning and clever tricks often caused their ruler, Araxos, to go mad with frustration.

The portal dwindled down to a point of light and vanished, leaving Xanos in her new home. She immediately regretted her decision. Perhaps remaining with the Sirens would have been the best course of action. They were already formulating ways to travel the realms which meant Kathazal would soon have access to such magic at his disposal. For the time being, there was nothing to do but wait and plot her next moves.

Xanos had barely decided which way to go when a gateway slashed open and a figure blurred through, striking her so hard she plummeted to earth and plowed through bodies and bloodstained soil. An iron vice squeezed her neck and lifted her only to slam her back down repeatedly until she began to lose consciousness.

The pummeling relented. A hand gripped her arm and flipped her onto her back. Her blurry vision cleared to reveal the enraged face of a goddess.

"Why?" Eve growled, tears streaming down her face. She ripped the crystalis from Xanos's grasp and held it before her nose. "Why would you destroy all that I have created, you ungrateful creature?"

Xanos tried to answer but blood bubbled in her mouth and spattered on Eve's face.

The goddess took no notice of the blood and wrapped a hand around Eve's neck. "Explain yourself, daughter!"

Xanos choked out a response. "Not...mine."

Eve's eyes narrowed and her gaze seemed to bore into Xanos's soul. After a long moment she nodded. "Not even you could possibly reach the primal core. You are neither a god, nor a child of paradise."

"Elohim's." Xanos tried to loosen Eve's grip on her neck. "Elohim's!"

The goddess relented, rising into the air a few feet off the ground. "Tell me everything, Xanomiel."

Xanos didn't like hearing her given name, for it meant Little Accident. The name she'd chosen for herself was similar but better—Clever One. At the moment, she didn't feel very clever. In fact, everything about her plans felt accidental.

She staggered to her feet and wiped the blood-crusted dirt from her eyes. "Can we go elsewhere for the story? I would—"

"No!" Eve screamed. "Face what you have wrought, little accident! Sit amidst the death you have caused."

"It is nothing compared to the death caused by my siblings!" Xanos shouted back.

A maniacal laugh erupted from Eve's mouth, echoing across the land and far beyond. "What you have done today dwarfs all deaths since creation, you clever little fool." The laugh morphed to sobs. "Over a million sentient beings dead, and tens of millions of innocent animals slaughtered."

"It was the crystalis!" Xanos said. "Elohim did this."

Eve shook her head. "No, Elohim was lured to this doom like everyone else."

How does she know? Xanos wondered.

"Tell me everything." Eve slowly smoothed the air with her hand

and the ground beneath her swallowed the dead. The blood drained, leaving pristine white sand. She drifted to the ground and sat cross-legged. "Tell your mother a story."

And so Xanos did.

When she was done, Eve spat in her face. "I fear undoing this will cause even more death and destruction." She examined the crystalis. "This was the center of it all—the very cause. Perhaps it is also the key."

"Not my fault," Xanos said softly.

"I cannot even sense the other dimensions anymore." Eve shook her head. "Our very existence has been knocked from its axis. Now I shall have no idea what the outsider gods are doing, or what we should fear."

"Then we Apocryphan are no longer your little soldiers." Eve had sought to make demigods for extra protection against the outsider gods, but the Apocryphan had turned into subjugators, instead of liberators. Xanos met her mother's gaze. "I have made us safe."

"You dare take credit for the apocalypse?" Eve laughed. "You should have never been born."

Help.

A weak voice echoed in her head. Movement caught Xanos's eye. Something struggled beneath the weight of a pile of corpses not far away. She stood and pushed the bodies of fae and beasts aside to reveal a unicorn. Blood stained its silver hide, and a long gash nearly separated its head from the body.

Somehow, it was still alive.

"Another victim." Eve bared her teeth. "Witness your great reward, Xanomiel."

"You can save it," Xanos said in a soft voice.

Eve shook her head. "No. I pray it stains your soul with regret, Little Accident." She slashed open a gateway and vanished inside, leaving Xanos alone with the dying beast.

2

The Sundering had been so long ago Xanos could not even guess what it meant in mortal years. A hundred-thousand years at the very least. And now it was soon to be over. Baal had reassembled his body, returning himself to flesh. The realms should have snapped back together in that very instant, but they hadn't.

And Xanos knew why.

When Justin had left her inside the time echo, Xanos had gone to ground zero. She wanted to make certain it was Elohim who held the crystalis. She was shocked to discover it had been Apollyon who wore it on a chain around his neck. Where he had gotten it from, Xanos had no idea.

When the Apocryphan attacked and Elohim responded, Apollyon had thrown himself between the attacks. Whether he'd hope to die or save his father was a mystery. Instead, the crystalis had refracted the attacks in one violent act of creation, shattering Earth into multiple dimensions.

Xanos knew where her historic self would be, but she had no desire to see her. Instead, she stood next to Apollyon. When he dove, she grabbed the crystalis, hoping to die. It seemed fitting that her end came at the moment of her greatest failure.

Her entire being felt as if it caught fire just before her consciousness blinked away to nothing. But some interminable time later, Xanos awoke. Something new burned at the very core of her being. It seemed the crystalis had created something within her. What it was, she didn't know.

She'd flown from the time echo, eager to tell the others, but Saila attacked her. Xanos no longer needed them, for she was once again a goddess. She'd opened a gateway and found herself in Pangea, home of the fae. The same place she'd lived after the Sundering.

The continent was thriving, full of diverse creatures both old and new—a stark difference from all those eons ago.

Now Xanos sat on a cliff overlook deep blue sea. She'd had time to contemplate a great deal over the past few days. Though Emily Glass had seemingly removed her powers, neither she nor Xanos had realized that there was a small part that was inseparable from the whole —a broken root of power. It might have eventually blossomed into full powers again after several millennia, but that wasn't certain.

What seemed certain was that the crystalis in the time echo had created life within that torn out part of her, regrown it in an instant. Her body had not regrown to its normal size, but it felt stronger and able to handle the strain of her powers. Xanos was once again free to do as she willed. She had learned what happened between Baal and Justin Slade and heard the theories put forth by Vitania.

They thought the Abyss and the Anchor Stone were keeping the realms from snapping back together. But that was not it at all. There was one key element missing, and it was the crystalis relic. Eve had taken it from Xanos on that fateful day and there was no telling what she'd done with it. If Baal found it, then the Mending, as he called it, would happen in a heartbeat.

If it was never found, the Mending would still happen, but much more slowly over years or decades. What Xanos couldn't understand was how the crystalis hadn't been drawn back to the origin like other relics. It was a mystery, and one she wanted to solve.

It seemed Xanos had a second chance to become a ruler over all. And if she had possession of the crystalis at the moment the realms slammed back together, she would wield the power of a god.

And the best part?

Elohim wasn't even aware of the crystalis. He didn't know it hadn't been his power that had Sundered Earth in the first place. Xanos shivered with delight. This was her second chance. She could recombine the Earth and redeem herself in her mother's eyes, then use the crystalis to remake it as she willed, becoming a true god even more powerful than Elohim and Eve.

But first she needed to find Apollyon and discover how and where he acquired the original crystalis. Perhaps she could gather more of them and become even more powerful. The poor boy was so dimwitted she could probably ask him outright. But first, she had to reach him before Elohim killed him.

It was almost certain that Apollyon was in Hell with his father. Xanos would have to be extremely careful going there because she was no match for Elohim. She stood and closed her eyes, listening to the waves crash against the cliff, the call of the sea birds, the distant roar of a beast in the jungle.

She envisioned the steps necessary to reach Apollyon, the words needed to coax the information from him. The keys to success would be stealth and speed.

A gentle whicker nudged her from her thoughts.

A unicorn with a silver hide and golden horn tapped its hoof on the rocks. *You have returned?*

Xanos blinked. "Astra?"

It is good to see you, old friend.

"I have not seen you since the dawn of the realms." Xanos shook her head. "I am hardly a friend."

You saved me and my kind on that fateful day. If not for you, we would have died. Not even Eve lifted a hand to aid us.

That day had been so chaotic, but Xanos could never forget the punishment Eve tried to lay on her shoulders. Xanos was not skilled at healing, but she had learned much from the fae and the Lyrolai who lived among them.

She stanched the blood flow with stasis, then dashed into the forest. It didn't take her long to find the red moss with magical healing properties, or the coppery root that numbed pain. She gathered ingredients and knelt by the injured unicorn, clumsily doing what little she could to thwart Eve's punishment.

When Astra was stable, Xanos had sought other wounded unicorns, healing and saving thirteen. They were the only survivors of a once mighty herd of hundreds.

One by one, Xanos carried the wounded creatures into safe glade where she fed and nursed them back to health. The day Astra stood and ate under her own power, Xanos had flown to the highest mountain and cried victory into the skies.

"I have beaten you, Mother!" Xanos raised a fist. "One day your little accident will rule your creations!"

Xanos couldn't look Astra in the eye because the guilt was too much to bear. She looked down. "I did not save you out of kindness. Your death was to be punishment from my mother and I could not allow her to win."

It only took you eons to admit that. Astra nickered and bobbed her head. *You have grown.*

"You knew?" Xanos looked away. "How?"

Astra's whicker almost sounded like laughter. *You did nothing that was not in your self-interest, Xanos.*

"What other reason is there for existing if not to advance yourself?"

I think you already know.

"How did you even know I was here?" Xanos asked.

On the day you saved me, our blood mixed and we bonded. Astra nuzzled Xanos's arm. *You are always welcome among our herd, clever one.* She turned and galloped away into the forest.

Xanos stared in that direction for a long time before turning back toward the ocean. She didn't like the mixed feelings stirring inside her. The thought of letting Elohim or Eve win filled her with anger and thoughts of revenge. There was nothing greater than outwitting more powerful opponents. No greater reward than watching them fall from their perch.

From this moment on, her existence would revolve around stripping Elohim of his powers and dooming him to die a mortal. With a crystalis, Xanos could achieve all her goals and more. Without Elohim and Eve, a mended Earth would become the ideal world it should have been long ago.

3

A massive torrent of green power slammed into Elohim's shield. Teeth bared in a feral grin, he summoned a counterstrike and unleashed it on the Apocryphan. His wide silver beam crashed into theirs, creating a miniature star where they intersected. Together, the Apocryphan were strong—stronger even than him.

He had no choice but to—

"Father!" Apollyon leapt into the air, throwing his body directly into the inferno.

"Pause." Elyssa stopped the playback from the ASE and jabbed a finger at the figure diving toward Apollyon. "That's definitely Xanos."

Shelton peered at the image like a man who needed reading glasses. "Hard to tell with the glare."

"I can't get it any clearer," Elyssa said. "There's too much interference."

"I think it's her too." I zoomed in for a better look, but the flare from the roiling star of destruction obfuscated the details. "It looks like she's holding onto something."

"That's what I thought." Elyssa narrowed her eyes. "Apollyon was wearing a chain with a diamond on it."

"Yeah." In all the excitement since seeing him in the time echo, I'd forgotten about that detail. "I don't think that was an ordinary diamond."

"How isn't she dead?" Adam scratched his head and leaned back his chair.

I shrugged and turned my gaze around the conference room. It had been a week since Baal finished reassembling himself from lost relics of Juranthemon and become a full-fledged god once again. Now he was Elohim, one of the old gods who'd created Earth and I didn't know how we could possibly stop what he'd put in motion.

Shelton grunted and projected a video from his arcphone. "The noms are in a real tizzy about it already."

A news reporter stood outside a perimeter surrounded by police and the Portuguese military. What had once been rocky terrain covered in scrub brush was now covered by shimmering tiles of the unknown substance used to construct Juranthemon's foundation. The massive pedestals that once held the statues of the Apocryphan were in various stages of reconstruction.

Ironically, the kneeling statue of Xanos was already complete.

The place where Elohim's reconstituted body once stood was empty as was Apollyon's. Both had returned to physical form. Another statue that had once been a person stood nearby. From what I could tell, Saila's former body was almost complete. All it lacked was her soul, a relic that currently resided in Cutsauce, the first hellhound I'd ever summoned.

"Jura is rebuilding itself," Elyssa said. "We have until it's completed before the realms snap back together."

I frowned. "The entire city, or just the area at the focal point?"

"We know from relics like the lost room that everything along the main thoroughfare was turned into a relic." Adam steepled his fingers. "The major artifacts were all in Unity Plaza at the time of destruction. I assume that many of the people present for the Sundering might also be resurrected."

"The gravity pulling me to my fate is almost unbearable." Saila wiped sweat from her brow. "The strain of remaining here is exhausting. I do not know how much longer I can hold myself in this body."

I shook my head. "Hang on as long as you can. There's got to be a way to stop this."

I won't let it take her, Justin! Cutsauce said inside my head.

Vitania stared at the frozen image of Apollyon, Elohim, and Xanos. "I would like to visit the time echo to see this diamond you speak of."

Adam tapped on his arcphone. "It reset a little while ago, so we've got about an hour until the main event."

Saila sighed. "I wish I could see it for myself." As a relic of Jura, she couldn't enter the time remnant.

There was nothing better to do, so I stood up. "Then let's go."

We filed out of the conference room and went down the corridor. The underground facility was nearly empty since Thomas had deployed all active Templars to Portugal. Even now, he and the Custodians were trying to cover up the massive anomaly. The magical rebuilding of an ancient civilization had already attracted international attention and it didn't seem likely there was any way to keep the cat in the bag.

And what was the point, anyway? When Earth recombined, it would completely alter the lives of anyone who survived.

We reached the travelling room, a large empty space set aside for opening portals. Vitania slashed open a portal to the burned-out mansion in the Fairy Gardens, a hop, skip, and a jump away from Arcane University.

Elyssa's phone dinged as we stepped through the portal. She tapped on her screen and grunted. "The Templars have deployed ASEs around the perimeter of Jura. They're going to deploy mass minders and illusion in their first attempt."

Minders were beings from the Gloom, a dreamland version of the real world. There, the minders harvested the dreams of sentient beings and converted the energy into aether. Every human had a minder in the Gloom, but not all minders had humans. When a human died, their minder typically faded away unless it was given new purpose. The Templars had long been employing orphaned minders as sentries for Overworld cities like La Casona that existed in the middle of the nom world.

Though they resembled floating brains with tentacles, minders weren't the stuff of nightmares. They could, however, alter the memories of humans and make them forget seeing things such as alien cities magically appearing in Portugal. Since they couldn't alter the memories of everyone who'd seen the images on the news, I had no idea how the Custodians planned to fix that.

Adam adjusted the floating platform supporting the portal generator. The large white ring had been constructed by Xanos's private army, Razor Echelon, so they could easily travel between realms in her quest to conquer the realmverse. Adam, Cinder, and Xanos had modified it so it could also hold open the portal between our world and the time echo.

Saila channeled liquid Stasis and poured it on the ground, revealing the scar in the fabric of space-time. Not even Adam or Cinder knew how to classify the bizarre anomaly. It had been created when Serena Thain used an anti-magic staff on Conrad and Ambria just as they used a blink stone, the most common sort of relic. It had transported them into an echo of the past only hours before the Sundering split the world.

We'd discovered a great deal of useful information from the time loop, but in the end it hadn't helped us stop Baal. To top it off, Xanos had somehow regained her powers and was on the loose. Anything and everything had gone wrong in our final attempts to prevent the end days and now all we could do was wait and pray the death toll and destruction wouldn't be as devastating as predicted.

Saila ripped open the portal to a white void.

Adam's forehead scrunched. He checked his arcphone, then looked back into the portal. "What the hell?"

Cinder activated the portal generator. The gems along the ring glowed. Beams speared from them and against the edges of the portal. The ring hummed and rose under its own power off the levitating platform. It rotated and aligned with the portal, then dropped onto it, forming a seal to keep it open.

Adam continued frowning and tapping on his phone. "There isn't anything on the other side."

"According to my chronometer, the echo should have reset." Cinder joined him at the portal. "After Xanos flew out of the time echo, we never deactivated the portal generator so it ran out of power and the portal closed. Perhaps that altered the anomaly."

Adam shook his head. "No, the gateway would have just closed."

I knelt at the hole in the ground and stared into the white void. "Vitania, can you help me test something?"

"Of course." The Siren joined me.

"Can you open a portal to Eden within the void?" The void was just the empty space where Earth had once been before being torn from its place in the multiverse and split into hundreds of pocket-dimension realms like Eden and Seraphina. Which meant she should be able to open a portal to the time loop version of Eden.

Vitania nodded and dropped into the hole.

Several of us shouted in alarm at her sudden maneuver, but instead of falling into the infinite space, she held out her arms and slowed to a stop. Then she traced symbols in the air and slashed her hand through them to open the portal.

Much to my dismay, nothing happened.

Vitania tried symbols to other realms, but none worked. She looked up at me. "I take it you've done this before?"

"Yeah." I shook my head. "I was able to visit newly formed realms."

She nodded and rose from the hole, levitating to firm ground next to me. "I believe I know what happened."

"But you haven't even read our whitepapers on the time echo," Adam said.

Vitania smiled. "I have knowledge that predates yours. It helped me form a conclusion with only a miniscule margin for error."

"I am curious to hear it," Cinder said.

"Though the image captured by your device wasn't perfectly clear, I believe the diamond is actually a crystalis." Vitania paused a moment as if to allow time for the inevitable query.

Saila gasped.

Adam scratched his head. "A what?"

I felt proud of myself for not blurting the obvious question before anyone else.

Elyssa nudged me. "You're losing your touch, babe."

I snorted. "Or maybe I'm learning a different touch."

"That sounds perverted."

I slipped an arm around her waist. "Oh, it is."

"A crystalis is a rare seed of creation formed in the nexus of the infernal and primal founts." She plucked a seashell from seemingly out of nowhere and projected an image from it.

Countless glowing lines branched in all directions with no beginning and no end. Some lines were blue, and others were orange. Orbs of energy occasionally flared where the blue and orange lines met. At the very center of the web was a single star that alternated between azure blue and orange. It took me a moment to realize that the lines represented the infernal and primal founts.

Vitania traced a finger along the lines. "In the beginning, there was a single point of incredible energy. It exploded, spreading outward, forming a web." She pointed to the central star. "The infernal and primal founts originally sprang from the universal core, spreading across every dimension, but also birthing smaller cores that have grown larger over the eons, giving them life of their own."

She traced back to the center. "Sometimes, a diamond-like object filled with incredible power forms at the core and finds its way through the network to a fountainhead. We call this object a crystalis."

"And they're extremely rare?" Elyssa said.

Vitania nodded. "The odds of one appearing on old Earth were much greater. With the world split into realms, the odds decreased exponentially."

I tried to wrap my head around her explanation. "If the primal and infernal founts spring from a common node, wouldn't that be a source of incredible power?"

Vitania nodded. "But only gods have the power to actually reach the nodes."

"Makes perfect sense." Adam tapped away on his arcphone, probably jotting everything down for his records. "Am I correct in guessing the crystalis could be used by other beings?"

"Yes." Vitania pursed her lips. "These so-called seeds of creation could be used by those of lesser power, though sparingly, lest they burn themselves out."

Elyssa tapped a finger on her chin. "How does this explain what happened to the time echo?"

"Adam told me that you could be harmed or killed within the time echo," Vitania said. "That indicates to me that this anomaly held full-fledged gods and demigods. It would also stand to reason that the crystalis carried by Apollyon also held its full power." She clasped her hands before her. "I surmise that Xanos tried to kill herself, but instead the crystalis rebirthed the powers stolen from her by Emily Glass."

I sucked in a breath between my teeth. "You're telling me we could have stolen the powers of gods from the time loop and used them ourselves?"

Vitania nodded. "It's even possible Emily could have stolen powers from the Elohim of the loop."

"What broke the time loop?" Adam said.

"My theory is that Xanos accidentally stole the power intended to create the realms. This broke the loop."

"Ah." Cinder nodded. "We thought the loop was unbreakable."

I groaned. "So, Xanos accidentally regained her powers because she wanted to kill herself. That is seriously messed up."

"No shit." Shelton sighed. "It's two girls one cup all over again, and Eden is the cup."

Adam gagged. "Worst analogy ever."

Cinder pursed his lips. "That would make Xanos and Elohim the two girls."

Shelton burst into laughter. "Oh, man, now that's a mental image."

I wanted to laugh. Wanted to forget the horror of what was to come. Knowing that we could have stolen Elohim's powers for our own only to have the opportunity stolen by Xanos made me sick to my stomach.

Vitania put a hand on my shoulder. "Do not let it trouble you too much, Justin. Wresting those powers from Elohim would have been nearly impossible, even for Emily. It's also possible she might not have been able to fully use them, just as your body cannot handle the full might of Apocryphan powers."

I threw up my hands. "I don't know what to do next. I feel like I'm watching a train wreck in slow motion."

Vitania's brow furrowed. "This reminds me of a memory long forgotten. Right after the Sundering, Xanos appeared in the newly created realm of Aquilis bearing a depleted crystalis." Her eyes widened. "I cannot believe I'm only now remembering this."

Shelton scoffed. "I can barely remember what I ate for lunch yesterday."

"Even the minds of Sirens can't possibly hold onto everything," Cinder said. "No matter how significant."

"There was so much happening so fast, and I didn't want to tell Kathazal that Xanos had been there." Vitania seemed to nod to herself. "It was not the raw power of the Apocryphan and Elohim that created the realms, but the crystalis caught in the middle of an enormous outpouring of destructive energy."

Adam looked up from his phone. "Was the crystalis itself turned into a relic of Jura?"

"Yes, it was." Vitania hissed. "And Xanos had it."

I looked back and forth between them. "Which means what?"

"I am unsure." Vitania turned to Elyssa. "I would like to review the ASE footage again."

"Sure." Elyssa pointed vaguely in front of her. "We'll need to go back to the Ranch."

Saila's eyes widened. She reached for me and collapsed. Her body convulsed and went still.

"Saila!" I knelt next to her and put a hand to her forehead. Before I even touched her, she began to morph, shrinking down to a small purple-toned Chihuahua.

Cutsauce whimpered weakly. *She is gone.*

4

"Oh, shit." I picked up Cutsauce. "Are you okay?"

Yes.

Shelton grimaced. "Please don't tell me—"

"Saila is gone." I swallowed hard. "We need to get back to the Ranch ASAP."

Vitania opened a portal and the group filed through back to the travelling room in the underground complex. I tuned into the nom news on my arcphone as I jogged down the corridor. There were even more soldiers guarding the slowly reappearing city of Juranthemon as the realms continued their inexorable collapse.

A female reporter pointed toward Unity plaza where Elohim, Apollyon, and Saila had been standing at the moment of the Sundering. "Something is happening!"

The camera zoomed toward the statue of Saila. The outstretched hands shaded light purple. The robes billowed in the wind. A moment later, Saila cried out and spun in place, clearly confused by the cameras. Orbs of destructive power coalesced around her hands. She shook her head and spun to face something off camera.

"Over there!" the reporter shouted.

The camera shifted as another portal tore open. Elohim and Apollyon stepped out, flanked by Olivia.

"Welcome back, sweet Saila." Elohim smiled broadly. "We have front row seats for the end days and room for one more if you'd care to join us."

Saila shook her head. "I will never join you, Elohim!"

"Holy farting fairies." Shelton grimaced. "Now we've lost everything."

"Not yet we haven't." I turned to Vitania. "Take us there."

Vitania shook her head. "Are you insane? We cannot fight Olivia, much less Elohim."

"I don't give a damn." I clasped my hands as if in prayer. "Please, Vitania. We can't let them take Saila."

Vitania sighed and concentrated on the image. "We must make this quick."

I nodded. "I'm ready."

Elyssa grabbed my arm. "Justin, get in, grab Saila, and run."

"That's the plan." I manifested into partial demon form, growing just large enough not to rip out of my clothes.

Cutsauce whimpered. *I can help!*

I shook my head. "Stay here. If this works it'll only take a second."

Vitania raised an eyebrow. "Ready?"

"Ready." I hoped my Daemos abilities would be enough since Olivia had muted my Seraphim and Apocryphan powers. I reached for them instinctively, but it was like trying to control a severed limb. Anxiety welled in my chest, but I pushed it back. Now was not the time for a panic attack.

Vitania ripped open a portal right next to Saila. I dashed out to grab her. A torrent of orange power blasted the earth in front of Saila. The shock threw me to the side.

Olivia burst into laughter. "Justin Slade, what in the hell are you doing here?"

I climbed to my feet. "Saila, into the portal now!"

Saila summoned a shield and blocked another attack from Olivia. "Justin?"

"Yes, it's me." I dodged a blast from Olivia. "Get into the portal."

"Come now, grandson." Elohim spread his arms wide. "Would you deny Saila a chance to view the apocalypse?"

"You're such a jackass, dude!" I raised a fist. "You got what you wanted, so why can't you just leave us alone?"

Elohim shrugged. "The universe favors me, boy. I believe it is long overdue for a makeover."

"Justin, get your ass in here!" Elyssa shouted from the other side of the portal.

Olivia blasted the earth around Saila's feet. "If you don't come with us, I'll annihilate all these pesky humans."

Despite the threat of obliteration, the news crews didn't budge. Maybe they didn't believe this was real. Maybe they thought it was an elaborate prank.

Saila's shoulders slumped. "I will go with them."

I wanted to object, but how could I? There was nothing I could do to stop Olivia from murdering every last nom in the vicinity.

Saila turned to me and murmured. "Look at Apollyon."

"Come this instant," Olivia said. "No heartfelt goodbyes."

"As you say." Saila rose into the air and flew toward them.

They went through the portal. Elohim smirked at me as it winked shut.

I took a good look at Apollyon just before the portal closed but couldn't understand what Saila had wanted me to see.

A group of soldiers, weapons at the ready, marched toward me, shouting commands in Portuguese. I held up my hands in surrender and backed toward Vitania's portal.

"Who are you and what's happening?" a reporter shouted from outside the lines.

I jumped back through the portal and Vitania closed it behind me.

"Son of a bitch!" I slammed a fist into my other palm.

"What did she say to you?" Vitania asked.

"She told me to look at Apollyon for some reason." I shrugged.

"He looked just like he did the last time I saw him—green-skinned and still wearing that nasty orange robe."

Adam peered at his phone. "The reporter I was watching looked at his face and started bawling." He flicked a finger across his screen. "Another crying reporter, and another. Geeze, you'd think they'd figure it out."

Apollyon was physically perfect, too beautiful to behold for mere mortals and even most immortals. But his power was corrupted, causing everything around him to degenerate into chaos. His only wish was for his father to kill him. I was surprised Elohim hadn't done it yet.

"What could she have meant?" Adam stared at the phone. "Apollyon looks like he did last time we saw him."

Cutsauce, now back in his purple Chihuahua form, growled as he stalked in circles. *I could have torn out Elohim's throat!*

Cinder pursed his lips and studied Adam. "I find it curious that viewing a recording of him does not affect you as it did when you met him in person in the time echo."

Adam sighed. "You're never going to let me live that down, are you?"

Shelton snorted. "I thought it was cute."

"Perhaps it is his corruption aura that causes the reaction," Cinder said.

Elyssa peered at the arcphone over Adams's shoulder. "Apollyon isn't wearing the rusty chain with the diamond."

Adam snapped his fingers. "That must be what she meant."

Vitania put a finger under her chin, eyes distant. "As I said, Xanos had the crystalis all those eons ago. It is possible that it hasn't rejoined the other relics."

I thought back to the moment Elohim and Apollyon were reborn. "I don't remember seeing it when Apollyon came back to life. That chain was hard to miss."

"Perhaps it is too powerful an object to be recreated." Vitania pursed her lips. "However, if it did turn into a relic and has not reappeared, then that could be significant."

That reminded me of the question I'd asked before Saila collapsed. "You said it might have been destroyed."

"Possible, but unlikely now that I consider the events." Vitania traced glowing lines in the air, weaving an equation that was too complex for my mind to comprehend.

Adam peered at it like a man trying to see the road through a foggy windshield. "Is that a multi-dimensional quantum equation?"

Vitania's eyebrows rose in surprise. "That you would even recognize it is impressive."

"I studied your notes in the quantum codex to help me modify Xanos's portal generator." He shrugged. "I still don't understand most of it."

She patted his head as if comforting her favorite pet. "You are a bright one, child. I wish Eve had given humans better brain capacity."

Adam frowned. "Thanks, I think."

Shelton grunted. "What she's saying is you're like a dog trying to learn basic math. There's only so far you can go."

Cutsauce growled. *One plus one equals two.*

I held up my hands. "What does this have to do with the crystalis?"

Vitania studied her equation for a moment then wiped it away. "Logic dictates that the crystalis created the realms in the most destructive manner possible because of the way in which it was inadvertently used. This act scattered the pieces of Jura throughout the newborn realms, not only giving them strange powers, but also making them immutable."

Shelton put a hand to the side of his mouth and murmured to Adam, "Immutable is a fancy word for indestructible."

Adam rolled his eyes. "The crystalis was technically part of Apollyon since it was on his person. If it was recreated, does that mean Elohim has an extremely powerful object at his disposal?"

Vitania nodded. "It means once Earth is mended, he can use the crystalis to recreate it as he sees fit."

"I think we're looking at this the wrong way." Elyssa bit her lower lip and stared into the distance. "If Elohim already had the crystalis, he would have bragged about it. What if the crystalis hasn't returned? What if its absence is the reason Earth didn't snap back together in an instant?"

Vitania flicked her gaze to Elyssa. "Yes, that would explain why the Mending is taking so much longer than expected. Not even the Anchor Stone and Abyss can account for the slow recall of the realms."

"But all the central figures in the Sundering are back." Shelton's forehead scrunched. "How could Apollyon be back together again if the crystalis is missing?"

"Considering how rapidly the other pieces have appeared all on their own, logic would also dictate that the crystalis should have reappeared almost immediately like Apollyon." Cinder tilted his head. "That would suggest a being powerful enough to resist the pull is holding onto the crystalis."

"Astute observations," Vitania said. "The only being with such power would be Eve."

I grimaced. "That woman is cray-cray."

Elyssa nodded. "To the max."

"If only the time echo weren't broken." Vitania sighed. "All the hypotheses in the world are worthless compared to first-hand observation."

I snapped my fingers. "Actually, there is a way you can see it first-hand."

"The slug?" Shelton shuddered.

I repressed a shudder of my own. "Yep."

Vitania looked perplexed. "A slug?"

"Let's go back to the Ranch and I'll show you." I hated not having access to my powers, but Olivia had muted them when I tried to stop Baal from completing his relic statue. Since Eve was more insane than usual the last time I saw her, it meant Emily was my only hope for restoration. Not even an Apocryphan had that ability.

Another anxiety attack began to build with soul-crushing force. I tried not to think about it, but that only made me think about it more.

Elyssa put a hand on my cheek. "It'll be okay, Justin. We'll get through this."

Her mere touch drove the vicious demons back down to my own personal hell for the time being. "I know."

Vitania shook her head. "Being stripped of an integral part of yourself is traumatic, like a healthy person losing one of their six senses."

"I can live without the Apocryphan powers, but not having my Seraphim abilities is driving me crazy." My fists clenched reflexively.

"You survived most of your life without them," Elyssa said. "You can survive until we find Emily."

"Well, when you put it that way, it makes me feel a little better." It didn't, but talking about it only made me think about it even more.

"Let me retrieve the portal generator." Adam tapped the controls on his arcphone. The hum of the ring ceased and the portal to the white void snapped shut. The apparatus lifted from the ground and settled back down on the levitating platform.

Vitania opened a portal to the Ranch.

Adam pushed the floating platform through the portal ahead of us.

"It'd be real handy if we could get that thing working right," Shelton said. "Vitania is the only one of us who can open portals to other realms right now, so we're screwed if anything happens to her."

"We will need to strip off the shell and access the ring itself," Cinder said. "Using Vitania's quantum codex, we can recalibrate it to open portals anywhere."

I whistled. "That'd be awesome, Cinder."

"I will also be venturing to Pangea to find out what is taking Lumia so long." Vitania looked worried. "You will need other travel accommodations while I'm gone."

Shelton sighed. "Does that mean we'll have to start using Voltis for inter-realm travel again?"

I grimaced at the thought. "We don't even have a ship anymore. Conrad's special boat is in Atlantis, I think."

"Ah, those were the days." Shelton sighed. "Sailing the Seraphim skies in our very own sky ship."

"Listening to Eor complain while Tahlee shouted at the top of her lungs?" I snorted. "Yep, those were the days."

We filed through the portal after everyone else, our progress slowed as Adam navigated the floating platform into the corridor.

Cutsauce limped alongside me, ears back, head down.

"Are you okay?" I asked him.

He looked up at me with mournful red eyes. *I feel so tired and strange with Saila ripped out of me.*

I knelt down and scratched behind his ears. "Go get some rest. I have a feeling the next few hours will be hectic."

Cutsauce whined, then headed down the corridor. We'd given him his own room since the last thing Elyssa and I wanted was a sentient hellhound watching us make whoopee. I stood and jogged to catch up with the others.

"Vitania, it would be helpful if you could give us some pointers on configuring this thing," Adam said over his shoulder. "Otherwise, it might take us weeks to figure it out."

The Siren nodded. "I will help, but first I wish to see this slug Justin mentioned."

Adam winced sheepishly. "Um, would you mind opening a portal to the Razor lab for us? All the tools for the portal device are there." He showed her an image on his arcphone.

Vitania didn't even bother using the travelling room, but opened a portal right in the middle of the corridor. There wasn't any other foot traffic except for us, so Elyssa didn't chide her for the breach of regulations.

"Thanks." Adam went through.

"I will assist him," Cinder said.

I nodded. "We'll be along after the slug viewing."

"I'm going to update my father." Elyssa shook her head. "This crystalis theory complicates things." She kissed my cheek and jogged down the hall.

Cinder and Adam returned moments later with a cart loaded down with equipment.

"We're headed to the lab." Adam patted the portal generator. "Maybe we can get this bad boy fully functional."

"I hope so." I looked over the dizzying array of stuff on the cart and was glad I didn't have to worry about it.

Adam and Cinder headed toward the levitator while the rest of us continued down the corridor to the repository room where dangerous objects were stored. The sword of Jura, Unmaker, had been in here until recently, but it had gone to join the other relics in New Jura, the unofficial name of the reappearing city.

I went to the window where an older gentlemen dozed, his head supported by his hand. I dinged the bell.

He flinched and his head bumped into the window. "Mabel, get the cat out of my office!" His eyes blinked open and he frowned. "Oh, sorry. I was just resting my eyes."

I frowned. "You're not a Templar."

He ran a hand down his face. "No shit, sonny boy. I was working with a Daemos feeder crew, then they asked for volunteers to staff non-critical positions since all the soldiers are getting ready for war."

"War?" Shelton scoffed. "Elohim could beat us with both hands tied behind his back."

The old man grunted. "What do you need, sonny?"

"Exhibit four thirty-one," I said.

"All right." He winced as he pushed himself upright and began to hobble away.

"Don't you need the paperwork?" I called after him.

He waved dismissively without looking back. "World's ending so who cares?"

Shelton grinned. "I like this guy. Maybe I'll adopt him as my long-lost pop-pop."

"Pretty sure that guy is you from the future." I shook my head. "What's the world coming to when Thomas Borathen doesn't care about protocol?"

"The end." Shelton shrugged. "Thomas is about to pull out all the stops, but I don't think the biggest army in the world can stop what's coming."

Vitania took a seat on the couch against the far wall and closed her eyes as if she thought napping was a great idea too.

The minutes ticked past as we waited for the grumpy clerk to return with the request. Elyssa jogged into the room around the five-minute mark, her face etched with concern.

"What's up?" I asked.

"My father isn't here." She glanced at the window. "He's not answering his phone either."

I was shocked. "Uh, aren't you the first person in the loop when it comes to operations?"

"He told me he was mobilizing troops, but other than that, I don't know what he's up to." Elyssa shook her head. "I think the strain of impending doom is weighing heavier than he wants to admit. He's been in the business of protecting noms and supers alike for a long time. It really eats at him when we're powerless to do anything about it."

I knew exactly how he felt because I was particularly powerless now, and there was literally nothing we could do to prevent billions from dying.

5

At long last, the old man returned with a black container. He opened the door next to the window and handed it to us with little more than a grunt.

Elyssa's mouth dropped open as if he'd just slapped her. "That's not protocol!"

"Little lady, I wasn't trained for this, it's not my job, and I'm too damned tired to care." The old man shrugged. "Besides, the world is going to end, so what's the fuss?"

Elyssa leaned on the counter in front of the window, her violet eyes flashing dangerously. "Never give up hope. We've saved the world plenty of times before and we'll do it again."

The old man pursed his lip. "I want to believe you, young lady, I really do. My grandfather fought in World War Two and nearly died a dozen times. He told me there were days he just wanted to give up, especially after seeing so many people around him die. But he just kept pushing forward, kept his head down, and made it back. Maybe that's possible now or maybe it isn't. But I'm too damned old for this shit, so let me nap in peace!"

Elyssa narrowed her eyes and tapped her comm badge. "Flava, are you in the facility?"

An answer came a moment later. "Yes, Elyssa."

"How are Conrad and Ambria?"

"They're ready to leave the infirmary, but I'm not quite ready to clear them until Numia finishes her psychological evaluations."

Elyssa nodded. "If you're free, I could use you in the repository."

"Tell me how to get there and I will come."

Elyssa told her and a moment later, Flava stepped inside.

The old man shook his head. "Am I in trouble?"

Elyssa took Flava aside and spoke to her for a moment. Flava nodded and turned to the old man. "What is your name, sir?"

He grunted. "Gerald."

"Would you like to no longer be tired? Would you like your youth back?"

Gerald burst into laughter. "Commander Borathen already offered me the blessing for my service, but I told him the same thing I'm gonna tell you. After my Francine passed—" His voice broke and a tear trickled down his cheek. "After she passed, I didn't see a reason for living. Helping the Templars gave me a purpose, but it doesn't change a thing. I plan to go on to the great hereafter and rejoin the love of my life when it's time."

Shelton seemed to swallow a lump in his throat. "Well, shit. I like this guy even more now."

I cleared my throat. "Gerald, I've been dead before."

He nodded. "I heard. Got any advice?"

"The afterlife isn't quite what you think. It might be hard finding Francine in all the chaos."

Gerald sighed. "You're not talking me into sticking around any longer than I have to."

"That's not the point." I nodded toward the arctablet on the desk in front of him. "I gave a complete account of my time in the afterlife in the Templar compendium. Maybe you'll want to read it so you'll know what to expect."

The old man nodded. "I will, son." He leaned back in his chair. "Now, get out there and save the world, will ya?"

Vitania opened her eyes and rose from her chair. "We shall endeavor to do our best, young man."

Gerald chuckled. "You immortals are quite the characters." He picked up the arctablet and ignored us.

I took the black box he'd handed us down the corridor to a small conference room where I set it on the circular table. "Make yourself comfortable, Vitania."

The Siren settled into the leather seat. "Now what?"

I opened the box and dumped out what looked like a giant rocky turd. The black object unfurled to reveal a slimy green booger the size of my hand. The slug extended its eyestalks, each one swiveling independently to view us. I wondered if seeing us sitting all around it made it nervous.

Three more pairs of eyestalks sprouted from the slug, each set choosing one of us to face.

"Dude, can this thing take us all in?" Shelton said.

"I guess so." I looked at Vitania. "We're about to go into Apollyon's memories. You can fast forward to certain periods in his life and so forth by wishing it to happen. Clap your hands twice and flick your nose to end the session."

"Interesting." Vitania looked at the slug. "How do I start?"

The eyestalks facing her lengthened. She stared back, nodded, and went absolutely still.

"Guess that means she's in," Elyssa said. "Might as well join the party."

I looked down at the eyestalks. "I'm ready." The eyes went black and I felt myself falling forward into oblivion.

I found myself sitting in the auditorium, a seat of stone surrounded by darkness. Apollyon sat on a stone next to me, the perfection of his entire being filling me with pain. I looked down.

"What want see?" he said. Apollyon's memory was perfect, but his speech was barely better than that of a three-year old's.

The vocabulary during his memories was perfectly normal, probably because I was interpreting it, not him. I wasn't sure if that was because my mind interpreted everything, or if Apollyon simply had a speech impediment.

Just as the last time I'd seen him in the auditorium of his mind, he was naked but for a loincloth. I touched the hollow of my neck. "Show me where you got the crystalis."

He blinked. "Pretty stone?"

I nodded. "Yes."

I LAY on my stomach at the edge of the burning waters. My tears sizzle as they fall into the infernal fount. I want to die. The lake bubbles and something floats to the surface. It glitters in the sun. I study it and am entranced by its beauty. Everything around me is corrupted, but something perfect and beautiful is here.

Did I created it as I created the demons?

A pair of gnurks fight over the body of a manikin, their gnarled limbs smashing against each other's heads. I wish they would stop, but most creatures in Hell love violence. A group of succubus cheer on the fighters. They are beautiful women on the outside, but their insides are dark and evil.

I push myself up and wipe away the tears. Hopefully, this beautiful new gem is not also brimming with evil. I step into the scalding lake of fire and swim out to the diamond. I reach out and grab it clumsily.

For an instant, I see the creation of the universe, witness, the birth of stars, planets, and feel myself reduced to nothing as I stand before an assembly of alien gods. Some are vast clouds of dark matter, others are short and stubby like tiny devils. Others look like the people of Earth, but not as many as the strange ones.

Then I am back in my own body, clutching the diamond and sinking into the fount. I consider letting myself sink forever, but not even these waters can drown me. Father says he is the only one who can kill me.

I swim to the top and climb out. One of the gnurks is dead. A pair of succubus cry out in pleasure as they mount the victor. I sigh and turn away, inspecting my prize.

Overcome by a strange urge, I clap my hands twice and flick my nose.

. . .

I WAS BACK in the auditorium with Apollyon. "Why did you take the diamond to Juranthemon?"

"Magic. Powerful." Apollyon seemed to struggle to say what he wanted.

"Can you think in complete sentences?"

He nodded.

"You just can't say what you want to say, right?"

He nodded again.

"Apollyon, this is not the real world and that is not your physical body." I watched him with my peripheral vision to avoid the pain of his beauty. "You don't have to use your mouth to speak."

"Oh, that is smart!" Apollyon laughed like a child. "This speaking without my mouth works!"

He didn't sound terribly intelligent. "Did Elohim not teach you very much?"

Apollyon shook his head. "I was alone but I learned from people I found. I also absorb things when I touch people. It helps me."

"Tell me about the crystalis."

"I found it. It spoke to me in dreams. Showed me pieces of creation. Showed me the outsider gods and worlds they made. Showed me father, Eve, Zeus, other gods who made Earth." He frowned. "Was a big universe god that split into other gods. Very scary."

I couldn't speak for a moment. There was too much to easily unpack and process, plus it wasn't relevant to what I needed. "Apollyon, you took the pretty stone, the crystalis to Juranthemon."

"For father to kill me." He gritted his teeth. "I tried to jump into death when Apocryphan and my father fight. The power caught me in the middle. The chain came off and the crystalis floated away. Then I wake up in another place."

"The Void."

He nodded. "I was something else. Something ugly and twisted like my power. There were many people, humans, Seraphim, Sirens, and more. I went into the mountains and hid. They built new cities, but over time they became crazy. I realized one day that I am worse than Apollyon. I am corrupting an entire world."

I wanted to reach over and console the poor guy even if it was just a representation of Apollyon. But now I had an answer to the question. "Show me the moments before the Sundering."

THE SKY GROWS dark with the approaching Apocryphan and their dragons. I look up in awe. They are magnificent giants, powerful and perfect. A light shines on father and someone shouts his name. I barely have time to comprehend what is happening when the Apocryphan strike.

Saila shields us, but only for a moment. Father forms a barrier and grins. He is mighty and the Apocryphan cannot kill him. But if they fight, maybe they can all kill me. Father lowers his shield and fires back. The energy of their attacks becomes a miniature sun twenty feet overhead. I see my chance and leap toward death.

I try to clutch the creation stone to make my wish for death, but the chain melts instantly in the inferno. The stone flies away to the center of the star. I reach for it, crying for an end to my torment. The stone explodes and everything goes white.

My mouth is filled with dust. Flies buzz in my ears. I push up and look around. Juranthemon is gone. Father is gone. I am in a blackened clearing surrounded by bodies and uprooted trees.

A beautiful Apocryphan steps from a ripple in the air. She was not with the ones in the sky. I hobble to her. "Who you?"

Her lips peel back in disgust and she flinches back. Something shiny falls from her hand and onto the ground. "What are you?"

"Me." I try to say my name, but it is too much for my lips to handle.

She bends over and picks up the glittering object.

"My stone!" I reach for it but she slaps my hand away. "Please kill me." She kicks me so hard, I fly far away and smash into trees. When I get up, she is gone.

A strange urge overcomes me. I clap my hands twice and flick my nose.

. . .

"HOLY SHIT BALLS." I turned to Apollyon just enough to see him from the corner of my eye. "You saw Xanos with the crystalis right after the Sundering."

"Yes, I see that it was her now." He slumped. "How did she get it?"

That was a damned good question. "I need to go. Can you—" My eyes blinked open and I was back at the table. The others were still staring blankly at the slug. "Hey, Sluggy, can you let them out?"

A chorus of groans sounded around the table.

"Hey, what the hell?" Shelton shook his head and rubbed his eyes. "Man, that was just getting good."

Elyssa wiped tears from her eyes. "Poor Apollyon. Seeing his childhood makes me hate Elohim even more."

Vitania looked quietly at me. "Did you discover something?"

"Yeah." I blew out a breath. "Apollyon found the stone in the infernal fount. It made him see visions of creation and destruction. He thought it was powerful enough to kill him if his father used it, so he took it to Juranthemon. When Elohim and the Apocryphan started fighting, he jumped between them, but lost the crystalis. It floated away from him and exploded, Sundering the world."

"Fascinating." Vitania leaned forward.

"That's not all." I told them about Xanos encountering the newly spawned Beast in the Void, the crystalis in hand.

"She stepped through a ripple in the air?" Vitania nodded. "The crystalis was the epicenter. It must have spawned portals to all the new realms. Xanos must have somehow found these portals and stumbled upon the crystalis while exploring them."

"Which confirms Xanos knew about the crystalis all this time." Shelton pounded a hand on the table. The slug took this as a cue and curled back into its imitation of a turd. "I knew that bitch was tricking us when she wanted to stay inside the time echo."

Elyssa's face burned red. "I should have known!"

I held up a hand. "It is what it is. What's more important, though, is where is the crystalis relic now?"

I grunted. "That's a damned good question."

"This proves that the crystalis is the linchpin of the Sundering.

Elohim's Mending cannot finish without it." Vitania nodded. "Wherever it is, it is safe from the pull of the Mending."

"Can we stop calling it that?" Shelton said. "Makes it sound like it's fixing things. It's more like the Blending, where creation is getting pureed by a giant blender and reconstituted into Spam."

"Our next steps are clear," Vitania said. "We must find Xanos and ask her. Alternatively, I suspect Eve might also know something."

"Both options sound equally dangerous," Shelton said. "We don't even have Emily, for god's sake."

"Then we must find her first." Vitania stared into space for a moment. "After she freed me from Dactia's clutches in Aquilis, she planned to report back to Eden. Something must have happened along the way."

"Well, at least we know Olivia didn't have anything to do with it." Shelton frowned. "The only other person powerful enough to waylay Emily is Eve."

"Then a visit to Eve's realm is next up," I said.

Vitania drew in a deep breath as if steeling herself. "Yes, I'm afraid it is. Let us hope she's saner than the last time you saw her, Justin."

Shelton scoffed. "Or this will be an awfully short one-way trip."

6

Vitania opened a portal to a meadow in Eve's realm a good distance from the cottage. After we stepped through, she held up a hand. "Let me speak to her first."

Shelton shrugged. "Hey, she's your friend."

"She was." Vitania's eyes narrowed. "It is strange how unbalanced Eve has become over the last few eons. This is not the first time she's lost her mind. The last time I'm aware of she married a mortal and birthed Victoria and Lydia."

Those women had borne Emily and Olivia, respectively. Lydia had given up her daughter, and Olivia had suffered severe abuse in the foster system. Once she'd come into her powers, she'd been a natural fit for Team Evil.

Shelton grunted. "Women."

Elyssa shot him a dangerous glare. "There's a difference between crazy and insane, Shelton."

He nodded. "I like my women a little crazy. Keeps things spicy."

"Then you must have really loved Aerianas." She bared her teeth.

"Ow!" Shelton put a hand to his chest as if he'd just been shot. "Did you really have to bring that up?"

The Daemas, Aerianas, had manipulated Shelton into some of the darker chapters of his life.

I waved off the chatter. "Earth was primarily Eve's creation, right?"

Vitania nodded. "The other gods filled in bits and pieces, geography, and so forth, but she was the primary architect. Elohim tried to take credit for it, but the other gods ridiculed him."

"You know this how?" Shelton said.

"Eve once showed me her memories of creation." She pursed her lips. "I believe the Sundering not only broke the world, but her mind."

"She literally put her heart and soul into creation." I shook my head. "Doesn't that mean the Mending—"

"The collapse," Shelton interjected. "Mending makes it sound like grandma stitching a hole in my pants."

I rolled my eyes. "Shouldn't Eve's mind be getting better?"

"A good question." Vitania pressed her lips into a thin line. "If it is, then it could be bad for us."

Shelton frowned. "How so?"

"Because what if Eve wants Earth back?" Elyssa grimaced. "Maybe she didn't realize what the Sundering did to her but now she does."

"All supposition, of course." Vitania waved a hand dismissively. "Perhaps the strain of creating Earth broke Eve's mind long before the Sundering ever occurred. Not long after creation, she vanished for a long while only to return much later and birth the first humans. This angered many gods, for they saw humans as inferior creations compared to Sirens, Seraphim, fae, and elves."

"I take offense at that," Shelton said. "I think some humans are pretty okay."

Elyssa snorted. "Like yourself?"

"I'm exceptional." He shrugged. "I think humans have evolved a lot more over thousands of years than the others."

"Only because humans started with nothing while we were given everything." Vitania frowned. "Perhaps that was the point."

I shrugged. "Maybe. Look, can we go find Eve? The collapse isn't gonna stop itself."

Shelton grinned. "Better name, am I right?"

I shook my head. "No, I just want you to shut up about it."

He clapped my shoulder and laughed. "See? You're evolving."

Vitania straightened her shoulders and approached the house while we waited in the forest. She went up to the door and knocked.

"What are you doing?"

"Waiting here like we said," I whispered, not looking back.

"Who said that?" Elyssa whispered.

"You did." I turned to face her.

She shook her head. "No, I didn't."

"I thought Elyssa said it too." Shelton shuddered and looked up and all around. "Oh, shit, are there ghosts here?"

"No, just me." A teenage girl seemed to melt out of the tree.

Shelton yelped and jumped back.

Elyssa's hand stopped halfway to the light bow sheathed on her waist.

"You are outsiders." The dryad cocked her head like a curious pup. "Why are you here?"

I put a hand over my chest and breathed a sigh of relief. "We're looking for Eve."

"Oh." The dryad's face saddened. "She was furious, screaming the name, Elohim, over and over, then said she would go to the primal fount and make sure he didn't win."

We collectively gulped.

"The primal fount on this world?" I asked.

She shook her head. "The one here is not strong because this world is not connected to the others. She went to the strongest fount, the one on old Earth."

Vitania turned from the door and saw the dryad. She hurried across the glade and into the trees. "Dryad, where is your mistress?"

"The primal fount on old Earth." Elyssa's eyes filled with concern. "I don't know what she's talking about."

"Don't worry, we'll be safe here," the dryad said. "This place is like Alden."

"Alden?" Eve had been raving about that name the last time I'd come here. "What is Alden?"

"A new world up there." The dryad pointed into the sky, but all I saw were clouds. "Or maybe it's over there." Her arm rotated ninety degrees. "She put it in the star forest."

Shelton shook his head like a wet dog. "You mean space?"

"The outside." She pointed up. "The star forest."

"Dryads think differently." Vitania took the dryad's hands. "How is this realm safe?"

"Eve said it was made in the after, brand new matter, not from the old world." The dryad shrugged. "I don't know what that means, but she said it was never part of Earth."

"A brand-new creation." Vitania nodded slowly. "I always wondered why the quantum tunnels here were different. Eve made a refuge."

"She went to the primal fount to make sure Elohim doesn't win. " Elyssa grimaced. "I don't know what she's up to, but it can't be good."

"How in the hell can she go to the primal fount on old Earth?" Shelton took off his hat and scratched his head. "Is it in the white void where Earth used to be?"

"I don't know." Vitania's forehead pinched. "She's never spoken of it."

I turned to the dryad. "When did she go?"

"Many days ago." The dryad stroked the bark of her tree. "A man came and spoke with the purple woman. Eve saw them and called him Elohim. The man took the purple woman and left. Eve was very upset to learn that Elohim knew of her world. She said she must end him before it is too late."

"That wasn't Elohim!" I slapped my forehead. "That was me. She went full-on crazy and attacked me."

"We must find the primal fount she speaks of." Vitania pursed her lips. "Perhaps she misspoke."

I turned to ask the dryad another question, but she was gone.

"She must have meant Eden." Shelton put his hat back on. "Isn't the primal fount on Eden near Kratos?"

I nodded. "Yeah I think—" and then it hit me. "She's in Atlantis."

Vitania frowned. "Yes, of course. I don't know why that didn't occur to me before."

Atlantis was, as far as we knew, the only surviving fragment of the original Earth. It sat in the middle of Voltis, a massive maelstrom that was essentially like one big malfunctioning portal.

I frowned. "There's just one major problem. I've been all over Atlantis and never heard of or seen the primal fount there."

"That's for sure," Shelton said. "None of the Sirens there ever mentioned it."

Vitania's expression soured. "Dolpha, Narine, and Balaena were once part of my inner circle. I have not spoken to them in some time."

For the mother of Sirens, "some time" could mean centuries, or millennia. I didn't really care. Eve's dastardly plans were at the top of my mind. "Vitania, can you get us to Atlantis?"

She stared into the distance, seemingly distracted, then snapped out of it and nodded. "Yes, give me a moment." Vitania slashed symbols in the air, then waved the flat of her hand across them as if wiping down a dirty counter. Gently undulating vortexes faded into view. Most were ghostly white, but a couple shimmered like gold. She examined them closely for a moment.

Shelton whistled. "Are these quantum tunnels?"

"Yes." Vitania pointed to a golden vortex. "This one is part of Eve's new creation. I believe it leads to Alden."

"Do we just hop into it?" Shelton said.

Vitania shook her head. "Opening a proper gateway is the only way to access them. For that, I require the symbols to Alden."

"Aren't most of the symbols related to the name of the realm?" I said.

"Usually, but not in this case." Vitania wiped the air and the tunnels vanished. "Perhaps she can tell us in person."

Shelton gulped. "If she doesn't kill us first."

Vitania slashed open a portal into a world of clouds. It took a moment for my gaze to notice the stone floor just on the other side. I stepped through and found myself in the observatory, a crystal dome atop Mount Olympus. An open doorway led to a room with three golden thrones where the Fallen had once given audience to the Archons, religious leaders from a city built further down the mountain.

Banished from Seraphina for rising up against their rulers, the Fallen had somehow ended up in Atlantis where they posed as gods. We'd later discovered they spent most of their lives seeking relics of Jura and scattering them among the realms to prevent the Armageddon Elohim had forced upon us.

"Dude, I'd forgotten about this view." Shelton pointed toward another mountain peak in the distance. "Good old Atlantis. Remember when I was finally able to make pizza?"

"Hard to forget after all those years eating glurk." Elyssa shuddered. "I really hated the food on Seraphina."

"You and me both." Shelton made a face. "That first taco we had in England was pure heaven."

Vitania closed the portal and looked around. "I can hardly remember the last time I came here."

"We scoured this place from top to bottom," Shelton said. "The primal fount definitely ain't around here."

I nodded. "The Fallen used this place to travel the realms but we never figured out how they did it."

"Yes, I spoke with them about their mission." Vitania pursed her lips. "I discovered Atlantis during my travels and explored it from one corner to the other. Following rumors of gods atop Mount Olympus, I went here, curious to see if the old gods still resided in this place. Instead, I found the Fallen. I believed their mission to keep the relics separated was worthy and tried to teach them how to make their own portals. They might have once had the strength, but the Sundering diluted the power of Seraphim more than most."

I'd wondered about that. "The Seraphim in the time echo seemed far more powerful than the ones these days."

Vitania nodded. "At the time, the Fallen were using Voltis as a means to travel. They did not understand an important fact about Mount Olympus." She tapped a foot on the ground. "It was chosen as residence for the gods because it was a place of great power due to the presence of the primal fount."

"The fount is on Olympus?" Shelton shook his head. "Like I said, we looked all over the place and we definitely would've noticed something like the primal fount."

Vitania pursed her lips and turned in a circle. "Olympus was a magnificent mountain with a city of gods. This Olympus is dead and barren."

"A lot went down over the eons." I shrugged. "Maybe Heval is the only thing left of the city that was once here."

"What you see is what you get." Shelton rapped his knuckles on the dome. "We scanned every inch of this place and didn't find any illusions, secret entrances, and definitely no hidden city of the gods."

Vitania nodded. "Did you go outside the dome?"

"Yep." Shelton folded his arms. "We used an Mzodi sky ship to examined the outside. We even had a gem that revealed illusions and scanned for caves."

"That can mean only one thing." Vitania began tracing symbols in the air much as she'd done in Eve's realm. She wiped a hand before her, revealing quantum tunnels. She sang softly and the tunnels vibrated like plucked strings on a guitar. Her gaze settled on one.

"What are you doing?" Shelton reached for the swirling vortex, but his hand went through it.

"This tunnel is a dead end." Vitania began singing to another tunnel, her words causing it to undulate this way and that. A symbol appeared in the air, then another and another until there were four. The Siren held out a hand and the symbols glowed with power. A portal slashed open to a sunlit meadow.

"Holy farting Olympians." Shelton peered through the gateway. "Where is that?"

"The real Olympus, hidden from mortal eyes within a pocket dimension." Vitania stepped through. Golden sunlight touched her face and a gentle breeze caught her hair. "Now I know why the Fallen remained atop this barren rock for so long."

"Because the barren mountain isn't really Olympus." I stepped onto the grass and sighed in relief at the pleasant warmth of the sun. The sweet scent of flowers drifted with the breeze and the temperature felt perfect.

"Hot damn." Shelton looked up and around. "So that's just a fake Olympus?"

Vitania nodded. "Faux Olympus."

"It's amazing!" Elyssa stared in awe at an orchard filled with fruit-bearing trees of all varieties. "This is paradise."

"Well, I wouldn't go that far." I'd been to paradise in the afterlife, and it wasn't quite that amazing here. "But it's definitely a place a god could call home."

An entire city of ancient Greek architecture lay before us, bathed in the mist of a massive waterfall that tumbled from the peak of the mountain. At the base of the waterfall was a great lake filled with azure blue waters glowing with power.

Shelton grunted. "The primal fount, I assume."

The wind cleared the mist hiding the center of the lake. It was there that I saw a frightening sight. Eve, the goddess of creation, stood on the water, lightning crackling along every inch of her body. She cried out and thrust her hands skyward, sending a torrent of power into the sky. The ground trembled violently, tossing us around while Eve remained steady.

"Eve!" Vitania rose a foot into the air and drifted toward the fount. "Eve, what are you doing?"

Eve gave no indication she heard Vitania. Her hands went back to her sides, gathering more power from the primal fount. The shaking in the ground subsided during her recharge.

"What in the blazes is she doing?" Shelton climbed to his feet. "Is she trying to bring down the mountain?"

Elyssa sucked in a breath. "I think it's worse than that. I think she's trying to destroy Earth and all the realms for good."

7

The dryad's words suddenly made sense. Eve's realm and Alden would be safe, but anything and everything pertaining to Earth was going into the trash bin.

I ran for the primal fount. "Eve, don't destroy Earth!" I blurred past Vitania and reached the edge of the lake. I knew better than to venture into the waters. Falling into the infernal fount had nearly killed me and I wasn't about to repeat the mistake with the primal fount.

That was when I noticed something in the water beneath Eve. It looked like another person but from this distance I couldn't be sure. I tried to channel my angel wings and hit a wall where my Seraphim powers used to be.

Vitania stopped at the edge. "I cannot venture into the fount." She shook her head. "Eve alone is not powerful enough to destroy all of creation. I do not understand why she even..." She abruptly hissed.

"What is it?" I said.

Vitania pointed to the figure under the water. "That is Emily."

Elyssa caught up with us. "Eve!" She jumped up and down waving her hands. "Eve, stop!"

The goddess was far too consumed with world destruction to even notice us.

"She has chained her power to Emily's." Vitania's brow furrowed. "She must be building up to a power surge that will shatter Olympus and destroy the realms along with it."

"Jesus, can't you guys wait?" Huffing and puffing, Shelton reached us and bent over, heaving for breath. "You know I can't keep up with you guys. I'm not too proud to be carried, man."

"Are you certain that's what she's doing?" Elyssa said.

"I cannot say for sure, but what else would she be doing?" Vitania's gaze went distant. "I have not seen such massive energy surges since the dawn of Earth."

"We've got to stop her." I desperately wished I'd brought along a flying broom. "Can you open a portal to the Ranch? I need to get a broom or carpet."

Vitania traced symbols and slashed a hand through the air. Nothing happened. "This much power is interfering with the portal. I'll have to return—"

Eve thrust her hands into the air. A bubble of energy greater than the last swelled toward us.

"Uh, are we about to die?" Shelton said.

Vitania sang and a shimmering dome covered us. The shockwave washed over it, sending cracks all up and down the surface. The ground bucked and heaved even more violently than the last time, tossing us around the confines of the shield like rag dolls.

When it finally ceased, I climbed to my feet. "We don't have time for brooms."

"Justin, you can't go into the fount." Elyssa grabbed my arm. "You'll never reach Eve."

"No, but maybe I can do something else." I called upon Kalesh. *Yo, I need something a little different.* I formed an image in my mind. *Can we do this?*

I don't see why not. He took control of our body. *Let's give it a whirl.*

I pulled off my shirt as my skin began to turn blue. Muscles coiled

around my arms and legs, but rather than swell to immense proportions, bone-wracking pain in my back drove me to my knees.

"Jesus H. Whippersnapper!" Shelton jumped back as tiny webbed
wings sprouted larger and larger from my back.

The pain stopped. I wobbled uncertainly as I tried to stand with
the unaccustomed weight on my normal-sized body. A simple
thought and the wings spread wide.

Elyssa gasped. "Justin, you've never used your demon wings for
anything but gliding."

I shrugged awkwardly. "Can't hurt to try." I took her hand and
kissed it. "Go get a broom if I end up killing myself."

"Justin, no!" Elyssa gripped my hand.

"Sorry babe, fate of the world and all that." I flapped my giant
wings and rose majestically into the air—at least for a drunk bird. I
hovered in place, tethered by her grip. "This is gonna work."

Lip trembling, Elyssa let go. "I love you."

I wasn't about to Han Solo my one true love. I blew her a kiss.
"Love you to Olympus and back." Then I rotated toward the goddess
and flapped my wings as hard as I could. She'd taken about five
minutes to charge before her last attempt at destroying creation. I
had to stop her or the next shockwave would probably barbeque my
flesh, broiling me in agony.

Then again, it was the primal fount, not the infernal one. Maybe
I'd die in ecstasy. I didn't really want to find out one way or the other,
so I flapped my wings like my life depended on it. Amazingly enough,
it wasn't nearly as hard as I'd imagined it, thanks to Kalesh's help.

These wings were able to support me when I spawned into an
eight feet demon with massive muscles, so it shouldn't have been a
surprise that they propelled my normal six-foot frame easily. With
Kalesh's help, I was able to maintain my balance with every powerful
thrust.

Energy crackled along the surface of the fount, tendrils reaching
toward me as if the fount despised an inferior being flying so close to
its surface. I rose higher to avoid being snared and aimed for Eve. My
plan was simple: ram her hard enough to make her stop. At the very

least it would give the realms a temporary reprieve. At the worst, I'd smack into her like an insect hitting a bug zapper and she'd never even notice.

Considering the amount of power flowing over her body, the latter scenario seemed more likely. "What in the hell am I thinking?" I muttered to myself. Eve was jacked straight into the most powerful source of magic that I knew of. It was time to rethink my strategy.

I ran through the few options available to me and came up with one that seemed more likely to work. Falling into the infernal fount had nearly ended me, so the same would probably happen if I took a plunge into the primal fount. But what if I just dipped an arm into it? Could I possibly snatch Emily from just beneath the surface and pull her away?

The tip of her nose looked as if it was just barely beneath the surface. Her hands also drifted at about the same depth, so it seemed possible to slow my momentum and pick her up instead of trying to play chicken with a god. I had no idea what would happen when I touched the water. It might burn away the flesh, leaving nothing but a skeletal arm, or simply singe the hair.

It doesn't matter. I have to try.

I closed to within fifty feet. Eve was so focused on her task she didn't even notice me. I was probably nothing but a fly in her periphery, a nuisance that posed no danger.

Thirty feet.

Eve's glowing eyes regarded me, but she made no move to strike me down.

Twenty feet.

Ten.

One of Eve's upraised arms lowered toward me.

I took that as a bad sign and banked sideways. I wasn't nearly as agile with wings as I was with a high-performance broom, but it was enough to keep me out of the crosshairs for the final few feet. I swooped lower, gritted my teeth, and envisioned grabbing Emily's hand. Eve swung her arm toward me. I took evasive action and swung hard left. It took me to Eve's opposite side, well away from Emily's hands.

I gritted my teeth and plunged my hand beneath the waters as a swept past Eve. My hand closed around Emily's ankle. Eve had apparently been expecting a direct attack because she gasped in surprise.

The waters of the primal fount burned my skin like cold fire. My hand went numb and I wasn't sure I'd actually snatched the target. I looked down and saw Emily swinging upside down beneath me. The skin along my arm was blue, but Emily looked no worse for the wear.

Eve shrieked and the power surging around her fell away. Golden flames licked her body as she focused all her rage on the fly who'd defied the spider.

"This isn't going to end well," I noted dryly.

Eve streaked after me, plumes of water flying off the primal fount in her wake. She would reach me in seconds and there was nothing I could do to outrun her.

Siren song drifted across the lake.

Eve slowed and turned to face the music.

I veered sharp left, making a U-turn back toward Vitania and the others then flapped my wings like there was no tomorrow. Which technically there wouldn't be if Eve got her hands on Emily again.

Eve continued hovering in place, entranced by the music. As I drew closer to shore, I noticed the strain on Vitania's face. It was probably taking everything she had to distract the goddess.

I landed awkwardly, stumbling forward. Emily thudded into the grass and rolled a few feet before coming to a stop.

Shelton grimaced. "Hot damn, you trying to kill her?"

I dropped to my knees and checked her pulse. It felt slow but strong. Pins and needles pricked up and down my forearm as feeling returned. Otherwise, I felt no worse for the wear. Only time would tell if that was the case.

Vitania's face reddened. Sweat beaded on her forehead and a vein in her neck bulged. She gestured frantically toward the portal. Elyssa picked up Emily and raced away, Shelton huffing and puffing behind her. I sprinted after them. I glanced back and saw Vitania stumbling weakly. She fell and the song faded to silence.

There was a brief heartbeat with only the sound of the waterfall and a bird crying in the distance. Eve blinked and looked across the lake at us. Her eyes widened. Then she screamed in rage and streaked toward us.

My bowels passed out and my asshole clenched to keep me from crapping myself. I summoned every ounce of strength I had and sprinted toward Vitania. Azure energy crackled along my arm and across my body. Suddenly I was hurtling across the meadow so fast that everything else seemed to stop.

Eve's flight slowed. Vitania looked frozen in place, hand outstretched in mid-fall. I reached her, stopped and scooped her into my arms. The world resumed movement, Eve flying, Vitania gasping in surprise as I picked her up.

"Where—" she didn't have time to complete the sentence before I raced back toward the portal, blue lightning coursing along my skin.

Shelton froze in mid-stride, one hand on his hat, the other gripping his staff. Elyssa moved in slow motion as I streaked past her and through the portal. I placed Vitania on the ground then raced back through the portal and snagged Shelton. I dropped him on the floor and Elyssa resumed full speed, dashing through after us.

Vitania slashed a hand. The portal closed, and she slumped.

Shelton staggered in a circle then dropped to his knees and heaved. "What in the actual hell just happened? I'm dizzier than a one-eyed monkey on a Ferris wheel."

Still holding Emily, Elyssa regarded me with wide eyes. "How did you move so fast, Justin?"

"We don't have time," Vitania said weakly. She traced symbols and a portal opened. "Hurry through."

I picked her up and crossed through the portal onto a sandy beach. Elyssa carried Emily and Shelton wobbled through last. Vitania closed the portal and sighed in relief.

A small cottage sat a short distance away, so I carried her toward it. "Are you okay?"

She nodded weakly. "It took everything I had to hold Eve at bay. Had she been in her right mind, I would have failed."

Emily moaned. Her eyelids fluttered and golden light filtered through the eyelashes. Elyssa quickly set her on the sand and backed up. "I have no idea what she'll do when she wakes up and I don't want to be the first person she sees when it happens."

"Smart." Shelton tugged on his collar. "I'm still feeling motion sickness from whatever Justin did."

"I moved faster than I've ever moved before, like the Flash!" My arm still prickled, but I wasn't sure it was because of the numbness going away. "It must have something to do with touching the primal fount."

Emily screamed. Torrents of golden energy poured from her eyes and speared harmlessly into the sky. Still holding Vitania, I turned tail and ran to give us a few extra yards of safety. I felt the power from the fount crackling in my muscles but I made sure not to run full out this time.

The scream stopped abruptly. Emily sat up and looked around, eyes wide. Her gaze froze on us. "Vitania?"

"It is me, child." The Siren patted my arm so I gently put her on her feet. She walked stiffly toward the demigoddess on the beach. "How do you feel?"

"Like absolute shit." Emily squeezed her eyes shut and rubbed them. "My skin feels chafed and sunburned."

Vitania nodded. "You were in the primal fount."

The rest of us approached.

"Emily, Eve was trying to destroy creation by daisy-chaining your power to hers." I shook my head. "I don't know if it would've worked, but it didn't look good."

With a groan, Emily pushed to her feet. She gasped. "Where's Tyler?"

Vitania shook her head. "I don't know. We only discovered Eve's awful plan thanks to a dryad."

Elyssa put a hand on her arm. "What's the last thing you remember?"

Emily's forehead tightened. "We were leaving Aquilis after freeing Vitania." She squeezed her eyes shut. "Olivia knew I was there. One of the Sirens must have sent her a message. We fought, and then Eve appeared, commanding us to help her. Tyler and I fled through portal after portal, but Eve was always right behind us. One of the portals opened randomly to a cliff. We fell into an ocean, and that's the last I remember."

"What realm was it?" I asked.

Tears formed in her eyes. "I-I don't know! I've lost him!"

Vitania sighed. "We will find him, dear." Vitania sagged. "I am too tired to open another portal for now."

"I'll go back to Aquilis and trace my portals from there if I have to!" Emily slashed a hand through the air. Magic surged from her hand, crackling like lightning. A dark cloud of energy coalesced in the air wailing like the horn of a distant train that was rapidly narrowing the distance. She shrieked and yanked back her hand but the power continued building.

I threw out my hands to make a shield—and nothing happened. *Oh yeah, I'm powerless.*

"It's a feedback eruption!" Vitania shielded her eyes with her hands. "Run!"

It was clear she was in no condition to run and besides, it was far too late to do anything about it, because an instant after she shouted, the storm imploded to a pinpoint. The air stilled and went quiet for an instant, and then the pinpoint blossomed into an explosion.

Instinct took over. I burst forward at full speed, azure lightning crackling across my skin. Once again, time seemed to stand still, all except for the explosion which was expanding relentlessly toward Emily. I snagged her first, then grabbed Elyssa in my other arm on the way out. I cross a hundred yards in an instant. There was no time to gently deposit them, so I dumped them unceremoniously in the sand without slowing, turned and ran for Shelton and Vitania.

The explosion was mere inches from Shelton when I reached him. I grabbed him and Vitania then blurred toward the others, skidding to a stop in the loose sand. The explosion flared to normal speed, a sphere of crackling energy followed by a sonic boom that flattened trees and tore the roof off the cottage.

Shelton dropped to his knees and started barfing.

Elyssa and Emily rose from where they'd rolled to a stop, spitting sand out of their mouths. Vitania looked a little sick herself, but managed to hold it in.

"Ugh." Shelton spat into the sand. "There goes everything I ate for the last three months."

Emily stared at me in amazement. "How did you move so fast, Justin? I've never seen anything like it."

I held up the hand I'd dipped in the primal fountain. Energy still crackled across my skin. "I guess maybe I'm supercharged from the fountain?"

I should have been excited, but instead I felt fear. Jeremiah once told me the primal and infernal founts chose who was allowed to touch them and take in their power. If someone tried to take power without permission, they died.

The infernal fount had nearly killed me even though I hadn't intentionally taken a bath in it. For all I knew the primal fount was eating me from the inside out and there was little I could do to stop it.

V itania touched my arm and jerked me from my frightening thoughts. "I'm simply too exhausted to examine you."

I grimaced. "You think I'll be okay?"

"I don't know. I need to rest before I can find out."

Emily stared at her own hands as if they were covered in blood. "What's wrong with my powers? I was just trying to open a portal, not kill everyone."

"I cannot say until I've rested." Vitania looked toward the cottage and sighed. "Well, at least the roof isn't completely gone."

Shelton wiped his mouth with the back of his sleeve. "Where are we anyway?"

Vitania took a deep breath as if talking were an effort. "Pangea."

"The land of the fae?" Shelton's mouth dropped open. "Pyra wouldn't let us set foot here. If the fae find us, we're toast!"

"This is unfae territory," Vitania said. "We will be fine."

"The unfae are the ones who kill people!" Shelton peered into the forest and shuddered. "They're gonna slice us open and use our blood for dark magic."

Vitania sighed. "The unfae are not like that."

I prayed she was right. "Let me get you to the cottage." I scooped her up again.

"Thank you, child." She leaned her head on my shoulder. "I'm afraid I greatly overtaxed myself."

The group shuffled to the cottage. It had been far enough out of the blast zone to avoid losing the roof entirely, but large chunks were missing from the front. The cottage looked nearly identical to Vitania's home in Iceland. Elyssa pushed open the front door and we stepped inside.

Aside from some conch shell chairs, there was very little furniture. Vitania's roommate, Lumia, had created most of the furniture in the Icelandic home by growing whatever she wanted or forming it from wood. She wasn't around to make a bed, unfortunately. I walked down the hallway and found a giant clam shell in a back room.

"This will do." Vitania nudged me to put her down.

"But, it's a shell." I rapped it to demonstrate that shells were hard. The shell opened to reveal a pool of crystal-clear water so deep I couldn't see the bottom.

She smiled at my confused face. "Not everything is as it seems."

"That's for sure." I dipped a finger in the water. It was pleasantly warm. "You're going to sleep underwater?"

"I am a Siren." Vitania climbed inside the shell and onto the water. A slight ripple was the only disturbance. She lay on her back and slowly sank beneath the surface, hair billowing gently. The clam shell closed.

"Uh, goodnight, I guess." The thought of sleeping underwater freaked me out. Then again, I was a simple land animal.

I returned to the front room to find the others sitting on the floor or in the conch shell chairs. Emily sat in the far corner, head down, her long, brown hair a curtain over her face. I didn't need to be a mind reader to know what was going through her head.

Elyssa, reclined in a conch shell, gave me a concerned look when I entered. "How's Vitania?"

"Tired." I shrugged. "We have to wait until she's recovered before we can get back to Eden." I walked over to Emily and sat on the floor next to her. "Would you be up to running some tests on your powers? We need you at a hundred percent."

She pushed her hair behind her ears, revealing a tear-streaked face and red eyes. "I'll do anything if it means I can search for Tyler. But I'm afraid I might kill someone."

"We'll keep it small." I stood and offered a hand. "Controlled experiments."

Shelton got up from a conch shell and slapped his hat on his head. "Amen to that. I don't want to sit around doing nothing while the world ends."

Emily took my hand and pulled herself up. "How long have I been gone? Did Baal do anything while I was captive?"

Shelton cleared his throat and winced. "Not sure how to break this to you, but Baal ain't around anymore."

She blinked. "Y-you defeated him?"

I grimaced. "No. Elohim is back."

"Bloody hell." Emily leaned against the wall for support. "What happened?"

"Kind of a long story." I opened the front door. "I'll tell you about it while we walk a safe distance from the cottage."

Elyssa hopped up from her seat. "I'm coming too."

As we walked, I told Emily the convoluted story. That Conrad and Ambria went missing and Shelton's investigations led to us finding a time echo of ancient Jura. That Eve had thrown Unmaker into the Void which led us to a dangerous showdown with the Beast. That Baal, the ultimate plotter, had tricked us into destroying the Void swarm so he could reach the Beast, a relic creature created from the essence of Baal and his son, Apollyon. Then I reached the end where Olivia muted my powers and made me watch while Baal completed his work.

"Elohim is back. His son, Apollyon, is back. Saila is back but is a prisoner of Elohim." I shook my head. "Apparently, the only thing keeping the realms from smashing together is the linchpin of the Sundering—a crystalis."

Emily ran a hand down her face. "After Eve took me, she muted my abilities and regaled me with her plans to scrap Earth and start over. She'd used part of a crystalis to create her home realm, Nova. Eventually, she found another full crystalis and used it to construct Alden."

Elyssa frowned. "I didn't realize gods couldn't create worlds without crystalis."

"They can, but it takes much longer." Emily reached the edge of the water at the beach and stared at the horizon. "She told me that our universe was created with the Big Bang, scattering seeds of creation all over. This eventually birthed the gods who then took their sections of the universe and molded them into what they wanted."

"Whoa." Shelton's mouth dropped open. "You're telling me the Big Bang ain't just a theory?"

"It really happened." Eve bent down, took off her shoes, and wiggled her toes in the sand. "Eve believes there was an overgod who made up all existence. The overgod eventually concluded that existence was meaningless all alone, so he destroyed himself, creating the universe from his body."

"Freaky." Elyssa bit her lower lip. "I guess that means we're all a part of god."

Emily nodded. "Maybe so."

Shelton snorted. "I know which part I am."

Elyssa grinned. "I doubt the overgod had an ass, but if he did, you'd definitely be the hole."

"Aw, you know me so well." Shelton shrugged. "I keep the shit from backing up."

"That you do." I clapped him on the shoulder and looked at Emily. "You ready to try something small?"

She nodded but her eyes remained uncertain. "Everyone should back away just in case."

Shelton paced about twenty yards away. "I still feel sick from Justin's last rescue so I want to give myself plenty of room."

Elyssa pressed her lips together. "Yeah, I felt like I'd just hit the drop on a roller coaster when he grabbed me. I've never moved that fast in my life."

I examined my forearm and noted that the slight azure glow had moved further up my arm. I tried not to think about what that might mean and flourished my other hand at Emily. "Let's get started." I took out my phone and began recording a video so we'd have something to examine.

Shelton tapped on his phone and aimed it at Emily. "I'm running a magic debug analyzer. I've never tried it on a demigoddess before, so no promises."

Emily held out her hand, palm upraised. A golden orb flickered into existence. The concern on her face morphed into relief when it continued to glow without exploding. The orb grew larger until it filled the palm of her hand. In that instant, the energy sparked wildly like a bare power cable in water.

Lightning flashed across the orb. Emily cried out and yanked her hand away. The orb should have been snuffed, but it seemed to take on a life of its own, crackling and growing, sounding like a rapidly approaching train, its horn blaring louder and louder.

Shelton was already running. The rest of us turned tail and chased after him. Emily easily paced Elyssa. I hung back behind them in case I needed to use my newfound super speed. The train horn reached a crescendo. The sphere of energy collapsed into a pinpoint of light. For a heartbeat, the world went silent before an explosion rocked the ground.

The detonation was barely ten feet in radius but left a small crater in the sand beneath the eruption. Anyone within that circle would've probably had their skulls turned inside out.

"Shit!" Emily clenched her fists and looked ready to punch a hole in the world. "I'm bloody useless!"

Shelton grunted. "Hey, if we need to kill a bunch of bad guys, we know how to do it."

"Along with a bunch of good guys." Elyssa shook her head. "It's almost as if your power gets stuck into a feedback loop until it overloads."

Shelton tapped on his arcphone and frowned. "I got some strange readings that don't make much sense."

I stood next to him. The screen displayed a close-up video of the energy in Emily's hand. Numbers and symbols danced across the display while thermal imaging showed cold and hot spots converging on each other beneath the golden glow.

"Well there's your problem." Shelton projected a holographic image so the others could see. "The power keeps spiking out of control. It's like you channeled conflicting energy types until they create a super storm."

I paused the video at the moment the fluctuations went critical and pointed to the blue and red spots. "I don't understand. Brilliance and Murk are hot and cold, but merging them together creates Stasis."

Shelton switched the filter on the video to reveal the actual colors of the orb. That was when I noticed the colors dancing across the surface.

Emily's eyes widened. "That can't be right."

I zoomed in on the jagged yellow energy. "Am I stupid, or does this look like you're channeling power from the infernal and primal founts?"

"That bitch!" Emily's face paled. "What in the hell did Eve do to me?"

"The two opposing powers are literally blowing up in your face." Shelton shook his head. "Man, this ain't good."

"Understatement of the eon," Elyssa said. "Is this something that fixes itself, or do you need to see a doctor?"

Emily sat in the sand and stared at the ocean. "I have no idea." She held up her hand and looked at it. "It means that I'm a menace."

Shelton studied the video for a moment. "Ah, now I see." He grunted. "Damn, I wish Nosti was here."

I looked at the frozen image. "What was your 'aha' about?"

"I figured out why the numbers are so hard to read." He swiped the hologram to display raw data that made no more sense to me than before. "These readings are usually caused by malaether, but since Emily is a demigoddess, the power levels are off the chart."

Elyssa pursed her lips. "You're saying that Emily is creating epic levels of malaether eruptions?"

Shelton nodded. "Nosti can confirm my findings when we get back to the Ranch."

Emily threw up her hands. "Doesn't bloody matter. The bottom line is I can't do anything."

I thought back to our retreat. "Your physical abilities don't seem to be affected. Maybe there are other facets of your powers that still work."

She narrowed her eyes. "You want me to restore your Apocryphan and Seraphim abilities."

I nodded. "Maybe that ability is controlled by a different part of you."

Emily looked at me for a long moment. "What if I reach inside your soul and flip the switch but set off a chain reaction? What if it causes you to explode?"

Shelton gulped. "It ain't worth the risk."

"Give me back the Apocryphan powers and we can go look for Tyler right away." I clasped my hands pleadingly. "Just give it a try."

"Justin, no." Elyssa gripped my arm hard enough to leave a bruise. "You're not going to be a guinea pig!"

"What's the alternative?" I waved a hand at the cottage. "Stay in Pangea until the realms collapse?"

"If you get yourself killed for no reason, then it won't matter!" Elyssa shot back. "Baal doesn't have the crystalis so we don't have to rush into anything."

I shook my head. "We played that game with the relics of Jura and look where that got us. Emily is out of commission and so am I unless she restores my powers."

Elyssa growled in frustration. "You killed yourself once already, Justin. Didn't you learn anything from that?" Tears streaming down her face, she gripped my shirt. "I fucking died that day! At least give us a chance to die together the next time!"

I was so shocked I didn't know what to say. Elyssa pushed past me and ran to the cottage, leaving me in a stupor.

Shelton took off his hat and sighed. "Dude, you're so selfless sometimes that you're selfish."

I blinked. "I'm just trying to get us back on track. Elohim is always so far ahead of us that we can't afford any delays."

Emily smiled sadly and put a hand on my shoulder. "I would do anything to find Tyler—almost anything. But I won't do that."

"Great, now she's quoting Meatloaf." Shelton snorted and turned toward the crater in the sand. "Let's consider other options before we risk blowing you up."

My fists clenched in frustration. "Emily, restoring my powers isn't the same thing as channeling energy. All you have to do is flip a switch."

"Justin, you don't know what you're talking about." Emily scoffed. "Muting and enabling powers means I have to reach into your very soul and adjust your aura. The power to do that is unimaginable compared to simply blowing things up." Her eyes narrowed. "I suggest you take a walk and really think about what you want and why."

"Get it through your thick skull that your friends don't want to see you die again." Shelton gently rapped his knuckles on the side of my head then walked toward the cottage.

Emily gave me one last hard look and followed him.

Frustration turned to anger and back to frustration again. "Why are they treating me like I'm a child?" I muttered. My gut instinct told me Emily could enable my powers, no problem. My brain told me that I had no hard evidence to back up that conclusion.

I'd rather die than sit here and do nothing.

9

You're a hypocrite.

I flinched. "Kalesh?"

No, I'm the other voice in your head.

I took a last look at the cottage and walked down to the water's edge. "Why am I a hypocrite?"

You claim you want to save lives but your actions would only lead to greater loss of lives. Elohim would win the endgame.

"Hasn't he already won?"

Obviously not if the realms still exist.

I took off my shoes and waded into the water. The sugary sand sifted through my toes and the water felt pleasantly cool. "Why don't you talk as much anymore?"

I feel us becoming one. Perhaps soon there will be no more us, but only you.

A pang of sadness stabbed my heart. "I don't like that. We used to fight all the time, but now we're a great team. You've taught me things I never would have figured out on my own."

I have always been a part of you and you a part of me. I once craved nothing but power and destruction, but you have helped me mature. Now it is my turn to help you.

I snorted. "You've helped me a lot. Our demonic abilities have gotten us out of a lot of scrapes."

And caused you to get into entirely new ones. For example, allowing Cephus to frame us for murder of the Trivectus.

"It was a learning experience." It had been a complete and utter bloodbath. "But it happened because I acted without thinking."

You've gotten better at that.

"The struggle is real." A golden fish flitted through the clear water and stopped to nibble on my toes. I leapt back in surprise and it darted away. "What do I do now? Just wait and pray Emily's powers start working again?"

I don't know. Maybe the fae will help.

I shook my head vehemently. "That's the worst idea ever. If Pyra finds out we're here, then god only knows what she'll do to us."

Oh, you didn't realize.

"Realize what?" I turned back toward shore and realized what Kalesh thought I'd already realized. A pair of fae hovered just outside the forest, wings humming. I'd been so focused on Kalesh that I hadn't heard them.

The one with long purple hair and an array of sinister tattoos on her arms narrowed her eyes and began speaking in Cyrinthian. "What human dares despoil our lands with his presence?"

"We shall roast your flesh and drink porridge from your skull, human!" the other one trilled. With her short pink hair and unmarred skin, I would have guessed she was the nice one.

I held up my hands. "I didn't come here by choice."

"And you shan't leave here by choice either!" The pink-haired one began weaving a pattern with her hands. "The fish will feast on your eyes!"

I put my elite naming skills to use and named them Pinky and Purply. "So, you're not going to eat me anymore?" I sighed. "Am I not good enough for you?"

She blinked, momentarily thrown off by my seemingly casual attitude, but quickly recovered. "Either way, you'll be dead." She thrust her hands forward and a web of black dust flew toward me.

I zipped to the side. "Missed me, Pinky."

The web veered toward me and the unfae grinned. "You can run, but you can't hide, human."

I blurred further away, my newfound speed the only thing keeping me out of reach.

"How is he so fast?" Purply said.

"Vitania brought me here," I shouted. "So, stop your stupid web thing and talk to her!"

"Lies!" Pinky jabbed a finger toward me as I began running a wide circle around them to stay out of reach of her spell. She spun around but couldn't keep up. "Vitania would never consort with humans."

"She's been living among humans for centuries!" I dodged out to the water and paused for a moment to let the spell catch up, then darted around it and back the way I'd come.

"More lies!" Purply began weaving a spell and I decided enough was enough.

I flitted straight at Pinky and grabbed her from behind, putting her between me and the spell. "Have a taste of your own medicine!"

"No!" she flung up a hand and the web dissipated.

Purply stopped forming her own spell and drew a wooden staff. She batted at me, but I dodged the blow easily. I snatched the staff from her hand and flung it toward the water. Something hard clobbered me over the head. I stumbled forward and felt warm blood trickling down my scalp.

Somehow, I maintained my feet and shot forward. Pinky grunted in exasperation. She'd drawn her own weapon while I'd faced Purply. I growled in anger and began to manifest into demon form. Muscles strained against my clothes. Pain stabbed into my forehead as horns began to grow. I swelled two feet taller, stretching my clothes to the max. Flexing my black-clawed hands, I rumbled, "Leave me alone!"

The unfae flinched in surprise and regarded each other.

"You are demon kind?" Purply said.

"I'm Daemos." My tail twitched with annoyance. "And no one to be trifled with."

Purply and Pinky stared long and hard, apparently considering their options. I bared my teeth in a confident grin, daring them to come at me again. Then the forest seemed to come alive. Towering tree creatures thudded onto the beach accompanied by dozens of bark-skinned dryads and fauns. Scores of unfae hovered in the air behind them, eyes glinting with anger.

I began to wonder if I should just start running to lead them away from the others, because this wasn't going to be pretty.

An unfae with glossy black hair and icy skin consulted with Pinky and Purply as the small army began to fan out around me. I was just about to get the hell out of Dodge when she raised a hand in the air and the army stopped.

She turned toward me. "You claim Vitania is here."

I nodded. "She's here, but asleep in a giant clam shell."

"Tell me more of this shell," she said in a calm but commanding voice.

"There's not a lot to say." I wasn't sure if this was a pop quiz or a stalling tactic so her forces could surround me. "There's a deep pool of water inside. She got in and sank out of sight. I don't know how to open it to prove my claim."

She pursed her lips. "Only a Siren can open the shell. For you to know what is inside means a Siren opened it in your presence."

I repressed a snarky reply about her Sherlockian skills and simply nodded. "Does that mean you believe me?"

"It means patience is required, demon kind."

"The name is Justin Slade." I'd already guessed who she was. "You must be Glacia, ruler of the unfae."

Her eyes flared for an instant. "I've heard of you. You are the one who returned Pyra from the human lands."

I nodded. "I freed her and Thal from Vokan's cantrap. Pyra refused to let me or my friends set foot in your lands."

"Yet, here you are." Glacia raised an eyebrow. "Why?"

"Vitania brought us here because we had a little altercation with Eve." I shrugged. "Nothing big."

Glacia's mouth dropped open slightly. "What would you know of Eve?"

"Way more than I want to, actually." I bit my bottom lip and considered what to tell her, then figured it couldn't hurt to pile on the facts. "Her granddaughter is with me as well. She's a demigoddess but Eve did something to corrupt her powers."

Her eyes narrowed. "You come bearing fascinating stories, child." Glacia fluttered to the ground and stood before me in all four feet of her glory. Then, like Thal had done before, she grew to match me in height, adding another inch just so she could look down on me.

In demon form I was a good two feet taller than normal already which would really make this really awkward when I shrank back down. So, I shrank down to normal size and craned my neck up at her. "Do you play basketball?"

Glacia blinked. "I don't know that word."

I'd said it in English because jamming the words together in Cyrinthian made even less sense. "Never mind. Would you like to go inside the cottage with me so you can see for yourself that Vitania is here?"

"My queen, it could be a trap." Pinky flitted toward us and hovered a few feet away. "Humans cannot be trusted."

"He is not quite human." Glacia smiled at her. "There is nothing he can do to harm me, dear one. Wait here."

Pinky scowled at me. "Unlike our fae brethren, we will kill you, demon man. Take care every hair on her head emerges unscathed."

"Aw, and I was going to give her a free haircut too." I mocked a frown. "Guess we'll have to stick with a shampoo and scalp massage."

My attempt at snark only confused her. Clearly, they didn't do haircuts in the land of the fae.

Glacia shrank until she was an inch taller than me then motioned for me to lead the way to the cottage. I did so, keeping a careful watch in case Pinky decided to do something rash.

The unfae queen misinterpreted my apprehension. "The treants and dryads will not harm you."

"I wasn't looking at them." I almost mentioned that I'd fought treants and dryads but decided now wasn't the best time to mention it.

Glacia paced alongside me. "How is Thal? I have not seen my niece for quite some time."

"She had tacos for the first time, so I'd say she's living her best life." Tacos was another word that faced an uphill battle at translating. Meat salad sandwich was about as close as I could get and that only made them sound disgusting.

Glacia grimaced.

I sighed. "It's an Eden thing. Tacos are amazing." This time I used the actual word.

"Tacos." Glacia said it slowly as if testing the word. She shook her head. "We have been isolated for too long and lost touch with everything that is not here."

"I thought the fae got their rocks off by messing with humans." I shook my head. "It must be awfully boring here."

"Dreadfully." Glacia scowled. "But I am not the fae queen."

Her statement triggered a memory, causing me to stop in my tracks. "Lumia was supposed to speak with Pyra about involving the fae in the fight against Baal. Did she ever make it here?"

Glacia's forehead wrinkled. "Yes, mother arrived." Despite her height and serious expression, she sounded like a lost child.

"Well, that's good." I waved a hand and noticed out of the corner of my eye that Pinky surged toward us for an instant before realizing I wasn't attacking Glacia. "Baal, the former grand overlord of Haedaemos reassembled enough relics of Juranthemon to bring him back to life as his former self, Elohim. Now the realms are slowly collapsing back into one world and the process will kill billions."

Her eyes widened and studied my face for a long silent moment. "That is hard to fathom. How do you know this?"

"It's a long story." I shook my head and started walking toward the cottage again. "I think it's best if Vitania explains." I was tired of telling and retelling the story, but I also figured Vitania's word would carry more weight with these people.

Glacia nodded. "That will cure my skepticism."

"I just hope we can wake her up." I hadn't considered how to open the clam shell bed.

I opened the door and tried to show some manners by letting her go first, but she waited for me to proceed, distrust plain on her face. I walked inside and found the others huddled around a seashell table they'd dug up somewhere. Shelton flinched and gave me a guilty expression.

"Great, so you're talking about me now?" I threw up my hands. "I'm not being greedy just because I want my powers back!"

Emily rose and held out her hands placatingly. "Justin, we think it might be a good time for you to step back for a while and not feel so pressured. You've been at the forefront nonstop. You deserve a break."

"Babe, it's for your own good." Elyssa stood next to Emily. "You've died once and we can't afford losing you."

"Is this a fucking intervention?" I roared with laughter and tried not to cry. "The realms are literally collapsing in on themselves and you want me to take a seat and chillax."

Emily opened her mouth then blinked and stared at something behind me.

I'd been so upset by the intervention that I'd forgotten Glacia, queen of the unfae was behind me. I stepped out of the way and flourished my hands toward the towering female. "This is Glacia, her royal highness, queen of the unfae, leader of warriors, sworn enemy of the dastardly humans, protector of truth, justice, and the American way."

Glacia cleared her throat. "What nonsense is this? Did Thal tell you all of that? And what is America?"

Elyssa bowed. "Glacia, forgive him. He's just upset at us for trying to keep him alive."

Emily followed suit. "A pleasure to meet you. Lumia told me so much about you."

Shelton was too busy snickering to even think about bowing. He flinched when he caught hard gazes from the women and managed an off-balanced bow. "Oh, uh, greetings your royalness."

Glacia flicked aside their greetings as if they were mere annoyances. "I would speak to Vitania."

"Right this way." I shot a dirty look at the others and led her past them to the hallway. When we reached the room with the clamshell, Glacia strode to it and gently stroked it with her fingers. It cracked open.

Glacia took my hand and pulled me onto the surface of the water before I could stop her. Rather than plunging into the depths, we sank slowly like wrecked ships.

"Hey, I can't breathe underwater!" I sucked in a breath as the water reached my neck and tried to pry my hand loose from her.

She smiled as if amused by my mortal fear. "Then I will enjoy the pleasure of your silence."

The water closed over my face before I could reply. Glacia tapped my nose and a bubble of air formed around my head. I drew in a breath and looked at the small bubble, wondering how long it would take to fill up with carbon dioxide and suffocate me. I exhaled. A stream of small bubbles trailed from the one around my head. A few breaths later, I realized that was how it released my exhalations.

Glacia formed a dome around her head as well as we sank into the pitch black. Minutes passed and I began to wonder just how deep this freaking water bed was when we stopped, hanging suspended in the water. A small light globe drifted from Glacia's finger, illuminating a figure beneath us.

Vitania floated just below our feet, hair billowing gently.

"She was exhausted when she went to sleep, so she might not wake up easily." Bubbles erupted from my air pocket.

Glacia frowned, apparently unable to understand what I was saying underwater.

I mimed yawning, drooped my eyelids sleepily, and then put my hands in the prayer position and pretended to go to sleep.

She stared at me, eyebrows pinched with confusion. Deciding I had nothing else to offer she tapped Vitania on the cheek.

The Siren blinked awake and shouted in alarm. "Glacia?" Despite the water between us, her words were clear as a bell.

Glacia nodded and spoke, but the water garbled her words.

Vitania looked from her to me and shook her head. Then she took our hands and we jetted up and out of the water, landing neatly beside the bed. Despite having just soaked our clothes, we were perfectly dry.

"How long have I been asleep?" Vitania said.

I gave her a sheepish look. "Maybe an hour."

She sighed. "Glacia, it is a pleasure to see you. I assume you were displeased to find humans on Pangea."

"The others were, but I do not care." Glacia shrugged. "I disguised myself many years ago and visited Utopia. I found the humans there exemplary creatures, better in many regards than some of my kind."

"That is quite a statement coming from you." Vitania touched the other woman's cheek. "I remember a much younger fae who thought all humans should be exterminated."

"These humans are better in every way than those scum on Eden." Glacia made a spitting noise. "Justin has made outlandish claims about Baal and the realms. I would hear the truth from you."

Vitania sighed. "Fine. But I am exhausted and require sleep so I will keep it short."

Glacia nodded. "A summation will do for now."

I glanced to the side and saw Emily, Shelton, and Elyssa huddled at the doorway. I turned away from them, not wanting to make eye contact after their little intervention.

Vitania told Glacia the highlights of Baal's activities and predicted a dire outcome if we didn't find a way to stop him. "If he finds the crystalis relic that enabled the Sundering and reunites it with Apollyon, then the realms will likely snap back together in an instant, killing billions as worlds collide."

Glacia put a hand to her chest. "How can we possibly stop this?"

"That's a good question," I said.

Vitania's shoulders sagged. "In fact, now that Elohim is resurrected, undoing the collapse may be impossible."

I rocked back on my heels at Vitania's unexpected declaration of doom.

Shelton gasped. "Whoa, impossible?"

Vitania shrugged. "How are we supposed to shatter Elohim, Apollyon, and Saila now that they are living, breathing beings again? It may be that there is no stopping the collapse, but at least we have time to consider options."

I looked for a place to sit down, but the open clamshell was the only furniture. "What options do we have? Retreat to Atlantis and wait?"

Vitania opened her mouth to speak, then narrowed her eyes as if remembering something. "But perhaps another crystalis would be powerful enough to stop the collapse."

I shook my head. "Uh, aren't they incredibly rare?"

She nodded slowly. "During the early days of my secret travels across the realms, I became a passenger on an Mzodi ship. Scuttlebutt, as they call rumor, was of a great find—a gem unlike any other discovered. I caught a glimpse of it as it was paraded around the ships of the fleet before being sent to Zbura to adorn the crown of the Seraphim emperor."

I did a double-take. "You think it was a crystalis?"

"It looked very much like the one from the time echo." Vitania's gaze became unfocused. "Like most of my ancient memories, it is faded, but probably accurate."

"Whoa." I tried not to get my hopes up. "So there might be a crystalis in Zbura, provided the emperor didn't use it."

"If it exists, it's likely in the palace museum, still adorning the royal crown." Vitania stifled a yawn. "I am too tired to discuss this further. Let me sleep and we will talk tomorrow."

Glacia put a hand on the Siren's shoulder. "You should know that Mother arrived in the fae lands weeks ago. Pyra refused to allow me an audience with her and I have heard nothing since."

"Troubling news." Vitania pinched the bridge of her nose and winced. "I was worried for Lumia already, but now my dreams will be nightmares." She fell back onto the water and began to sink. "There is much to do when I awaken." She sank out of sight and the shell closed.

Glacia turned and put a firm hand on my shoulder. "I must know every detail Vitania omitted."

"You sure you'll believe what I have to say?"

She nodded. "Now that you are vouched for."

I glanced at my friends and tried not to scowl. "Let's go outside."

"Justin—" Elyssa reached a hand toward me.

I shook it off. "We'll talk later." I was too pissed to think straight about the situation. Maybe they were right. Maybe Emily would inadvertently kill me if she tried to restore my powers, but we were past the endgame and into the death throes of the realms. Doing nothing wasn't an option.

Outside the cottage, mushroom chairs and tables had already sprouted. Fae crowded around the tables, drinking from dainty flower teacups. Fauns played a haunting melody on pan flutes while dryads pranced around treants. A massive grinning cat perched atop one of the tables, eyes glittering in the sunlight.

I paused a moment to take in the bizarre sight then followed Glacia to a tall mushroom table with stools of woven vines. A massive purple caterpillar crawled from beneath the mushroom, giving me quite a start. I yelped and jumped back as it curled up on the table before the unfae queen. A hookah of flower petals and stems poofed into existence and the caterpillar lit it.

Glacia took a long puff, held it in, and exhaled the smoke. She patted the mushroom next to hers. "Join me."

The smoke smelled like cinnamon apples and smoked bacon. "What's in that thing?"

"The leaves of blue ferns," she replied. "The smoke tastes and smells like whatever you crave."

"Neat trick." I sat on the proffered stool and took the pipe. I carefully inhaled and was surprised by how soothing the smoke felt. It was almost like a light mist just before the rain. And it tasted just like the special smoked bacon Shelton had made during our time in Atlantis. "This is amazing."

Glacia nodded. "It clears and relaxes the mind to allow for clearer thinking."

"Where has this been all my life?" I took another draw and let it sit in my lungs.

Shelton and the others approached the table but the extra vine chairs shrank into the ground and vanished.

Shelton looked hurt but stopped a distance away.

Glacia took back the pipe and tapped it against her lip. "Tell me why you are upset with your companions."

I told her. "Do you think it was unreasonable of me to let Emily try to restore my powers?"

"You're very driven, Justin." She folded her arms on the table. "Like any leader, you are willing to do everything necessary to protect those in your care, even if it means sacrificing yourself."

I let the sentence bounce around in my head for a moment before speaking. "So, I'm right?"

"You are clearly not the only leader." Glacia's eyes settled on Elyssa whose violet eyes glared dangerously at the two of us.

"Granted, Elyssa is the better leader. I'm ready to act while she wants to sit back and plan."

Glacia nodded. "What would happen if you died?"

"I died once and they did okay without me." I held up a hand. "That's not to say I want to die again."

The unfae queen frowned. "How did you die and return to life?"

"Oh, boy. That's kind of a long story."

"We have time." She took another puff from the hookah.

I'd become a fairly proficient storyteller thanks to situations like this, so I gave her a rundown on my adventures in the afterlife and continued with more details about how Baal had collected the relics of Jura and restored himself and his son to life.

Several other fae drifted close as I told the story, many frowning in disbelief. Others took their cues from Glacia's reactions. The queen seemed to believe me without reservation since Vitania's support gave me street cred—or forest cred as it was.

As the sun began to set, new vegetation began to sprout. Giant sunflowers blossomed, shining golden sunlight down on us. The fauns gathered driftwood and dead limbs to build a towering bonfire near the water. The caterpillar produced more hookahs, handing them out to the fauns and fae. Judging from the odor of the smoke, most of them weren't using blue fern leaves.

Glacia clasped her hands on the table and pursed her lips after I finished speaking. "You are not a leader."

I blinked and forgot what I was going to say next.

She continued before I recovered. "You are a bull dragging your keepers by the ropes around your horns."

My jaw went slack. "Wow. You really think I'm that bad?"

"You excel at making snap decisions, and barge forward without considering long-term consequences."

"I've gotten better over the years." I shrugged. "I try to be more careful in my decision making now."

"You are a protector, a shield." Glacia nodded as if agreeing with her own words. "If you die, the shield is gone and those behind it will suffer."

"I see your point, but we can't afford to do nothing while the realms collapse all around us." I sighed and watched the fauns dance around the fire. Though the treants stayed well away from the flames, the dryads had no such reservations and joined the festivities. I'd seen such a celebration in the Fairy Gardens at Arcane University, so I knew this party was headed for an X-rated climax.

Glacia continued. "I agree. The fae have remained in isolation for too long. I believe it is in our best interests to help you." She nodded as if to reaffirm her position. "Tomorrow when Vitania awakes, we will visit Pyra and demand an audience with Lumia."

I fist pumped. "Now, that's what I'm talking about." I felt marginally better about our situation, but we were still a long way off from being fine. Vitania was our only means of travel between realms. Mine and Emily's powers were borked. Elohim was working to restore Earth at the cost of billions of lives, and Eve, it seemed, was intent on destroying it and starting over from scratch.

Even with all our powers operating at top efficiency, I questioned whether we had the ability to defeat one god, much less two of them. Hell, even Olivia seemed nearly impossible to defeat despite Emily's best efforts.

As the festivities grew wilder, I took my leave and walked down the beach until the sounds of music faded in the distance. I knew it was stupid to be mad at Elyssa and the others, but I couldn't bring myself to go back to them just yet. I sat on the sand and let the waves lap my feet. I closed my eyes and laid on my back, listening to the soothing sounds. Before long, calm replaced my anxiety and worry.

The problems before us seemed insurmountably huge so I tried to cut them into smaller, more manageable chunks, *tried* being the key word. How did one slice and dice destruction on an interdimensional scale into bite-sized pieces that mere mortals could digest? How could we possibly save billions of beings from the collapse of the realms?

Doomsday was creeping toward us all and the denizens of most realms were probably completely unaware of it. Atlantis was presumably the only safe place to be when the final collapse occurred, but billions of humans wouldn't fit there unless we utilized every square inch of ocean. Initiating such a bold plan would also require telling the noms of Eden about magic. There was no telling how they'd react.

But at this point, it seemed we were running out of options. We had to implement an exodus on a biblical scale before time ran out. Leaving the noms in the dark and allowing them to die without a chance of saving themselves was unconscionable.

I wished I were as clever as Elohim. It had taken him eons but he'd successfully resurrected his physical body, outsmarting Eve and the rest of us in the process. His machinations had manipulated so many lives I couldn't even count them all. He'd even used Eve to lure us into the Void so we could do the dirty work of reaching the Beast for him.

If only there were some way to pit Eve's wrath against Elohim. Unfortunately, she was too mentally unbalanced to be much good to us. Then again, if Elohim discovered Eve's intent to destroy Earth and start over with Alden, he might act and that would buy us time to plot a route out of this mess.

But I couldn't just pick up a phone and call Elohim, nor could I casually mention Eve's plans in a conversation. He had to find out about it through one of his minions. The most likely kind would be an infernus, which led to another question. Now that he was back in the flesh, could Elohim control his infernus the same way he had before?

As Baal, he could see through their eyes, direct their actions, and even possess them to experience a taste of physical life. That led me to another revelation. The grand overlord of Haedaemos no longer existed. Elohim was now flesh, meaning he'd left a tremendous power vacuum in the spirit realm. Then again, Haedaemos might not be around for much longer once the collapse was complete. I wondered what that meant for those of us with inner demons. Would Daemos cease to exist as they currently did?

I mentally yanked myself back on track. This tangent was a bottomless pit of questions that I couldn't answer. The only actionable idea from my mini-brainstorming session was spreading the rumor that Eve was trying to destroy the realms. Even if Elohim could no longer see through the eyes of infernus, he would still hear about it. That might get one monkey off our back.

I sighed in mild satisfaction. This wouldn't save the world, but it would preserve it a bit longer. "Things are looking up," I announced to no one. Before I had a chance to congratulate myself too much, something stung my neck. I jerked upright and staggered to my feet.

Pinky fluttered a few feet away, a scowl marring her face. "You will not change our ways, human."

"Change your ways?" I scoffed. "I'm trying to save the damned..." the final word refused to form on my lips. *That bitch drugged me!* My vision went blurry and the beach swayed back and forth. My limbs refused to respond to my commands. Strong hands gripped me before I toppled over sideways.

"He's heavy and he stinks," a male voice said. "I do not like this plan, Trusha."

"Quiet, Moss. You take his feet and I will get his arms."

"Pyra will not restore you to the fae for this." Moss sighed. "Once you have spilled blood, there is no going back."

"Will you help me or not?"

Moss sighed again. "Yes, of course I will."

I couldn't feel anything in my limbs except the pressure of someone gripping them. They flopped me onto my belly. The sand blocked my nose and mouth. I couldn't see or breathe. Without control of my limbs I couldn't even roll back over. My heart pounded a panicked rhythm as I struggled to draw breath. Just when I felt consciousness slipping away, the ground fell away.

The buzz of fairy wings told me Moss and Trusha were airlifting me to the one place I didn't want to be without Glacia's protection. Pyra was going to burn me alive.

I faded in and out of consciousness as we traversed miles of forest. Daylight invaded the darkness behind my eyelids. Cold stone pressed against my face. My eyelids felt glued shut. I tried to clear them with my hands, but my arms barely moved. I managed to open one eye. Someone's foot blocked the view.

"Unacceptable," a female growled. "Glacia's commands do not supersede mine."

It had been a while since I'd heard that voice, but I recognized it. "Pyra," I hissed. My mouth felt drier than a cotton factory.

Someone jerked me upright. "Perhaps we used too much toad venom," Moss said from somewhere nearby. "He looks terrible."

Thrusha's face appeared inches from mine, teeth bared. "Tell my queen why you are here, human."

I could barely form a response. "Water."

"Get him water," Pyra said from somewhere behind Thrusha.

Thrusha released me and I collapsed back to the ground. Moss helped me up a moment later, a large cup-shaped flower in hand. He trickled water into my mouth. It tasted so sweet to my dehydrated tongue I slurped loudly without caring about the audience.

"His tongue is swollen," Moss said. "And the whites of his eyes are yellowed. We nearly killed him."

"You are unfae." Pyra stepped into view, a haughty sneer on her face. "You are already sullied by spilt blood."

Moss stiffened but said nothing.

My regenerative abilities were probably the only thing that kept me alive. "Thank you," I muttered to Moss.

"He speaks at last." Thrusha pushed Moss aside and took my chin in her hand. "Tell Queen Pyra why you are here."

I met Pyra's gaze. "I saved your life and this is the hospitality you show me?"

She flinched as if I'd struck her. "I forbid you from setting foot in our lands and yet here you are."

"Vitania brought us."

Pyra's eyes flared. "Did she come for Lumia?"

My muddied mind took a moment to process the unexpected question. "Is Lumia here?"

"Answer the question, human."

I managed to shake my head. "Vitania brought us here for safety."

"Then she brought you to the wrong place." Pyra paced away, staring into the distance. "What was she thinking?"

My eyesight was still blurry, but we seemed to be on a hill or mountain because a valley spread out before us. "Glacia is bringing her here today. Ask her yourself."

Pyra shook her head. "There will be no discussion. Glacia will carry out her duties and execute the invaders for touching fae soil."

Thrusha scowled. "What if Glacia refuses, my queen? She has already spoken in opposition to your plans for Utopia."

"Then I will anoint another queen of the unfae." Pyra turned to her. "Someone who is unquestioningly loyal."

Moss grimaced but Thrusha beamed. "I would be a most excellent queen."

"Perhaps." Pyra turned and regarded me for a moment.

"I saved your life, damn it." I tried to move but I was still too weak. "Vokan was going to drain your soul."

"There is no reprieve for breaking covenant, human." Pyra glared at me. "The sentence is death."

11

Pyra's death sentence was a real nice capper to the evening. My tongue was still swollen and nausea squirmed up my esophagus, thanks to the paralyzing agent Thrusha had given me. Pyra didn't seem inclined to make me more comfortable. She snapped her fingers. Thrusha and Moss gripped my arms and dragged me away. My bones ached as they thumped down a long spiraling staircase. Moments later, my captors dumped me into a dark room with a dirt floor.

"Water, please," I gasped through dry lips.

The doorway sealed shut, leaving me in darkness. My demonic night vision kicked on, casting the small space in bluish light. The walls looked like rough-hewn stone. I was probably underground somewhere. Any attempts at escape would have to wait since I could barely turn my head, much less move my arms and legs.

Concentrating with all my might, I managed to make my left index finger twitch. *Well, that's a start.* I couldn't even properly talk to myself since my throat felt like the Sahara Desert. I tried sleeping off the effects of the drug, but my heart raced with anxiety.

Some interminable time later, the doorway opened. The light outside cast a long shadow into the dim space, but I couldn't see who it was. The figure knelt next to me and spoke. "Here's some water. Can you drink it yourself?"

"Moss?" I croaked.

He gripped me beneath my arms and dragged me away from the door until I was propped up against the wall. The stone was uncomfortably cold and dug into my back, but it felt like heaven compared to my raw throat.

Moss trickled water into my mouth. I manage to swallow most of it, but my throat muscles weren't working at top efficiency so some went down the wrong pipe and made me cough.

"Why help me?" I said after a coughing fit.

"I don't like suffering." He set a pouch near me. "There's more water and some food in there for later when you can move on your own." Moss stood and walked toward the door.

"Pyra is wrong." I sounded like an old man but at least it didn't hurt to speak.

Moss paused at the doorway but closed it without answering.

Now that my throat felt better, my back started to complain about the rough stone wall pressing into the skin. I concentrated and made my right arm flop. It wasn't great, but it was progress. My stomach rumbled and another sensation worked down through my guts.

"Oh, shit." I strained with all my might to regain control of my body. "Please not this. Anything but this!"

Judging from the warmth filling my pants, it was too late. Forget escape. I was ready to die. But in my current state I couldn't even kill myself. The paralytic must have really upset my stomach, or else I'd eaten some fae food that hadn't sat well in my stomach. Either way, I didn't plan on letting Pyra execute me with a load in my pants.

I had to escape.

I reached out to Kalesh. *Got any tricks up your sleeve?*

That fae must have used enough paralyzer to subdue a dragon. Even our regenerative abilities are straining to overcome it.

I sighed. *Just great.*

Kalesh continued. *I have other troubling news.*

Oh boy, I can hardly wait.

He chuckled. *Waiting is all you can do right now.*

I flopped my arm in defiance. *Not for long. So, what's this bad news?*

Juranthemon in Haedaemos is slowly vanishing. All that is left of Unity is a white void. This void seems to be spreading.

Cold fear gripped my heart. *As Jura is reappearing in Eden, it's erasing Haedaemos behind it.*

Kalesh gulped. *We will all be wiped from existence?*

The collapse of the realms is causing it. Have any spirits been affected?

There are rumors of some greater demons vanishing, he said. *But there is also a war among the overlords, each one vying for Baal's throne.*

I shook my head. *At this rate, there won't be a throne left by the time someone wins.* I tried to reason out what this could mean, but theoretical magic wasn't exactly my strong suit. *Since Baal and Apollyon returned to life, maybe other beings sent to Haedaemos are also being reincarnated.*

Most of us were created long after the Sundering, Kalesh said. *Does that mean we face oblivion?*

That was a good question. *I really don't know.* I was tired of hearing his voice in my head, so I closed my eyes and entered a state of deep meditation. A studio apartment coalesced around me. It had changed since the last time I'd been here. Though it was a product of my imagination, Kalesh could also shape it.

Where there had once been a single bed and an old-school television with video game consoles, there was now a gray room with a couch and a big screen television. Kalesh stood behind a kitchen counter pouring alcohol into a shaker. He put in some ice and began shaking it. "Want some?"

I shrugged. "What is it?"

"What do you want?"

I pondered that difficult question. "Hennessy and Coke."

Kalesh groaned. "Please tell me you're joking." Aside from the blue skin and small horns on his forehead, he looked identical to me. Even his voice sounded the same, though it was a bit deeper. Even the skin on his arm sparkled like mine, thanks to the primal fount.

I stepped up to the counter. "Surprise me."

He produced two glasses from nowhere and poured an amber liquid into them.

I took mine and sipped. It was slightly bitter with a refreshing aftertaste. I held out the glass and examined the drink. "Wow, it's good. What is it?"

Kalesh took a sip of his own. "I don't know. I just thought about what I wanted to tickle my taste buds with and created it." He rapped his knuckles on the counter. "That's the advantage of crossing over from Haedaemos and into your head."

I pointed out his sparkly arm. "Did the primal fount infect you too?"

He nodded. "It infected us all the way down to the soul."

I conjured a barstool and sat down, sipping my drink and spinning idly. "Well, my soul will be making a return trip to the afterlife shortly."

Kalesh cocked his head. "Do you really think Pyra will execute us?"

"I have zero doubt."

He nodded. "How much time do we have?"

I shrugged. "Eight to ten hours maybe."

He leaned on the bar. "Then perhaps we have time."

"Time for what?"

"An adventure." Kalesh grinned. "Remember when Baal brought us into his palace in Juranthemon to gloat just before you died?"

I nodded. "Hard to forget."

"After you faded away, I grew very weak and faded out of consciousness for a time. When I woke, I was still in the room where he'd kept us."

I frowned. "He just left you there?"

Kalesh shrugged. "The demon spirits of most Daemos are so closely intertwined with the human soul that the spirit fades away. I think that's because it goes to the afterlife with the soul, but I could be wrong."

I frowned harder. "You didn't go anywhere."

"I know." He tapped a finger on his lips. "I think I briefly faded out during your transition to the afterlife, but since we are not completely merged, I remained behind."

"Makes about as much sense as anything in this crazy life." I took a gulp of my drink. "What happened next?"

"I wandered the halls looking for a way out while avoiding Baal's minions." He stepped away from the bar and looked toward the window. "I found a room with a massive demon pattern in the floor. I've never seen anything so complex."

"Uh, there are demon patterns in Haedaemos?" I scoffed. "I thought those were just for summoning demons in physical realms."

"They are which is why I became extremely curious." Kalesh set down his drink. "When I touched the edge of the pattern, it was as if thousands of voices and images filled my mind. I could barely make sense of it all, but I knew without a doubt that I'd touched the infernus network."

I sucked in a breath. "Holy shit balls. That's how Baal controlled his infernus?"

Kalesh shook his head. "I think it's how his minions control them. Baal didn't need an interface as far as I know."

I tried to polish off my drink but it was apparently bottomless. "I'm in."

Kalesh blinked. "But you haven't even heard my plan yet."

"Dude, I'm paralyzed back in the real world." I rubbed my hands together and nodded at the window. "Let's go on an adventure."

He grinned and clapped my back. "There might be a problem."

I quirked an eyebrow. "And that is?"

"The last time you crossed over, you were dead." He shook his head. "It might not work this time."

I shrugged. "Projecting my consciousness should work whether my body is dead or alive."

Kalesh bit his lower lip. "Then let's see what happens." He climbed through the window and stepped out onto a narrow bridge. It led across a dark void to a window in a building on the other side. When I'd been dead, a storm of consumed souls in the afterlife had challenged my crossing. This time there was nothing but eerie silence.

The first few steps were easy but became progressively harder as I neared the midway point until it was like pushing through an invisible bog. It had been this way during my initial attempts to cross from the afterlife.

"You're not physical, remember?" Kalesh stepped across the midpoint without issue. "You're spiritual energy, not flesh and blood."

It hadn't been that long since my afterlife adventure, but my physical brain had been all too eager to forget what death had been like. I paused and allowed myself to remember what allowed me to cross over last time. *I am not flesh and blood. I do not need to breathe. I am energy. An astral projection.* I hovered a few inches off the bridge, floating like a ghost. The invisible resistance vanished.

"There you go." Kalesh grinned. "We're getting better at this."

Without moving my legs, I drifted across the barrier between my world and Haedaemos. Every molecule of my being tingled, and the weight of gravity tugged down on me once again. Even though Haedaemos was a spiritual realm, it was still bound by rules like those of physical realms.

We crossed the bridge and ducked through the window leading into the other building. A small, minimalist apartment was inside. There was a couch in the middle of the den and a television against the far wall. A bowl of fruit sat atop a counter in the kitchen. All in all, it looked like an apartment you'd find in the real world.

I ran a hand along the white leather couch. "Is all this real?"

"Real enough." Kalesh turned on the television. On it, the Cookie Monster was devouring a pentagram made of chocolate-chip cookies. Unlike the Cookie Monster I'd seen as a kid, this one wasn't a puppet. "Some parts of our existence mirrors that of the real world."

I grimaced. "Can you mold reality like I could in the afterlife?"

He shook his head. "Only very powerful demons can do that. The laws of magic and physics still apply here."

"Does that mean we have to take a car to reach Juranthemon?"

Kalesh snorted. "No. We're on the opposite side of the world from

Juranthemon, but we can still reach it quickly."

My forehead pinched. "How?"

Kalesh went to the apartment door and opened it. A cacophony of chaotic booming and grinding of stone and metal echoed from the hallway beyond. "Bedlam, of course."

I'd only caught a glimpse of Bedlam the last time I'd been here and it was like watching an M.C. Escher painting come to life. Just around the corner, a dizzying array of walls and stairs shifted and rotated at seemingly random intervals. The floor rumbled and shook, rolling like the waves on a stormy ocean.

I rubbed my eyes to keep them from crossing. "How do we get through that without being ground into burger meat?"

"Just follow my lead." Kalesh stepped toward chaos.

I gripped his arm. "Hang on a minute. Is there a pattern? What if we get separated?"

"There is no pattern." He pointed toward a stationary door about three stories up. It vanished behind a wildly spinning staircase an instant later. "But if you're any good at Mario Brothers, this is a piece of cake."

I face-palmed. "Dude, playing a video game is one thing, but trying to do all that jumping in real life is something entirely different, especially when there aren't any magic mushrooms around to help." I threw up my hands. "I don't have any extra lives."

He smirked. "Didn't you use one to come back to life the last time?"

I hadn't thought of it that way. "Yeah, but if my astral projection is smashed, I think it's game over."

"Like I said, just follow my lead." Kalesh stepped to the edge of the undulating floor as the concrete walls ahead slammed together hard enough to blow his hair back. The instant they opened, he dashed through.

I saw no other option but to follow. Thankfully, my super speed was intact, so I stuck to his heels. He leapt up the side of a moving wall, rode it sideways, and sprang to a rotating staircase. I kept pace but nearly rolled an ankle when the staircase reversed rotation the moment I landed. It rolled sideways but Kalesh didn't even try to run to the other side. Rather than fall thirty feet to the floor, we remained on the stairs. Apparently, gravity didn't operate like normal here either.

We ran up the stairs, connected with another stairwell as it rotated into place, then scaled a wall. Just as it began to drop out from beneath us, we leapt to another stairwell. Kalesh and I bounced back and forth between a pair of walls to reach the third story, then ran along a spinning staircase and dove through the open doorway.

Kalesh flourished his hands and shouted, "Parkour!"

"Parkour my ass." I put a hand over my racing heart. "That was terrifyingly fun."

"Yeah, it helps pass the time when I'm bored." He turned and entered the narrow corridor beyond the doorway. We soon reached a vast plateau of hexagonal stone columns. They measured anywhere from ten to thirty yards across. Some jutted at irregular angles, rising higher than the others around them. Some were gone, leaving dark, seemingly bottomless pits. A dim orange sun rotated in place beneath a sky so black it seemed to absorb the light.

I shivered in the sudden cold. "What is this place?"

"It's a part of Nowhere." Kalesh knelt and rapped on the ground. It thumped hollow like a timpani drum. "It's a juxtaposition of chaos and order that allows us to bend the rules of physics a little."

"Is it different than the part of Nowhere I've been?" I asked.

He nodded. "Nowhere is vast. I walked for days in one direction until I hit a dead end."

"Like a cliff?"

Kalesh shook his head. "It looked like a wall of translucent water, but it wasn't liquid. When I rapped on it, the darkness on the other side scattered."

I grimaced. "How does darkness scatter?"

He stared into the distance as if trying to come up with a way to explain it. "It was like a swarm of roaches was covering the other side and I scared them off. When I did, dim beams of sunlight came through the cracks."

"That is creepy as hell."

Kalesh shuddered. "Yeah. I decided to turn around and go the other way."

I frowned. "How am I able to summon you when you go on these little trips?"

"The window in your soul always opens wherever I am. Nowhere operates as a middle ground for the physical and spiritual, so it follows me here too."

"What happens when I release you?"

"I usually end up right back where I was." He looked up at the sun. "We should get going."

I nodded. "Lead on."

Kalesh jogged along the uneven terrain and stopped about a mile later. He knelt at the edge of the next hexagonal column and traced a symbol on the surface. It rumbled and rose a few feet, revealing a cavity in the stone. Ultraviolet light pulsed from within, thrumming softly in rhythm. I followed Kalesh into a small room where a large crystal sat atop a pedestal.

"What is that thing?" It didn't resemble anything I'd seen before, not even the gems created by the Mzodi.

"I have no idea." Kalesh put a hand on my shoulder. "But touching it will take us just outside Juranthemon. Getting inside the city will be another matter."

"How do we get back?" I asked.

"I'll show you." He touched the crystal and the world flickered. The next instant we stood inside a dim room, lit only by a pulsating light just before us. Kalesh waved a hand at cave walls. "We're in an underground chamber. The light in the middle of the room is connected to the crystal." He touched it and we were back in the hexagonal room with the crystal. "You just touch the node and boom, you're back."

"Wow, that's pretty cool." I touched the crystal and the cave flashed into existence around us. "Is this how people get around in Haedaemos?"

"I've never seen anyone else use them, so they might be my little secret." Kalesh shrugged. "Moving around Haedaemos is risky so most demons wouldn't do it anyway. Crossing into another overlord's domain is just asking to be assimilated."

"Yeah, this realm ain't no paradise." I looked around. "Guess we'd better get moving."

He nodded. "Juranthemon is off-limits to everyone except Baal's minions, so we'll have to be extremely careful."

"I gotcha." I took a deep breath. "Let's go."

Kalesh followed the contour of the cave wall until he located a small tunnel barely three feet high. He dropped to his knees and crawled through.

I assumed the position. "Don't fart."

His laughter echoed from ahead. "Demons don't fart."

As I crawled behind him, however, the faint scent of brimstone grew stronger and stronger until it overwhelmed everything else.

Kalesh stopped. "Something's wrong."

"Isn't Haedaemos supposed to smell like brimstone?"

"Not like this."

The ground shook and dust rained down on my head. "Earthquake!"

The ground shook again and again.

"Fuck." Kalesh picked up the pace. The tunnel exit appeared not far ahead after he exited.

I crawled as quickly as I could and emerged in a forest of massive trees. Orange flames licked the dusky sky. The ground shuddered as another giant tree collapsed with a boom. A monstrous roar echoed. A swath of trees crackled and snapped like toothpicks beneath the weight of a gargantuan creature. A one-eyed demon with a horn the size of a semi-truck on its snout reeled backward beneath the onslaught of an even larger demonic opponent.

Shouts and screams rose above the roars of the goliaths as armies of smaller but no less horrifying demons collided on a field just beyond the tree line.

The war for Juranthemon was raging.

12

Kalesh pursed his lips. "This could be a good thing."

I blinked in confusion. "Say what?"

He scaled a tree with his demon claws and peered out at the landscape. I climbed a neighboring tree the same way and looked for myself. A horde of purple demons fought a giant lizard-shark just beyond the battle closest to us. Goliath demons smashed and bashed each other in yet another test of might not far from the purple demons.

"All four overlords are throwing everything they've got into taking the city." Kalesh grunted. "They haven't waged war like this in eons."

"Do they even realize that the city and this entire realm are going away?"

He shook his head. "Obviously not." Kalesh flicked his gaze toward me. "Infiltrating the city will be even riskier than I thought. Are you sure we want to do this?"

"If this works, it'll be epic." I shrugged. "It's worth a try."

He nodded. "At the very least, Elohim will never see it coming."

I looked at the towering city walls. "How do we get in?"

"The same way I got out." Kalesh pointed toward a pair of giant demons battling near the wall. "There's a secret entrance over there."

My jaw went slack. "Behind those demons?"

"Yep."

I shook my head. "That's a pretty big wall. There's got to be another way in."

"Probably, but I don't know where else to look." Kalesh flexed his glowing arm. "Maybe we can run fast enough to avoid being eaten."

I reflexively reached into my pocket to check the time, but my phone was back in Pangea on my physical body. "I don't have much time before Pyra has me executed, so let's get started."

He nodded grimly. "Let's go."

We jogged out of the forest. The field was crawling with demons of all configurations. A giant blob rolled over demons, sucking them inside and dissolving them into gaseous vapors as it assimilated them. Scorps and crawlers skittered into battle. Massive starfish with maws of razor teeth on their limbs sucked up small scorps, devouring them like crawfish.

It was a literal field of horrors, the stuff of nightmares, and we had to dodge through it without becoming demon fodder ourselves. I reached inside and touched the primal force crackling in my soul. Kalesh and I burst forward at top speed.

The battle seemed to slow to a crawl.

We zigged around the starfish demons, zagged between the legs of a monstrous manbearpig, circled around a squad of purple demons that were fleeing a one-eyed, one-horned flying purple demon eater, and then dashed beneath the shiny black carapace of a giant scorp facing a horde of crawlers.

The combatants were tightly packed around the section of the wall we needed to reach. It was impossible to go through them, so we leapt atop the crowd and used their heads as stepping stones.

"There!" Kalesh pointed to a section of wall that looked no different than the rest, and jumped back to the ground. He traced a demon pattern on the wall. The slick surface bulged as if a giant face were trying to break free of a sheet of plastic.

The battled resumed around us. Nearby humanoid demons did a double-take as they noticed us seemingly appear from nowhere. A score of crawlers, sensing fresh prey, hissed and screeched before skittering toward us. I could barely kill the things in the real world, much less here without powers.

"What now?" I shouted.

The face in the wall opened its mouth and moaned in agony.

"Jump through!" Kalesh grabbed my arm and shoved me into the gaping orifice.

I barely had time to yelp before stumbling into the pitch black. The air inside was dank and humid. Thick liquid dripped from above. I gibbered with disgust, my feet slipping and sliding across the damp ground. Another body collided into me and we tumbled through the darkness. An instant later we rolled onto cobblestones. A face bulged from the wall on this side too, mouth agape.

The shrieks of pursuit echoed from the darkness. Countless eyes glowed within the tunnel and the shadows writhed with spiky legs. Kalesh traced a pattern on the wall and then unexpectedly bitch-slapped the face. The moaning mouth clamped shut, crunching down on the pursuing crawlers like a mouthful of nuts.

"Ew!" I shuddered. "Are they dead?"

Kalesh shook his head. "Weakened perhaps, but nothing here dies without being assimilated into another demon."

"This place is freaking weird." I looked up and around at the crystalline buildings nearby. I hadn't seen the entire city of Juranthemon, but this resembled the architecture I'd seen inside the time loop. "I can't believe we made it."

Kalesh looked up and down the street as if expecting company, but there was no sign of life. He frowned. "Where are the defenders?"

"The wall looks pretty sturdy." I shrugged. "Maybe Baal's people don't think they need to guard it."

"You mean Elohim's people?"

I shook my head like a wet dog. "Yeah, whatever. I guess they aren't his people anymore."

"Let us hope that's the case." Kalesh headed down an adjacent road. "The palace is this way."

I paced alongside him, keeping an eye out for demons, but the streets were empty. The city was a labyrinth of canals, walkways, bridges, skyways, and buildings. We had to double back on several occasions because of dead ends. Kalesh huffed and puffed angrily when we circled through a plaza for the third time.

"How exactly did you escape last time?" I raised an eyebrow. "You can't find your way through the city, much less discover a hidden passageway."

He sighed. "I didn't quite tell you the whole story about how I escaped."

I raised my other eyebrow. "Well, spill it."

Kalesh leaned against a wall and crossed his arms. "I was captured by a ruby spirit."

I grimaced. "Aren't they super strong demons?"

"Yes, some of the most powerful humanoid demons." He bit his lower lip. "This particular ruby used to be a knight for Domathus."

That name knocked loose a memory. "The mastermind behind the Demonicus Incident."

"Exactly." Kalesh's gaze went distant. "This demon went by the name Astra, but her true name is Astranamastia."

"You were able to use her true name to escape?" I asked.

He waggled his hand. "She recognized me and told me she was part of a plan by another overlord to disrupt Baal's plans."

I frowned. "She was a mole?"

"Yes, I believe so." Kalesh pushed off the wall. "She was surprised to see me still alive since the palace was filled with gossip of our demise."

"I'll bet." I tilted my head. "Why did she help you escape?"

"Because she thought it would throw a wrench into Baal's plans." Kalesh sighed. "And what did we do? We came back to life and helped Baal achieve his goals."

"Don't remind me." I looked up and around at the buildings hemming us in, then pointed at a skyway. "If we can get up there, maybe we can find our way to the palace."

Kalesh shook his head. "Unless you have your Seraphim powers, we can't operate the skyways."

I threw back my head and stifled a shout of frustration. "We don't have hours to wander aimlessly. I don't want to cross back over only to find myself bleeding out from a fae dagger."

"We could use our super speed to search faster."

I shook my head. "We'll just end up running in circles faster. We need a vantage point." I tested the wall of a nearby skyscraper, but couldn't find a door. "Do I need Seraphim powers to open the freaking doors too?"

Kalesh regarded the structure. "I don't know, but I suppose we could climb one of them."

I ran a hand along the smooth surface of the skyscraper. "There's nothing to hold onto."

He pursed his lips. "What if we ran really fast up the side?"

The tower looked at least a hundred stories tall. I tried to calculate how that would work and failed. "How do physics work here?"

He shrugged. "Haedaemos is a shadow copy of old Earth, so gravity probably works the same unless you're a super powerful demon."

"Which means if I run at this wall and then up it, centripetal force will keep me on the wall for only a few seconds. Even moving super-fast, we won't have enough time to scale the entire building."

Kalesh nodded. "Getting back down would be tricky too."

"Can we sprout wings in Haedaemos?"

He nodded. "But we suck at flying so it would take forever to reach the top."

"We could just use our wings to glide down." I concentrated on growing my demon wings but didn't feel the slightest itch in my back to indicate anything was happening.

"Oh, yeah." Kalesh blew out a breath. "I'm the one who lets you grow wings." Large black batwings unfurled from his back. "I forgot about that little detail."

I face-palmed. "Well, there goes that idea."

"Not necessarily." His wings beat, lifting him off the ground. Kalesh held out a hand. "Grab hold."

"This isn't gonna work." I took his hand anyway.

With great effort, he lifted me a few feet off the ground and held us there for a moment, then nodded in satisfaction. "I'm strong enough for us to glide."

I released his hand and dropped to the ground. "What happens if we fall?"

Kalesh shrugged. "We won't die, but we'll be incapacitated for a while."

"We don't have a while."

He nodded. "I know."

"Then don't let us fall." I walked across the courtyard as far from the skyscraper as possible, Kalesh pacing beside me. I held out a hand. "Should we hold hands while doing this to be safe?"

Kalesh snorted. "That would look really stupid."

I waved a hand around the courtyard. "It's not like anyone is watching us."

He shook his head. "If we blew up a building, would you look back when we walked away?"

"Hell yeah. That's half the fun."

"Lame." Kalesh blew out a sigh. "This is why we never get style points." He nodded toward the building. "Grab my arm macho style when we jump off, okay?"

"You mean grabbing each other's forearms?"

"Yup." He held up three fingers and counted down. "Three, two, one."

We blurred toward the building. At the last instant, I realized I hadn't timed exactly how to shift my momentum so I could run up the side. Kalesh executed it perfectly. I stumbled slightly but managed to plant my first foot against the side of the building. The stumble caused me to fall behind and lose some speed. Kalesh peaked at about ten floors up and jumped. I panicked and jumped at an angle toward him.

Kalesh left his wings folded and dove to meet me, hand outstretched. I gripped his wrist with both hands, clinging on for dear life. His wings unfurled, jolting us to a near stop, and then we glided over smaller buildings, angling for a courtyard a few blocks away.

My demon shook his head and gave me a look of disappointment. "If this was an action movie, you'd be the comedic relief."

"Dude, I don't care." I looked over nearby rooftops and spotted a vast white void to the south. "That must be where Unity was."

Kalesh nodded. "The Palace is at the opposite end of the street." He turned his head north. "I think I see which way we need to go." He guided us to a rough landing in a plaza a few moments later. Rather than repeat our previous attempt, we jogged in the general direction of the palace until we hit another dead end.

I looked up at a nearby crystal tower and rubbed my hands together. "I'll do better this time, I promise."

"I'm not expecting any miracles." Kalesh counted down and we blurred toward the building.

I timed my approach better this time and planted my feet on the side of the obelisk-shaped structure. The sloping sides allowed us to get even higher before jumping. I leapt in unison with Kalesh and caught his forearm in the manliest man-grip of my life.

He nodded somberly with approval. "Epic, bro."

"You got it bruh." I fist-pumped with my free hand to show how manly and unafraid of falling I was.

Kalesh released my forearm. I yelped in surprise as my grasp slipped.

He roared with laughter. "I like comedic relief better."

I scowled up at him. "Do demons have balls? Because I'm about to punch you in the crotch."

Kalesh's smile vanished as his eyes settled on something ahead. "Oh, shit."

I was facing the wrong way and had to twist my body around to see what he saw. "Oh, shit."

He banked hard to the left, but a shout from below told us we'd been spotted. A pair of dark red demons leapt into the air on equally red wings and sped toward us. The first one snatched me from Kalesh's grasp as easily as taking candy from a baby, and swooped away. I heard shouting, but couldn't see what happened to Kalesh. A moment later, the other ruby spirit coasted next to us, her hand gripped around an unconscious Kalesh's neck.

Before I could come up with anything snarky to say, they dropped us into the plaza just in front of a sprawling palace. There was nowhere to run. Nowhere to hide. Because we were surrounded by at least fifty other demons.

It seemed Pyra would be executing an empty body, because my soul wasn't going to make it out of here alive.

13

The crowd of demons surrounding us were mostly ruby and sapphire spirits sprinkled with a few yellow caustics.

Kalesh moaned and rolled onto his knees. He rubbed his eyes and looked around. "We're screwed."

"That's putting it mildly." I stood and took in the crowd. I didn't sense anger, but there was a whole lot of suspicion and confusion.

A caustic worked his way to the edge of the circle, licking his lips like a hungry dog. "I call point of privilege for the sapphire spirit."

One of the rubies glared at him. "You were not given permission to speak, dog." She approached me. "What manner of spirit are you?"

Kalesh stepped in front of me. "He is my child."

She shoved him out of the way with little effort. "No, there is something different about him." She took my hand and inspected it. Her eyes flared. "He is not a spirit!"

Another ruby spirit pushed through the crowd. "That's because he is Daemos." She planted herself just behind the other ruby. "He is Justin Slade, grandson of Baal."

A round of gasps rose from the surrounding demons. The caustic who'd approached earlier backed away as far as he could.

"Greetings, Astra." Kalesh bowed. "It is an honor to see you."

Astra raised an eyebrow, but said nothing.

I wasn't sure if she was here to doom or save us, so I kept my mouth shut.

A male ruby spoke. "Our master has sent you to continue his work?" He practically spat the words at me.

"Justin Slade is an enemy of our master," a caustic shouted. "We should devour him."

The male ruby pursed his lips. "An enemy?"

I sensed an opportunity and took it. "I tried to stop Baal from destroying Haedaemos." I straightened my shoulders. "I make no apologies for trying to save the realms."

A sapphire spirit pointed down the long road leading to the blank spot where Unity once stood. "That is why the world is vanishing?"

"Yes." My voice cracked like a pubescent teen, because any one of these demons could consume me and there was nothing I could do about it. "Baal destroyed Haedaemos so he could return to his true physical form as the god, Elohim."

"Lies!" A caustic scrabbled through the crowd, his hands grasping for me. "Devour him!"

Astra gripped the caustic and casually flung him over the crowd and somewhere out of sight. "I will devour the next demon who does that."

The male ruby turned toward her. "You believe him?"

"I do, Lethamene. Baal led us to believe that he was merely seeking dominion over Eden." She shook her head. "Never did he mention he would sacrifice our realm to do so."

"It's not just Haedaemos," I said. "The realms are collapsing back into one Earth. Since Haedaemos is a spirit copy of the old Earth, it will cease to exist once the process is complete."

Lethamene pinched his chin between thumb and forefinger. "Baal was incarnated into Elohim?"

"Reincarnated," I said. "Baal's origins go back to the Sundering when the realms were created."

Confused looks passed among the demons.

"What is this Sundering you speak of?" Lethamene replied.

Kalesh frowned. "Baal never told you how Haedaemos came to be?"

A sapphire shook her head. "Baal told us it was a mystery lost to the ages."

I snorted. "Bullshit. He was at the very heart of it."

"Devour the liar!" someone shouted.

A caustic echoed the sentiment, but the ruby and sapphire spirits ignored him.

"What do you know of history?" Astra said.

"A lot." Before I could continue, something invisible seemed to press against my chest. I staggered backward into Kalesh. Just as quickly as it had come, it was gone.

His eyebrows pinched. "What's wrong?"

I put a hand over my chest. "It felt like someone was standing on my chest."

"Your body," he hissed in a low voice. "They might be trying to rouse you or even kill you as we speak."

"I don't have time for this," I muttered. I straightened and met the confused looks from the demons. "The Apocryphan, Xanos, lured the god, Elohim, to Juranthemon with rumors of a great battle. She lured her siblings and father with tales saying Elohim seeking to claim dominion over the Earth, displacing the Apocryphan rulers." I pointed toward the blank spot down the road. "When both sides appeared in Unity Plaza, she instigated a fight. The epic battle shattered Earth into multiple realms. Many of the citizens of Jura were killed instantly, but instead of going to the afterlife, they became the denizens of this spirit world, a copy of old Earth."

Murmurs of confusion and disbelief echoed from the throng.

Astra pursed her lips. "Why would we not go into the afterlife?"

I shrugged. "We think the afterlife was also disrupted and possibly reset."

"This is quite a tale," a female sapphire said. "You claim Baal was once this Elohim?"

I nodded. "Elohim and his son, Apollyon, were together at the center. Baal was a combination of the two, though Elohim's personality was dominant. Apollyon became the Beast, a pitiful creature trapped in the Void. At least until recently."

The murmurs grew louder.

"The Great Devourer has escaped?" Lethamene exclaimed.

I shook my head. "No, he was reincarnated by his father's side."

"Then perhaps we shall be reincarnated," the sapphire said.

Astra narrowed her eyes. "Yes, what would prevent us from being reincarnated?"

I knew the answer—sort of. "Did any of you exist before the Sundering?"

The blank stares and downcast eyes told me the answer.

"Domathus claims he was," Astra said. "Some overlords have been alive for eons."

"If you weren't alive during the Sundering, then you don't have a physical body to go back to." I pointed toward the former location of Unity. "And once this realm is reduced to a white void, I don't know if you'll be trapped here or simply wiped out."

"We threw a caustic into the void," Lethamene said. "He screamed piteously and faded to nothing."

Kalesh chuckled. "Well, that answers that."

I couldn't laugh because it felt like someone dropped a truck on my chest. I fell to my knees, gasping even though I technically didn't need to breathe here.

Astra stepped closer. "What is wrong with him?"

"The fae are probably trying to wake him." Kalesh dragged me to my feet.

"The fae?" Lethamene's eyes widened. "I have never been able to gain a foothold in their world."

"Utopia." A caustic spat the word. "Many of my kind were drawn there by a powerful magus named Vokan. None of them returned."

The pain eased from my chest and I rose. "That's because I devoured them."

The caustic scowled. "You?"

I nodded. "It was like eating raw liver and onions."

"Why are you a prisoner of the fae?" Astra asked.

"I don't have much time to explain." I braced myself for another invisible attack. "Kalesh and I need to leave so I can return to my body and face what's happening in Utopia."

Lethamene narrowed his eyes. "Why would you risk your very soul by journeying to the world of the damned?"

Astra nodded. "Yes, why come here?"

I put a hand on Kalesh's shoulder. "Because we need your help to stop the end of the world."

The murmurs in the crowd faded to silence.

Lethamene nodded. "I am listening."

"Inside the palace is the pattern Baal used to control all his infernus." I jabbed a finger at the building even though it was right in front of us. "As Elohim, we don't think he can control them anymore."

"You are right," Lethamene said. "That is why we are here to transmit his orders to them."

"We control them," a caustic snarled. "He allows us to inhabit some of them as our reward."

I scoffed. "What a lousy reward. He expects you to keep working for him while your entire world disintegrates."

The caustic raised a finger as if to denounce me, but a ruby gripped his throat and flung him out of the circle.

Astra shook her head. "I grow weary of those foul creatures."

Lethamene crossed his arms. "Instead, you expect us to work for you while our world ends?"

"My goal is to save the realms." I shook my head. "I don't know how I'll do it, but I'll figure it out."

Astra gave me a doubtful look. "Is it not too late now that Elohim once again walks Eden?"

I shrugged. "I don't know. There is a piece of the original puzzle missing from Baal's design, and that missing piece is the only reason the realms didn't instantly collapse, killing billions and erasing the other realms." I didn't trust them enough to mention the crystalis.

"Let me see if I understand." Lethamene clasped his hands before him. "The collapse will recombine the realms into one Earth. The physical beings have a chance at survival, but we have none?"

"I don't know." I sighed. "There's so much I can't answer. All I can do is promise that I'll try to stop what Baal put in motion."

Astra shook her head. "At this very moment, the armies of three overlords are fighting for control of the city so they can control Baal's vast network of infernus in the mortal worlds. The walls are stout, but even they cannot withstand an army."

I looked toward the white void. "How quickly is that spreading?"

Lethamene answered. "A few feet a day. Within a week, the palace will be consumed, and with it, the infernus control pattern."

I pinched the bridge of my nose and thought furiously. "Can you possess the infernus?"

"The earlier ones, yes." Lethamene scowled. "Baal changed the design so the soul spark would reject demonic possession because one of the caustics took one for himself and tried to escape."

"Only a special infernus could house a ruby or sapphire for long," Astra said. "And even if you could create such a thing, our presence has adverse effects on the physical world. There is something about our essence that is incompatible with life."

"It's because of Apollyon," Kalesh said. "His aura placed a taint on Haedaemos, giving it the same brimstone odor that Hell has. His corruption aura created the demonic creatures of Hell and is probably why the beings of Haedaemos have similar characteristics."

"But he and Baal are gone." Astra tilted her head to the side. "Would that mean the taint is gone?"

Kalesh shook his head. "I don't think thousands of years of saturation will just go away overnight."

Lethamene waved his arms and the circle around us cleared a path toward the white void. He stared at it long and hard. "You've said nothing to sway me and I cannot simply believe that you weren't sent here by Baal to deceive us into helping him yet again."

"We're telling the truth!" I held out my hands imploringly. "If you control the infernus network for us, it will give us a chance to stop all this."

"How?" Lethamene gripped Kalesh by the throat and lifted him from the ground. "Do not lie, little man! Tell me the truth or I will devour your demon!"

Kalesh struggled futilely in the ruby demon's grasp.

I held up a hand. "I'm not lying!" I decided it was time to lay all the cards on the table. "When the world was sundered, those at the epicenter of the blast weren't completely destroyed. Their bodies, nearby buildings, and more were blown apart and scattered across the realms. But rather than being annihilated, they were transmuted into indestructible pieces."

"So that is how the relics of Jura were created." Astra nodded. "What does this have to do with you helping us?"

"The Sundering wasn't just caused by the Apocryphan and Elohim." I took a breath and hoped this gambit paid off. "It was something called a crystalis—a powerful seed of creation that rarely spawns where the infernal and primal founts meet. Apollyon unwittingly wore one on a chain around his neck. The attacks caused it to explode in an intense act of creation that led to the Earth splitting into newly formed realms."

"I have heard of a crystalis before." Lethamene dropped Kalesh almost as an afterthought. "Baal searched high and low for one for eons before embarking his plan to collect the relics of Jura."

"The crystalis that created the realms may have also been turned into a relic—a relic that Baal never found." I pushed home the final point. "So long as it's missing, the collapse of the realms will be slow. But if Elohim finds it, then the collapse will probably be instantaneous, and Haedaemos will cease to exist."

Lethamene towered over me. "How will controlling the infernus help?"

I decided to lay a few more cards on the table. "Vitania believes there's a crystalis in Seraphina. If we can recover it, we might be able to save existence as we know it. But to reach the crystalis, we'll probably need an army."

"Baal controls Seraphina with a dragon army." Lethamene scoffed. "What good is even ten thousand infernus against such odds?"

I straightened my shoulders. "We don't need ten thousand. We only need a few dozen."

"A few dozen?" He stared at me blankly. "What madness is this?"

"I specifically need infernus who control nom governments." I gave them the hook that I hoped would reel them in. "What if the dragons faced the combined might of the Overworld and nom war machines?"

Lethamene's jaw went slack. "Missiles and nuclear weapons would be formidable against dragons."

I nodded. "We can defeat the dragon army, get the crystalis, and stop Haedaemos from being destroyed."

The sassy sapphire who'd spoken against us earlier nodded. "I believe the boy. After Baal abandoned us to our fate, I would love nothing more than to crush the skulls of his dragon army."

Kalesh pumped a fist. "And hear the lamentations of their women!"

"Lamentations are music to my ears." Lethamene nodded sagely. "I would almost rather use the infernus to destroy Eden completely rather than let Baal have it. The infernus could unleash nuclear war."

My insides went cold. "Elohim will live on no matter what. From what I understand, he wants to destroy everything so he can start over. Without your help, without the crystalis, Haedaemos has no chance to survive."

"Lethamene speaks from a place of great anger," Astra said. "I am willing to endorse your plan, for it seems to be our best chance."

"As am I," the sapphire said.

Many other voices rose in agreement. Only a lone voice in the back jeered and shouted at us. His comments cut off with a choking noise and yet another caustic was hurled away from the others.

Those guys are hopeless.

Lethamene remained quiet for a long time before speaking. "I was Baal's top knight, destined to become a lord with my own fiefdom. As a demon, it is my duty to let my overlord use me for his will, so long as it does not lead to my own end. But for the grand overlord of Haedaemos to doom his entire realm to oblivion is unthinkable." He put a huge hand on my shoulder and squeezed tighter than he needed to. "I will support your plan. But know this—if I sense deceit on your part, I will rain nuclear weapons down upon Eden and in every realm where we have infernus. There will be nothing left but dust when I am done."

I gulped. "I have nothing but the best intentions, Lethamene. I have known almost nothing but war and strife for the past several years and would do anything to finally see peace."

Several demons scowled.

"I like war," one muttered. "It makes existence interesting."

Lethamene bared his teeth. "Nothing stirs the spirit like a brutal war. I have inhabited the bodies of many a soldier over the eons just to feel alive."

"Uh, well, you can fight all the wars you want after we avert the collapse." I decided a change of subject was in my best interests. "I can communicate with you through Kalesh?"

Kalesh nodded. "I will remain here."

An invisible force drove me to my knees. The fae were trying to wake me again, it seemed. "I need to get back to the window," I gasped.

Kalesh knelt next to me. "The window exists wherever I am." A thin crack in the air split open before me. "Please don't let the fae kill you." He shoved me into the breach. I tumbled into a dark tunnel. A light beckoned from the other end.

Kalesh gripped my arm and dragged me like a corpse until we reached the light. The studio apartment waited beyond the exit. Another firm shove sent me through. The apartment vanished as I jerked back to consciousness.

A pair of gleaming green eyes stared down at me. I slowly registered whose they were. Thrusha knelt on my chest, a bloodied stone dagger gripped in one hand as she carved something on my chest.

It didn't look like I had much time left.

14

The next thing I noticed besides the murderous unfae on my chest, was the awful odor filling the small room. The load I'd dumped in my pants hadn't gone anywhere.

Thrusha smirked. "He still lives. Clean him and prepare him for his fate."

My arms and legs twitched and spasmed. I wiggled my fingers and felt them respond. The paralytic had nearly worn off, but when I tried to rise, my rubbery arms had no strength.

A pair of male fae hauled me up off the floor and dragged me up the spiral staircase I'd unceremoniously been dragged down hours ago. One opened a door and the sound of flowing water emanated from the room beyond.

The room turned out to be a vast cave. Light sparkled from crystals jutting from the floor and ceiling. Water poured from somewhere above, casting rainbows where it struck the crystals. Beams of sunlight entered the cavern through holes in the roof far above, lighting a pool of crystal-clear water. Runoff from the pool formed a stream that continued further into the cave.

My raw throat ached for the bounty of water and my soiled pants cried out for justice. If this was the fae idea of a shower, I was all in.

My escorts hauled me past the waterfall and along the stream until we reached a dark pool of bubbling water. They dropped me on the hard stone floor, roughly stripped me naked, then plunged me into icy cold waters.

Slimy flesh writhed against me. Tiny mouths nibbled all up and down my flesh, even in my butt crack. I shouted in terror and disgust, flailing my limbs in a vain attempt to gain control of my body. Foul-tasting water filled my mouth. Despite my thirst, I had no desire to drink it.

"I don't think he likes the eels," one of the fae said with a grin.

"This is where the unfae bathe when they're here." The other one knelt next to the pool, holding my hair to keep me from going under. "Not even the eels can clean the filthy creatures."

They gripped me beneath my arms and yanked me out of the pool, leaving me sprawled on the stone floor.

"Let him dry a moment," one said to the other.

I shivered violently, not only from the cold, but from the memory of the eels squirming against my tender bits. Red marks covered my skin, but admittedly, I did look and feel pretty damned clean. Warmth filled my chest, working its way out to my arms and legs. I flexed my hands and they responded immediately.

The fae were looking away from me, talking to each other in low voices, so I climbed to my feet. I was hungry as hell, but otherwise I felt right as rain. Apparently, the eels did a lot more than clean the flesh—they purged the toxins from my body too. The wounds dug into my chest by Thrusha were already starting to heal.

I restrained myself from growling in anger. These fae bastards were going to pay for what they'd done to me. I reached for my inner demon and manifested.

The fae abruptly stopped talking a moment later, as if some instinct told them danger was near. They slowly turned, eyes on the ground where they'd left me. Instead of a weak, incapacitated prisoner, they found something else. Terror slowly filled their eyes as they took in the towering beast with horns and flames in its eyes standing behind them.

Before they could scream, I backhanded the nearest one. He slammed into a crystal and slumped to the ground, unconscious. The other one sprouted wings and tried to fly away. I snatched his foot and plunged him face-first into the pool of eels.

He kicked and flailed like a child in a roach nest. I pulled him back to the surface. A tenacious eel clung to his nose. The slimy gray creature was no more than a foot long and no wider than my finger. It had no eyes and its teeth were flat and smooth, but it still looked terrifying to me.

I plucked it free and dropped it back into the water, then held a long, black claw to the eye of the fae. "Tell me how to escape, or I'll turn you into a fairy pirate."

His eyes widened. "There's only one way out."

"No back exits?" I splashed a hand in the pool. "Does this stream go to the surface?"

"I don't know." He gripped my wrist, straining to pull free, but I was far too strong.

"Keep that up and you'll lose an eye," I growled in guttural, demonic tones.

He stopped struggling and his eyes filled with resignation.

I spoke once he grew still. "Is Glacia here yet?"

"Her retinue just arrived," the fae said in a trembling voice.

I didn't think Glacia would willingly kill me, but she might not have a choice if Pyra commanded her. My thoughts latched onto something Pyra had said earlier. I shifted my grip on the fae, taking his arm firmly in my hand. "Are there other prisoners here?"

"Only one," he said.

"Who is it?"

"I don't know." He shook his head. "They are in isolation, not to be spoken to or viewed. Their food is dropped into a slot and left."

"Where is their cell?"

He gulped. "In the deepest reaches of the dungeon."

I had a good feeling about this. "Take me there."

His eyes widened. "I thought you wished to escape."

"Yeah, and this is part of the plan." I set him roughly on his feet. "Lead the way."

The moment I released him, he made a break for it. I lunged forward at super speed, hands reaching for his shoulder. Instead, I struck him in the back of the head and sent him skidding across the stone floor. He rolled to a stop, bloodied and unconscious.

"Just great," I bellowed. I knelt next to him and gently slapped him in the face. I could probably dunk him in the eel pool and wake him, but maybe I didn't need him. The spiral staircase seemed to be the only way into and out of this place. Maybe all I had to do was follow it to the bottom to find the cell of this mysterious prisoner.

I slung the small fae escorts over my shoulders like sacks of potatoes and carried them back to the stairs and down to my former cell. The room reeked of poop, especially to my hypersensitive demon nose. I dropped them inside and closed the door, dropping a thick wooden beam in place to bar it shut.

Then I jogged down the winding stairs, passing several doors on either side until I reached the bottom. A wide tunnel led to three doors. I removed the bar from the first and looked inside. It was empty, as was the second one. I found who I was looking for behind the third door. They were emaciated, pale, and stank to high heaven. Rotting clothes hung from their frame, and they mumbled incoherently.

But it was exactly who I'd thought it would be. Pyra's secret prisoner was her mother, Queen Lumia.

"Oh, that bitch is gonna pay," I muttered. I cradled Lumia in my arms and hurried up the stairs.

Her eyes blinked open and stared vaguely into mine. "I know you."

"Do you?" I didn't think she recognized me in demon form.

"Yes, young Slade." She drew in a long breath. "Even with the horns."

I reached the shower room and took her toward the waterfall.

Lumia shook her head weakly. "The eel bath."

I shuddered at the idea, but obliged. She was too weak to stand on her own, so I lowered her gently into the cold waters. The water squirmed with activity. Eels rubbed against my hands and fingers.

"Put me under," Lumia said.

I submerged her head and left her there for a few seconds before pulling her back up. She nodded, and I hauled her out of the water. Not a shred of her tattered clothes remained. Bite marks covered her bare skin and shaved head, but she was able to stand on her own. It felt extremely awkward since I was still stark naked too.

Lumia took my arm for support and pointed toward the waterfall.

I tried to imagine I was fully clothed, instead of my demon willy dangling free alongside a nude female who wasn't Elyssa. This was not the time for BDDE, as Elyssa jokingly called it—Big demonic dick energy.

Lumia reached between crystals and withdrew silken robes that seemed to be all the rage among the fae.

I hastily put on mine and felt relieved to conceal my demonic tender bits. "How long have you been held captive?"

Lumia's gaze went distant. "I have no idea. I went straight to Pyra when I first arrived. My loving daughter drugged me and threw me into the dungeon for daring to suggest we join the other races in the fight against Baal." She pursed her lips and regarded me. "Why are you here?"

I released my demon form and shrank down to normal size. The robes magically shrank with me. "Vitania brought us to Pangaea to recover. Glacia discovered our presence, and after some discussion, decided to help us speak with Pyra. But a pair of fae kidnapped me and brought me to Pyra. They'd planned to execute me when Glacia arrived."

Lumia scowled. "I never meant for my people to become xeno-phobes. I don't understand my child. What turned her into such a little monster?"

Her daughter was hundreds of years older than me, so calling her little sounded strange. Then again, most parents continued seeing their children as kids all their lives. Pyra certainly acted like a spoiled kid when it came to humans setting foot in her precious kingdom.

"I'd be willing to bet Vokan turned her mistrust of humans into hatred." I shook my head. "God only knows how long he held her in a cantrap."

"Vokan is not representative of the Utopian humans." Lumia sighed. "But I think you are correct. There was a time even Pyra was curious about humans. Times when she wished to venture into their lands and see them. I forbid her from doing so because I did not trust the humans. Little did I know how different these humans were from those of old Earth."

"Well, if she hates humans enough to throw her own mother into the dungeon, it means we can't reason with her." I bit my lower lip. "We'll have to take over by force."

Lumia laughed mirthlessly. "A coup against my own flesh and blood to reclaim the throne I abdicated long ago."

I burst into song. "Isn't it ironic, don't you think?"

Lumia frowned. "Yes, of course. Did I not just point out the irony?"

I cleared my throat. "Sorry, bad joke." I rubbed a hand on my chest. Most of the wounds had healed, meaning Thrusha hadn't used a magical dagger to slice me up. "How, exactly, are we going to overthrow Pyra?"

"Very carefully." Lumia held her hand over a crystal and the inner light glowed brighter. "I am weakened, but should have enough strength to get us out of here."

I waved a hand at the magnificent waterfall. "Why does a prison have such an amazing shower room?"

"This was once my palace." Lumia sighed softly. "After I abdicated the throne, Pyra had her own palace built and turned mine into a prison. I suppose she wanted to make a name for herself rather than rule in her mother's shadow."

"Makes sense." I headed toward the door. "We'd better start moving. It won't be long before they wonder why I haven't been brought to the executioners."

Lumia nodded. "Yes, but be prepared to fight if I fail to help us escape unnoticed."

I led the way upstairs. Despite Lumia's assurances that she could keep up, she lagged behind unless I slowed considerably. Rather than carry her, I scouted ahead. Most of the other doors along the passage had been walled off with stone.

"The old entrances to the throne room, dining hall, and other places," Lumia explained when I asked.

The ground rumbled. Beasts bellowed, and trumpets sounded from somewhere above. I hurried and reached a door at the end of the stairs. It sounded as if a herd of horses were galloping past outside. Lumia caught up and pressed a hand to the door. It slid aside and into the stone.

The air outside was thick with dust and smoke. Metal clanged. Voices cried out in anger and defiance.

"There's enough dust to keep us hidden." I couldn't see more than a few feet ahead. "Let me carry you and we can get out of here."

Lumia put her arms around my neck as I lifted her diminutive frame. "The safest route will be west along the edge of the flower forest and then north toward the dark lands where the unfae reside. Whatever you do, don't step into the flower forest."

I grimaced. "Why not?"

"The monstrous bees and carnivorous flowers do not care for trespassers."

"Enough said." I stepped out of the doorway and leapt back just as a herd of centaurs stampeded past.

One of them reared up and spun on its hind legs to face me, its face contorted with rage. I should have felt fear, but all I could focus on was the massive package flopping around between the centaur's hind legs. There was no corresponding package below the humanoid torso.

I grimaced and jumped back. "Well, that just answered a question I didn't even know I had."

The centaur sheathed a massive battle axe on his back as his forelegs stomped impatiently. "Take the wounded to the stone tree. The queen has recalled all troops."

Lumia gasped. "Centaur, what is happening?"

"I do not ask questions, lady fae. I follow orders." He galloped off after his comrades.

Lumia shivered. "This is terrible. The last time I assembled our warriors was to fight off the orc hordes of the swamplands."

"Well, I'm not going to complain if Pyra is under attack by orcs." I peered into the dusty landscape. "Escaping in the chaos shouldn't be too hard."

She shook her head. "This has nothing to do with orcs, and everything to do with you."

I blinked. "How does this have anything to do with me?"

"You said Pyra planned to make Glacia kill you." Lumia sighed. "I suspect there was a difference of opinions. One thing led to another, and I fear the worst."

My brain slowly connected the dots. Pyra was probably furious that Glacia had hosted me and my friends. She'd likely sent a bluntly-worded message to Glacia, demanding she present herself to the court. The dutiful sister had presented herself only to be berated by Pyra. An ultimatum had been presented: kill Justin Slade or Glacia would no longer be queen of the unfae. Glacia had refused. It was anyone's guess what had happened after that, but it seemed a full-fledged civil war was underway.

15

Chaos seemed to follow me wherever I went. We'd never defeat Elohim if every place I visited was at war. I couldn't shake the looming dread of defeat. "Pyra needs to lighten up or there won't be a kingdom to fight over anymore."

"My daughter was once so full of light and love." Tears trickled down Lumia's face. "That was why I felt comfortable leaving the kingdom to her. She used to write to me on occasion to let me know how our people fared. But then her letters stopped and ugly rumors told me a different story."

"Did she act like that before Vokan captured her?" I said.

Lumia pursed her lips. "Her last letter was perhaps a century before Vokan captured her. Her words seemed normal, but it's possible she was lying."

"A century?" I blinked. "How long were the intervals between letters?"

"By human terms, a lifetime." She smiled sadly. "When you have lived as long as I have, a hundred years does not seem so long."

"That's kind of depressing." I blew out a breath. "I wonder if all that time trapped in Vokan's cantrap screwed up her mind." Another thought hit me, but it seemed less likely. Could Baal have replaced the real Pyra with an infernus? It fit his modus operandi perfectly. "Or maybe the Pyra in charge isn't the real one."

Lumia's eyes flared. "You think Baal replaced her?"

I blew out a breath. "It's a possibility."

A stiff breeze began to clear the dust and smoke, so I sprinted west toward a forest of giant flowers. Frighteningly large bees hovered over the blooms, seemingly oblivious to the sounds of battle coming from the fae village. There were no signs of life in the mushroom homes or tree houses at the outskirts of town, probably because everyone had retreated to the stone tree, whatever that was. I turned north well before reaching the flower forest, unwilling to test my luck with the bees.

If not for the doors in the sides of trees and mushrooms, I never would have known this forest was a city. Some of the fae lived up in the trees while others made their homes in the trunks or under-ground like Lumia's former palace. The center of town was a grassy meadow, now flattened and muddied from centaur hooves.

The stone tree rose from a clearing not far from the meadow, its leafless black branches spreading over the fae city like an umbrella. Dozens of centaurs and short elephantine creatures formed a perimeter around the base while fae hovered overhead on gossamer wings.

Lumia stared at it and shuddered. "I should have known from the moment I laid eyes on that monstrosity that no fae queen would call that home."

An equally large force gathered to the north of the tree, this one of green-skinned humanoids with thick tusks protruding from their mouths, towering cyclops, and lumbering humanoids with clubs. Fae armed with bows and crystal swords buzzed above their heads.

I stopped in my tracks and set Lumia on her feet. "Are those goblins, cyclops, and ogres with the unfae?"

"And orcs." Lumia's eyes flared. "I don't understand."

"Because they're enemies of the fae, right?"

She nodded. "Since the dawn of time, orcs, goblins, and their allies have hunted fae for our pixie dust. On old Earth, the elves were our close allies, but we were forced to make other allies after our move to Pangea."

I grimaced. "If our former enemies are helping the unfae, that can only mean one thing. Glacia is the bad guy."

Lumia slumped against a tree. "I should never have left. It is my fault the kingdom has become a wretched hive of villainy."

It seemed the entire fae nation was on the verge of extinction with or without the collapse. I had to stop this war before it began. But how was I supposed to stop a clash between mortal enemies? The unfae had formed a dark alliance with their mortal enemies. The orcs, goblins, etc. wanted nothing more than to crush the fae. The centaurs and other fae allies would probably fight down to the last creature.

A pep talk from Lumia wouldn't stop them since the orcs were unlikely to listen to the former fae queen. Glacia would probably order them to war no matter what. The only thing that might appeal to both sides was their own instinct for self-preservation. True, it hadn't worked very well so far, but it was worth another try.

As the unfae forces marched closer to the stone tree, I dashed into the hundred-yard space between the two armies and threw up my hands. "Stop! You're making a terrible mistake!"

Tinkling laughter emanated from somewhere behind the first row of orcs. A female fae I didn't recognize fluttered into view and perched atop the boulder-shaped head of a cyclops. "Nothing you say or do will stop this, human. Pyra and her ilk have doomed themselves."

Even though the orc army continued their steady march toward me, I held my ground. "Doomed themselves how?"

"They took our queen captive and tried to replace her." She held up a tiny fist. "This is the final grain! We will not be treated as second-class citizen because we chose to defend our homeland. We shed blood so these weak cowards could remain safe in their vaunted city of light. They have done nothing to protect the fae, yet they judge those of us who made the ultimate sacrifices and call us monsters. We will force them to fight until all fae have blood on their hands!"

Orcs roared in approval and cheers rang out from the flocks of unfae hovering in the air overhead.

"We have remained silent too long," another unfae shouted. "They call us killers and banish us from their cities. We will no longer serve those who do not deserve our protection."

Another unfae spread her arms. "Centaur brethren, do you really wish to die for those who hold you in such contempt? The fae will use you and throw your lives away."

As she continued, I felt myself somewhat swayed by her speech. Pyra hadn't done herself any favors by being such a bitch, either.

The unfae army marched relentlessly forward. Soon they'd be right on top of me. I surged into demon form, growing as tall as I could. Massive bat wings unfurled from my back and my tail lengthened to nearly ten feet.

In the past, turning this much control over to my inner demon would have resulted in an uncontrollable rampage as my consciousness took a back seat to his. Instead, I felt more like a co-pilot in my demonic body.

Raising massive hands in the air, I roared, "There will be no battles today."

The cyclops and orcs stopped in their tracks at the sight of the giant smurf-colored demon blocking their path. Then I realized they were looking at something behind and above. I looked back and saw Thrusha shoving Glacia out onto a limb of the stone tree, a dagger drawing blood from the unfae queen's neck.

Gasps rose from the unfae. Orcs grunted and stomped their feet angrily. It took a moment for me to process that they looked genuinely concerned for the health of Glacia.

"Cease your theatrics, Willow!" Pyra appeared behind Thrusha, face twisted into a snarl. "Your army will disperse at once or Glacia dies and Thrusha will be your new queen."

"Never!" Willow raised a dainty fist. "Return Glacia to us bathe in a lake of blood."

"I am your queen!" Pyra raised her fists. "Submit!"

"Enough!" a weak voice called out. Lumia staggered across the field toward me. "I cannot see my children tear themselves apart like this."

My spiraled horns fell off and thudded to the ground as I shrank back to normal size. I helped Lumia cross the field until we both stood between the armies.

Willow's eyes flared. "Queen Lumia, you have returned?"

"Please do not fight, children." Lumia leaned against me for support. "The realms cannot afford it."

"What is wrong with you?" Willow flitted down to us and took Lumia's hands in hers. "My queen, you look ill."

"I will be better soon." Lumia forced herself upright and off me. "I returned for a matter of great import. This world may soon cease to exist, many of its denizens killed as our realm collides with others."

Willow blinked several times. "I do not understand."

"The realms are ending." I balled my hands and mimicked colliding worlds. "The Sundering that created them is being undone, causing them to collapse back into one world. Our only chance at stopping it is by finding a power source as intense as the one that created it."

Her forehead furrowed. "What is this man creature talking about, my queen?"

"Listen to him." Lumia's breathing became labored. "I have not recovered my strength."

Willow shook her head. "Since her return from the human lands, Pyra has become a tyrant. The unfae cannot abide such behavior. What would you have us do, queen?"

"No fighting." Lumia grasped weakly at her arm. "Give us time to explain."

"Do not listen to that creature," Pyra called out. "She is not Lumia, but a fake created by humans to deceive us!"

Lumia groaned. "I would dearly love to slap my daughter's face right now."

Willow's eyes darted back and forth between me and Lumia.

I groaned. "Please don't tell me you believe Pyra."

She took Lumia's hand and examined it, as if trying to discern that the fae queen was genuine.

"It is truly me." Lumia put a hand on her face. "Please don't attack."

"Attack!" Pyra threw a cloud of glittering dust into the air. "Destroy the invaders!"

The centaurs roared and charged. The elephantine creatures bellowed and tromped after them. The air buzzed as the giant bees from the flower forest swarmed toward the armies.

Willow's eyes flared. "Defensive positions!"

The orcs and cyclops formed a line. Unfae hovered overhead, weapons drawn, crimson pixie dust glowing in their hands. The fae gathered around the giant stone tree watched from afar, unable to kill lest they also be deemed unfae. This was going to be a bloodbath and we were caught square in the middle.

There was nothing I could do to stop this now. At best, I could grab Lumia and get us out of harm's way. Before I could scoop her up, a massive bipedal ox stepped forward from the centaurs and stomped the ground. The earth trembled. Orcs staggered to keep their feet. Lumia and I fell to the ground. The centaurs and their allies continued their charge, seemingly unaffected by the earthquake ox.

The ground undulated like a giant waterbed at an orgy, making it virtually impossible to stand. My only chance was to manifest and try to fly out of there before the two armies crushed us into pasta sauce. One of the ground waves caught Lumia, tossing her through the air. I leapt and caught her in mid-air, landed heavily, and rolled onto my back. The centaurs were less than a hundred feet away. There was no way I could manifest and get us out in time. I'd been through too much to just give up, so I unleashed Kalesh and swelled into demon form, shielding Lumia with my body.

Centaurs raised up to strike me with their hooves. I gritted my teeth and braced for broken bones. The blows never came. The earth stopped rippling and the thunderous charge of hooves went silent. An eerie song floated through the air, causing centaurs, orcs, and others to go still.

"Vitania." Lumia's voice filled with hope.

I tried to move, but my muscles refused to respond. Lumia pressed a hand to my temple. A tiny shock jolted through my body and my limbs suddenly worked again. I still felt the weight of the song pressing down on me, but whatever Lumia had done gave me the ability to push forward.

"How dare you interfere, Siren!" Pyra shouted.

I rose to my feet, Lumia cradled in one arm and squeezed between the still forms of the opposing armies. Some of the unfae seemed unaffected by the song, but many drifted to the ground and stood there, eyes alert, but bodies perfectly still. I made it out of the danger zone between the armies and saw a sight that made my eyes water.

Elyssa, Shelton, and Emily flanked Vitania. The Siren continued singing as she advanced toward the stone tree.

"Justin!" Elyssa dashed forward, but Vitania held her back and shook her head.

I dashed over to my friends. The moment I stepped behind Vitania, I no longer heard the song. I stopped, backed up, and stepped in front of her. The song switched back on. It seemed Vitania could project sound in only one direction if she chose to do so. If Elyssa had stepped in front of her, she would have been rendered motionless like the others.

I set Lumia on her feet. "Sup, babe."

Elyssa leapt into my big blue arms and kissed me furiously. "I was so worried about you!"

"Sorry, Thrusha kidnapped me." I scowled up at the distant Pyra. "She was going to make Glacia execute me."

"I'm afraid I slept far longer than anticipated," Vitania said, somehow continuing to sing. "When I heard Glacia had been summoned and that you were missing, I feared the worst."

"Yeah, well it's always the worst when it comes to Justin." Shelton clapped me on the back. "Loving the silky robes, by the way. They make your demon form look sweet and innocent."

I snorted. "That's what I was going for."

"Makes your ass look bigger too." He grinned. "Glad you didn't get executed."

"It goes pretty well with your BDDE, too," Elyssa murmured in my ear. She slid out of my arms and back to the ground. "How are we going to stop the battle? The moment Vitania stops singing, they're going to slaughter each other."

I looked up at Pyra. Thrusha, unaffected by the song, still held the dagger to Glacia's throat. "We need to get to them."

"What, by flying?" Shelton scoffed. "They'll slit Glacia's throat before you get close."

I shook my head. "No." I felt the energy of the primal fount electrifying my body. "By running." Before anyone could object, I kicked into hyper drive. The world seemed to stand still as every molecule of my being vibrated at a higher frequency than real time.

The soundwaves from Vitania's song rippled like translucent waves across the clashing armies. I looped around them, taking care to avoid the sound waves. I didn't know if they could affect me at this speed and didn't feel like testing the theory.

The stone tree was a massive structure with a base large enough to hold a pride of elephants. Though it appeared to be made of polished black stone, a closer inspection revealed bark. It was as if someone had petrified a living tree, freezing it for eternity. The great trunk rose for fifty feet before splitting into limbs only marginally smaller.

I dodged between the fae standing outside and entered the doorway. I skidded to an abrupt halt inside, astonished by what I found. The interior was vast, much larger than it looked on the outside. Orange light filtered through sparkling dust drifting through the empty space. There were doors and holes in seemingly random positions far above, but no stairs or ladders to reach them. The floor of the great hollow was covered in a layer of giant leaves.

It made sense. The fae could fly and had no need of stairs. Unless I morphed into demon form, how was I supposed to reach the top? And how was I supposed to know which door led to Glacia? I couldn't even begin to estimate how high I needed to go.

"Intruder!" someone shouted from above. "Subdue him!"

Fae leapt from nooks and doorways above, pixie dust flying from their fingers. In seconds, I'd be snared in their net. There was no way I could fly with them attacking me.

I closed my eyes and envisioned the view from outside. Pyra, Glacia, and Thrusha were on a limb about two-thirds of the way up. There was only one way to climb the tree and avoid being captured. Physics was about to become my best friend.

I raised a fist at the attackers. "You'll never get me, because I have science on my side!"

That declaration earned me some confused looks. I didn't give them a chance to recover and burst forward at top speed, running in a circle. To any observer, it looked like I was going nowhere fast, but I had a plan. After my third lap, I planted a foot on the wall. The circular shape of the trunk and my speed kept my feet on the wall with the power of centripetal force.

Angling slightly upward, I began to climb in a long, wide spiral. The attacking fae looked frozen in mid act, faces morphing toward confusion in slow motion. Most were out of my reach, but others were directly in my path. I was tempted to tear off their clothes when I ran by, but the force might seriously injure them. These fae weren't the bad guys. They were just following the orders of their crooked queen, Pyra.

By the time I was halfway up the trunk, I'd completely disoriented myself and had no idea which side of the tree was which. A miniature orange sun hovered not far above, and beyond that there was nothing —no trunk, no doors—just empty space. I had no idea where to go from there.

I had no choice but to stop.

Dodging into the final doorway, I paused to get my bearings. I heard nothing, not the distant shouts of Pyra, not the fae who'd attacked me below. There was nothing here but absolute silence.

In my haste to save Glacia, I'd wandered into unknown territory and was completely lost.

16

The silence settled onto me, a heavy, suffocating blanket of nothingness.

A lone sound penetrated the shadows, a slow, distant thump. At first I thought it was my own heartbeat, but then I realized it came from somewhere else. Was it ahead? Behind? It could have been above or below, but there was no telling in this place.

Abject fear gripped my heart. *I have to get out of here!* I turned to leave, but the doorway I'd entered was gone. "No!" I stumbled forward and found thin air. The interior of the trunk appeared around me as if a veil had been lifted from my eyes. But now I was falling.

My hand snapped out and caught the lip of the ledge just in time. The smothering anxiety lifted an instant later, leaving me frightened and confused. "What in the hell was that place?"

Still dangling, I shook my head and tried to rationalize what I'd seen. It only took a moment to realize what it was. The corridor was enchanted, designed to keep away those who didn't belong, like an aversion spell. That meant it had to be the doorway leading to Pyra and the others. I just had to man up and run through before it could frighten me off again.

The fae below were now searching for me. To their eyes, I'd

simply turned into a blur and vanished. It wouldn't be long before they turned their gazes upward and spotted me dangling from the ledge.

I pulled myself up, stood at the very edge of the entrance. I hadn't crossed into the umbra, the shadow of the spell, yet so I could still see the interior of the tree. Once I entered the darkness, there'd be no turning back if I hoped to save Glacia. I had to run as fast as possible until I reached the other side.

Then again, what if there were obstacles hidden in the darkness? I'd snap legs off if there were tripping hazards. There might be other physical traps concealed by the spell. I put a hand on the wall so it could guide me in a straight path. I'd have to take my chances and run at a normal pace. Unless there were wall spikes, I'd survive any collisions.

I stepped forward.

A cloak of oblivion covered my eyes and ears. I couldn't even hear myself breathe. My hand touching the wall grasped at nothing. Fear welled in my chest. Soul-crushing anxiety slithered around my guts, squeezing harder and harder. I sensed something evil and malevolent set its cold gaze on me.

Move forward. I forced myself to onward. The next step came slightly faster, then the next and the next. I broke into a jog even though every instinct told me to turn and run the other way. The distant thump grew louder and louder. A dim green light glowed through a thick mist. I used it as a beacon, praying it wasn't guiding me to a grisly end, but the exit from the dreadful room.

I heard voices, distant shouts and cries, and dared to hope that I was about to find myself outside just behind Pyra. The mist cleared and the darkness faded as I stepped into the halo of green light. There was no exit, no sanctuary waiting for me. A cry of horror tore from my throat and my knees went weak.

A creature unlike any I'd seen before was pinned to a stone obelisk before me, its chest pried open by a web of thorns. The light emanated from a pulsating organ inside the thorax. Viscous green liquid circulated inside translucent arteries. The creature wasn't even remotely humanoid, with four limbs attached to an upper shell and four legs protruding from the abdomen. The head had no eyes, only several rows of glowing pinpoints.

Simply standing in its presence filled me with terror, but that was only part of this room of horrors. Dozens of fae were pinned to the walls by their wings, their chests torn open, hearts gone. This place was soaked in pure evil.

Cold sweat trickled down my back. What in the hell was this room? Was Pyra responsible? I abruptly remembered my objective and snapped out of my trance. Whatever this was could wait. Sunlight glinted off stone in the back of the chamber. I zipped forward, eager to leave the strange creature behind me.

I emerged on a limb outside and sighed with relief. The armies were still frozen by Vitania's song. Twenty feet below and to the left, Thrusha still held the dagger to Glacia's throat. I angled myself to land behind Pyra and leapt. She must have heard the change of the wind because her gaze flicked straight toward me.

Pyra threw out a cloud of dust an instant before I landed. My feet touched the limb. Thrusha gasped, raised the dagger, and stabbed it toward Glacia's neck. I burst into super speed and the dust froze in mid-air. I dashed past Pyra and reached Thrusha an instant later. I was nearly overwhelmed with the desire to snatch the dagger and slash her nasty little throat with it, but there were good reasons to keep her alive.

She was Pyra's right-hand unfae. She might have answers to the mysteries of that horrific room. I tore the knife from her gasp and knocked her on the back of the head with the butt. Still maintaining my speed, I reversed and did the same to Pyra, hoping it was enough to knock them both out.

I entered normal speed. Pyra slumped unconscious. Thrusha staggered, gasping in surprise, hand pressing to her head where blood welled from the blow. I wrapped an arm around her neck and squeezed. She struggled and flailed, squealing and hissing like a cat being murdered. Just when I thought she'd never pass out, she went limp.

"Holy shit balls." I let her slump onto the broad limb. "What is wrong with that bitch?"

Glacia tumbled over sideways and lay unmoving. Fearing the worst, I ran in front of her. Blood trickled from flesh wounds, but she was still breathing and a pulse still beat in her neck. She'd probably been drugged with the same stuff used on me and Lumia.

The armies below burst into motion again, their front lines crashing into each other. Vitania had apparently stopped singing. I gripped Pyra by the back of her neck and lifted her before me. "I have your queen. Surrender or she dies!"

The armies kept right on fighting because they couldn't hear a word I said from way up here. Pyra had been using an amplification spell to make herself heard earlier. I cleared the cobwebs from my memory banks and tried to remember an Arcane spell to dust off, but it had been so long since I'd used Arcane magic, I couldn't remember one.

A sonic wave swept between the armies, shoving them apart. Vitania's voice thundered above all the noise and confusion. "Pyra is our prisoner. Lay down your arms and surrender immediately."

Centaurs, earthquake oxen, and the freaky elephants turned their gazes on me holding their queen. Cries of dismay rose from the fae on the lower branches of the stone tree. The creatures of the fae army threw down their weapons. Guttural cheers rose from the unfae allies. Even from this distance, the hatred on the faces of the centaurs was plain as day.

In less than twelve hours, I'd witnessed two wars. That was far too many for comfort.

Vitania's voice rang out once again. "Queen Lumia has returned and hereby reclaims the fae throne. May every creature of the fae lands kneel in the presence of the mother of the fae."

Lumia rose into the air surrounded by a nimbus of white light. I was surprised she had the energy for it, but then I saw Shelton holding his staff out, face strained in concentration. The light show worked. Both armies kneeled, joined by the unfae. The fae seemed more reluctant, probably because they'd been born long after Lumia left. But murmurs and shouts from those who remembered soon forced the stragglers to their knees.

I didn't know what else to do for the time being. Glacia, Pyra, and Thrusha were unconscious and I sure as hell didn't want to go back to that room of horrors right away. The throne room was through the doorway behind me, so I scooped up the fae one by one and took them inside.

The interior spread out before me, far larger than possible given the outside diameter of the tree. I wasn't even surprised this time. The interior was so large there was a small forest of trees and vines inside. A dais held a throne woven from the living branches of saplings. Hammocks made of flower petals and vines hung from the small trees. Butterflies fluttered about, going from one flower to another, sparkling dust trailing from their abdomens.

I whistled in appreciation. "Pyra knows how to decorate at least." I placed Pyra, Glacia, and Thrusha in flower hammocks, then settled into a hammock of my own and waited for the others to appear. I must have dozed off because Shelton nudged me awake sometime later.

"Wakey, wakey, sleepyhead."

I leapt up with a start. "How long have I been out?"

"Took us thirty minutes to get up here." He tipped his nose toward the other hammocks. "What's with the trio of sleeping beauties?"

Lumia and Vitania, surrounded by an entourage of fae, entered the room. Lumia hurried over to her children, gently stroking their foreheads like a mother checking for a fever. She smiled gently at me. "Thank you, Justin."

I nodded. "Thrusha needs to be locked up immediately."

Lumia motioned over a pair of fae. "Lock her up nearby."

They picked up the unconscious fae and carried her away.

"I was concerned something happened to you." Vitania approached me. "Once I entered the stone tree, I realized why it took you so long to reach Pyra."

I waved my hands around at the interior. "Is this place using pocket dimension magic to make it larger?"

Lumia frowned. "This is not fae magic." She cast a sprinkling of dust into the air. "I've never seen anything like it."

"Nor have I." Vitania traced her fingers through the air as if stroking invisible threads. "There is a juxtaposition of time and space that resembles nothing I've seen before."

My mind wandered naturally back to the bizarre horrors in the rooms above the throne room. "Is everything settled here for the time being?"

Vitania's eyebrows rose. "Why do you ask?"

Before I could answer, someone slammed into me from behind, nearly bowling me over. Strong hands spun me around and Elyssa's violet eyes glared at me. "You leapt without looking, Justin! How many times do I have to tell you to stop doing that?"

"Yeah but—"

"No buts." She gripped my robes. "You vanished inside and were gone for fifteen minutes. I thought you'd died or been captured."

"I'm trying to explain!"

Eyes flashing dangerously, Elyssa bared her fangs and yanked me closer. "Don't make me bite you, Justin."

I grinned. "That sounds fun actually."

She rolled her eyes and pulled me in for a ferocious kiss. "My adorable little idiot."

I batted my eyelashes innocently. "Aw, I'm adorable?"

"He's as bad as Tyler." Emily stood behind Elyssa, arms folded. "I don't know what we did to deserve such smartasses."

"Jackasses," Elyssa corrected her.

"You two are such bullies." I held up my hands in surrender. "Now, back to Vitania's question." I turned to the Siren. "Something evil is going on in this place. I don't even want to try explaining it. You just have to see it."

Lumia's eyes pinched with concern. "Evil in the palace of the fae?"

I pointed up. "We need to go up a level."

She nodded. "Lead the way."

I paused. "How did everyone get up here without wings?"

Lumia quirked an eyebrow. "We rode the leaves."

I crossed the throne room and went to the central hollow of the tree. I looked at the long drop to the bottom of the tree hollow below. A fae drifted upward not on wings, but aboard a giant leaf, floating and twirling as if driven by gusts of wind. I'd run right over them without even realizing their purpose. Then again, my method had been a lot faster.

There were leaves on the throne room floor, so I stepped on one and willed it to carry me out into the hollow. It responded, floating up like a magic carpet and out into the great hollow. I got my bearings and spotted the passageway of evil just below the miniature orange sun. The others floated out on leaves and clustered around me.

I pointed to the opening. "It's there."

Vitania and Lumia floated up ahead of me. Emily, Elyssa, Shelton, and I followed close behind.

"Gird your loins," I told the others. "This is the corridor from hell."

Shelton frowned. "Dude, after fighting a war in the Void, nothing can faze me."

Vitania and Lumia vanished into the infinite darkness. I took Elyssa's hand. "Make a chain." Emily took her hand. Shelton rolled his eyes, but followed suit with Emily. I led them inside. The blanket of silence wrapped around me. Elyssa suddenly gripped me tighter. I forged straight ahead, fighting the swelling terror and anxiety squeezing my insides.

I finally saw the glow from the green heart and followed it until the mist and darkness were gone. Lumia and Vitania stood still, eyes wide with horror at the bodies pinned to the walls.

"Oh, fuck!" Shelton, white faced and breathing heavily, stumbled into me. "What the hell is this place?"

Elyssa shuddered. "I've never experienced anything like that corridor. What kind of magic is that?"

Vitania wiped a sheen of sweat from her forehead and turned toward me. "This being is not of our universe. It is the minion of an outsider god."

I gulped. "A what?"

"When the Earth was whole, there were gods from other dimensions and other worlds who hungered for the life force of its creation. But our gods protected Earth." She shivered. "The Sundering removed us from the trans-dimensional realm and cut us off. Some of the outsiders must have been on Earth when it happened."

"Elyssa and I met the spirit of a creature named Voxx during a visit to the Abyss." I looked at the floor to avoid staring at the bodies around me. "It told us it came from the outworlds. But its spirit had been trapped in the Abyss for eons."

"What kind of alien is it?" Shelton said.

Vitania shook her head. "The body is alive, but I sense no soul or spark within."

I shifted to demon vision and saw a faint green halo rippling the air around the body. But there was something strange about the glow around the heart. There were multiple auras, squirming and roiling within like a sack of maggots. As Vitania stepped closer to the body, they stiffened, pointing straight at her like arrows.

"Stop!" I grabbed Vitania and yanked her away just as a wormlike creature burst from an orifice in the heart and sprang toward her.

17

The creature's circular mouth opened and closed rapidly, popping like suction cups as it sought a target that was no longer there. It plopped on the floor, wriggling helplessly for a few seconds before it shriveled and died like an overheated earthworm.

"Holy farting aliens!" Shelton gibbered like a germophobe in a virus laboratory. "That ain't no ordinary worm!"

"That thing's heart is full of those little monsters." I threw up a little in my mouth. "Maybe I've seen too many alien movies, but I think it was going to burrow into your chest and make a baby."

Emily looked at the bodies pinned to the wall and gagged. "Is that what happened to all these fae?"

"If that's the case, this place would be crawling with alien babies." Shelton shook his head. "Nah, this is classic Ceti eel territory. That worm was going to burrow into your ear and let Khan control you."

Vitania and Lumia looked absolutely perplexed.

I snapped my fingers. "Thrusha and Pyra must be infected."

Lumia blinked from her confusion. "My child is under the influence of this outsider?"

"Only one way to find out." I looked back down the corridor of darkness. "Is there any way to dispel that?"

Vitania frowned. "Perhaps, but it will take some time to study."

"We must help my child first." Lumia took Vitania's hand and led her back into the darkness.

I was tempted to jump out of the window again, but Shelton couldn't exactly follow me, so I formed another chain with the gang and we made our way down the little hall of horrors to the main hollow where our leaves waited.

Shelton boarded his leaf and hugged himself on the way down, probably contemplating life and his poor choices, like becoming best friends with me.

When we reached the throne room, Glacia and Pyra were awake. Pyra glared angrily at her sister, but Glacia coldly ignored her.

"Mother!" Glacia rose to her feet. "I heard you were back, but Pyra refused to let me see you!" She embraced Lumia and kissed her cheeks. "Your other daughter has run the kingdom into the ground since her return from captivity."

"I have run it as I deemed fit!" Pyra scowled at them. "I will not shirk my responsibilities."

I shifted to demon vision and studied her aura. It was slightly dimmer than that of her mother's but I didn't sense anything strange about it.

Elyssa nudged me. "What do you see?"

I shook my head. "Nothing."

Pyra's scowl flicked to me. "Why did you say that? Why are you looking at me?"

"Where's Thrusha?" I said.

Lumia motioned toward a pair of fae. "Take us to the prisoner."

They led us to a thicket of vines in the far reaches of the throne room. The vines parted to reveal Thrusha bound inside. She hissed and spat. "Release me!"

I ignored the outburst and examined her aura. At first it looked as normal as Pyra's, but a tiny speck of green caught my eye. It was so small it was nearly unnoticeable. I reached a tendril of my essence and touched her halo. Cold dread, the same I'd felt in the corridor leading to the outsider's room, filled me almost instantly.

A gasp escaped my mouth as I staggered back and released her. "She's infected."

Thrusha shrieked in fury. "You know nothing!"

That much was certain. The revelation that creatures from another dimension were dispersed among the realms scared the crap out of me. As if we didn't have enough going on already.

Vitania observed with a detached expression. "Is it in her brain?"

"Maybe." I shrugged. "It's a speck of green aura in her head, so probably so."

"Like she's possessed?" Emily stepped closer. "Maybe I can help."

"Uh, your powers are on the fritz." Shelton put a hand on her shoulder. "And we sure as hell don't want our resident goddess getting infected by whatever's inside her."

"It is more likely a physical possession, not spiritual." Vitania pursed her lips and nodded. "Better that you not test your luck."

"What is wrong with her?" Pyra pushed between her mother and sister, a worried look on her face.

I examined Pyra once again to make sure I hadn't missed a green speck in her aura. As she neared Thrusha, an arc of green energy crackled between the two of them. Pyra's eyes went cold and she raised a hand. "Guards, arrest these people!"

The fae guards looked at each other uncertainly.

Lumia frowned. "Pyra, do not make me—"

The intensity and frequency of the green energy between Pyra and Thrusha increased. I noticed other arcs of power probing Lumia and the others nearby, but they seemed to have no effect.

"I will see you all destroyed!" Pyra growled. "Release my faithful servant this instant!"

"There's a psychic connection between them," I said. "That thing is probing all of us."

Vitania backed away, pulling Lumia with her. "This explains much. The entity controls this one and heavily influences the other."

Lumia glared at the prisoner. "Why did you murder those other fae?"

"They were unsuitable for habitation." Thrusha strained at the vines holding her. "Release me!"

"How long have you infected this host?" Vitania said.

Thrusha looked away. "I have nothing else to say."

I stepped closer to her. "Tell me, or I'll burn the body of that creature we found upstairs."

She gasped. "No. I am still alive!"

That response confused me more than I was willing to admit, so I forged on. "The body is alive?"

Thrusha remained silent for a moment before reluctantly answering. "My consciousness exists, but the body is dead."

"You can spread your consciousness among multiple beings?"

"Yes. It is how we assimilate information." She tilted her head at a strange angle. "Release me and I will tell you everything."

"Nuh uh, no way!" Shelton made a sign of the cross. "There's no telling how many fae that thing's infected. We need to burn this place to the ground!"

"Not necessary." Vitania pursed her lips. "If we destroy the body, that will sever the control it has over this unfae."

"No!" Thrusha screamed. "What would you have me do?"

"You murdered dozens of my people!" Lumia clenched her fists. "You desire mercy when you have given none to us?"

"I did not intend for them to die." Tears poured down Thrusha's face. "This host is the only one that survived more than a month or two."

"Monstrous!" Lumia wiped away tears of her own. "Why must you have more than one body?"

"Eons ago, I discovered the Earth dimension while plane-shifting. I had not been here long when a great explosion tore the world apart. I survived for several more days. As I neared death, I cast my preservation rune. It placed me into deep hibernation and preserved my essence." Thrusha hesitated. "One of your creatures found me and infected himself. I learned about the rulers of this land and discovered the only way to heal my body was with powerful magic."

Lumia folded her arms over her chest. "What magic guards the corridor to your room of death?"

"An aversion aura powered by a rune on my exoskeleton." Thrusha's head twitched like that of an insect. "Our magic users carve runes into the bodies of warriors and explorers, granting them enchantments to keep them safe."

"Insanity." Shelton pinched the bridge of his nose. "If we don't stop the realms from collapsing, the next thing on our plate will be invasion of the insectoid body snatchers."

Thrusha's eyes twitched toward him. "In my short time since regaining consciousness, I have absorbed information about the realms, but there is much I don't know."

"How do I disable the aversion rune on your exoskeleton?" Vitania said.

"You cannot." Thrusha blinked. "I have disabled it."

Vitania nodded. "Release the unfae whose body you hold captive."

"And return to a disembodied state?" She shuddered. "Why would you deprive me of the perfect host?"

"Because you nearly destroyed the fae kingdom!" Lumia thrust a finger toward Pyra. "And you can influence her too."

Vitania took a deep breath. "We cannot abide this diversion. Now that Lumia rules the fae once again, we can assemble the full might of her people."

"Is Seraphina our next move?" I asked.

"It seems to be the only move left available to us." Vitania sighed. "Elohim's dragon army is certain to control Zbura, so we will need every possible ally if we're to take the city and the crystalis."

Elyssa grimaced. "What do we do with that alien? It's wrong to let it keep control of Thrusha."

"Vitania is right." Emily stared at the prisoner. "We've got way too bloody much on our plates to negotiate with this thing. Let's retrieve the crystalis and fix the realms, then we can decide what to do with the creature."

Lumia turned to the guards. "Secure the prisoner in a stasis pod and cut off all access to the level above this one. No one is to enter, not even you."

The guards nodded and gripped Thrusha by her arms as they dragged her away.

"No!" Thrusha flailed and screamed. "Please release me and I will help you!"

Shelton shuddered. "Last thing we need is help from a body snatcher."

Once the screams faded, Lumia spoke. "I will send word to the far reaches of Pangea and assemble my army. I will also send emissaries to Utopia and tell them to be ready."

Shelton's eyes brightened. "Will there be unicorns?"

"Of course." Lumia sighed. "I hope that this is enough. There is little hope without the help of the Sirens."

Vitania nodded sadly. "Perhaps Dactia is also possessed by an alien."

"Is it really an alien?" Shelton said. "It's from another dimension, not another planet."

"It is not of our world," Vitania said. "It is an alien."

"An insect that uses magic." Shelton shook his head. "How in the hell did Earth survive as long as it did before the Sundering?"

"Eve, Elohim, and the other humanoid gods were very powerful and possessive." Vitania shrugged. "I'm certain they fought many divine battles to keep their creations safe."

Interdimensional god battles sounded epic, but all things considered, I preferred to keep our dimension nice and disconnected from the outsiders. I raised a hand. "I had a little adventure during my captivity." I told them about the foray into Haedaemos and our new alliance. "Baal's former knight, Lethamene is willing to use the infernus network to help us. Maybe we can use nom missiles and weaponry to take down the dragon army."

Elyssa frowned. "Are you suggesting we let the noms in on the Overworld?"

I shrugged. "Maybe we can use the infernus to steal the weapons and the noms will never know."

She nodded. "With Juranthemon appearing bit by bit on live TV, the cat may already be out of the bag anyway."

"Not to mention the portals and magic used when Justin tried to save Saila." Shelton grunted. "Like Vitania said, we're gonna need every ally we can get. A few hundred thousand noms with their weapons might be the edge we need to stop global extinction."

"We need the Sirens," Lumia said. "Perhaps I can convince Dactia to join now that my people are willing to join the fight."

Vitania shook her head. "Dactia formed an alliance of like-minded Sirens who believe waiting out the collapse in a safe place will allow them to rise to power afterward. She will not be swayed."

Shelton scowled. "Let's get our alien mind-bender to infect her and then we can control them."

"The Sirens have already abandoned Aquilis, departing for parts unknown." Vitania tapped a finger on her lips. "The only safe place for them to go is Atlantis."

"Or Nova, or Alden." Emily bit her lower lips. "If they were created outside of the realms like the dryad said, then they should be safe from the collapse."

Vitania's gaze went distant. "During my captivity on Aquilis, I overheard talk of a new world. I believe Dactia knows of Alden, or at least suspects it exists. She may have set her sights on it."

Shelton frowned. "Won't Eve have something to say about the entire Siren nation descending on her new world?"

"Frankly, I don't know whether Eve will care or not." Emily shook her head. "She might still be in the primal fount on Olympus or scouring the realms for me so she can finish what she started."

"There is also the matter of finding Alden." Vitania clasped her hands at her waist. "I will need to probe the quantum tunnels on Nova until I decipher the matrix."

"Huh?" I stared blankly. "What does that mean?"

Vitania smiled gently. "It is how I discover the symbols opening the quantum gateway to Alden."

Shelton frowned. "How are Alden and Nova reachable from our dimension?"

"Even I am unsure how Eve created an adjacent dimension," Vitania said. "But once it existed, she already knew the quantum symbols for the Earth realms, so she burrowed a quantum tunnel back to the known realms, leaving a secret passage."

"We accidentally found Nova a long time ago using Voltis." I shuddered at the memory of those days. "Are you sure it's really so safe?"

Vitania nodded. "Alden and Nova are reachable from our realms, but they are outside the realmspace that is collapsing, and therefore safe."

"Ah, okay." I nodded. "That makes sense."

Shelton tapped a finger on his chin. "If the realms collapse does that mean her new realms will exist cut off from normal space-time dimensions forever?"

"I do not know." Vitania's gaze went distant. "However, since she connected Nova to our realms, it will also be drawn back toward the old Earth dimension as well. Which means once she starts thinking clearly again, it is likely she'll sever the quantum tunnels."

Elyssa folded her arms across her chest. "How are we supposed to reach Alden without those tunnels?"

"It may be possible to burrow a new tunnel since I already know the location of Nova in the quantum matrix." Vitania traced her fingers in a pattern, as if working out a math problem in her head. "Alden and Nova exist in the same realmspace, so it's likely Eve will maintain the quantum tunnel between them."

"Well, you already found the quantum tunnel from Nova to Alden." I shrugged. "So, the next step is going back to Nova and divining the symbols, right?"

"Precisely." Vitania continued doing her invisible math in the air. "There are several things that must happen in the meantime. We must assemble all the forces we can muster in a staging area and prepare for the invasion of Seraphina. I will seek out the quantum location of Alden so we might use it as a refuge during a worst-case scenario."

"We might not even need to invade Seraphina." Elyssa pursed her lips. "I think a covert mission to probe Zbura's defenses is the best next step."

Vitania nodded. "Absolutely. You should do that immediately."

Shelton raised his hand. "Uh, how are we supposed to sneak into Seraphina without you here to open a portal?"

"I will open a portal and then reopen it in the same place twenty-four hours later." She pressed her lips together. "That should give you enough time to probe Elohim's defenses."

"Why not open a portal right inside Zbura?" Shelton said. "We could be in and out in no time."

"I have no image of Zbura to use, and even if I did, it has likely changed drastically since the dragons took control." Vitania turned to me. "What do you need to ready yourself for the mission?"

I looked at Elyssa. "Good question."

Shelton held up a finger. "Hey, maybe we don't need Vitania after all. Cinder and Adam might have Xanos's portal generator up and running by now."

"It's worth finding out." I really wished my Apocryphan powers were working, because relying on Vitania was totally lame. "Send us to the Ranch and we'll be ready to go in three hours."

The Siren slashed open a portal to the Templar compound. "I will open it again in two hours." She opened another portal to Solan in Utopia. "In the meantime, we will assemble our allies."

Elyssa, Shelton, and I stepped through the portal and onto the grassy front yard of the Ranch. The gateway winked shut behind us an instant later. Templars melted out of the forest around the house, closing in on us almost instantly.

"Raven alpha niner." Elyssa held up a hand. "Stand down, soldiers."

They vanished back into the forest as quickly as they'd appeared.

Shelton snorted. "Everyone's on high alert, huh?"

"That's normal procedure for people appearing through unknown portals on the front lawn." Elyssa headed into the large barn to our right. "Let's get down to Cinder's lab." She stopped abruptly and yanked her vibrating arcphone from her back pocket. "Looks like someone was trying to reach me while we were gone."

I took out Nookli and was a little sad to have zero notifications, aside from a recommendation for a nearby Indian restaurant. Then again, my friends were usually right by my side when I got into sticky situations. I peered over Elyssa's shoulder. "Nothing bad, I hope?"

She shook her head. "Michael is back in town and wanted to talk to me. When I didn't respond, he got worried."

A hulking figure in dark clothes emerged from the barn. "Ninjette!"

"Michael, I'm sorry." Elyssa hugged her big brother. "While you and dad have been gallivanting around the globe to assemble the Templars, we've been a little tied up in the other realms."

Shelton scoffed. "A little tied up? We just averted a major civil war in Fairyville!"

Michael grunted. "I'm not surprised. What happened?"

"Where's Dad?" Elyssa headed toward the barn. "I'd prefer to debrief everyone at once."

"He's in the war room." Michael followed her inside the barn. "He's not in a good headspace right now. I think he's lost hope."

"That goes for all of us," Shelton said. "Baal gave us a galactic wedgie and left us to die."

Elyssa looked worried. "This isn't like him at all. Did your mission not go well?"

"We went to every Overworld city and barely managed to recruit a hundred supers." Michael shrugged. "Victus's first reign as overlord purged thousands of supers and drove legitimate Templars underground. His second reign threw everything back into chaos just in time for Xanos to come along and nearly wipe it out. We're scraping the bottom of the barrel and our numbers are at an all-time low."

"God, I'd really hoped more of the old guard would show up." Elyssa sagged. "I guess there just aren't any left."

Michael nodded. "Truth be told, there's a sense around here of accepting the inevitable."

Intense dread wrapped around my insides. Thomas was supposed to be unbreakable—the one person we could all count on to never give up. If he was losing hope, then the future was doomed.

18

"I need to talk to him." Elyssa marched ahead. "Elohim hasn't won yet."

The barn floor dropped open into a ramp, descending into a vast underground parking garage where the Templars kept their flying cars and other magical vehicles. Once we reached the bottom, the ramp closed to conceal the secret entrance in the highly unlikely event noms or other uninvited guests took a stroll into the Templar compound. Since our return from Seraphina, all the aversion wards, illusions, and a crack team of Templars once again guarded the perimeter, so I wasn't too worried about it.

At the opposite end of the garage we took the levitator down into the maze of tunnels comprising the bulk of the secret compound. "I'm going to Cinder's lab." Shelton tipped his hat and took the levitator to the lower levels. The rest of us continued down the corridor.

Thomas was inside the war room, a large stadium-style conference room, staring blankly at the holographic projection of a giant green moon opposite a black hole. Sandwiched in between were hundreds of smaller orbs, some slowly orbiting the moon, while others played ring around the Rosie with the black hole.

It was a live view of the realms from the Glimmer, the world that had been shattered and used to make the Anchor Stone by the Sirens. Between its gravitational pull and that of the Abyss, the realms had been stabilized. Otherwise, they would have drifted so far apart, travel between them would have become impossible. Now that they were being pulled back together, none of us would have minded a little extra distance.

Some of the realms near the Abyss were already dangerously close to its gravitational fringe, their orbs brushing the darkness.

I sighed. "This can't be good for your mental health."

Thomas looked across the table at me. "I've watched four realms collide already. I don't even know which ones they were."

"Most of the ones near the Abyss are unexplored," I said. "There's no reason to think they're all inhabited." Unfortunately, my other favorite realm, Utopia, was one of those about to be swallowed.

"Dad, there's still hope!" Elyssa strode around the table and put a hand on his shoulder. "Remember what you always told me every time I thought I wasn't good enough?"

"This is too big for us." Thomas shook his head. "We might as well be ants trying to stop the world from spinning."

"I nearly died on multiple occasions because I wanted to date your daughter against your wishes." I raised my eyebrows in challenge. "Me, an insignificant kid against the insurmountable might of the Templars. But I never gave up. Then we faced Daelissa and an unstoppable army of Brightlings. But we didn't give up." I pounded a fist on the table. "We've saved our world and other realms time and time again. The stakes are higher than ever, and we're up against a full-fledged god, but even gods have weaknesses. Even gods fall short." I pounded the table again. "Thomas, you can't give up on us yet."

Elyssa wiped tears from her eyes. "This isn't like you at all."

Thomas stood and put a finger near a pair of realms not far from Seraphina. "Those are the reptile and the yeti realms you traveled through while searching for Emily. They've got days, at most, before the Abyss swallows them, and there's not a thing we can do to save them."

I sat down. "Maybe there is."

He pursed his lips and stared at me with his ice-blue eyes. "Explain."

I gave him the four-one-one on crystalis and how one caused the Sundering. "Glacia believes a crystalis exists in Zbura, the former capital of the Brightling Empire. If we can retrieve it, we might be able to use it to stop the collapse from happening."

Some of the hopelessness faded from Thomas's eyes. "But Seraphina and especially Zbura, is controlled by Elohim's dragon army. We simply don't have enough units to invade."

"Then it's a good thing we found Emily and Vitania to help us." I leaned on the table. "We stopped a civil war before it began in Pangea, and now Lumia is queen of the fae again. She's gathering her people to fight even as we speak."

"Coupled with the Utopian forces, that's an excellent start," Elyssa said.

"Perhaps." Thomas shook his head. "But this won't be a ground war. We'll need a significant airborne presence."

"That's where this bit of good news comes in." I grinned confidently. "We now control Elohim's infernus network."

Thomas leaned his forearms on the table, interest gleaming in his eyes. "You're telling me we have control of the entire infernus network?"

I nodded. "Obviously, dealing with demons isn't as simple as all that, but Kalesh is my proxy there. We can use the infernus to gain access to nom weaponry—missiles, anti-aircraft batteries, nukes, and so forth. We can blast dragons out of the sky before they even get close to us."

"Nom weapons?" Thomas frowned. "Revealing the Overworld would be nearly unavoidable if we start stealing massive amounts of weapons from noms. Revealing the Overworld would incite panic among the nom governments. Rather than recruit another ally, we would only make new enemies."

I nodded. "Normally, that would be true. But Baal planted infernus throughout nom governments. That might give us a way to take nom weapons without anyone being the wiser with black ops methods."

Thomas shook his head. "I've studied nom military forces. They are huge, unwieldy, and crippled by bureaucracy. But even infernus can't cover up millions of dollars in missing hardware, and stealing nukes would create a different kind of panic. They'd blame other governments and possibly go to war with each other."

"You might be right," I said, "but dealing with panicked noms is easier than defeating a dragon army."

"Is it?" He pursed his lips. "Bringing the noms into this war might create a far greater immediate threat. Noms are not stupid. They would eventually track missing weapons to the infernus, discover that they aren't human, and that would lead them to the Overworld. There's no doubt in my mind that the governments of the world would unify against us and we'd have to fight unwinnable wars on two fronts."

"Then we minimize the theft," I said. "Any little bit will help."

Thomas nodded. "That might work. We could even explore creating shadow organizations within governments that would give us our own nom black ops, but we don't have the time to invest in such a venture."

His logic, as usual, was solid and it made me really sad. "If we stole one nuclear missile, it might be enough to destroy the entire dragon army."

He put a hand under his chin and considered it a moment before shaking his head. "Nukes are simply too well guarded and accounted for even in Eastern bloc countries. We also might risk setting off the crystalis and cause a new disaster."

I clicked my tongue. "Oh, yeah."

Elyssa clasped her hands together. "Not to mention the radioactive fallout."

I sighed. "Fine. No noms."

"Minimal noms," Thomas said. "We'll figure it out." He switched the holographic image to a map of Seraphina. "For now, we need a plan to infiltrate Zbura and see what we're up against."

"I'm on it," Elyssa said.

I stepped away from the table. "I'm going to Cinder's lab for an update on the portal generator. Things will be a lot smoother if that's working."

Elyssa nodded. "Text me when you find out. We can use it for this mission if it's ready."

I blew her a kiss. "Will do." I left and went down the corridor to the levitator. It took me down to the level where a warehouse had been converted into a lab. Shelton, Cinder, and Adam clustered around a white table that had been liberated from one of Xanos's labs. A robot arm held a white ring that was far too small to be the portal generator I remembered.

I hurried over to the others. "Where did that come from?"

Cinder turned and approximated a smile. "Harry told me about your recent trials and tribulations. I am happy you made it back alive." He awkwardly clapped my shoulder, using enough force to make me stagger sideways.

Shelton winced and put a hand on his own shoulder. "Cinder, you gotta practice your friendly gestures on crash test dummies before you dislocate someone's shoulder."

Adam snorted and clapped my other shoulder. "Cinder thinks he's mastered facial expressions, so now he's moved on to invading personal space."

"I do not think friendly gestures are an invasion." Cinder pursed his lips. "Perhaps I should conduct a survey of the compound population and arrive at a consensus."

I sighed. "Maybe you can do that after we save the universe."

"Indeed." The golem turned toward the white ring. "To answer your question, this is the core of Xanos's portal device. We stripped electrical shielding and power cells and found this alabaster core in the center."

"Alabaster?" I touched the shiny surface of the ring. "Like the alabaster stone the arches are made of?"

He nodded. "It appears she used a captive Siren to sing the stone into shape and enchant it with the Cyrinthian symbols for the Abyss. Using an arctablet, we discovered a way to activate the ring while simultaneously imprinting the destination symbols into its matrix, thus allowing travel to any realm for which we possess the Cyrinthian symbols."

"Dude, that's awesome." Shelton rubbed his hands together. "Why did Xanos have that thing bound up in all that shielding?"

"She couldn't power it unless it was directly over a leyline." Adam pushed a finger up his nose despite not having worn glasses for quite some time. "Xanos wanted a mobile portal generator, so they built an array of power cells around it."

"We determined that a few grams of black aetherite will power the ring for hours." Cinder produced a chunk of the black rock, mined exclusively from the inside of Voltis, the massive aether storm in Seraphina. During our time with the Mzodi, we'd mined tons of the stuff to power their flying ships.

Aetherite, simply put, was magical energy solidified by high pressure and violent power surges in the aether vortexes in Seraphina. The Mzodi mined them and enchanted them for various purposes. Black aetherite was thousands of times more concentrated due to the insane conditions inside Voltis. Once we'd figured out how to harness its power, it had become an invaluable resource.

And now it was proving itself yet again.

I clapped my hands. "This is great. Can it open portals at specific locations in other realms?"

"It operates by the same rules as omniarches in that regard." Cinder produced a slim cylinder of black aetherite. "Once you imprint the proper symbols, you precisely imagine the destination and will the portal to open."

"Let's give it a test then." I took the aetherite. "Where does this go?"

Adam took the aetherite and pressed it to the side of the ring. "The entire surface draws power from the nearest source." He produced a roll of gray tape and wrapped it around the aetherite and the ring.

Shelton guffawed. "Did you seriously just use duct tape to power an interdimensional portal device?"

Adam shrugged. "Sometimes simpler is better."

"It's rather unsightly, but quite functional." Cinder turned to me. "Place a hand on the ring and imagine the Cyrinthian symbols for your destination. That will activate the device and cause it to draw power from the aetherite. Then precisely picture the destination and the portal will open."

I nodded. "Let's give it a shot." I touched the cool surface. It felt metallic, not stone, probably because it was so polished. I envisioned the symbols for Utopia. The ring hummed to life. An electric current ran through my arm, nearly causing me to lose my concentration. I envisioned the silver towers of Solan, a sight I still remembered perfectly.

The ring vibrated and an invisible force pushed me back several feet. Power thrummed, and beams of light speared from the ring, ripping open a portal a few feet away from the device. But this portal wasn't an oval roughly the height and width of a doorway. It spanned nearly half the width of the lab, at least forty feet wide and just as tall.

"What in the blazes?" Shelton leapt back, staring at the Utopian horizon on the other side. The silver towers rose about a hundred yards in the distance. Cars screeched to a halt just on the other side of the portal and pedestrians stared open-mouthed at us from the other side.

The Utopians knew about and used magic, but not even they were prepared for a massive gateway opening along a busy roadway.

"Turn it off!" I shouted. "Turn it off!"

"Simply will it to close," Cinder said.

Close! I thought. The portal shrank to a dot of light and vanished.

"Holy smoking goats." Shelton took off his hat and fanned his face. "I ain't never seen a portal that big. It was even bigger than an Obsidian Arch."

Cinder and Adam looked unconcerned.

"Well, it was still a good first test," Adam said. "The shielding around the ring also focused the portal into a smaller or larger size.

Unfortunately, the aetherite was incompatible with the shielding apparatus, meaning we don't have a way to change the size of the portal aperture."

"Without a regulator, the ring draws as much power as it can from the aetherite at once." Cinder tapped the cylinder of aetherite. "Perhaps by reducing the point of contact where the aetherite touches the surface, we can alter the size of the portal."

I removed the duct tape from the ring and examined the aetherite. Adam had placed the long side of the cylindrical stone against the ring. I set it upright so the bottom of the cylinder touched the ring and secured it with more tape.

"Justin is doing science," Shelton said. "Everyone get back."

I rolled my eyes at him. "Tell that to the Utopians who just watched me open a portal large enough to drive a herd of elephants through."

Adam winced. "I didn't know that would happen."

Shelton snorted. "The look on Justin's face was priceless though."

"Hilarious." I rolled my eyes again. "Let's see how it goes this time." I once again opened a portal, this one to the place in El Dorado where Altash and Lulu used to live. The earth dragons, unfortunately, weren't there, but the portal was less than half the size of the previous one.

"See?" Adam grinned. "Works as advertised."

"Yeah, no more ginormous portals." Shelton mimicked pinning a medal to my shirt. "Scientific achievement unlocked."

Adam and Shelton continued with their jokes, but I was too deep in thought to care. Ever since our last encounter with Lulu, I hadn't given much thought to the earth dragons. But if they were out there, we needed to find them. I made a mental note to look them up once we were done with the covert mission to Zbura.

On the upside, the portal generator allowed us to transport thousands of troops at once, scaling the portal size by using more aetherite. Another amazing thought occurred to me.

Shelton abruptly stopped talking. "Uh-oh. Justin's got that look."

I nodded. "I just figured out how we're going to save millions of lives."

Shelton raised an eyebrow. "Let's hear it."

I patted the ring. "This bad boy can fit thousands of people through it all at once. Once Vitania finds out how to reach Alden, we could transport refugees there. If we could get her people to make more of these rings, we could take them to multiple realms and possibly save hundreds of millions of beings and maybe even ecosystems too."

Cinder nodded. "That is an excellent idea, Justin. But do we have enough time to implement it?"

"Maybe?" I threw up my hands. "I don't know. Utopia and several other realms are about to be eaten by the Abyss, so we could start with them. Eden and the noms would present its own set of challenges."

Shelton shook his head. "If we devote that much effort to moving people to Alden, then there's no way we'll have the resources to fight the dragon army and steal the crystalis."

"Agreed," Adam said. "This is an either-or scenario, Justin."

I pondered that. With just one ring, we'd have to move it to Utopia and start evacuating people immediately. That would hinder using it to transport troops to Zbura and would tie up all our logistical efforts. The Utopians would be easy to evacuate compared to the other civilizations we'd seen. The yeti and reptile worlds were also near the Abyss and I didn't have the first notion about how to communicate with them, much less convince them to trust an alien species that they should abandon their worlds.

"Dude, wouldn't it be better to just concentrate on finding the crystalis?" Shelton held out his hands imploringly. "If we stop the collapse, we save everyone and nobody has to uproot their civilizations."

"But if we're defeated in battle, then we won't have time to save millions of refugees," Adam said. "It's the all or nothing scenario."

Shelton scoffed. "I thought you were on my side."

"I am." Adam held up his hands to placate him. "But fighting a dragon army to get a crystalis is definitely the riskier of the two plans."

"High risk, high reward," Shelton shot back.

"We must also consider that the proper application of the crystalis has yet to be determined," Cinder said. "Who will wield the power to stop the collapse, and will it truly work?"

I blew out a breath. "When you put it that way, it sounds like we're gambling with millions of lives."

"Either way is a gamble." Adam folded his arms over his stomach. "Imagine going to the yeti world, announcing that the end is nigh, and then convincing them to pick up their entire lives and go through a portal to an alien world."

"Tough sale." Shelton nodded. "They might react violently and we'll have another battle on our hands."

"We've spoken with the yeti," Adam said. "They've seen humans and would actually have some reference to go on. Imagine going to the reptile realm where we've had zero contact with the sentient natives, and trying to convince them that we're not alien invaders."

"Seeing humans for the first time would be a terrible shock," Cinder said. "We also don't know what language they speak. There would be significant barriers to gaining their trust."

I held up a hand. "Fine, fine, I see your points. We face significant hurdles either way. But I see a third way that might work."

Adam tilted his head to the side. "And that is?"

"We take a lesson from the Voyager missions and send info capsules to all the realms we can, giving them a chance to mentally prepare for what's coming and what's at stake."

Adam pursed his lips and looked at Cinder. "That's actually an excellent idea."

Cinder nodded. "It could easily be done with ASEs, provided we are granted adequate supply."

"They're manufacturing them by the handful now," Shelton said. "I'll bet Thomas would give us all we need."

"Let's find out." I left the lab and made a quick trip back to the conference room where I told Thomas, Elyssa, and Michael our plan.

"It's an excellent idea." Elyssa tapped her comm badge. "Lieutenant Horton, report to the war room."

"Yes, Commander," a female voice replied.

Horton, a thin woman with a buzz cut, appeared at the door moments later. She entered and saluted, hand across her chest in Templar fashion.

"Horton, we need the communications department to create an information capsule that can be understood by beings completely unlike humans." Elyssa described the reptile, yeti, and snake person realms to her. "Cyrinthian is the most universal language, but let's also include pictograms. I will compile a hologram with other information to include."

Horton nodded. "We can enchant ASEs to seek out sentient life and put the information on a loop."

"Let's plan for multiple ASEs per realm to increase the chances," Thomas said.

Horton nodded. "We'll have something ready within four hours."

"Excellent." Thomas nodded. "Dismissed."

Horton saluted and left.

"I'm headed back to the lab." I couldn't stop a grin from spreading. "I feel really good about this."

Elyssa returned the smile. "Me too." She put a hand on my shoulder. "The infiltration plan is almost ready. I think it's best if just the two of us go. With your super speed, we should be able to get in and out without the dragons noticing."

I nodded. "Sounds good. I'll go tell the others." I scooted back down to the lab and found Shelton, Adam, and Cinder still talking excitedly near the portal generator.

"What's the verdict?" Shelton said.

"Project ASE is green-lighted." I gave him a thumbs-up. "And Elyssa told me that the Zbura infiltration is a two-person job."

He snorted. "I figured it'd just be you two lovebirds. You move like greased lightning, so the two of you will be hard to catch."

I checked a bin full of aetherite. "Cinder, can you carve a very slender piece of aetherite? We need the portal to Zbura as small as possible."

Cinder nodded. "Of course, Justin."

Adam fiddled with his arcphone a moment then showed me a picture of an island floating in the air. The skylet was a few miles off the coast of Zbura, home to an Alabaster Arch that no longer functioned since Victus Edison had sabotaged the Grand Nexus. "This is probably the best entry point. Zbura was heavily damaged even before we left Seraphina, so any images we have of the city would likely be inaccurate."

"Agreed," Cinder said. "Zbura was built on a mountain—an ideal breeding ground for dragons. The buildings have likely been converted to nests."

"Probably filled to the brim with dragon shit." Shelton shook his head. "No telling what you'll have to wade through just to find the crystalis."

Adam grimaced. "Wear hip waders just to be safe."

Elyssa strode into the lab, every delicious curve of her body highlighted by skintight nightingale armor. She tossed me a strip of cloth and leaned a pair of flying brooms against a shelf. "Is the portal generator ready?"

Adam waved. "Good to see you too, Elyssa."

She flashed a smile. "Sorry. We just got the most recent calculations and time is running shorter than we thought."

I frowned. "What do you mean?"

"Utopia should be orbiting away from the Abyss, giving it a couple of extra days, but apparently the Abyss is closing in on it." She checked a timer on her arcphone. "In two days, Utopia will be swallowed whole and crushed like a pea."

Shelton gulped. "No way! But we weren't affected by time dilation when we were there the last time."

"Because it's outside the fringe." Elyssa displayed a holographic video of the realms. "This is an accelerated projection." When she started playback, The Abyss began drifting toward the Anchor Stone, vacuuming in realms as it went. As it reached the outer ring of realms orbiting the Anchor Stone, the giant moonlike creation fractured. As the two massive bodies collided, a massive explosion left behind a single blackened orb.

"Holy intergalactic Pac-Man," Shelton breathed. "The collapse is going to destroy all life everywhere."

19

"The going hypothesis is that ninety percent of life will be snuffed out in the collapse." Elyssa tucked away her phone. "The Abyss and the Anchor Stone were crafted by the Sirens from bits and pieces of other realms after the Sundering. If the realms were in their original configuration, then the collapse might be far less destructive, but with these two heavyweights on either side, everything in between will likely be crushed."

Shelton turned to Adam. "Well, what are you waiting for? Get these people a portal to Seraphina!"

I hunted through the bin of black aetherite and found a chunk with a sharp tip. "This ought to work. Just put the tip against the ring and the portal will be small."

Shelton snorted. "Just the tip, please."

"Knew he was going to say that," Elyssa said.

Cinder nodded. "There was a ninety-nine percent probability."

The rest of us burst into laughter while Shelton shrugged in typical uncaring fashion.

I removed the cylindrical aetherite from the ring and carefully attached the new chunk so only the sharp point made contact with the edge.

Elyssa gave me an amused look. "Duct tape?"

I shrugged. "Whatever works, right?" I jogged behind a nearby shelf, stripped to my underwear, and wrapped the piece of black cloth she'd given me around my waist. A pinch on the lower edge sent nightingale armor spreading down my tender bits and all the way to my feet. I pulled up on the upper edge and the armor covered me to my neck. The cloth was different than I remembered, slightly shiny with tiny honeycomb patterns. Apparently, they'd changed the formula with the new armor. It looked funky, but I liked it.

Elyssa wore only the holster with her compacted light bow outside her armor. This was supposed to be a covert mission, and weapons wouldn't do us much good against dragons anyway. Even my Seraphim powers had trouble against the magic-resistant hides of the massive reptiles.

I strutted back and forth, admiring my ass in the tight uniform. "Where'd you get the armor?"

"Commander Salazar set up a new enchantment facility in Los Angeles, Colombia." She shifted to her left foot, hip jutting out. "They're slowly ramping up production."

"Thank god." Shelton tipped his cowboy hat back. "I don't like the way it emphasizes my manly belly, but it's nice having extra protection."

Adam snorted. "It's the tacos and burgers that emphasize your belly, Shelton."

Cinder nodded sagely. "Why is it men enjoy curves on females, but women do not appreciate curves on men's stomachs?"

Elyssa rolled her eyes. "Thicc bellies aren't exactly sexy."

Shelton patted his belly. "Hey, I have a great dad bod and didn't even have to have a kid to get it."

I imagined Shelton would be a better father than he thought. I'd seen the way he treated Conrad's friend, Max, bolstering his confidence and teaching him how to use his Arcane powers. It was a nice thought, almost tragic considering how many families would perish if we didn't stop the collapse.

That sobering thought got me back on track. "Let's get going, shall we?"

Elyssa nodded. "Open the portal once every hour so we can check in." She tapped the comm badge on her collar. "We'll let you know if we're ready to return."

Adam put a hand on my shoulder. "Good luck."

"Thanks." I picked up one of the brooms Elyssa had brought and whistled appreciatively. The black leather saddle was hand-stitched with red wings, the stirrups were powder-coated black, and the throttle was brushed nickel. It was a gorgeous piece of work, and these were no ordinary brooms.

Elyssa grinned at the look on my face. "You like?"

"I likey so much." I gasped. "These are boomsticks!" The high-performance brooms had been a huge boon to the Overworld forces during the Second Seraphim War, but had become quite a rarity during our long exile to Seraphina. "Where did you get boomsticks?"

Elyssa grinned. "You remember our friend, Rai?"

"Of course, how could I forget the guy who got us boomsticks in the first place?" Underborn had actually been the one to introduce us all those years ago. It felt like a lifetime had passed since then.

"He's been in hiding for nearly a decade because Victus tried to have him killed a few times during his reign of terror."

I grimaced. "Dark days."

Elyssa nodded. "Yeah. But he's back now and set up shop near Arcane University." She shrugged. "Maybe the Skywraiths can do a reunion tour."

I thought about all the people who'd fought by our sides during the war against Daelissa. About those we'd lost and those I hadn't seen during our time trapped in Seraphina. "It would do us some good to get the gang back together again. I haven't seen Lanaeia, Joss, or Otaleon in ages."

"They're with the Seraphim refugees in Utopia." Elyssa gripped her broom. "Let's save the reminiscing for later and start the mission."

I nodded at Adam. "Ready when you are."

He touched the edge of the ring and stared at an image on his arcphone. A gateway about five feet in circumference slashed open before the ring, its edges flickering gently. I peered through and confirmed the destination was on the other side. Bathed in the orange light of a dying day, the Alabaster Arch still stood in a field of blue grass. Elyssa and I crept through and surveyed the floating island. Aside from a golden dove roosting in a purple-leaved tree, there was no sign of life.

I shivered, not because I was cold, but because of the flashbacks from being trapped here. Seraphina was a beautiful world, but there was no place like home. Eden had tacos and that was something the world of angels would never have.

"Looks clear." I gave a thumbs-up to Adam.

He returned the gesture and the portal winked off. Elyssa and I double-tapped our badges to synchronize the timers.

"It's been a while since I've worn nightingale armor. Do the new suits work like the old ones?"

Elyssa nodded. "You can use the heads up display without covering your face, but that's the only difference."

"Cool." I pinched the collar and the armor crept up to cover my head, leaving my face exposed. The fabric was transparent from the inside, but I'd found it helpful if others could see my facial expressions. If they could tell I was about to crap my pants, they'd know it was time to get the hell out of Dodge.

We mounted our brooms and sped north toward Zbura.

Elyssa's voice sounded in my ear through the comm badge. "Underneath the front edge of the saddle, you'll feel slight indentations."

I probed with my fingers and found a row of them lining the seam underneath. "What are they?"

"Rai told me they're programmable runes. Only the first one is working right now." Elyssa and her broom shimmered into near invisibility. "We put a camouflage spell on it. Double-press the rune to activate it."

"Sweet!" I did as instructed, and the air around me rippled. I could see everything just fine, but the spell refracted light waves, bending them around me and the broom to make us nearly invisible. But there was one major problem with such spells—they required tremendous amounts of energy to maintain. "How long can it last before it needs recharging?"

"The brooms use an aetherite core, so they can go hours before depleting the energy. Rai integrated Mzodi arcnology to improve their design." Elyssa's camouflage rippled off. "These are just prototypes. When I told him what we're up against, he said he'd get to work on weaponized versions."

I rubbed my hands together. "Dude, I can hardly wait!" I deactivated my camouflage. "We should be able to sneak into the city no problem."

"That's my hope." Elyssa tapped the armor covering her temple. "The HUD tells me we'll reach land in fifteen minutes. Let's hit silent mode in five, okay?"

I tapped my temple. Numbers and trajectory lines appeared before me. For some reason I flashed back to the time I'd portaled onto a mountain, skied at breakneck speeds down dangerous terrain, and deployed a parachute at the last minute to stop my father from marrying Kassallandra. *Those were the good old days.*

Even though I'd fought a monstrous scorp and Aerianas had nearly killed me, that experience paled in comparison to covertly invading dragon territory. Without my Apocryphan or Seraphim powers, I had little chance of defeating even a single dragon.

We activated camouflage and moments later, Mount Hein appeared through the mists, its sides dotted by alabaster buildings. A great crystal palace still adorned the peak, seemingly undamaged despite the dragon war that had driven the Seraphim from their lands.

The HUD zoomed in at my mental command and I was flummoxed by what I saw. Seraphim in colorful robes walked the streets, going about their business as if nothing had ever happened. The friend information display, FID, on the HUD allowed me to see Elyssa's confused look through the camouflage.

"Something isn't right." Elyssa sounded as concerned as I felt.

I went with my first thoughts. "We couldn't take all the Seraphim with us. The ones left behind must have made a truce with the dragons." Despite the evidence, something about the scene below didn't feel right.

"Well, we're staying out of sight until we figure out the truth of the matter." Elyssa slowed to a stop. "Let's see how close we can get to the palace."

We maintained relative altitude, climbing gradually higher toward the palace at the peak of the mountain. The streets were sparsely populated, but the people below were going about their business as if there had never been a dragon invasion. An outdoor market was the most crowded area I noticed.

Moments later, we reached the palace walls at the peak and paused outside. A pair of men sat in the courtyard drinking and laughing. I couldn't hear what they were saying, but it was obvious that security wasn't an issue here.

"Where in the hell are the dragons?" Elyssa said. "None of this makes sense."

The air whistled overhead. Sleek red missiles fell from the sky just overhead. It took me a moment to realize they were dropping straight toward us. "What are those things?"

The answer revealed itself an instant later. Massive leathery wings unfurled, revealing dragons that were too small to be wyverns and too large to be drakes. Elyssa took evasive action, diving toward the ground. I abruptly realized she was shouting in my ear for me to follow her.

I twisted the throttle and shifted sideways, spiraling away from the pair of dragon claws stretching out to grab me. Elyssa dove down a narrow ravine. I went in after her, the rough cliff sides close enough for me to touch if I stretched out a hand. We flew beneath a great alabaster mansion straddling the ravine, then veered right, following the insanely steep streets as we dodged down alleys and avenues alike.

A quick look back told me the red dragons were right behind us, keeping pace even with our turbo-charged boomsticks. Elyssa was twenty feet ahead of me. The nearest dragon was fifty feet back, give or take. At this speed, it couldn't possibly hit me with fire. Elyssa was angling toward the purple canopy of a forest at the base of the mountain. Once we reached the cover of the trees, we had a much better chance of evading our pursuers.

Narrow beams of red energy flashed over my shoulder. The heat singed my cheek even through the armor. I glanced back as the lead dragon unleashed another blast. A quick dodge to the right saved me from becoming dinner. "Elyssa, these things can shoot lasers from their eyes!"

"I noticed!" she shouted back. "Keep going. We're almost to the trees."

No sooner had she given me that assurance when a purple dragon and a dark blue comrade burst through the treetops and into the air before us. Even from this distance, it was clear they were roughly the same size as the miniature wyverns after us. We weren't just regular screwed. We were super-duper screwed.

"Shit!" Elyssa exclaimed. She took a sharp right down a steep alley. "There's only one chance."

We headed back out to sea. The last chance she spoke of were the heavy mists of aether floating like clouds over the ocean far below.

I had the boomstick throttle twisted to the max. We had to be going over a hundred miles per hour, a speed that dragons simply shouldn't be able to maintain. The only dragon I'd seen move faster was Drakara, the massive black dragon who ruled the dragon nation. I was beginning to wonder if these smaller wyverns could also shoot energy out of their assholes to fly faster.

Dodging back and forth to keep from being charbroiled by laser beams, I dearly wished once again for my Apocryphan powers so I could blast these mofos from the sky. I hated feeling helpless.

The few minutes it took to reach the aether mists felt like an eternity, but at long last, we reached it, four dragons still on our tails. We hadn't been gone from the skylet for more than forty minutes, meaning Adam wouldn't open the next portal for another twenty minutes. The time in the HUD further dashed my hopes by showing me twenty-two minutes until the next portal.

It seemed we'd have to play keep away for a small eternity until our escape opened up. Elyssa, already planning ahead, steered into a thick cloud of aether, showing up as a green dot in my HUD. I went in after her, and vision dropped to five feet. Following her indicator, I went into a steep dive then doubled back seconds later.

"I think we lost them." Elyssa slowed to a stop. "It'll take us ten minutes to reach the skylet from here. We'll make a break for it eleven minutes before the portal opens."

I hovered beside her, nervously checking our environs. She looked like a ghost through the mists. I switched to thermal vision, but the dense aether garbled the spell. I went back to normal view, feeling like a blind man floating in shark-infested waters. "How did the dragons see through our camouflage?" I hissed.

Elyssa put a finger to her lips then pointed to her mouth and mimicked talking.

We hadn't been talking very loudly near the palace, but it was possible these small dragons had amazingly sharp senses and had heard us. Even the Mzodi with all their years of fighting wyverns native to Seraphina didn't know much about the physiology of dragons.

Drakes were small dragons, not much larger than cats. Wyverns varied from car-sized to the girth and length of a city bus. Most of them came in three flavors: red for fire, green for poison, and light blue or white for frost. There were also sea dragons, but I'd never seen any great number of them in our battles against Drakara and her minions.

These weird little dragons were something new altogether, and I didn't like not knowing anything about them. I'd never seen purple and blue dragons. What flavor of lasers did they shoot, grape and porta potty?

I desperately wanted to talk about it, but maintained radio silence, counting down the minutes and seconds before we could make a break for the portal. Elyssa shrieked an instant before a pair of claws wrapped around my arms. I was whisked away, instantly losing sight of her in the mist.

"Elyssa!"

"Justin, I'm here," she said through comms.

We broke through the edge of the mist moments later and I saw her again, arms gripped by a red dragon, the seatbelt still holding her securely to the boomstick. But neither of us could reached down to use the throttle of our brooms, and even if we could, I didn't think they were powerful enough to break us free.

We were dragon fodder.

20

The purple and blue dragons flew behind their red comrades, watching us with curious tilts to their heads. If these were ordinary wyverns, they would have torn us to shreds by now. There was something about these creatures that made me think they were much smarter than the average dragon.

By the time we reached the palace courtyard, my arms were aching from the tight grips on my biceps. The dragons eased us down in the courtyard while a pair of Seraphim unbuckled our seatbelts and removed the brooms. I gave thought to snatching Elyssa and using my super speed to get away, but there was no sense wasting an opportunity for answers.

A female with short orange hair appeared from behind the other Seraphim. "You do not smell of our people. Who and what are you?" Her Cyrinthian dialect wasn't one I'd heard before, but it resembled those I'd heard in and around the far southern reaches of Sazoris, the southern continent.

The question and her accent threw me off, leaving me speechless for a moment. "Since when do Seraphim smell people?"

Her eyebrows rose in unison and it was her turn to look confused. "Seraphim?"

"Yes, Seraphim." Elyssa pointed toward the city. "Why did the dragons allow you to remain unmolested?"

The other Seraphim looked just as confused as the female, foreheads pinched, eyes narrowed.

The orange-haired female recovered first. "I will ask again. Who and what are you?"

I decided to keep things simple. "We're humans from Eden. Where are you from?"

That raised eyebrows even further. I glanced back and noticed the dragons were gone, replaced by more Seraphim.

The orange-haired female began speaking to the others in a language I didn't understand. One male shook his head vehemently though the others seemed to agree with what she said.

"What language is that?" Elyssa whispered to me.

I shook my head. "No idea."

"I am Kroa," the orange haired female said. "Tell me your names."

It was a strange name for a Seraphim, but I was starting to think these people were anything but what I'd thought they were. "I'm Justin and this is Elyssa. May I ask where you're from?"

"What are humans doing on Seraphina?" Kroa circled around us, a predator examining potential prey.

Considering these people were allied with dragons, I grasped for a lie and failed miserably. "Uh, just a little sightseeing. I heard Zbura is lovely this time of year."

"Zbura." Kroa said it slowly as if she found the word hard to pronounce. "This city is now called Drathon." She pronounced it *Drah-thone.*

I frowned. "Sounds like something you just made up."

She blinked. "You are impertinent for someone who is our captive."

I decided to cut to the chase. "Why are you allied with the dragons?"

She and her comrades chuckled as if that were the dumbest question they'd heard.

"Allied with the dragons?" Kroa shook her head. "You are not familiar with our kind, are you?"

"With what kind?" Elyssa said. "You're humanoid, but you're not Seraphim or human?"

"We are drygon, the alpha species of the dragons." Reptilian wings flared from her back. Her skin morphed to shiny scales, her head elongated, and her the pupils of her eyes became long slits. Within seconds, an orange dragon stood before me, its body not much taller or larger than Kroa's. The dragon form melted back into human form.

My mouth dropped open. "Shape-shifting dragons?"

A blue-haired male cleared his throat. "Kroa, we should take them to Mother so she can decide their fate."

"Agreed." Kroa turned and began walking. The other drygon herded us ahead of them.

I glanced at our brooms and again considered making a break for it. I might be able to super-speed us out of there, but without the brooms, we had no way of reaching the skylet and the portal. That wasn't the only reason I decided not to run. I was also extremely curious to learn more about the drygon and Mother. Neither Altash nor Lulu had ever mentioned them, and as far as I knew, Altash had fought Drakara to prevent her from usurping the dragon mother's throne.

If they were the alpha species as claimed, did that mean the drygon existed before wyverns, drakes, and other dragons?

I noted every turn we took through the crystal halls, making a mental map that would guide me back to the courtyard. Once my curiosity was sated, I'd grab Elyssa and super-speed back to the brooms. That would hopefully give us enough of a head start on our captors and allow us to book it back to the skylet for the next portal.

The route to the throne room seemed unnecessarily complicated until I realized we weren't going to the throne room. Instead, we entered a shaft and rode a cloudlet to the top of one of the towers I'd seen from the outside. The room at the top was barren aside from a hooded figure standing on a balcony overlooking the city.

Kroa knelt. "Mother, we have captured human intruders. What would you have us do with them?"

The figure turned and gazed upon us with bright red eyes that seemed as old as the universe itself. She lowered her hood to reveal a plain face and perfectly bald head. Her appearance certainly wasn't what I'd expected from the dragon mother.

Mother watched us in silence with her piercing gaze. Her eyes weren't solid red, but alternating hues, like roiling lava in a volcano. Her gaze turned to Kroa and the others. "Why did you capture them?"

Kroa blinked. "They were intruding upon palace grounds, Mother. And they are not of our kin."

"Did they harm anyone?"

"No, Mother."

Mother turned to Elyssa. "Why are you here?"

Elyssa seemed to ponder her response for a brief moment before answering. "We are here on a mission of mercy so we can stop the realms from collapsing and destroying all life."

Kroa gasped. "Collapsing realms? What nonsense is this?"

Mother nodded. "I sensed something was amiss with the world. Unfortunately, I am powerless to do anything but watch and wait."

"Baal is the one who set this in motion," Elyssa said. "He has reincarnated into Elohim and seems content to let the realms implode so he can start over."

"That is very much in keeping with Elohim's philosophy." Mother stepped closer and took Elyssa's hands, turning them this way and that in hers. "You are quite beautiful, child. Very nearly an example of perfection in humans. Yet, Eve will do nothing to save you and Elohim will happily watch you perish."

Elyssa blushed. "Thank you, Mother."

"It is not a compliment child, simply an observation." Mother turned to me. "This one has many imperfections and the taint of Haedaemos upon him." She sniffed delicately. "I assume he is your manservant?"

I opened my mouth to speak, but Elyssa shushed me and spoke

instead. "He has his issues, but he's a good person who wants to stop the collapse."

"I see." Mother took my face in her hands, turning it this way and that, then peeled back my lips to examine my teeth. "He is healthy, at least."

I felt like a horse being evaluated for the glue factory. "Mother—"

Mother put a finger over my lips and turned to Elyssa. "If you came seeking my help, I'm afraid there is little I can do. I was once a goddess, an equal to Eve, Elohim, Zeus, and the other old human gods, but I no longer have the power I once did once Drakara took it."

Elyssa bit her bottom lip. "Mother, we did not even know about the drygon. We came here for another reason."

Mother's eyebrows rose. "Oh? Did you believe Seraphim still lived here?"

"No. We came here looking for an artifact rumored to be in the palace."

The drygon pursed her lips. "You believe an artifact can stop the collapse?"

I desperately wanted to shush Elyssa from spilling the beans to someone who might very well be an enemy coaxing vital information from her. But Elyssa usually had much better judgment when it came to things like this, so I kept my mouth shut and let her do her thing.

Elyssa pivoted the conversation. "Mother, how did you lose your power?"

Mother turned to Kroa and her comrades. "Leave us."

Kroa looked like she wanted to disagree, but she and the others bowed, turned, and left without a word.

Mother went back to the balcony and Elyssa followed. I sauntered after them, casually staying close enough to hear everything without relying on my enhanced demon hearing.

"My daughter, Drakara, believed that our dragon form was superior and that there should be no human form." Mother shook her head. "She absconded with several of my eggs and returned thousands of years later with an army of wyverns and drakes. Drakara had mutated herself into a monster that defied all proportions. She threatened to destroy all drygon if I did not give up my powers of creation." Her shoulders sagged. "So, I abdicated my power to her. Since then, she has kept us around like pets, forbidding us from producing offspring."

I couldn't help myself any longer. "How do Altash and Lulu fit into all this?"

Mother turned slowly toward me. "Altash was my favorite son." A smile touched her lips. "When the Earth was still young, he realized that for magic to thrive, it required healthy leylines all across the globe. He and a group of other drygon took the responsibility upon themselves, over time morphing into earth dragons and losing the ability to return to human form."

"So your people can just become whatever they want?" I shook my head. "How do you go from this size to a goliath like Drakara?"

"It takes thousands of years to evolve oneself. They can return to original form by evolving back, but it takes just as long." Mother looked from me to Elyssa. "Tell me the truth. Why are you here?"

I gave Elyssa a look and shook my head.

Elyssa shook her head back at me. "I think we can trust her, Justin. At this point, what do we have to lose?"

"Everything," I said. "What if she tells Elohim what we're up to?"

Mother hissed and her eyes blazed brighter. "I would never help that monster."

Elyssa looked Mother in the eyes. "We're looking for a crystalis that was rumored to be in a treasure room or museum in the palace."

The drygon's gaze went distant. "I do not know of this treasure room, but some Brightlings were unable to flee when Drakara descended upon this city and still live here. One of them was a servant to a former king. Perhaps he would know something."

"Did he serve King Skazaeleus? I asked.

Mother nodded. "I believe so. He has told me stories of the war in Eden and how he and the Brightlings returned in defeat."

"May we speak with him?" Elyssa said.

"Of course." Mother reached out a slender finger and channeled orange energy into a gem on the wall. "He will be here momentarily."

"Thank you," I said.

Mother watched Elyssa closely. "A crystalis is an object of immense power. Wielded properly, it can create worlds. Wielded improperly it can destroy creation."

"So I've heard," Elyssa said. "Have you used a crystalis before?"

"Only a little at a time. It was Eve who used one to form the Earth." Mother's gaze went distant. "Even after the primordial mass formed, it took countless eons and many gods to shape it into what it became. Very few gods have the power to use that much power at once. Eve always was the most powerful creator, much to Elohim's disgust and dismay."

"Yeah, he's a jealous little bitch," I muttered.

Elyssa pressed her lips together in a look that told me she'd made up her mind to go all in on this new relationship. "Mother, if we find the crystalis, can you help us use it? Eve is insane, and the only other person who could use it is having problems with her powers."

Mother frowned. "I am sorry, child, but I abdicated my powers of creation to Drakara. There is nothing I can do but offer advice."

I wasn't even surprised. "At this point we'll take what we can get."

"What good is the crystalis if we can't use it?" Elyssa threw up her hands. "We've got to restore Emily's powers somehow."

"Who is Emily?" Mother asked.

"Eve's granddaughter." Elyssa stared at a mural depicting a blond-headed Seraphim torching an army with beams of Brilliance. "She's a demigoddess."

"What is wrong with her powers?"

Elyssa shrugged. "Eve took her to the primal fountain in Atlantis and chained their power together so she could destroy the realms."

Mother pursed her lips. "I have heard Atlantis is the only remaining fragment of the original Earth. Is that true?"

Elyssa nodded. "It is."

"Then the primal fount there still retains the original pure power." She tapped a finger on her lips. "In the right hands, using a crystalis there could possibly halt the collapse."

"Why there, specifically?" I asked.

Mother regarded me for a moment before answering. "Because it is the true center of the realms for the primal fount for Earth, just as Hell is the true center for the infernal fount. But the primal fount is more closely aligned with creation."

It made about as much sense as anything else did, so I just nodded and accepted it. Unfortunately, I knew without a doubt that we'd only just started the adventure to find the crystalis. The Brightlings had probably cleared out the treasure room and hidden the valuables throughout Seraphina. The servant we were about to speak with would no doubt have a treasure map and a list of challenges we'd have to face to collect clues leading to the location of the prize.

Roleplaying as Indiana Jones wasn't exactly what I'd hoped for, but at this point, I'd do anything to lay my hands on a crystalis.

I sighed and paced around the room while Elyssa and Mother spoke. Daelissa's conquests of Eden were the primary subject of the murals in the room. There were portraits of Skazaeleus, the former king of the Brightling empire, but several had been slashed or burned, probably by Daelissa when she'd visited here years ago to draft her army for another Eden invasion.

"I am here, Mother." An elderly seraph knelt at the threshold to the room. "How may I serve?"

"Come, Morriss." Mother held out her hand.

"Morris?" I chuckled. "What kind of Seraphim name is that?"

He frowned. "I am descended from the house of Issa. My name proudly upholds the ancient tradition of passing on the names of my ancestors."

"Oh, it's got an extra s in it." I gave him a sheepish grin. "It sounds like a human name."

He scowled. "That is a great insult to my house."

"Enough," Mother said in a commanding tone. "Morriss, what became of the relics in the treasure room?"

"We sent them to Utopia on an Mzodi ship, Mother." He bowed. "We feared everything would be destroyed if we did not take steps."

Elyssa took out her arcphone and displayed a holographic image of the crystalis from the time echo. "Did any of the relics look like this?"

His eyes widened. "That is the Star of Ussor."

Here comes the quest, I thought. "Was it on the ship too?"

Morriss shook his head. "I'm afraid it vanished years ago. We suspect Daelissa took it when she made her grand return over a decade ago."

"Son of a bitch!" I face-palmed.

"Are you certain it wasn't simply misplaced?" Mother said.

Morriss scoffed and immediately flinched as if remembering who he was addressing. "The Star of Ussor puts off such a glow that it would be impossible to misplace. I noticed its absence only a few days after Daelissa left with her army. The Divinity Scepter and several other items were also gone."

Elyssa blew out a long sigh. "Great. I guess we can cancel the invasion because we're officially screwed."

"Invasion?" Mother scoffed. "You planned to fight Drakara's army?"

"We thought we'd have to fight our way into Zbura to reach the crystalis," Elyssa said. "Turns out there's nothing for us here."

"So Seraphina is left to her dismal fate." Morriss slumped. "Daelissa's warmongering weakened our armies and left our realm ripe for the plucking."

"Yeah, well there's more to it than that." I shook my head. "All the realms are doomed without that crystalis."

"All the realms?" Morriss's eyes flared. "What do you mean?"

"The realms are collapsing back into one Earth." I gave him a brief history. "The Star of Ussor is possibly a gem of great power used by the gods to create worlds. It was our last hope to stop the collapse."

Morriss dropped to his knees, a seraph suddenly faced with the prospect of the destruction of his entire world. "But I am barely three-hundred years old. I still have so much to live for!"

Elyssa knelt next to him. "Are you absolutely certain you don't know anything about the missing relic?"

He squeezed his eyes shut. "Those days were so chaotic. The entire city guard was mobilized and taken from the city. So many unfamiliar Seraphim came through here that any one of them could have taken it. I cannot—" Morriss abruptly went silent. "There is one thing that was strange. Not long after Daelissa embarked for Eden, I encountered a very odd seraph in the palace. His clothing was like nothing I'd seen and his skin was sickly looking. He told me it was from his long time on Eden."

"Sickly?" I asked. "In what way?"

"His skin looked grayish." Morriss shook his head. "That was the last time I saw him. I don't know why that would have anything to do with the theft of the Star of Ussor, but it has stuck in my mind all these years."

"Hmm," I said as a line slowly formed between a giant pair of dots —his information and some facts of my own. I suddenly knew where the crystalis had to be.

21

"I know where it is." I paused to let the tension build, but Elyssa was having none of it.

"Spit it out, Justin."

"Party pooper." I sighed. "Fjoeruss has it."

Elyssa raised an eyebrow. "You think he sent a gray man here to retrieve an ancient family heirloom?"

"It makes sense, doesn't it?" I turned to Morriss. "How long was the Star of Ussor here?"

"Eons. History says that when Ussor vanished from Seraphina, he left behind marvelous relics. Among them was the star. It was moved to the palace museum for safekeeping."

"Fjoeruss is Ussor." I turned to Elyssa. "The moment he found out the Grand Nexus was functioning again, he must have sneaked one of his gray men into Seraphina to retrieve the star. It would have been easy with Daelissa moving so many troops around."

Elyssa pressed her lips into a thin line. "What would Fjoeruss need with a crystalis? He may be powerful, but he's not a god."

"We need to pay him a visit and find out." I turned to Mother. "Provided we're free to go, of course."

Mother nodded solemnly. "Your efforts could save all the worlds, so of course you are free to go. How did you reach Seraphina in the first place? The Alabaster Arches no longer work."

"We have another way." I was hesitant to tell her too much. Just because she was letting us go didn't make her an ally. "It's possible we could evacuate your people from Seraphina and give them a new home away from Drakara."

"That is a kind gesture, but no place is safe with the realms collapsing." Her shoulders straightened. "And Drakara would hunt us relentlessly. She has the capacity to travel the realms, though the energy cost of opening a rift large enough to give her passage is incredible. It is more likely she would send her minions after us."

I grunted. "If she can open rifts, I wonder why she hasn't invaded other realms yet."

"Oh, she has," Mother said. "She has a swarm of nearly a million drakes and wyvern, but even those numbers spread thin over several realms."

"A million?" My mind boggled at those numbers. Drakes were small, but still deadly. There was no way in hell we could hope to defeat that many dragons if it ever came down to an invasion. Freeing Seraphina seemed like an insurmountable task. Then again, if we didn't stop the collapse, there's be no Seraphina to free.

Morriss sobbed. "We're doomed!"

I hated to say it, but he was probably right. Even if we stopped one apocalypse, another was right over the horizon. "Thank you for your help, Mother." I bowed to the mother of dragons.

"Yes, thank you." Elyssa offered a Japanese-style bow. "If we can get our brooms back, we'll be on our way."

"At once." Mother sent Morriss scurrying away to get the drygon who'd captured us and then ordered them to give us an escort to our destination. Kroa seemed less than enthused to just let us go, but did as ordered.

Within moments, we were back on our brooms and zooming for the skylet. Kroa and the rest of our escort turned back once we cleared the mists and the skylet appeared on the horizon.

"Not even a goodbye?" I shouted after them.

None of them so much as looked back.

Sixteen minutes later, the portal opened right on schedule. We went through and found Adam, Cinder, and Shelton waiting with bated breath.

"That was fast," Adam said. "You were only gone three hours."

"Felt like a lot longer." I shook my head. "So, you're never going to believe what we found out."

"We've seen way too much shit to not believe you," Shelton said. "Let me guess, you met the Flying Spaghetti Monster and he's destroy Elohim and the dragon army."

"Nailed it!" I leaned my broom against a shelf. "We can just sit back and relax now." I headed toward the exit. "See you guys on the beach."

"Justin, are we certain this Flying Spaghetti Monster will help?" Cinder hurried to catch me. "I am concerned that a being made of pasta will be unable to withstand the might of Elohim."

Adam and Shelton burst into laughter. I doubled over with belly laughs until tears of mirth streamed down my cheeks. "Cinder, you're a national treasure."

He frowned. "Ah, so the pasta god is not going to help us?"

"He doesn't exist." I patted him on the back. "It was a joke."

"Yeah, the Pastafarian religion isn't big on violence anyway," Shelton said. "Make lasagna, not war."

That got Adam giggling again.

Elyssa wiped tears from her eyes. "I needed that, especially after what happened to us in Seraphina."

A Templar entered the room, Vitania and Emily in tow. He saluted Elyssa and left.

Vitania strode over to the alabaster ring and examined it. "What happened? I opened a portal at the scheduled time, but you weren't there."

Emily nodded. "I was worried something awful happened."

"We just got back from Seraphina." I shook my head. "We hadn't exactly planned to do what we did."

Vitania pursed her lips. "That seems to be a pattern with you."

"Oh, it is," Emily said. "But they usually get good results."

Shelton's smile faded. "Well, tell us what happened."

Elyssa told the story of the drygon, Mother, and the missing crystalis. "Our last hope is that Fjoeruss might have the Star of Ussor."

Adam groaned. "He's such a pain in the ass to deal with."

"He'll make us jump through a dozen hoops and then tell us he doesn't have it." Shelton made a spitting sound. "Provided we can even find him."

I turned to Vitania. "Any luck helping Emily?"

She shook her head. "I was unable to unweave the corruption in her aura. Whatever Eve did to her cannot be easily undone."

Adam held his arcphone toward Emily and tapped the screen. His eyes flared. "Holy smokes, the readings are off the charts. It's similar to the readings I got from Justin, but hundreds of times greater."

"Meaning what?" I said. "We're like charged batteries?"

He shrugged. "The likeliest theory is that Eve's destruction pulse combined with the pure magic of the primal fount imprinted on your auras, changing them. It's possible only another godlike being could reverse it."

I examined the shimmer of power along my skin. "I like super speed, but I'm a little concerned there might be negative side-effects."

"It's possible even if you had your Seraphim powers right now, they'd be corrupted like Emily's are." Adam tucked his phone away. "I'll study the readings and see if I can figure out anything."

"First things first." I set Nookli on a table and projected a holographic map of the world. "Let's find Fjoeruss. How did we track him down last time?"

Elyssa took out her arcphone and tapped on the screen, probably scoping out a complicated plan that would give us the most efficient path to finding the elusive Seraphim. She then put the phone to her ear and started talking. I tried to listen in but Shelton and Adam were talking so loudly that I couldn't filter them out.

"Let's send Templar agents to all his businesses," Shelton said. "Demand he turn over the crystalis or we'll burn it all to the ground!"

Adam shook his head. "We could hack into the arcsys servers at one of his locations and use it to track him. Avoid making a big scene."

"If he's on Eden, I could sing a song to locate him," Vitania said. "Unfortunately, I'm exhausted again. I need more rest before using too much magic."

Elyssa looked at her phone screen, grunted, and showed it to Adam. "Open a portal to this location on Eden."

Adam raised an eyebrow. "What's there?"

"Fjoeruss." She flashed a grin. "I called him and he's agreed to meet."

His eyes flared. "Well, that was super easy, barely an inconvenience."

I couldn't believe she had a direct line to Fjoeruss. "When did you get his number?"

"He negotiated an agreement with the Templars not to abuse magic in his business practices with noms. Part of the agreement was that he give us an emergency number." Elyssa shrugged. "I figured now was as good a time as any."

"Wow, wow, wow." Adam chuckled. "Emergency numbers are tight."

"Dude, you've been watching way too many pitch meetings." Shelton shook his head.

Adam took a step back. "I'm gonna need you to get all the way off my back about that."

"Pitch meetings?" I hadn't a clue what they meant.

"Adam, the portal please?" Elyssa tapped her foot impatiently.

"Oh, yeah." Adam walked to the alabaster ring and put a hand on it while concentrating on the image Elyssa gave him. Beams of energy flashed from the ring, tearing open a portal a few feet away.

Cinder stared at the gateway in quiet apprehension. "I will remain here. I have several theories about stopping the collapse that I wish to examine."

Shelton clapped him on the shoulder. "Perfectly understandable.

Fjoeruss had created Cinder as a gray man long ago, but a freak accident had cut the puppet strings and given Cinder sentience and free will. Even though he had a working relationship with his creator, he still wasn't completely comfortable around him.

"Fascinating." Vitania examined the ring. "This was certainly crafted by Sirens."

I stepped toward the portal. An ordinary office waited on the other side. Men and women in business attire glanced at us, but otherwise kept on working as if this were something they saw every day.

I shifted to demon vision and soon learned why. None of them had soul auras because they were all golems. Fjoeruss was the only individual I knew who could make such lifelike beings. Baal's infernus were virtually identical to living humanoids, but they were made from demon flesh, not synthesized from scratch like these.

We filed through, leaving the portal on behind us. A man with gray skin stepped from within a cubicle and motioned us to follow. He led us into a hallway and to a corner office at the end. I'd expected to see a cityscape, but there was nothing outside except vast white tundra.

Shelton pressed his nose to the window. "Where in the hell is this place?"

"My arctic safe house," A familiar voice said from behind us. Fjoeruss stepped into the room, leaving the door open behind him. "After the events of the Crystoid Incident, I decided it was time to make my own secret militarized base." His gaze settled on Vitania for an instant longer than the rest of us.

"That explains why we hardly hear from you anymore." I frowned. "Why a business office, though?"

"I have a portal system connecting this place with my other companies around the globe." He spread out his hands. "Think of it as a nexus of sorts."

"Hold on, a portal system?" Shelton turned away from the outside view. "Mind explaining how that works?"

"After Daelissa's defeat, I collected and studied many of the relics found in the storerooms at Thunder Rock, El Dorado, and the other waystations with Alabaster Arches." Fjoeruss clasped his hands over his waist. "I discovered a small cache of black cubes that act as portal nodes. Once activated and bound, they create a mesh of quantum tunnels that form doorways from one to another."

"Are you kidding me?" I stormed toward him. "We could have used that kind of arcnology to fight Xanos and Baal."

Elyssa gripped my arm to stop me. "Justin, he offered it to us, but there are limitations that made them less optimal to use than omniarches."

I blinked. "What? When did he offer it to us?"

"Shortly after our return from Seraphina." Elyssa shrugged. "The nodes have to be static, and once they're connected, can only lead to one place. The omniarches worked much better."

"Why didn't anyone tell me about this?"

"Because by then we were all over the place trying to fight Xanos." Elyssa shook her head. "It was just a bullet point in one of our daily briefings."

"Oh." I felt somewhat mollified.

Fjoeruss nodded at Vitania. "You look a bit pale, Queen Vitania. Perhaps we should go to the Templar compound to continue this conversation."

Something in his voice made me think he didn't like having a Siren in his secret base.

Vitania showed no surprise that he knew who she was. "I have overextended myself as of late, Ussor, but we may proceed here."

He studied her for a moment then turned to Emily. "Something feels off about you as well, Miss Glass." He looked at the group. "Where is Mr. Rock?"

"Unavailable," Emily replied curtly. "Missing, if you must know."

"My regrets." Fjoeruss spread his hands. "I still owe him a favor from some time ago and would be pleased to offer my services in finding him."

Emily's gaze turned hopeful. "He may not even be on Eden, but I would be grateful for any help."

Fjoeruss nodded. "I will put my network on it at once."

I barged into the conversation. "Do you know why're here?"

"Of course." Fjoeruss sat at one end of the conference table. "I would like to know why you want the Star of Ussor."

Elyssa sat down. "We need to see it first to confirm it is what we think it is."

He raised an eyebrow. "What do you think it is?"

Information was Fjoeruss's favorite currency. Elyssa knew how to play his game, but instead of playing it slow as normal, she pulled her trump card out first thing. "We need to skip the normal negotiating and get straight to it. The star may be able to stop the collapse of the realms if, as we hope, it is a crystalis."

Fjoeruss frowned. "What is a crystalis?"

I gasped. "You've never heard of them?"

"Just because I was among the first of the Seraphim doesn't mean I know everything." Fjoeruss offered a terse smile. "I have probably forgotten more than you've learned in your short life."

"Thanks, Grandpa." I shook my head cynically. "A crystalis is a super powerful diamond like gem formed where the primal and infernal founts meet."

"A force of creation," Vitania added.

If my familiarity offended him at all, he didn't show it. Fjoeruss pursed his lips. "I was unaware such a thing existed."

"It's apparently a very rare power source the gods used to fuel or accelerate creation," Adam said. "In fact, a crystalis was what caused the Sundering in the first place. We think using another one can halt the collapse."

"We need to see the Star of Ussor." Elyssa leaned her elbows on the table. "No negotiations, no indecision. It could save billions of lives."

Fjoeruss nodded. "It will be here shortly." With his army of gray men and other golems at his beck and call, he didn't even need to issue verbal commands. "In the meantime, perhaps you would like to bring me up to date on your efforts."

"Efforts?" I snorted. "Baal played us like fiddles, clapped our cheeks, and called checkmate. Now we're just trying to keep the board and pieces from being tossed in the fire."

Fjoeruss raised an eyebrow. "An apt description."

"What have you been doing all this time?" I said. "Everything you've built is about to crumble to dust."

He leaned back in his chair. "Ensuring my continued survival."

"And nothing else?" Shelton scoffed. "It's gonna be mighty boring without anyone but golems to boss around."

Fjoeruss steepled his fingers and offered no response.

Vitania cocked her ear and her gaze went distant for a moment. When her focus returned, she bored it into the Seraphim. "Where are they, Ussor?" She stood, casting about as if looking for something mortal eyes couldn't see. "They are nearby, but not here. I can hear them!"

Fjoeruss sighed. "Had I known you would be among my guests I would not have brought you here."

"What in blazes are you talking about?" Shelton said. "What do you hear?"

"Sirens." Vitania scowled. "And they are singing the song used to create Alabaster Arches."

22

Shelton's jaw dropped open. "Fjoeruss has Siren prisoners?"

Fury glowed in Vitania's eyes. "Well, Ussor, are they prisoners or allies?"

The Seraphim clasped his hands on the table. "The Sirens are allies."

"You will tell me everything." Vitania stalked toward him, eyes glowing. "Right now!"

For the first time in a long while, Fjoeruss looked moderately concerned. A fight between the first Siren and one of the original Seraphim wouldn't be pretty. "You would threaten me in my own—"

"Yes!" Vitania roared in disharmonic union with several voices at once. "I will sing this place to the bottom of the Arctic Ocean if I must!"

Fjoeruss went very still, apparently regretting a few life decisions recently made. "Very well, but you will not like the answers."

A low, crazy laugh, like the kind a man hears when he tells his wife to calm down, floated across the room. "I already do not like the questions, Fjoeruss." Vitania leaned toward him and spoke in a low hiss. "So, answer me now."

Shelton whistled and leaned toward me. "Holy farting fairies, dude. I nearly crapped my pants and she's not even talking to me."

Emily nodded in worried agreement. "Vitania can be scary."

Adam wiped a bead of sweat from his forehead. "Reminds me of that time I told my girlfriend she was being unreasonable."

Elyssa's eyes flared. "You have a death wish, don't you?"

Fjoeruss's words interrupted our little aside. "Using the portal nodes, I have bound together locations across the globe. My golems have been recruiting the best of the best humans and supers. We have collected animal life, fauna, and flora to preserve as much as possible. My activities caught the attention of Sirens stationed on Eden. They reported to Dactia that I was creating an ark, so she approached me about an alliance."

Vitania scowled and took an empty seat near him. "It is good she sees the value in preserving as much life as possible, but she refused to help me stop the collapse."

"Dactia sees that as a hopeless task," Fjoeruss said. "She saw the ark as a worthy goal."

"A real modern-day Noah." Shelton scoffed. "How can you build a big enough ark to save a planet's worth of life? And what about the hundreds of other realms out there?"

"That is why the Sirens sing the song to create arches." Fjoeruss paused a moment, as if wishing he didn't have to give away so much information for free. "They are constructing nodes to connect multiple realms—open doorways—so to speak, that will allow us to identify more life to preserve. But we have run into one major issue."

Elyssa pounded a fist on the table. "You've got nowhere to run, do you? Atlantis might be the only safe place to be in the final moments of the collapse, but it's not large enough to contain everything you've preserved."

"For the love of god, please don't preserve glurk, or any of that nasty Darkling food from Seraphina." Shelton gagged. "As long as we have ingredients for tacos and burgers, I'll be a happy man."

Elyssa stared pointedly at Shelton and put a finger to her lips before turning to Fjoeruss. "What's your endgame?"

"Yet to be determined," he admitted. "Dactia's people are working on an inter-dimensional gateway—one that will lead us completely out of here. But because Earth is broken, we are off our dimensional axis, cutting us off from the multiverse. We believe it may be possible to bridge the gap in the final days of the collapse."

Vitania pursed her lips. "There is no need. I already know of a safe space. But if I give you that information, you will have to aid us."

"In what way?" Fjoeruss shook his head. "No conventional war will win this battle."

A gray man entered the room and placed an ebony box on the table in front of Fjoeruss.

Vitania sucked in a breath and stared at it, eyes filled with uncertainty.

Shelton rubbed his hands together. "Moment of truth."

I realized I hadn't taken a breath for several seconds as anxiety spurred my racing heart.

Fjoeruss put a hand on the lid. "You truly think this can stop the collapse?"

"Open it, damn you." Vitania glared at him. "Or I will open it myself."

He lifted the lid and set it aside. Vitania reached inside and pulled out large diamond pulsating with its own inner light. She closed her eyes and murmured to herself for a moment, then reverently placed the diamond back in the box and closed it.

Elyssa leaned against the table. "Well?"

Tears trickled down Vitania's face.

"No, no, no," Shelton moaned. "We're so screwed."

Adam slumped. "Damn. I really thought we had it."

A smile shone through Vitania's tears. "Salvation is at hand, for we have a crystalis."

Suddenly all of us were jumping, whooping, and hugging each other. All except for Vitania and Fjoeruss. Even the latter couldn't help but look somewhat relieved.

"You truly think this will save us?" Fjoeruss asked.

Vitania nodded. "It is our best hope. We must take it to the primal fount in Atlantis and pray Eve is no longer there."

Elyssa's smile faded. "What if she is?"

"I'll lure her away somehow." Emily took a deep breath. "Whatever it takes."

"Well, whatever we do, it needs to happen ASAP," Shelton said. "Utopia is on the verge of being wiped out along with most of the other realms near the Abyss."

"We've already established a node in Utopia." Fjoeruss tapped the conference table and an arctablet emerged. He swiped the screen and projected a holographic image of the realms. Dozens had lines connecting them to Eden. "This is the current map."

"You don't sound so hesitant to give out free information anymore," Elyssa noted.

"That is because we have hope, Miss Borathen." Fjoeruss studied Utopia's proximity to the Abyss. "The node is in their capitol city of Solan. Perhaps we could start a general evacuation. The node gateways are marginally smaller than that of an Obsidian Arch. We can expect to get a few thousand humans through at the most before the realm is destroyed."

"If we stop the collapse, it's a moot point," Shelton said.

"Better to be safe," Elyssa shot back. "We need to start a general evacuation."

"Though I have nodes there, I am not politically connected to the natives." Fjoeruss turned to me. "It may require a personal visit from you to initiate such a major undertaking."

"We have emissaries they trust." Elyssa tapped on her phone. "We need to arrange clearance so our people can come and go through the nodes as needed."

Fjoeruss hesitated, then nodded. "Very well. But such clearance expires when this endeavor ends in victory or defeat."

Elyssa scoffed. "I'd expect nothing less from you." She took Fjoeruss's arctablet and scooted her chair closer to him so they could hammer out the details.

Vitania rose from her seat. "There's much to do, but I must rest if I'm to be of any use."

Fjoeruss summoned a gray. "It will escort you to a bedroom."

"Thank you." She followed it into an elevator.

I tried to help Elyssa with negotiations, but quickly started yawning out of boredom. This was my least favorite part of trying to save the world, but it had to be done.

"Well, isn't this quite a reunion?"

The familiar voice jerked me from my bored stupor.

The man who entered the room looked almost no different than the last time I'd seen him, though the wicked smirk I remembered was absent. Underborn regarded us with a hint of amusement. "Justin, it's good to see you again."

"Is it, though?" I stood but didn't approach him. "What in the hell are you doing here?"

"I formed an alliance with Fjoeruss, of course." He folded his arms over his chest. "I formerly possessed several relics Baal needed and came to the one person who could help me hide them."

Shelton snorted. "That didn't work out so well, did it?"

"I'm afraid that not even I could win the long game against a god." Underborn shrugged. "The last time we all stood in a room together was when we allied to take down Daelissa." He sighed. "Ah, for simpler days."

"The Slade boy has once again given us a last chance at victory, Underborn." Fjoeruss opened the box to display the crystalis. "This may stop the collapse, provided we can find someone powerful enough to use it."

Underborn raised an eyebrow. "And what, exactly, is this trinket?"

"A crystalis," Elyssa said. "A seed of creation forged where the primal and infernal founts meet."

He frowned. "I've never heard of such a thing."

I grinned. "It feels good knowing something you don't."

"Damn straight," Shelton said.

"Tut, tut, children. Even I can't know everything." Underborn took a chair against the wall. "How does this crystalis work?"

I shrugged. "All I know is we need someone with godlike powers to use it to stop the realms from collapsing."

He glanced at Emily. "I assume you are that person, Miss Glass?"

"Not at the bloody moment." Emily scowled. "Eve tried to use me to destroy the realms and left my powers corrupted. If I tried to use the crystalis now, I'd likely blow everything to bits."

Adam's eyes widened. "Wow, could you imagine the malaether backlash that much power would cause?"

Shelton shuddered. "We'd rip our universe a new asshole, that's for sure."

"Maybe even create a new negative universe!" Adam rubbed his hands together like a kid with Halloween candy.

"Uh, don't look so excited." Shelton snorted. "I think Nosti just had a nerdgasm in his pants."

"Third one today." Adam grinned.

Underborn ignored their banter. "Perhaps Conrad Edison could do the job?"

I blinked. "Conrad? He's not godlike."

"But he has an intimate connection to the primal fount." The assassin's gaze lingered on me. "I'm surprised he's not with you."

"He's attending important matters in the Glimmer." I decided not to elaborate.

Underborn's eyes flicked from me to Emily and back again. "How interesting."

I frowned. "You'll have to be more specific."

"Three destinies, all interwoven." Underborn nodded to himself. "From the moment I met young Conrad, he reminded me of you. Oh, he was certainly less precocious and far more serious, but he seemed driven by forces beyond his control toward that final moment where he ended his father's life."

He turned to Emily. "And you, a direct descendant of Eve, a demigoddess who stopped a massive infernal invasion while Justin was occupied with Daelissa's many plots. And somehow fate pulled you all together to face a threat to our very existence."

Fjoeruss looked up from his negotiations with Elyssa. "So, Underborn, you subscribe to my theory now."

The assassin nodded. "It's clearer than ever now even with just two of them together."

"Theory?" I looked from Fjoeruss to Underborn. "What theory?"

Fjoeruss spoke. "Many of the Overworld's great prophets died during Victus's rise to power. Of the few that survived, there were whispers of a coming savior. My people gathered as much information as possible, cobbling together a new foreseeance that was not realized until nearly a decade later when Conrad killed his father."

I blinked. "Conrad had his own version of Foreseeance forty-three eleven?"

"Most cataclysmic events are seen by prophets," Underborn replied. "But Victus had many of them executed when they began speaking of a savior."

"There were other major foreseeances besides forty-three eleven." Fjoeruss idly tapped a finger on the conference table. "One foretold of a massive demonic uprising. Another spoke of a new god that would lead us to a new world, but only if the trinity overcame the trials of the Abyss."

Emily gasped. "You think this trinity refers to me, Justin, and Conrad?"

Fjoeruss nodded. "Most of us were so focused on Foreseeance forty-three eleven, that we didn't even notice the events of the older prophecies. It was not until you threatened to take my powers from me all those years ago that I realized you must be the new god."

"But I'm not a full-fledged god," Emily said. "I'm a demigoddess at best, and one whose powers are malfunctioning."

Foreseeance 4311 had ruled my life up until the day we'd defeated Daelissa. Like most prophecies, there was far too much room for interpretation when it came to certain things. But everything Fjoeruss said led me to one inevitable conclusion. Emily might be the goddess who would lead us to the new world of Alden. But what did that mean for Eden and the realms? Did it mean they were doomed and our only hope was to start over on Alden?

Fjoeruss looked down at his tablet and read. "Only the union of the three and the bonds they have forged may hope to prevail when the old god seeks to remake all in his image."

I waited with bated breath for more, but he seemed to be finished. "That's it?"

He nodded.

"So, the rest of us are useless," Shelton said. "Guess we might as well go home."

"Not true." Underborn looked amused. "The bonds they have forged refer to all of us." He motioned around the room. "We are all connected, all drawn together for this fight."

Elyssa nodded. "Justin couldn't find a matching pair of socks without me."

Shelton snorted. "Well, when you put it like that, I'm in."

"Me too!" Adam clapped his hands together. "Now we just have to figure out how in the hell we get our heroes back in working order again."

"Ain't that the truth." Shelton shook his head. "Any hero mechanics around here?"

"I'm no bloody hero." Emily sighed. "I just want to find Tyler and enjoy life instead of constantly being on the run from my psychotic sister or having the universe collapse into a ball of fire around me."

The things Fjoeruss and Underborn had said rattled around in my head, slowly shaking out into a more coherent image of things to come. Our trials and tribulations since returning to Eden from Seraphina made sense in retrospect. Conrad had been the one to bring us back from our long exile only for us to immediately have a showdown with Xanos and Razor Echelon. That had taken us on a wild goose chase across the realms to find Emily.

Once together, we'd defeated Xanos and survived the trial of the Abyss. Meanwhile, Baal had nearly completed his ten-step program to take over the world by ascending back to godhood. In our rush to stop him, we'd unwittingly helped him accomplish his goals by destroying the Void swarm and allowing him to collect the last true relic he needed: The Beast.

Instead of stopping Baal, now Elohim, we'd helped him achieve his goals. So how in the hell were could we be certain our future actions weren't also part of Elohim's grand scheme to blot out all life in the realms and start over? To make matters worse, it wasn't just Elohim we had to worry about. Now Eve was all aboard the death and destruction train.

Emily and I needed to get our powers back and there was only one person who might possibly agree to fix things, provided she gave me a chance to reason with her instead of instantly striking me down.

I had to talk to Emily's evil sister, Olivia.

23

My mission was so stupidly insane that in the past I would have tried to sneak off and do it in secret. Elyssa had just given me a verbal beat-down for my stunt in Pangea, and I didn't feel like going for a round two. Besides, if I couldn't convince Elyssa, my love and closest ally, that this mission was our only chance, then how could I expect to convince Olivia of anything?

Fjoeruss and Elyssa took a break from information sharing and planning when a gray man entered the room bearing food and drinks.

"Hamburgers!" Shelton rushed toward the grub at superhuman speed, cutting off Emily in his haste.

Emily could have yanked him back by his leather duster but seemed to admire his enthusiasm.

I skirted the commotion and took Elyssa's hand, kissed it, and led her to the opposite corner of the room.

She sighed. "You've got that look again. Somehow I feel like you want to do something even dumber than rushing into the fae fortress to take down the tyrannical queen without asking me first. "

"Bingo!" I snapped my fingers. "But I'm being a good boy and telling you about it before I rush off and do something rash."

Elyssa sighed. "At least you're trying, babe." She leaned against the wall. "Dish."

"Emily needs her powers if we stand a chance at this plan working. Eve is hell-bent on universal destruction and there's no one else we can even remotely trust to help us."

She raised an eyebrow. "But..."

"But maybe we can convince an enemy that it's in their best interests to help us." I paused to let that sink in, but Elyssa was already ahead of me.

"Olivia." She pursed her lips.

"It's crazy, I know, but hear me out." I'd compiled a short list of pros to make my case and shut down any counter arguments Elyssa made. Technically, my list of pros was only two bullet points long, and the second one was so bad it was almost a con.

Before I could list my pros, Elyssa spoke. "I think it's a good idea, Justin."

My mouth remained open for a good ten seconds while I processed her quick response. "Say what?"

Elyssa gently pushed up on my chin to close my mouth. "Emily told me how Olivia was churned through the foster system. How she was raised by some of the worst people imaginable, raped, nearly killed several times, but managed to live through it all. She's a survivor, plain and simple. If we tell her the collapse will destroy all life except the gods, then she might be willing to help us stop it so she can become one of the new gods."

I hadn't even considered that even though it should've been at the top of my list. "Uh, yeah. Your pros are better than mine."

"What were you going to say?" she asked.

I bit my bottom lip. "Well, it sounds kind of stupid now."

"Humor me."

"Uh, I'm super-fast so if she tried to kill me, I could run away."

Elyssa repressed a grin. "Uh-huh. And what else?"

I really didn't want to say it but did anyway. "I look just like Cain, and she liked him."

"Because Cain was your evil doppelganger." Elyssa snort-laughed in her attempt to hold it in. "You took Cain away from her, so she's more likely to hate you. I would have definitely put that in the list of cons."

I sagged. "Yeah, well I was already grasping at straws."

Elyssa hid her grin. "It's okay, babe. You tried, and that's what really matters."

I shrugged. "What you said makes a lot more sense as usual."

Elyssa took my hand. "Olivia has almost no sense of humanity left in her. But as much as she flaunts her demigoddess-ness to appear superior, I think she still feels like that beaten little girl who was told she was worthless for most of her childhood. You'll have to convince her that giving Emily back her powers to stop the collapse is about her survival and proving her superiority, not about saving people."

I grunted. "Maybe I should just ask her to stop the collapse. She might be more willing to do that than fix her sister's powers."

"Trusting her to help Emily is one thing but giving her a crystalis could be every bit as catastrophic as the collapse." Elyssa shuddered. "Olivia might corrupt everything with one stray thought and make reality a living hell for the rest of us."

I grimaced. "Yeah, you're right." I paused. "I just realized you didn't say 'we' have to convince her."

"That's because you're the only person who can get in and out of her presence with super speed." Elyssa rubbed my hand. "Even if she agrees to help Emily, we'll have to be extremely careful to make sure it's not a trap."

"Yeah, that's the gamble, isn't it?" I sighed. "Well, here's hoping."

She kissed my cheek. "If anyone can give us hope in a hopeless situation, it's you."

"I *hope* you're right." I cupped her cheek and drew her in for a kiss. "Thank you for being the smart one."

Elyssa giggled. "Thank you for not being stupid and running off without telling me."

My mood sobered. "The next question is, how in the hell do I find Olivia?"

"Yes." Elyssa grinned.

I blinked. "Huh?"

"She's probably in Hell." Elyssa sighed. "The question is whether or not we can make a portal going there."

I reached out to Kalesh. *I need an image of Hell so I can portal there. Can any of our new allies help?*

I will ask. A moment later, Kalesh responded. *Yes, there are infernus there. Astra is showing me how to access one.*

There was a brief instant of disorientation and suddenly I felt as if I were seeing through two sets of eyes. I closed my eyes and the double images went away.

Do you see what I see? Kalesh said.

Yes! Holy shit, dude, this is freaky!

Elyssa spoke. "Justin, what's wrong?"

"Kalesh linked me to an infernus in Hell. Give me a sec." I tried to move the infernus, but nothing happened. *Can you walk around? I want to see the layout.*

Of course. The infernus started strolling down a tunnel. The walls sparkled with diamonds and other gems. Gold and other precious metals veined the rock. The tunnel branched in countless places, some leading to vast caverns cast in dusky twilight.

Where are we going?

Up to the mansion, Kalesh replied. The infernus stepped into a cone of light in the middle of the room. We abruptly shot straight up on an invisible levitator. Elevator doors dinged and opened to reveal black marble floors. The infernus stepped into a corridor that made Grand Central Station look small.

The only decorations in the corridor were giant windows and the orange sunlight painting the walls. The infernus hopped onto a battery-powered scooter and rode it down the hall. Aside from distant echoes and occasional animalistic sounds, there were no other signs of life.

How did you know where the levitator was? I asked.

The infernus knows the layout of the mansion, Kalesh said.

The infernus drove the scooter up a long spiraling corridor and stopped at a doorway in the top. Bodies sprawled across nearly every inch of the bedroom beyond, most of them completely naked. Some stirred, giving me hope that these people were still alive and not murdered in a fit of rage by Olivia.

A discarded shirt read, *Baal's Little Bitch*. These were the same people we'd seen searching the Abyss. Now that Elohim no longer needed their services, they were back in Hell, both literally and figuratively.

A low moaning caught my attention. The infernus tip-toed between the bodies and rounded a corner. Olivia was on the other side, pressing the head of a man into her hoo-hah while mercilessly slapping and scratching his face.

I winced and wished I could shut off the image. The infernus ducked back out of sight and left the room.

Got any eye bleach? I asked.

Kalesh chuckled. *It seems Olivia has nothing better to do than throw wild sex parties.*

Yeah, so let's hope my latest crazy plan works.

Using a wickedly sharp fingernail, the infernus scratched a small symbol on the wall.

Its strength surprised me. *Is this one of Baal's personal infernus?*

Yes. They're stronger than the average bear.

I memorized the marble-veined wall and the symbol. It was an old trick we'd used during the war against Daelissa to help us open portals to locations that looked virtually identical to others. Since Hell was in Eden, all we would need was an omniarch or Adam's portal generator.

I gave Kalesh a mental fist-bump. *Thanks, bro.*

You got it, bruh.

The connection to the infernus flickered off. I opened my eyes and grinned at Elyssa. "Looks like this plan is good to go. Kalesh used an infernus to take me on a walk through the Hell mansion."

Elyssa pursed her lips. "Maybe we should have used the infernus to talk to Olivia."

I shook my head. "We don't want her to know that we're in control of the infernus. She could probably astral project to Haedaemos and take back control."

"Good point."

I nodded my head at Fjoeruss. "Do we tell the others about this plan?"

Elyssa nodded. "Let's get this partnership started off on the right foot."

I took a deep breath and walked over to the others where I announced my desperate scheme.

"Justin, you're insane!" Emily shook her head vehemently. "Olivia is a monster. She'll never help us."

"I think it's dangerous, but worth a try," Adam said. "Plus, with Justin's super speed he can get in and out easily."

I grinned. "Yeah, that was one of my pros."

"It was your only pro," Elyssa said.

Shelton grunted. "It ain't a good plan, but it ain't a terrible one either."

I frowned. "Uh, thanks, I think?"

"I don't know enough about Olivia to make a judgement call," Underborn said. "But if she is our last hope to restore Emily's powers, then there's no other choice."

"Agreed." Fjoeruss sipped a glass of whiskey. "Are you certain none of us could use the crystalis?"

"The power required to stop the collapse is beyond imagination," Adam said. "Anyone without a god-level fuse would be snuffed out."

"It's like me using Apocryphan powers." I sighed. "My body and soul aren't designed for that kind of power."

"This plan is horrid. I just hope you're quick enough on your feet to escape when Olivia tries to kill you." Emily scowled. "And even if she agrees to help, it will only be to lure me into my death."

"Probably." I shrugged. "But we've got no choice. Not unless you think we can convince Eve to help."

Emily paled. "No, that would be an even worse idea."

"We can use the portal generator to get you there," Adam said.

I nodded. "Babe, you staying here?"

Elyssa nodded. "Be careful, okay?"

I hugged her and took a moment to enjoy it before kissing her and backing away. "See you soon."

Adam, Shelton, Emily, and I took our leave and went back through the cubicles to the open portal. Cinder was still in the lab, a hologram of the realms hovering before him. He turned toward us. "What was the outcome of your meeting?"

"Ba-da-bing!" Shelton clapped his hands. "We have a crystalis."

"Now we just need a god to use it." Adam told Cinder my plan.

The golem nodded. "I may have another option, but it would only work as a last resort."

"Another option?" I walked around the hologram. "I'm all ears."

"Though I have no measurements to back up my theory, I have made projections based upon anecdotal evidence." He wiped a hand through the hologram and switched it to a view of the solar system. "Based upon the stories we've been told, the stars and some heavenly bodies existed before the gods began creation. Using the existing matter available, they crafted the Earth and other planets, molding them as they saw fit. That leads me to believe a crystalis contains extremely concentrated energy, enough to spawn a new planet with life, but not enough to create a star."

Shelton shrugged. "Makes sense, but what's the point?"

"The point, Harry, is the magnitude of energy contained in the crystalis may not be equivalent to that of a sun." Cinder zoomed in on Sol and displayed some incomprehensible numbers, then panned over to Earth with what looked like smaller numbers. "I believe that ordinary supers could tap into the energy from the crystalis and give the realms a nudge. Many such nudges would reverse the course of the collapse and perhaps stabilize it."

Adam snapped his fingers. "Dude, you're right. It would be like rocket thrusters gradually slowing a space ship instead of one giant rocket booster burning through all its fuel at once to do the same job."

Cinder switched back to the view of the realms and highlighted the Anchor Stone and Abyss with a tap of his finger. "In fact, I believe the Sirens tapped into a crystalis to tether the realms together in the first place. If we can replicate their success, then perhaps we can save the realms ourselves."

"Yeah, but if that's the case, why hasn't Vitania mentioned it?" Shelton said. "She was running the show back then."

"Probably just one more thing she's forgotten over the eons." I considered Cinder's proposal for a moment. "Let's ask her when I get back."

Shelton winced. "Yeah, let's hope you get back."

Emily touched my shoulder. "Justin, don't relax for a moment. Olivia will toy with you, give you hope, and then kill you. I think this plan is madness."

"But there's a glimmer of hope it might work." I squeezed her hand. "Olivia might not care about others, but Elyssa made a good point—she's a survivor and will do what it takes to live."

Emily sighed. "I truly hope you're right."

I closed the portal to Fjoeruss's arctic hub and focused on the symbol on the wall in the Hell mansion. "If Olivia gets a crazy look in her eyes, I'll just super-speed away." The ring glowed and a portal opened to the Hell mansion.

"You do that." Shelton expanded his staff. "We'll come running if you give the word."

I shook my head. "Absolutely not. If something happens to me, close the portal." This might be a one-way mission and I didn't want my friends to die for nothing. I hopped through and blurred away before they could argue the point. It didn't take long for me to retrace the steps taken by the infernus. I reached the bedroom and skirted around the naked concubines. Olivia had thankfully finished with her sexcapades and was resting on a couch in an adjoining area while sipping on a glass of red wine.

Her eyes flared when she saw me. "Cain!" She jumped up, arms open wide before jolting to a stop. The look of delight morphed into a scowl of anger. "Justin, you piece of shit."

I held up my hands in surrender. "I come in peace."

"And you'll leave in pieces." Fiery energy gathered at her fingertips.

24

I prepared to blur away. "Hear me out or you'll die with the rest of us!"

"Die?" She paused. "I'm listening."

"The realms are collapsing—"

"Billions will die, blah, blah, blah." Power sparked between her hands. "You think I give a shit?"

I took out Nookli and showed her a hologram of the projected outcome of the collapse—the Abyss and Anchor Stone crushing the realms, leaving Earth blackened and lifeless. "Not just billions. Everyone except Elohim and Eve."

The energy bouncing between her hands flickered out. "You're lying."

I shook my head. "Think about it. The Abyss and Anchor Stone didn't exist before the Sundering. They were created to counterbalance each other and keep the realms from drifting apart. But the Abyss is devouring realms as it snaps back toward the Anchor stone, snuffing out anything living as it goes. It will do the same when it hits the inner realms like Eden. By the time it reaches the Anchor Stone, there won't be anything left alive."

"A force only gods could survive." Olivia spat on the floor. "Elohim is such a jackass."

"He didn't even mention this possibility, did he?" I allowed myself to relax a little. "Look, I know you don't care how many die but if you help your sister, we might be able to stop the collapse. Then you can continue to live, laugh, love while using sentient beings as your playthings."

Her smirk spread into a grin. For a moment, she looked nearly identical to Emily, aside from the aquamarine hair. "You think the combined might of two demigoddesses can stop the collapse?"

"Yes." I wasn't about to tell her about the crystalis. "But Emily has a problem with her powers. Eve tried to use her to destroy the realms and now her powers are corrupted."

Olivia howled with laughter. "Have all the gods gone mad?" She doubled over, tears of mirth trickling down her cheeks. "Eve wants a do-over too?"

I shrugged. "Elohim and Eve are bat-shit crazy. Maybe it's time you and Emily activated your Wonder-Twin powers and showed them who's boss."

She leapt up, her robes falling away to show off everything beneath. "I'll do it!" Olivia rubbed her hands together eagerly. "Then we can rid ourselves of Elohim and Eve and rule the realms together. Emily can be the yang to my yin. The devil to my divinity." She sighed. "Oh, this'll be fun."

I didn't dare mention just how backward she was on her metaphors because I didn't want to ruin the moment. Even so, I remained suspicious. "You're not just saying that so I can bring your sister here for you to kill her, right?"

She blinked and looked offended. "Any other time, I absolutely would. But this opportunity is just too good to pass up. Go get my sister."

I backed slowly away nodding. "I'll be right back." Once I was around the corner of the partition and out of her sight I blurred back to the portal and dashed through.

Emily flinched and jumped back, apparently surprised to see me pop up so suddenly. "Did you have to flee for your life?"

I shook my head and told the others about my conversation. "Olivia is all about overthrowing Elohim and Eve, so I think she's telling the truth."

Shelton nodded in agreement. "She's a bitch and a liar, but this sounds genuine."

"Straight from her evil heart," Adam said.

Cinder regarded us silently for a moment. "I do not have sufficient data to make a determination, but I will trust your judgement."

Emily steeled herself. "Moment of truth, then. Let's go see my lovely sister." She stepped through the portal.

I paced alongside her. "I'll scoop you up and run us back here if things go sideways."

She was so lost in thought she didn't even hear me. Gaze distant, hands rubbing together nervously, Emily took a deep breath and finally nodded. "I trust you, Justin. Maybe my sister will finally do something halfway good even if it is for her own gain."

The floor was completely clear of concubines when we reached the bedroom. An ornate throne that hadn't been there before now sat in front of the bed. Olivia skipped from behind the partition, red robes flowing behind her. She leapt and landed in the center of the cushioned throne. Spreading her hands grandly, she smirked. "You like it, sis?"

Emily swallowed uncomfortably. "It's lovely, Olivia."

"Glad you like it." She flourished a hand. "Kneel before your goddess."

I sighed. "Look, can we skip the theatrics and get on with saving the universe?"

"Of course," Olivia said sweetly. "As soon as you kneel, bow, and scrape the floor. Then we can get on with the main event."

Gritting her teeth, Emily dropped to a knee and bowed. I rolled my eyes and did the same.

"Both knees," Olivia said. "Then bow all the way to the floor like you mean it."

I braced for a sneak attack, readying to speed us away, then scraped the floor like she wanted us to.

Olivia clapped her hands and giggled. "Perfect! Now we can get started."

Emily rose. "Thank you, sister."

"No, thank you." Olivia's smiled turned cold and tears trickled down her cheeks. "Thank you both for taking away the one person I loved in this miserable fucking existence."

My insides froze at the sudden change of demeanor. "What are you talking about?"

"Cain." She spoke in a whisper, but the pain rippled across my demonic senses like the ocean tide. "You killed him."

"He was never alive to begin with," I said. "He was a part of Baal's essence injected into the body of my father."

"He was my only love." Olivia wiped away the tears and continued speaking in that deathly quiet voice women use when they're about to destroy someone. "So, I took someone you care about."

Emily's breath audibly hitched in her throat. "Olivia, what did you do?"

Her sister motioned with her hand and several male concubines carried in a hooded figure. The muscular body was covered in cuts, bruises, and a sickly sheen of liquids I didn't want to identify. One of the concubines brought in a metal chair and set it next to the throne. The others placed the figure on it.

Olivia plucked off the hood.

Emily cried out and rushed forward but a shield knocked her back. "Tyler!" she screamed.

Olivia burst into cruel laughter that slowly devolved into sobs. Tears poured down her cheeks despite the manic smile on her face. "I fucking love that look on your face, Em." She wiped the tears from her face. "After our little meeting on Aquilis, I chased after you and Eve, but only found poor Tyler floating alone in the ocean. You can't even imagine how I've used and abused him since then."

"Tyler!" Emily pounded her fists against the shield, sobbing. "Let him go. You can have me. Do anything you want to me, just let him go."

Tyler stirred. "Em, is that you?"

"It's me, baby!" She slumped against the translucent shield. "I'm here."

Despite the swollen lips and cheeks, he managed to smirk. "You didn't even let me freshen up before stopping by to visit?"

Olivia's smile faded. "As much as I've enjoyed watching your pain, sister, it's just not quite enough." She turned to me. "It's your turn to pay the piper, Justin." She pointed to the bed. "Go fetch your little girlfriend and bring her here because I want you to put on a show. I want you to pound me like Cain used to do. Pull my hair, spank me, and choke me while she watches everything."

"No!" Emily screamed. "No more games, Olivia. You've made your point, now release Tyler and help us."

Olivia ignored her and made a shooing motion at me. "Go get your little bitch and bring her back."

"You never planned to help us, did you?" Emily backed away from the shield. "You want to make us suffer like you suffered when we took Cain. Then what? You planned to kill us and just let the world be snuffed out?"

"Get Elyssa now!" Olivia gripped Tyler's throat. "Do it, or I'll kill him."

I held up my hands in surrender, desperately thinking of a way to save Tyler. The shimmering air across the room told me there was no way around the shield. The only possible option would be running back into the hallway, finding an open window, and somehow reaching the window near the bed.

With my super speed I could do it. I'd whisk Tyler away before Olivia even knew what happened. I backed up slowly, taking Emily with me. "Fine. I'll go get Elyssa and do what you want."

"My sister stays here," Olivia said.

Emily shook herself free from my arm and stepped forward. "I won't leave Tyler."

"I know."

She shook her head. "Justin, don't come back. After she's had her fun, she'll kill us."

"No, I won't." Olivia held up her pinky finger. "Pinky swear!"

I almost extended my middle finger at her but controlled myself and backed out. Once I was out of sight, I found a window at the end of the hallway and blurred over to it. The material was transparent, but it wasn't glass. I pounded on it until it finally cracked, making enough noise to wake the dead. There was no way in hell I'd break through the window in the bedroom before Olivia saw me coming, but I had no choice but to try.

I spawned into demon form and used a massive fist to punch through the window. It crumbled like stone. A hot, arid breeze touched my skin and my demon form felt right at home. I leapt from the window and spread my bat-like wings. The house perched high on a cliff overlooking lakes of bubbling water. Misshapen demon forms clustered around a flawless man at the shore of the nearest lake.

Elohim's son, Apollyon, looked up at me. He didn't look remotely surprised. If anything, he just looked sad.

I wasn't surprised to find him here. It was his corruption aura that had turned this place into Hell eons ago. Elohim apparently figured this was the best place to keep him for now.

The hot air lifted me and carried me around the corner and toward the bedroom window. I wouldn't have the luxury of punching it until it broke. The only way to make this work was in one quick, decisive motion. I climbed higher and flew further away from the mansion until I had sufficient distance and angle, then aimed my head at the window, tucked my wings, and dove.

I felt like a big blue brick from an airplane bathroom, unfurling my wings just enough to keep me angled toward the window. I angled my demon horns at the last instant and plowed through the transparent material. I had more than enough momentum. The window exploded into pieces. My horns plowed into the floor, shattering tiles and grounding concrete to dust. Using all my demonic strength, I stopped my skid.

Olivia and her concubines regarded me in shock. Emily's eyes went wide when she saw me. Everything around me slowed as I sprang into hyper-speed. Arms outreached, I grasped at Tyler. The air shimmered around him and my hands met another shield. Running my hands around desperately, I realized he was completely encased in another barrier. I tried to lift the shield, but Olivia's godlike powers made it immovable.

I reached back with my massive fists and pummeled the barrier. With a desperate roar, I unleashed everything I had. The shield cracked, but it wasn't enough. Still moving at super-speed, I jackhammered the shield until it was nothing but a spider web of cracks. Even then, it refused to break.

I stopped to catch my breath and the world resumed moving.

Olivia's cruel laughter cut through the air.

"How cute." Olivia gripped me by the throat and threw me at the shield bisecting the room. I went through it and smashed against the wall.

"Can't blame me for trying." I released my demon form, shrank back to normal, and rose unsteadily to my feet. "I'll go get Elyssa."

"Too late." Olivia made a slashing movement with her finger. A blade of orange energy formed at Tyler's throat.

Emily's screams thundered in my ears. "Tyler!"

Tyler grinned. "I love you, Em. Kill this bitch for me, okay?"

The blade slashed his throat. Blood poured down his chest. His body spasmed and toppled over.

Golden energy blazed around Emily and her eyes lit like twin suns. "Tyler!" Her pain and rage shook the room. Malaether crackled around her aura like a thunderstorm. A low hum began to build. Emily roared and pounded against Olivia's shield. Her sister smirked but sweat beaded on her forehead as the shield began to crack and shatter.

An orange blaze formed around Olivia and she rose into the air. Concubines scattered in all directions. The shield holding Tyler fell. I blurred forward and grabbed him, hopeful I could get him to a healer in time.

A trail of Tyler's blood seemed to freeze in midair as I streaked through the hallways and back to the portal. I blasted into Templar compound without stopping, ran straight to the healing ward, and laid Tyler on a bed. "I need a healer now!"

Meghan hurried from the back of the ward. "What is it?"

"His throat was cut. Save him!" I had no time to waste and hyper-sped back to the portal and into the Hell mansion. I'd barely made it through when the low hum from Emily's malaether buildup reached a fever pitch. There was a moment of deathly silence and a bright light. Heat washed across me, hurling me out of the hallway window I'd broken earlier. Spinning out of control, I spawned demon wings and managed to break my fall.

Gliding on the superheated breeze, I circled away just as the entire side of the mansion exploded, hurling chunks of marble and bodies in all directions. Olivia and Emily grappled in midair, two goddesses burning bright as meteors in the hellishly orange dusk. Olivia thrust her foot against Emily's midriff and pushed her away. Beams of golden energy speared from Emily's eyes. Olivia countered with orange beams of her own. The energy boiled into a miniature sun between them, golden light tarnished by rust.

Another malaether wave was already building, this one ten times louder and larger than the last. Apollyon and the Hell demons watched from a distance, captivated by the pure power on display. I flapped my wings to put as much distance between me and the fight as possible, lest I be crushed like a fly.

"Tyler!" Emily's scream echoed the pure pain and agony of losing her one true love. The ball of energy between her and Olivia shaded completely gold and shot toward her wicked sister.

Olivia screamed in terror at the last moment as the energy engulfed her. Emily screamed louder, veins of golden and blue energy rippling beneath her skin. The flesh around her eyes became nearly translucent, revealing a ghostly figure of energy beneath. It wasn't just her aura, but something else I couldn't identify.

Olivia streaked out of the flames, her skin blackened and bleed-ing. She flew higher, smoke trailing from her charred clothes and seared flesh. At the last instant, she seemed to realize she was flying straight at the event horizon of the malaether eruption.

She juked away, diving as Emily's golden rays followed her. The massive sphere of malaether imploded into a pinpoint of light and the world went silent for an instant. Then it erupted like a nuclear weapon. I was nearly half a mile away, but even then, I wasn't sure if it was far enough.

Olivia thrust out her hands and tried to shield herself, but she looked like an ant trying to fight a supernova. The explosion washed over her. Superheated air blasted across the mansion and the massive building folded in on itself like a house of cards. The cliff it sat on began to quake and crumble. Dust and rubble rained down on the plains below.

Black smoke trailed a small figured as it plummeted earthward. I realized Emily's golden glow was no longer visible. Both she and Olivia were gone. My breath caught in my throat and tears burned my eyes. "Emily!"

25

I tried flapping my wings at super speed, but rather than propel me faster, it just made me hover in place. I angled toward the distant place where smoke rose from the ground and dove. It took a seeming eternity to cross that half mile where I found the smoking remains of Olivia in a small crater.

"Oh, Jesus." I pinched my nose against the stench of burnt flesh.

Olivia's face was a seared mess. One eye was completely gone, the other missing an eyelid. The eye twitched toward me and I shouted in alarm. Something rattled from Olivia's throat. I couldn't understand what she was saying any more than I could comprehend how she was still alive. She convulsed and black liquid trickled from her mouth. Then she went still.

Shuddering, I switched to demon view. Her aura drifted up from her body, dwindling until it vanished. I couldn't believe it. Olivia was dead. I would have taken a moment longer to let that sink in, but I had to find Emily. I rose into the air, circling in a search pattern. By the time I reached the rubble where the mansion and cliff had been, I had to admit the truth. Emily was gone too. The cliff and mansion were now her monumental cairn.

Tears burned my eyes. I dropped to the ground and fell to my knees. Not only had I lost a friend, but the realms had lost their last hope to stop the collapse.

"What happen?" Apollyon suddenly appeared at my side though he'd been on the opposite side of the mansion only moments before. "You okay?"

I didn't dare look at his perfect face. I knew from my experience in the time remnant that seeing him only invited madness. Physically, he was absolute perfection, but he had a speech impediment and a corruption aura that ruined everything living around him.

"No, I'm not okay." I shuddered with another sob. "My friend is dead."

"The goddess?" He touched me gently. "I saw her fall." Apollyon took my hand. "Come!" He dashed ahead like an excited child and only my super speed allowed me to keep pace with him. We circled the rubble and found a smoking crater nearly hidden from above by leaning pillars of stone.

Another sob tore from me and tears clouded my vision. Apollyon released my hand and we slowly encroached on what I felt certain was Emily's charred corpse. A slab of stone lay inside the crater, covering it. I almost didn't want to remove it for fear Emily was crushed as well as burned.

Apollyon lifted it as one might lift a paper plate and tossed it aside. A hand jutted from dusty soil. I rushed into the crater and knelt, digging through the earth until I uncovered a face, arms, and the body. The clothing was charred. Emily's flesh was black as soot. I gently pulled her burnt body from the shallow grave and carried her up and out of the crater.

When I set her down in the sunlight, I realized her skin wasn't charred, but covered in soot. Apollyon knelt next to me, spitting on her skin and wiping it off with his shirt. I grimaced, but figured it was actually kind of sweet—for a child. Though his aura was hideous, Apollyon was actually a very nice boy.

Emily moaned and stirred. Eyelids fluttered open. She sputtered and sneezed, clearing the dust from her nose. She looked up at me with a blank stare that slowly resolved into comprehension. "Justin?"

I nodded, wiped the tears from my face. "I can't believe you survived that."

Tears tracked mud down her cheeks. "Tyler."

"I took him to Meghan. If anyone can heal him, she can."

Apollyon clasped his hands pleadingly. "Goddess, can you kill me too?"

Emily automatically looked toward him. She gasped gently at his perfect face. "Why do you want to die?"

I waited for her to burst into sobs of madness, but his beauty apparently had no effect on her as it had before. I risked a peek and felt insanity shredding my emotions within seconds. I looked away just enough to give myself relief.

"Am bad." Apollyon shook with sobs of his own. "Father promised but he lied."

"Olivia?" Emily whipped her gaze toward me. "Where is she?"

"Dead." I kept my tone somber, not sure how Emily would react.

She squeezed her eyes shut. "I wish I could say she deserved it, but she didn't."

"Not sure if I agree," I said.

Emily put a hand to her head and winced. She seemed a little out of it, which was perfectly normal considering the hell she and Olivia had unleashed on each other. I wanted to comfort her, but our next major step involved making like Mary's little lamb and getting the flock out of there. I looked up and found the outline of the portal several hundred feet up. I couldn't ask Emily to fly us up there because we didn't need to risk another nuclear explosion.

I pulled out my phone but Nookli was a useless brick. Apparently, the malaether wave had sent my phone into the afterlife. "Nookli, no." With a trembling hand and heavy heart, I slid her back into my pocket.

Emily pushed to her feet. "I need to see Tyler. I need to know he's okay."

I pointed up. "We have to get up there first." Averting my eyes, I turned back to Apollyon. "Where is Elohim, by the way? Do I need to worry about him seeing me?"

"He with Seela." Apollyon pointed up. "He want to find Eve and kill her."

"Saila?" I clarified.

He nodded. "He kill Eve, but not me. Why?" Apollyon's shoulders sagged. "Hell already bad. Now I make it worse."

I put a hand on his shoulder while keeping my eyes off his face. "You are a good person. Maybe we can fix you, because I think killing you will be nearly impossible."

He gasped. "Fix me? Please!"

"For now, you have to stay here." I pointed up at the portal. "We need to get back there somehow. Unfortunately, I can't fly while carrying another person."

"Oh there?" Without warning, Apollyon gripped my shoulders and flung me straight up. I rocketed toward the portal at incredible speed, screaming in alarm at the top of my lungs.

Emily's shouts trailed just behind mine. I looked down and saw her only a few dozen feet behind me. I overshot the portal by a quarter mile before losing momentum. I spawned my wings as large as I could without bulking into demonic form. Held out my hands as Emily closed in. "Grab them!"

She latched onto my hands and dangled. "I take it you don't want me to fly on my own?"

I shook my head adamantly. "The last thing we need is a malaether eruption in Cinder's lab."

Though I couldn't gain altitude, I was able to take us into a gentle spiral back to the portal. I heaved Emily through as I passed it, then flapped my wings at super speed to hover in place so I could glide in.

Shelton and the others were hiding behind a shield generator in a far corner. Rubble from the mansion was scattered in a cone pattern outside the portal and much of that part of the room was blackened and destroyed.

"Holy exploding ass bombs!" Shelton turned off the shield generator and marched toward us. "What the hell happened? If Cinder hadn't heard the malaether building up, we would've been deep fried or squashed."

Adam jogged up behind Shelton. "Emily, did you use your powers?"

Emily pushed past them. "Where's Tyler?"

I scooped her into my arms and super-sped her to the healing ward. Meghan sat in the front lobby, face pale. She rose when we entered. "Emily, I'm so sorry."

The scream that tore from Emily's throat seemed to come from the center of a universe of agony. She ran into the back room. "Tyler!"

I followed behind, a knot forming in my throat when I saw the still, bloodied form of Tyler Rock on the bed.

"He was too far gone," Meghan whispered behind me. "The magic damage was extensive and the body had already bled out. I'm so, so sorry."

I wiped the tears from my eyes and nodded. "I understand."

Emily kissed Tyler's blue lips. Tears rained on his face, leaving tracks in the blood.

Justin.

I flinched at Kalesh's sudden intrusion. *What is it?*

Tyler is still a demon spirit. With the death of his body, perhaps he will return to Haedaemos.

I nodded. *I don't think that will be of consolation to Emily. Is there any way to locate him?*

He is probably in the correlating area of Hell in Haedaemos. I will ask the others for help.

Thank you. I approached Emily and gently touched her shoulder. "Emily, maybe Tyler is still alive."

She looked up at me, her face a mess of blood, mud, and tears. "What do you mean?"

"His demon spirit." I tried not to sound too confident because I didn't want to give her false hope. "Tyler might be back in Haedaemos."

Emily nodded, but she didn't seem any happier. "He was completely bonded with the body. For all I know, he's in the afterlife."

Which meant it was one more person she could only visit in Nowhere, the place where the physical and spiritual intersected. "I know it doesn't make you feel any better, but at least he's not gone forever whether he's in the afterlife or Haedaemos. I asked Kalesh to find him."

She leaned against the wall, slid down until she sat on the floor.

I didn't know what else to do, so I sat down next to her and put an arm around her shoulder. She buried her face in my shirt and sobbed and sobbed until she could cry no more. It could have been minutes later or an hour. In my own grief, I'd lost track of time. I hadn't been terribly close to Tyler, but having thought I'd lost Nightliss before, I knew the absolute devastation of such a loss.

Emily took a deep breath, stood, and nodded somberly at me. "Thank you, Justin." She reached down and pulled me to my feet. "If Kalesh finds him, maybe there's hope after all."

"I truly hope so, Emily." I took her hands. "Let's get cleaned up. Take all the time you need, okay?"

She sniffled. "I've already done that. Unfortunately, life goes on and the clock is ticking. If Tyler is back in Haedaemos, we need to stop the collapse to save him. Can you please show me where to clean up?"

"Of course." I took her to mine and Elyssa's private quarters. "There's a shower in there. I think you can wear one of Elyssa's uniforms." I found one of the black unitards and set it on the bed.

"Thank you." She went into the bathroom.

I grabbed a change of clothes and went into the common shower room down the hall. I scrubbed and scrubbed as if I could clean away the day's events, but those scars were likely burned in for the rest of my life.

Emily was ready to go when I returned to the room and we went to the lab. Shelton and the others were cleaning up when we arrived.

"Dude, what happened?" Adam ran over to us. "Emily said something about Tyler?"

"I thought I saw something blur through here earlier," Shelton said. "Was that you?"

I nodded, uncertain if bringing up Tyler would tear open Emily's wounds again.

"Tyler is dead at the hands of my sister." Emily shuddered. "Olivia is dead too."

Adam grimaced. "Tyler's dead? Olivia had him all this time?"

I sighed and told them about the tragic events. "Olivia did just as Emily feared and toyed with us. She was a lot more broken up about Cain's death"—I made air quotes—"than we realized."

"Fucking bitch!" Shelton smacked a fist into his palm.

"Incredibly tragic." Cinder awkwardly patted Emily's arm. "I offer my condolences."

"Thank you, Cinder." Emily was obvious repressing hard. Her eyes were dry, but her breath hitched in her throat. "We need to get back to work. See if there's another way to save the realms."

I sadly took out Nookli. "The malaether blast fried her."

"Nookli died too?" Shelton hissed and seemed to hold in whatever he wanted to say.

Adam took her from me. "It was probably the EMP effect. Let me have a look at it—"

"Her," I corrected.

He nodded. "I'll look her over."

I swallowed the knot in my throat. "Who's going to tell me where the Indian restaurants are?"

"Justin, it's a damned phone." Shelton sighed. "Look, we need concrete ideas to move forward. There's got to be something we can do."

A Templar entered the room and saluted. "Commander Slade, we have an incoming portal request. Do you accept?"

"What? Who?" I cleared my thoughts. "Yes, I accept."

The Templar tapped his comm badge. "Proceed."

A portal flashed open. Conrad, Max, and Ambria spilled out with Evadora and Ivy close behind.

"Justin!" Ivy rushed across the room and squeezed me in a bear hug. She was still a tiny thing, but with her demonic strength coming online, she was growing stronger with every passing day.

"Shelton!" Maxwell Tiberius ran over and shook hands with his favorite hero.

Shelton drew him into a hug, then cleared his throat uneasily and clapped him on the back. "Good to see you, kiddo."

"It's terribly good to see you again, Emily." Ambria offered her a curt nod. "Where is Commander Elyssa?"

"She's in Fjoeruss's secret arctic fortress." I hadn't spoken with Conrad or Ambria much since their recovery from a brush with madness. "How are you two feeling?"

"Much improved." Ambria smiled uneasily. "The dreams are less frequent, thankfully."

"Being trapped in that white void. The world ending over and over again." Conrad squeezed his eyes shut and sighed. "It was more than my mind could bear."

"I think it sounds like fun!" Evadora leapt into the air and twirled, drifting slowly back to earth like dandelion fluff. "I want to watch the world blow up every day!"

Adam backed away from her. "Uh, okay then."

"We tried to stop it several times." Blue energy crackled across Conrad's skin. He trembled and rubbed his hands together. "I thought for sure being right at the center of the blast would end it all one way or the other."

Shelton peered at Conrad's hand. "What's up with the glow?"

"I don't know." Conrad held up both hands to show the faint azure glow. "The healers seem to think something in the time remnant affected my powers, but the spells they use to measure AP don't work on me."

"Arcane potential doesn't apply to your real power." Adam took out his arcphone and tapped on the screen. "I scripted an entirely new spell to gauge people like you." His face wavered between surprise and a frown as he scanned him.

"What is it?" Conrad asked.

"There's no corruption in your energy like there is with Emily."

Ambria flinched. "Emily's power is corrupted?"

"Eve screwed it up in the primal fount." Shelton huffed. "Shit has gone sideways and inside-out the past couple of days."

Cinder watched over Adam's shoulder. "This is fascinating. It would seem Conrad's power reserves are growing even as we speak. It is as if something sparked rapid growth within him."

"Hang on a sec." I put up a hand. "Conrad, did you and Ambria actually go to the source of the Sundering in the time remnant?"

"He did," Ambria said. "I tried to stop him, but he just wanted to end it all." A tear trickled down her cheek. "In retrospect, I can't blame him."

Adam snapped his fingers. "What if the crystalis in the time remnant actually affected him? What if it supercharged his growth and connection with the primal fount?"

Shelton's jaw dropped open. "You think Conrad is turning into a god?"

"Maybe?" Adam shrugged. "Or maybe he's just more in tune with the fount."

"Holy shit balls in paradise." Shelton clapped his hands. "That's the answer. Maybe Conrad can use the crystalis!"

26

E veryone burst into excited conversation all at once.
Adam threw up both his hands. "Hold up!"
The room went silent.

"Conrad's power levels are nowhere near Emily's." Adam projected a holographic line graph that meant nothing to no one except maybe him and Cinder. "The blue line is Conrad's power capacity." He pointed to a yellow line that was far above the blue one. "This is Emily's."

"We theorize that the capacity to channel energy levels is somewhat in line with this graph." Cinder pointed to Emily's line. "Even at this level, it is only a fraction of what might be necessary to generate enough force for stopping the collapse."

Emily wiped her eyes. "Even if my powers were fixed, I'm useless?"

"It looks like I certainly am." Conrad sighed.

I frowned. "What about your theory of chained power and nudging the realms to a halt?"

Adam shook his head. "I looked through my calculations and realized I'd forgotten to account for the full gravitational attraction between the Anchor Stone and Abyss. It would take an incredible burst of power to slow the realms down."

"What if we chained our powers together?" I put a hand on Emily's and Conrad's shoulders. "Maybe together we'd have enough power to do the job."

"Maybe." Adam waggled a hand. "Unfortunately, Seraphim powers aren't compatible with Siren powers, Conrad's powers aren't compatible with Emily's, and so forth."

I stared at the hologram. "Where's Apocryphan power on that scale?"

Adam added in two more lines, green for Apocryphan, and golden for Eve. The Apocryphan line was just below Emily's, but Eve's was three times greater.

"When did you measure Eve?" I asked.

"I haven't," Adam said. "That's an estimate. It could be much higher."

Shelton grunted. "Probably a lot higher."

Emily sighed. "Provided my powers can be fixed, how much power do I need to nudge the realms back into place?"

Adam switched the hologram to an image of the collapsing realms and zoomed in on the Abyss. "The gravitational pull between the Abyss and the Anchor Stone is incredibly intense. You would have to push against both of them at the same time, slow and stop them within a very short window of time. Otherwise, they'll simply accelerate again." A white line appeared on the chart, this one between Emily's and Eve's. "My estimates indicate this is the minimum power required to do the trick."

Evadora giggled and clapped her hands together. "Or else it's squish time!"

"The very objects created to keep the realms from drifting apart are the ones that will destroy all life." Ambria shook her head sadly. "Even if Emily stops them in place, what's to keep them from drifting again?"

"That's a really good question." Adam panned through the various realms. "The patchwork of physics and magic making up the Abyss and the Anchor Stone are just about impossible for us mere mortals to decipher. I still don't understand how the Sirens pulled it off."

"There's only one choice left." Emily straightened her shoulders. "I must appeal to Eve and beg her to help."

"And give her a chance to use you as a realm destroyer again?" Shelton scoffed. "That's insane."

"If she finds out we have a crystalis, then it's game over." I shook my head. "She might use it to snuff out existence in the blink of an eye."

"Contrary to popular belief, the gods are not all powerful or omniscient." Emily set her hands on her hips. "Eve probably can't end creation with a thought. Even with a crystalis it took her longer than seven days to make the Earth. It's a risk, but we're at a dead end. My powers are corrupted, and no one else has nearly the power we need."

Shelton shook his head. "It can't possibly end up worse than what just happened with Olivia, right?"

Emily shuddered. "It's not like we have a choice."

"I hate to admit it, but you're right." I put a reassuring hand on her shoulder. "We'll convince Eve somehow."

"Vitania and Lumia must come with us." Emily nodded as if reassuring herself. "They've been friends with Eve almost since the beginning. It might be enough to snap Eve into a lucid state."

"I want to talk to Eve!" Evadora skipped in a circle around us. "I like crazy people."

Shelton shook his head. "That's because you're bat-shit crazy already, kid."

"No, she isn't." Ivy harrumphed. "Evadora just thinks differently."

"Differently?" Shelton scoffed. "That's one way of putting it."

I gave Emily's proposal some thought and came to the same conclusions she had. Without a full-fledged god, not even she had the capacity to stop the collapse. I checked the time. "Vitania is resting and won't be of much use until tomorrow. I'll get her and Lumia tomorrow and then a small group of us can track down Eve."

Emily nodded. "Let's hope she hasn't gone far from the primal fount."

There wasn't much else to do at that point. I wasn't tired but figured getting some shuteye was a good idea.

Shelton clapped his hands together. "I don't know about you all, but I'm starving. So I ordered some pizzas and tacos and they should be here in a few minutes. What say we go up to the main house and enjoy ourselves for a little while before committing suicide by insane goddess?"

Adam raised a fist and whooped. "Pizza and tacos!"

"Yay!" Evadora gripped Ivy's hands and they danced in a circle.

I opened a portal back to Fjoeruss's arctic fortress and interrupted Elyssa's meeting with him and Underborn to tell her what happened with Olivia.

Elyssa's mouth dropped open. "Olivia and Tyler are dead?"

I nodded grimly. "Our only chance now is to convince Eve to help us."

Underborn pursed his lips. "Scraping the bottom of the barrel for options?"

"Yeah." I shrugged. "Emily's powers are corrupt and no one else has the power needed to stop the collapse."

"It's worth a try," Fjoeruss said.

I thought of something that hadn't been mentioned earlier. "Did Dactia mention Alden to you, Fjoeruss?"

He nodded. "She said once she discovered its location we could start relocating the inhabitants of the ark there. Unfortunately, I have not heard from her in over twenty-four hours, so I haven't received a status update."

"I have a feeling Alden will be our fallback if everything else fails." I shrugged. "On the upside, there's a pizza and taco party at the Templar compound if you want to come."

Underborn smirked. "When all else fails, throw a party?"

I nodded. "You got it."

"I must decline." Fjoeruss rose. "I need to locate Dactia and ensure she hasn't run afoul of any problems."

"Phissilinth and I also have plans." Underborn nodded at me. "But thank you for the invitation."

I was a bit relieved they hadn't accepted the invitation.

Elyssa took my hand. "I'm totally down for pizza."

"Then let's go join the party." I led her back through the portal and closed it.

We took the levitator to the parking garage and exited the barn just in time to see a very nervous delivery guy handing a stack of pizza boxes and paper bags to Michael. Elyssa's brother looked positively gigantic compared to the teenager. The moment everything was out of his hands, he scurried toward his car.

Michael chased him down and towered over him. "You forgot something," he said in a menacing voice.

"I'm sorry," the delivery guy whimpered. "What's missing?"

Michael handed him a stack of dollars. "You left before I gave you your tip."

The man took the money and sped off in his car.

Shelton snorted. "What the hell was he so scared of?"

"I was just stepping outside for some broadsword practice when he drove up." Michael shrugged. "Guess he wasn't expecting to see a man with a sword."

"Talk about serial killer vibes." I sniffed the delicious aroma of pizza. "Let's get this party started."

We went inside the house, unpacked the food, and laid it out on the long table in the open-area dining room while Adam concocted frozen margaritas with the aid of magic.

The front door opened and Bella stepped inside. "Harry!" Despite being petite and two heads shorter than him, she gripped Shelton in a bear hug and lifted him a foot off the ground.

"Christ almighty, woman!" Shelton tried to free himself but her dhampyr strength was too much. "At least let me pretend to be the man in the relationship sometimes."

Bella giggled and set him down, then jumped into his arms and kissed his face. "Like this?" she said playfully.

"Now, that's more like it." Shelton pecked a kiss on her nose, then cleared his throat nervously and looked around. "How about the rest of you mind your business?"

Evadora burst into laughter. "It's more fun minding your business!"

I looked at the impressive spread on the table and my stomach grumbled. "Shelton, you can make out with Bella all you like, but I'm gonna eat." I sat down at the table and helped myself to a variety of tacos and a slice of pizza.

Within seconds, everyone else crowded around the table.

"Shelton, what kind of evil streak made you order this?" Adam held up a slice of pineapple pizza.

Shelton snorted. "I ordered the devil's pizza for my woman."

"Oh, Hawaiian pizza!" Bella hopped down from Shelton's arms and helped herself. "Thank you, papi."

"You got it babe." Shelton grimaced as she took a big bite. "Though I will never understand how you can like that stuff."

Adam tossed ingredients into a large cooler and cast a spell. "Frozen margaritas a la Nosti are now served!"

I poured a cup of the frozen mix and tasted it. "Wow, this is really good."

Adam grinned. "I've been tweaking that recipe since we were trapped in Seraphina."

We sat down at a table and got our pizza and tacos on. By the time I finished the first glass of Adam's margarita, my senses were buzzing. "What's in this stuff?"

"Fermented amber from Seraphina." Adam held up a bottle of golden liquid. "It tastes similar but is saturated with aether to give it an extra kick even if you're a super."

Shelton rose and staggered drunkenly toward the pizza buffet. "Must be the only good food to come out of that blasted realm."

"Take it easy there, big guy." Adam kept him from falling over and propped him against the kitchen counter. "How many drinks did you have?"

"A couple." Shelton held onto the counter for support. "Maybe make drinks for us mere mortals next time."

Bella patted Shelton on the ass. "Perhaps I should get you into bed."

Elyssa came up behind me and laced her arm in mine. "Hate to admit it, Shelton, but this was a great idea."

I nodded. "Yeah, it was."

Shelton shrugged. "I just go with my stomach and everything always works out."

Conrad, Ambria, Max, and Cinder were playing Monopoly at the coffee table in the den. Michael observed them quietly from the couch, looking relaxed for once in his life.

Ambria pounded the table in frustration and glared at Max. "Don't you dare charge me for landing on Boardwalk!"

Max grinned. "Pay up!"

It looked like Monopoly was well on its way to ruining more friendships.

Shelton sighed and nearly lost his grip on the countertop. "Damn, this was fun. I hope we can save the universe and do this again sometime."

Elyssa chuckled. "You and me both, Shelton."

THE NEXT MORNING, I woke up feeling surprisingly clear-headed despite going to bed practically drunk. I showered and headed into the mess hall for a quick breakfast, then went to the war room where I knew I'd find Elyssa.

She was debriefing Thomas and Michael when I entered, a holographic projection of the realms hovering above the table.

"Fjoeruss has already started evacuations from Utopia, but his arctic facility can only hold so many people." She pointed to the other realms near the Abyss. "Within the next twenty-four to forty-eight hours, these will all be wiped off the map."

Thomas turned toward me. "Recruiting Eve is extremely dangerous. If she turns on us, she could wipe our most vital pieces off the board."

"Believe me, I'm painfully aware of that." I sighed. "But we've run out of alternatives. Even if we had coordinates for Alden, Eve might prevent us from sending refugees there and that's just as bad. We're on the cusp of a no-win scenario with only one play left."

Thomas pursed her lips. "Can we neutralize her?"

I shook my head. "She's a goddess, for god's sake. I don't think we can exactly hit her with knockout gas or a drugged dart. Emily might stand a chance of surviving a knockdown fight like she did against Olivia, but I wouldn't count on it."

A Templar escorted Lumia and Vitania into the conference room. Lumia nodded at Thomas. "A pleasure to see you again, Commander Borathen."

Vitania took a seat at the table. "I came as soon as I received your message. It seems we have reached a moment of true desperation."

"I'm afraid so," Elyssa said. "We can't fix Emily's magic problem, and even if we did, Adam thinks she wouldn't have enough power to counteract the gravity between the Abyss and Anchor Stone."

"It seems the tools of our salvation will also be the means of our doom." Vitania studied the hologram of the realms. "The Abyss was never meant to serve as a counterbalance to the Anchor Stone. Rather, it was to orbit the stone along with the realms. But in order to make it escape-proof for demigods, our only solution was the intense gravity fields of the fringe. Now that the delicate orbit of the Abyss has been upset by Elohim's plot, it will take an act of immense power to stop it."

"How did you make it in the first place?" I said. "Could you possibly destroy it the same way you created it?"

"Unfortunately, no." Vitania sighed. "We used the combined might of the Apocryphan to construct their own prison."

I shook my head in confusion. "How in the world did you manage that?"

"After the Sundering, no one knew exactly what had happened, but the realms were still very close together, dimensionally speaking." Vitania sang softly and an image of the newly sundered Earth appeared before her. The orbs representing the realms were practically all on top of each other. "I soon discovered that certain geographical areas overlapped on other realms, allowing me to step through and back again. But as I learned about the quantum tunnels connecting the realms, I quickly found that they would soon drift so far apart, the tunnels would snap. I went to Kathazal and told him about my findings. He commanded me to discover a way to travel among all the realms."

"Had you already figured out how to use symbols to make portals?" I asked.

She shook her head. "No, but I was already quite familiar with transdimensional portals before the Sundering. I also knew that giving the Apocryphan the knowledge of creating portals would be extremely dangerous, so I opted to make an overly complicated network of arches that would hinder them from freely travelling the realms."

Elyssa nodded. "The Alabaster Arches."

"Precisely, child." Vitania wiped away the image and illustrated a large obsidian arch striped with alabaster. "My inner circle and I constructed a master arch that would later become known as the Grand Nexus. I told Kathazal that we required Apocryphan power to enable them. We created a special stone inscribed with hidden symbols and told Kathazal that it would store energy like a battery and allow us to use it later. Little did he know that when he channeled into the stone, it was scanning for a special realm that could be used to imprison him and the others."

"Oh, snap." I blew out a breath. "You tricked him into finding his own prison."

"Except the perfect prison didn't exist." Vitania summoned another holographic image of dark realms further out from the others. "We found clusters of dead realms imbued with strange gravitational readings. It was then that we formulated a plan to construct the Abyss, a small realm with a vast gravitational fringe. We altered the symbols on the stone and then had several Apocryphan channel into it at once to give the spell enough power to draw together the dead realms and combine them. Step by step, our plan finally came to fruition."

"That's amazing." Elyssa shook her head in disbelief. "They were so cocky they never once thought that double-crossing them was even a possibility."

"True, but because of the power used to create the Abyss, only a god could muster the power needed to destroy it." Vitania regarded the hologram with sad eyes. "We must hope against hope that Eve will regain her sanity and help us stop the collapse, or at the very least, destroy the Abyss."

"Are you feeling rested?" I asked.

She nodded. "I am in full vigor."

Lumia yawned. "I'm not. Being a queen again is exhausting. I have tasked my people with collecting all manner of specimens for a general evacuation. The Mzodi's largest sky ships are transporting everything they can to Solan. But with the limited time left before the Abyss devours Utopia, there's no way we can evacuate everyone."

"That's why we're so desperate." I couldn't bear the thought of so many lives snuffed in an instant. "We'll lose everything one way or the other. At least you and Vitania have a chance of bringing Eve to her senses."

Vitania straightened her shoulders as if steeling herself. "Agreed. Let us hope she is in a good frame of mind."

"Let's keep this party small," Elyssa said. "Justin, Vitania, and Lumia should go first. Let's keep Emily away for now just in case."

"Sensible as always, child." Vitania rose. "I'm hopeful we'll find Eve in her small realm. That is her retreat—a place where she's found some modicum of serenity throughout the eons."

I shuddered. "Does everyone eventually go mad if they've been alive long enough?"

"Eve's boredom led her to do many things that were unhealthy for her sanity." Vitania sighed. "Living a lifetime as a mortal and birthing the Apocryphan were two of the worst things she could have done."

"We've all made mistakes." Lumia brushed her hands together as if ridding herself of unspoken memories. "Let's see if we can stop Eve from allowing another to happen."

Apparently ready to get the show on the road, Vitania slashed open a portal leading to the small cottage on Eve's world. I kissed

Elyssa goodbye then followed Lumia and Vitania through. The portal blinked shut behind me.

Bright moonlight cast the unlit cottage in eerie shadows. It seemed no one was home. A pair of golden orbs appeared in the darkness of the front porch and a shadowy figure rose. My heart skipped a beat and my asshole clenched.

Eve was home.

27

"Vitania? Lumia?" A golden nimbus ignited around Eve as she stepped from the porch. Lanterns hanging from the surrounding trees ignited, glowing brighter until it was bright as day around the cottage.

"It is us, old friend." Vitania clasped Eve's hand. "Forgive me for getting to the point, but why are you trying to destroy all that which you created?"

"Elohim," Eve said in a ragged voice. "His stain has seeped into the very fabric of my creation. During his long existence as Baal, he corrupted the humans and turned Eden into a cesspool of ignorance and evil."

"And yet the humans of Utopia exceeded all expectations," Vitania countered. "Perhaps those on Eden simply evolved differently. It does not mean you need to destroy them and start over."

"You would kill the fae as well?" Lumia took Eve's other hand. "What of the Lyrolai and other folk of the wood? Are we unworthy of existence?"

"I have already made a place for them, but my plans to salvage the worthy was ruined when he took my Emily." Eve's glowing eyes settled on me. "The beings, plants, and animals from four realms were already relocated before Justin interrupted my plans."

I blinked. "We thought you were destroying the realms, not saving them."

Eve jerked her hands free from Vitania and Lumia and backed up a step. "Oh, I was destroying realms. Eight with no redeeming qualities were ground to dust. There are three more worth saving and the rest will be annihilated."

I gulped. "Which three?"

"Eden is not one." She pursed her lips. "The fae from Utopia were on my good list, but perhaps the humans from there are worth saving as well."

"The good list? You're not Santa Claus." I shivered. "If the collapse continues as it has, the Abyss will devour everything before smashing into the Anchor Stone, leaving nothing but a dead planet where Earth used to be. If that happens, Elohim wins."

A ragged laugh erupted from Eve. "Elohim took credit for all I did, parading himself before mortals as their god until most of the fools believed only in him. But he could never create free will and sentience as I did. Apollyon was his only success, if you can call that abomination a success."

I could tell from the looks on Vitania's and Lumia's faces that this was going downhill fast, so I clamped my mouth shut and let them talk to her.

"Eve, we can save your creation and spit in Elohim's face all at once." Lumia held out her hands imploringly. "Please, let your oldest friends help you save your beautiful creation."

Tears trickled down Eve's cheeks. "I-I thought I could repair the damage on my own. But my spark has dimmed, leaving me but a pale shadow of the goddess I once was."

Vitania rubbed Eve's hand and nodded. "You have been too harsh on yourself. But we may have a way for you to not only salvage the realms, but shape Alden into an amazing new world for refugees."

Eve blinked. "You know of Alden?"

"You've mentioned it before, dear." Lumia offered an understanding smile. "Perhaps you could give us the quantum coordinates and we can assist you."

Eve reclaimed her hands and shook her head. "No, no, no. I must do everything myself. Only the chosen may go there."

Vitania's lips pressed together. "Are we not chosen, Eve?"

"Yes, of course." Eve's frown brightened into a smile. "But you two are meddlers and I cannot have that. Not this time. You will see it when the time is right." Her smile abruptly vanished. "You said I could salvage the realms. How?"

Lumia met Vitania's gaze and paused before answering. "Emily's powers have become erratic since you used her in the primal fount. We need her whole again. This will enable the two of you to stop the collapse."

"No, it won't." Eve pursed her lips. "I tried to slow the collapse when we were linked, but I simply don't have enough raw power at my disposal. There was a time when I could stop the Earth from rotating, or even adjust its orbit by degrees to warm or cool it. But the Sundering diminished my powers as it did all the gods who were on Earth at the time. Ironically, I will only have the power to stop the collapse once it is over and the damage to this dimension is undone."

I couldn't stop myself from asking. "The Sundering made you weaker?"

She rose slightly off the ground, hovering in place, and looked down at me. "All gods lost power that day. Our selves were shattered along with our creations. Elohim lost the most since he was at the epicenter."

"We may have another way to stop the collapse." Vitania regarded the hovering goddess calmly. "A power source that will allow you to fix it."

Eve's eyes flashed brighter for an instant. "You possess a crystalis?"

Vitania's composure faltered. "We may know where to get one. If we succeed, will you promise to stop the collapse?"

The goddess spun in a circle, giddy with excitement, a hint of insanity gleaming in her eyes. "Yes, yes, a thousand times yes! Fetch it and I will fix everything!" She dropped to the ground. "Better yet, tell me where it is, and I will fetch it myself."

Lumia nodded. "First, we need Emily's powers repaired."

"Done."

Vitania narrowed her eyes. "And we need the Abyss demolished so the gravitational fringe no longer threatens or affects nearby realms."

"Easily done." Eve shivered in delight. "When your people cobbled it together, you overlooked a major structural flaw."

Vitania flinched as if someone just insulted a cardigan she knitted for a nephew. "What do you mean?"

"Why, the plug, of course." Eve closed her eyes and sucked in a breath of absolute joy, like a junkie about to get a hit of heroin. "The Abyss is joined to the infernal fount which powers the fringe. Simply dismantling the connection will reduce the Abyss to rubble, and the fringe will dissipate."

Vitania's gaze went distant. "How could I have overlooked such a mistake?"

I wanted to reassure her, but Eve continued rambling.

"It will all be so beautiful." She sighed. "Daughter, come here. We can finally finish what I started."

Lumia cleared her throat. "Daughter? Do you mean Emily? Shall I fetch her?"

"No, she means me." A figure stepped out of the cottage and approached.

The voice sent chills all the way down to my bones. "Xanos!"

The purple demigoddess stepped into the light and nodded. "Once I regained my powers, I sought out my mother and begged her forgiveness for my evil deeds. She nearly killed me, but reconsidered and made me her apprentice."

"Xanos is but a shadow of her former self," Eve said. "She regained most of her power, but alas, it is too little to ever allow her to rise to true godhood. Even so, she can still use those powers to create rather than destroy."

Xanos dropped to one knee before me. "I am sorry, Justin. In my hubris I ignored your advice, thus allowing Baal to complete his plans unhindered. The destruction of the realms will be as much my fault as his."

I didn't for a moment trust this sudden change of heart by Xanos. "You're a mistress of manipulation and an excellent liar. I don't think I could ever trust a thing that comes out of your mouth."

"Truth," Lumia said. "You have always been a jealous creature, plotting in the shadows and unleashing havoc upon the world, Xanos. I cannot believe Eve trusts you."

"I relived the Sundering in the time remnant," Xanos said. "When I thought to end it all, it instead returned my powers and gave me a new lease on life. I felt as if the universe were telling me something. As if it deemed me unworthy of death and my punishment was to undo what I have done."

I shook my head. "I'm still not buying it."

"I found the crystalis at the center of the Sundering—or at least the relic which is all that remains of it." Xanos bit her lower lip. "It is safely in Alden where it cannot be found by Elohim or used to speed up the collapse."

My mouth dropped open slightly. "Does it have any powers like the other relics?"

Xanos shook her head. "None that I know of. Then again, I hid it eons ago and never touched it again until recently."

I breathed a sigh of relief. "Well, let's hope it stays hidden there because it could undo everything we've worked for if it returns to the realms."

"Yes, yes, yes." Eve's gaze looked glassy and unfocused. "Undo it all." She looked around. "Where is Emily? Where is my lovely grand-daughter? Together, she and I will use the crystalis to make the realms whole again."

"Vitania, dear, let's get Emily." Lumia put a hand on the Siren's shoulder.

Vitania regarded Eve and Xanos uncertainly. "We will fetch Emily and return soon." She didn't sound like she meant it.

"No need." Eve took Lumia's hand. "Let's go together. You will tell me where to find the crystalis and then we will fix everything."

I really didn't like her newfound manic enthusiasm. I hoped that in her excitement, Eve didn't go overboard. I also wondered if she were only telling us what we wanted to hear so she could get her hands on the crystalis.

Vitania looked from Xanos to Eve and back to Xanos again. "We must have absolute assurances that you will abide by our requests, Eve. There can be no lingering doubts that you will go against our wishes. I also cannot trust Xanos with a crystalis."

"I promise I will do anything to help," Xanos said.

Vitania stared at her as if trying to bore into her very soul to divine the truth.

"The realms will be saved, my sweet." Eve kissed Vitania's cheeks and held her at arms' length. "But I will also use it to finish Alden."

Vitania nodded. "Very well."

"I will allow nothing of the sort." A thickly muscled figure with black hair and chiseled jaw emerged from the forest. He stood as tall as an Apocryphan, bordering on ten feet tall, with a frame to match.

It took a moment for me to realize who it was. "Good god almighty. Did you start taking steroids?"

Elohim smiled grandly. "Good god almighty, indeed. I have simply allowed myself to return to my natural size and height rather than remain the puny size of mortals."

Eve swelled to match his size. "There is nothing special about our original forms, Elohim. You still think too much of yourself. I am willing to bet your performance also still leaves much to be desired."

I snorted. "That was cold." I resisted the urge to high-five Eve since she'd probably leave me hanging. "Elohim, do you seriously think you can stop Eve from doing what she wants?"

Gaze unwavering, he nodded. "I was going to be patient and simply savor the collapse as it wiped out the realms one by one, knowing the immense pain it would bring Eve." His eyes narrowed. "And then I sensed a great disturbance—"

I couldn't help myself from blurting, "In the Force?"

"In the fabric of space time." He frowned. "Eve, my dear, I did not realize you had a backup plan. I rushed here, but you were nowhere to be found, so I left a minion behind to alert me when you returned." Elohim smirked. "A midget Apocryphan, a Siren and a fae all in one place. It seems I came just in time to prevent another vain attempt to stop the collapse."

Xanos looked as if she wanted to swell to their size, but apparently, returning her powers hadn't undone the curse Eve had laid on her after she'd lost her powers. "Elohim, leave us alone and enjoy your victory."

"I can directly thank you for everything, dear." Elohim spread his arms as if inviting her in for a hug. "Join me and leave this insane goddess to rot."

"You cannot stop me." Eve straightened, rising to her full Amazonian height. "Do not test me, Elohim. We both know who is strongest."

I raised a fist. "Death by snu snu."

Vitania shot me a severe look.

I shrugged. "Seems appropriate."

Elohim ignored my outburst. "Eve, you are barely a shadow of your former self. Though the Sundering weakened me, my time in Haedaemos allowed me to absorb countless souls and sprits. I have more than regained my lost power." Energy crackled in his hands. "You cannot defeat me this time."

"Try me, fool." A nimbus of golden power surrounded Eve. "This time I will not spare you."

I gulped. "You two have fought before?"

They didn't answer because Elohim abruptly flew at her, fists extended like a giant Superman. He slammed into her midriff and a shockwave tossed the rest of us through the air like rag dolls. I only managed to stay upright because I slammed into a tree. Vitania and Lumia recovered gracefully, but Elohim and Eve smashed through the cottage, plowed into the forest, and vanished from sight. Xanos had been standing right next to Eve, but she'd also vanished.

The ground trembled. A mountain in the distance cracked down the middle, sending dust and rubble into the sky. Golden beams slashed at a distant figure in the air. Elohim fired back with silver beams. Thousands of birds erupted from the treetops. Panicked deer, squirrels, giraffes, and a herd of elephants stampeded through the meadow, vanishing into the forest on the other side.

I rubbed the back of my head and felt a bump forming. Blood wet my fingers. I wondered if the stampede had been a hallucination from the blow to my head, but another elephant bearing a gaggle of monkeys dashed past followed closely by a rhinoceros and two bears. I staggered over to Lumia and Vitania hoping they had answers, but they both looked as panicked as I felt.

"We have to help her somehow." Lumia fluttered into the air as another quake shook the ground. The lanterns above the cottage flickered out. Explosions lit the night sky. Silver and gold streaked overhead like errant comets playing a cosmic game of tag. Except every time they tagged each other, it felt as if the world would split apart.

"If they're this powerful right now, I can't imagine what it would be like for them to have their full powers back." I staggered to catch my balance as the earth continued to quake. The peak of the distant mountain exploded in a brilliant flash of light.

Vitania began to sing. A great sense of peace settled over me. Everything was fine—just fine. What I really wanted to do was find a nice tree and take a nap beneath it. A part of my brain knew the song was responsible for this feeling, but my body was too relaxed to resist.

Apparently, the song didn't work on the battling gods.

A golden meteor smashed into the cottage. The shockwave knocked us off our feet. Burning wood hurtled in all directions. Silver streaked into the meadow, plowing a smoking furrow from one end to the other, stopping in a mound of earth at the far end from the cottage.

The song stopped. Contentment morphed instantly to dread.

"Eve!" Lumia flew toward the burning remains, Vitania close behind.

Burning trees lit the meadow. I spotted a still figure resting against the mound. *Elohim*. Without hesitation I blurred across the distance, morphing into demonic form as I ran. I had no weapons and no magic. Infernal strength would have to suffice.

Elohim groaned and began to push himself to his knees. God help me, I had no choice but to seize the moment. Drawing upon every fiber in my body, steeling my soul against the evil I had to commit, I gripped Elohim's head and savagely twisted it.

His neck cracked like thunder. His body went limp, slumping over.

I released him, guilt flooding me for the cold-blooded murder, even if Elohim was responsible for so much death and destruction. "I'm sorry. I had no choice."

Elohim's shoulders shook and a low chuckle filled the air. He rose to his feet, flexing his neck. "Thank you, Justin. I haven't had a chance to visit my chiropractor in some time."

"No fucking way!" I looked down at my massive demonic hands, as if confirming that I'd just used everything I had to snap his neck.

Despite his smirk, Elohim's face was crusted in blood and dirt. One of his arms bent at an awkward angle and he was missing most of his hair.

"Yes way, son." Elohim raised a hand. Silver energy gathered at his fingertips but fizzled out. He scowled. "That's inconvenient."

"You egomaniacal bastard." I growled deep in my throat. "What's inconvenient is wiping out all the realms just so you can put your name brand on creation."

"I must say I'm a bit peeved you killed Olivia." He brushed dirt from his ragged robes. "I'd thought about keeping her around for a few millennia, at least until I decided what direction I wanted for the new Earth."

"You're keeping the name too?" I scoffed. "Not an original bone in your body, is there?"

"I named Earth, boy." Elohim straightened his shoulders. "Who do you think terraformed it into its original shape?"

"Earth just means dirt." I scoffed again. "Looks like you're just as bad at naming things as I am."

He winced and doubled over, as if something inside him just broke. "Eve put up a good fight, but in the end she told me what you'd planned, boy. Even if you have a spare goddess available, I'll make sure you never reach the primal fount in Olympus." A portal tore open behind him. A dragon as big as a mountain loomed in the distance on the other side, its scales as black as night.

Those skies belonged to Seraphina, and the scales belong to Drakara. A wyvern on the other side of the gateway peered curiously at us.

Elohim managed a smirk. "Perhaps it's best if you remain here, boy. This small realm was created by Eve after the Sundering and will survive the collapse. I might just let you live in peace if you don't piss me off again." He stepped through the gateway. "If you come to Olympus, you'll find my dragons waiting." The portal snapped shut.

My body shrank down to normal size. There was no anger. No guilt. No sadness. I felt empty. Then I saw Lumia and Vitania huddled over a still form on the ground and hopelessness filled the void.

Eve was dead.

28

I flashed across the distance between me and the others. Eve's body was a twisted, burnt mess. Images of the dying Olivia flashed before my eyes. Vitania held Eve's one good hand and Lumia held the fallen goddess's head in her lap. Tears poured freely down their cheeks.

"Mother!" Xanos limped from the forest, her face bloodied and bruised. She knelt on the opposite side from Vitania.

"Where were you?" I said. "We could have killed Elohim!"

"The last thing I saw was Elohim flying into Eve and everything went black." Xanos shuddered. "An explosion awoke me."

Eve's eyes fluttered open. Golden light shone from within, but they stared blankly into the skies she'd created. Little by little, the light began to fade.

"I'm sorry, Eve." The words caught in my throat and tears burned my eyes. I wasn't mourning Eve. I was mourning humans, fae, Sirens, Seraphim, squirrels, giraffes, and especially tacos. Our last chance to stop the collapse was dying in our arms.

Eve's body trembled and her gaze snapped into focus for a brief instant. She reached out and squeezed my hand with bone-crushing force.

I float in the sea of stars, a golden orb of life given life by the death of its creator. I know nothing, yet I am filled with purpose. I must create. But there is nothing suitable here to build with, so I travel toward a pinpoint of light. As I travel through an expanse of dust and rock, I discover another sentient being. It orbits a pair of rocks, bumping them together as if that might bind them into one coherent piece.

It stops and approaches me. No words are spoken, but I hear it saying, "This is mine. You are not welcome here."

I respond. "You do not know how to build, much less create." Then I move on, pulled inextricably by the distant star, leaving the being behind.

It occurs to me that linear travel in the void is useless. At this rate, it will be eons before I reach it. I sense that the emptiness can be bypassed somehow. I only know this because the echoes of the grand creator have given me a basic knowledge. I shift perception and a vast network of glowing lines fills my view. I tug gently on one and feel the vibrations of a star on the opposite side of the universe. It takes me some time but I finally locate the one leading to my destination.

"What are you doing?" The other sentience circles me, pulsating with malevolent curiosity. "I have created all that you see. You are not welcome in this domain."

"I do not want to be here in this dismal place." I pluck a thread and feel the pull. "Goodbye." The void folds and I am instantly in the orbit of the golden star that drew me to this place. I have never been here, but it feels like home. Planetoids, asteroids and cosmic dust are all the raw materials I need to create.

"Let me out of here!" I jerked back to the real world.

Eve's eyes closed. A brilliant flash blinded me for an instant. When the spots faded, there was nothing left of the goddess but fine gray ash.

Lumia and Vitania hugged, sobbing softly. Xanos sifted the ashes through her hands, eyes full of disbelief.

"What the hell did she do to me?" I said. "I think I saw Eve way back in the beginning even before the Earth was made."

"She must have imprinted her memories on you," Vitania said. "Can you recall anything?"

I closed my eyes and concentrated, trying to summon other memories, but only the brief moments I'd seen were there. "No. I just see what was in my vision."

"His mind could not absorb it." Lumia's shoulders shook with sobs. "All that knowledge, lost forever."

"Why the hell did she try to give it to me instead of Vitania?" I threw up my hands. "I don't want to be the reason it was all lost."

"It is not your fault, child." Vitania rose on unsteady feet and slashed open a portal. "Eve has only herself to blame."

Emily stood on the other side of the portal, eyes wide and concerned by the mourning Siren. "What happened?"

"Eve is dead."

"Is that Xanos?" Shelton shouted.

Murmurs of surprise rippled through the others, but Emily saw nothing but the ashes of her dead grandmother. She dropped to her knees and cried out in sorrow and pain. Elyssa and Ambria hugged her from both sides. I swallowed a sharp lump in my throat. Eve and Emily hadn't exactly been close, but Emily had just lost the love of her life hours before, killed her sister, and now her grandmother was gone.

"Jesus Harvey Christ." Shelton took off his hat and stood next to me. "What happened?"

"Elohim." My words sagged with despair. "I thought I could kill him, Shelton." A maniacal laugh-cry burst from my throat. "He was weak from the fight. I tried to break his neck with every ounce of strength I had and all I did was give him an adjustment."

"Dude, he's an OG god." Adam stood to my other side. "What did you think was going to happen?"

Shelton scoffed. "If Eve couldn't kill him then I don't know who could."

"Xanos could have helped," I muttered.

Xanos shook her head. "Only a god can kill a god."

Vitania cleared her throat. "We have suffered a great loss, but there is one last hope remaining."

That was news to me. I frowned. "What hope is that?"

"I will find my sisters so we can uncouple the Abyss from the infernal fount and destroy it. That will prevent it from devouring the other realms." She took a deep breath as if keeping sorrow at bay. "Perhaps we can also remove the gravitational magic from the Anchor Stone and lessen the speed of the collapse. Life will be lost, but not all life."

"How many Sirens will it take to uncouple the Abyss?" I asked.

"Nearly all of us. I must implore Dactia to at least do this." Vitania closed her eyes for a moment. "Unfortunately, I have no idea where she might be."

"I do." Lumia sighed. "Alden. The Sirens from Aquilis were probably among the first to be relocated."

Vitania nodded grimly. "Then I shall get to work." She traced symbols in the air and wiped her hand across it, revealing the golden tunnel she'd found our last time here. "This must be the quantum tunnel to Alden. As with any unexplored tunnel, I cannot simply enter it. First, I must divine the symbols that unlock it."

Adam looked intrigued. "How do you do that?"

Lumia shook her head. "The process takes weeks or months to complete. It took her centuries to compile her realm codex."

"Utopia doesn't have that kind of time," Shelton said. "Hell, Eden might not have that long left."

I turned to our purple companion. "Xanos probably knows them."

She shook her head sadly. "Eve wouldn't give me the coordinates. She only trusted herself with that information."

I glared at her. "You'd better not be lying."

"I have no reason to lie!" Xanos shouted. "What do I have to gain except annihilation?"

"There is no way to speed the process, I'm afraid." Vitania shook her head sadly. "I should begin."

Adam snapped his fingers. "We can just find the scar and open it."

"Exactly." Shelton clapped him on the shoulder. "We just need Ivy and Alysea to help Justin—" He stopped speaking as if remembering I didn't have my powers. "Er, Nightliss can help."

It seemed to be our last best hope, but it would take some time to bring everyone here. Then I thought of something else. I turned to Lumia. "Can you summon the local dryads?"

She tilted her head curiously. "I believe so, why?"

"I need to talk to them."

Lumia put a hand to the ground and closed her eyes for a moment. "I have requested their presence."

A moment later, shadowy forms in the forest separated from the trees. Females with bark-like skin shyly made their way toward us while others remained at the fringe of the meadow.

I wasn't sure how to start, so I got straight to the point. "Dryads, Elohim has murdered Eve."

"Yes we know," a tearful dryad said. "We saw her fall."

"I am sorry for asking so soon after her death, this but it is imperative that we find the key to Alden." I spread my hands imploringly. "It's vital we reach the Sirens there so they can help us prevent the utter destruction of the Earth realms."

Gasps rose from some in the crowd. The few nearest the front seemed less surprised. Eve might have talked to them, or perhaps they'd overheard her ranting about Elohim.

"How can we help?" the first dryad said. "We cannot open portals."

I nodded. "But if any of you saw Eve open a portal to Alden, you could show us the symbols."

"I saw many symbols," another dryad said.

"As did I!"

"Yes, me too!" another said.

"Can I get you to draw them for me?" I said.

Lumia cast glowing orbs into the air to light the vicinity.

The first dryad frowned. "Draw?"

"Yes, make the symbols on the ground." I knelt in the dirt and drew symbols. "Like this."

"Yes, I can do that." She knelt and started scratching symbols in the dirt. Several other dryads dropped to their knees and began doing the same. Before long, the furrow left by Elohim's fall was full of drawn symbols.

Vitania began reviewing them. "Most of these are for Eden." She pointed to another. "Utopia. Aquilis. Seraphina." She continued down the long row, naming each grouping as she came to them. Many weren't correctly drawn, perhaps because that particular dryad hadn't remembered correctly or hadn't seen them all. Moments later, Vitania looked at the last set and shook her head. "Alden's symbols aren't among these."

"Do you mean the golden land?" One of the shy dryads in the back stepped forward. "The one with the silver city?"

"Perhaps, child." Vitania smoothed over a place in the dirt. "Please show me."

"I cannot." The dryad looked down. "Whenever Eve traveled there, I had trouble remembering how she opened the portal."

Adam hissed. "She must have protected the symbols by making anyone in the near vicinity forget they saw them."

Emily sagged. "Why does she have to make everything so bloody difficult?"

I put a hand on her arm. "We'll figure this out somehow."

Emily's mouth dropped open in horror and the whites of her eyes went completely black. I tried to move my hand but my muscles were locked in place. Emily screamed. I screamed. Just as suddenly as the moment had begun, my hand came free and Emily stumbled backward, falling into Adam's arms.

I held up my hands and looked at them. "What the fuck was that?"

Emily straightened, a realization dawning in her eyes. She slashed her hand through a series of patterns, her movements almost robotic. A portal ripped open. Golden sunlight poured through the gateway and into the meadow. Emily took a step back and turned to us. "Justin, I don't know what you did, but the answer just came to me."

Vitania gasped. "Perhaps the memories weren't meant for Justin, but for Emily."

"Memories?" Emily looked from her to me. "What memories?"

"Eve gripped Justin just before she died and gave him a vision of the time before creation." Lumia shrugged. "He couldn't remember anything else."

"I certainly didn't remember symbols for Alden." I frowned as I tried to remember the symbols Emily had just used to open this portal. "And I still don't remember what you did."

"Neither do I," Vitania said. She scowled. "Perhaps you can write them down for future reference."

Emily flinched and shivered. "I'm starting to remember things that aren't from my own memories." Emily squeezed her eyes shut. "There's too much. It hurts!"

Lumia put a hand on her shoulder. "Just relax, dear." She massaged Emily's temples, her fingers sparkling with magic.

Emily sagged with relief. "Thank you, Lumia."

While they were doing that, I peeked through the portal to Alden. When nothing killed me, I stepped through. A glorious valley adorned with lush green grass and trees in fall colors of orange, red, and blue spread out before me. A bright blue river bisected the valley, running all the way to a sparkling ocean. A silver city straddled the river, spanning it with crystal bridges and alabaster webs that connected the towering buildings.

"It's gorgeous." Xanos stepped through and spread her arms as a light breeze brushed back her hair. The rest of us piled through the portal, awestruck by the world on the other side. The sweet scent from a nearby field of lavender flowers tickled my nose. The air was pleasantly cool, balanced by the warmth of the golden sun.

"It's amazing!" Conrad plucked a blade of grass and sniffed it. "Everything is so fresh."

Ambria took his hand. "It's like Heaven."

"Perhaps if you weren't here it would be." Max stuck out his tongue at her.

She smiled and playfully poked her tongue back at him.

Ivy and Evadora danced in a meadow of red and gold flowers, giggling like children even though they were both well into their teen years.

Shelton peered at the distant city with spectacles. "I don't see anyone or anything down there."

Vitania closed her eyes and drew in a breath. "It reminds me of old Earth, but it seems even better."

Lumia wiped a tear from her cheek. "It takes me back to when the world was new, and Eve was the sweet goddess we adored."

"Indeed, it does, dear." Vitania slipped an arm around Lumia's shoulders and kissed the top of her head. "Considering her state of mind, I'm absolutely amazed she could make this place."

"It's incredible." Lumia sighed in contentment. "I would love to see more."

"Maybe you could ask them for a tour." Shelton pointed toward distant specks in the sky. "We're about to have visitors."

Lumia frowned. "Did you sing the song of summoning?"

Vitania seemed to steel herself. "I did."

"Is Dactia with them?" I zoomed my vision but even if I saw faces, I wouldn't know what Dactia looked like.

"Almost certainly." Vitania glanced back at the portal as if reconsidering her idea. "She is not one to sit idly. That is why she makes a fine queen."

"Sounds like a meanie to me," Ivy said. "She threw you in jail and everything."

"She is a bit single-minded in her pursuits," the Siren replied.

"We're here to back you up this time." I punched my palm. "She won't take you without a fight."

As the water dragons bearing the Sirens drew closer, I stiffened in surprise because I recognized three of them. Balaena, Dolpha, and Narine, the Sirens who we'd met in Atlantis had apparently come to Alden.

The dragons landed and the Sirens disembarked gracefully. They seemed to flow toward us, their hair and gowns rippling and waving as if underwater. The lead Siren's hair was aquamarine with hints of red and orange glinting in the sunlight. She had the face of a middle-aged matron and an expression that warned others not to mess with her. Her resting bitch face was so intimidating, I felt like a kid about to get a spanking.

The other Sirens looked with alarm at Xanos, but the one I

assumed was Dactia remained cool as a cucumber. It probably helped that Xanos wasn't her old ten-foot-tall self anymore.

"Maybe I'll wait on the other side of the portal." Shelton began edging away.

Adam gripped his arm. "You can change your diapers later, man."

Vitania nodded. "Queen Dactia, I hope you're settling into your new home."

"We have not, Vitania." Dactia raked her gaze over the rest of us. "You have come to gloat I suppose? I foolishly allowed Eve to relocate us without complete information."

Vitania maintained a smooth façade. "What do you mean? Alden looks glorious."

Dactia frowned. "Did you not just come from Eve's world? Did she not tell you?"

"I have terrible news, I'm afraid." Vitania sighed. "Our beloved Eve is dead, murdered by Elohim."

The other Sirens gasped.

"No, this cannot be!" Narine cried.

Dolpha scowled. "Eve spent the last of her sanity creating this place, but it was all for nothing."

Even Dactia looked shaken. "We are truly done for, I'm afraid. I have led my people to the edge of oblivion."

I held up a hand. "Hold up. Can you explain what's wrong with Alden?" I waved a hand around. "It looks perfect to me."

Dactia looked ready to lecture me but regarded me patiently for a moment before responding. "This world is incomplete, unfinished."

"What do you mean?"

"Only a hundred square miles is complete. The rest is nothing but volcanic rock and an ocean devoid of life." Dactia shook her head. "This region is nearly perfect, but the rest of the finished area is nothing but a patchwork of flora and fauna Eve transported here from other realms in her vain attempt to salvage what life she deemed worthy."

"Well, anything is better than staying on Eden or the other realms," Shelton said. "Cause they're all about to die."

"How did you open a portal to here, Vitania?" Dactia stepped closer. "I had hoped to bring more sea creatures and ocean plants from Aquilis with us, but we dared not leave since Eve refused to give us the symbols to Alden."

"Why not leave the portals open?" I suggested.

"Portals between this dimension and that of the realms are unstable." Dactia pointed to our portal. "Even now, yours is beginning to break down."

She was right. The edges of the portal were flickering and filling with static. It looked ready to collapse at any second.

"I will happily supply you with the symbols to Alden," Vitania said.

Dactia stiffened. "And in return, you'll want me to abdicate the throne."

Vitania shook her head. "No, but I will require you to help us do everything possible to salvage the Earth realms."

The other Siren pressed her lips into a flat line and went silent. "I will not send my people into senseless battle, but I will help you transport other beings and creatures here to save as much life as possible."

"You must help me destroy the Abyss and the Anchor Stone," Vitania countered. "That will at least lessen the impact of the collapse."

"Is that even possible?" Dactia shook her head. "We used the power of the Apocryphan to create them. How will we manage with none?"

Xanos stiffened. "You have me."

The Siren queen faced her. "You are in full possession of your powers?"

"Mostly." The Apocryphan looked down. "After Emily Glass took my powers, Eve removed my natural form and made me small like humans. But my height does not impact my powers."

"Can you enable my powers?" I asked.

Xanos shook her head. "I cannot. The Apocryphan were not granted soul powers."

I groaned.

"Saila is out there somewhere," Adam said. "If we can find where Elohim is keeping her, maybe she can help."

Shelton scoffed. "Yeah, well if we're going to find her, it looks like a return trip to Hell is in order."

I hated to think about it, but he was right. If finding Saila increased our chances of saving lives, then we had no choice.

29

E mily sagged as if the thought of returning to the place Tyler died was too heavy to bear, then straightened and steeled herself. "I will go if there's a chance of finding Saila."

"Maybe Apollyon knows where she is." I turned to Vitania. "Can you open a portal to Hell?"

"I would not do it from Alden," Dactia said.

Vitania nodded. "Dactia, let us gather every Siren, then journey to the Abyss."

"You're destroying the Abyss from the inside?" Shelton scoffed. "That's like demolishing a building while you're still in it."

Vitania shook her head. "We will start the process from within the Abyss and then move through the portal in the infernal fount and finish the process from Hell itself."

"You don't think Elohim will stop us?" I said.

"Elohim has likely moved all his forces into Atlantis." Vitania nodded to herself. "I doubt there will be much of anything or anyone there to stop us."

"Oh, this is going to be amazing." Ivy clapped her hands. "Can we record the Abyss blowing up?"

"You can only witness it from within the Glimmer," Vitania said.

"If you wish to see it happen, go there and gaze up at the Anchor Stone."

"Can you send us there, Vitania?" Evadora clasped her hands pleadingly. "I don't want to miss it."

Vitania wordlessly opened a new portal to the realm of eternal twilight. Evadora and Ivy skipped through. She closed it then turned to me. "Do you wish to wait here while we collect the other Sirens?"

I shrugged. "Might as well." I didn't know what else we could do in the meantime.

She and Lumia followed the Sirens to their water dragons and climbed on behind them. The group lifted into the sky and flew out to sea.

Ambria ran from the forest at the edge of the meadow. "Has anyone seen Conrad?"

I frowned and looked around. I saw Shelton, Adam, Max, Elyssa, Emily, Xanos, and Cinder, but no Conrad. I hadn't even realized he and Ambria had left the group. "Where did you go?"

"He got this strange look on his face and said he wanted to explore the forest." Ambria looked panicked. "He was walking right next to me one minute, and the next he was gone!"

Shelton groaned. "This is exactly what we need now."

Xanos rose into the air, a green nimbus around her. "I will begin an aerial search." She zoomed toward the forest.

"Yeah, me too." I began to morph into demon form when a wave of dizziness washed over me. I staggered backward but Elyssa caught me before I fell.

"Justin, what's wrong?" Elyssa pushed me upright.

I leaned on her, shaking my head to clear the cobwebs. "I don't know."

"Dude, your other hand." Shelton pointed to my left hand.

The faint azure glow had apparently spread to my other side. I touched the neck of my Nightingale armor. The glow covered my chest and was nearly all the way up my neck. I tried to morph into demon form and once again nearly passed out. "It wasn't like this an hour ago."

"That's for damned sure." Shelton tentatively touched my hand as if it might shock him. "We need to get you fixed."

"I wonder if Eve transferring her memories accelerated it." Elyssa pressed a hand to my chest. "Maybe you should take it easy until we figure this out."

"Maybe so." My heart raced, fueled by newfound anxiety. Now I'd truly lost all my powers. I was completely useless.

Elyssa kissed my cheek. "Justin, I know what you're thinking. We'll figure this out, I promise."

I slipped on a fake grin. "Ah, I'm not worried."

"You sure look worried," Shelton said. "Can't blame you. I'd be shitting bricks if I lost all my powers."

"That's exactly what he needs to hear right now." Adam sighed in disbelief. "There must be some scientific way of diagnosing his issue and curing it."

"Man, I hope so." Shelton gazed at the forest. "Our heroes are dropping like flies."

I started walking toward the forest. "Let's hope Conrad isn't having an episode."

"He's not, Justin," Ambria said in a very certain tone. "Both of us are totally fine now. This is something else. It's almost as if he were being drawn toward something."

Shelton frowned. "What on Alden would draw him to it? This place is totally new to us."

Max looked uncertainly ahead. "Does Alden have a primal fount?"

"I think every world has a primal and infernal fount," Adam said. "Everything is connected."

"Bloody hell, you're right, Max." Ambria stopped walking. "Conrad was drawn to the primal fount by Ezzek Moore before. Maybe it's happening again."

I shrugged. "That's fine and dandy, but how are we supposed to find it? It might be deep underground and unreachable unless the fount wants you to find it."

A green streak plummeted to the ground next to us. Xanos looked troubled. "I found him standing outside a cave in the forest.

He refused to return with me and said I should bring Emily and Justin."

Emily approached us. "What did she say?"

"Conrad requests yours and Justin's presence at a cave," Xanos said.

"Well, that's not creepy at all." Emily straightened her shoulders. "Lead the way."

I nodded at Xanos. "I'm ready."

"Why don't you cradle Justin gently in your arms and fly him there?" Shelton smirked. "He can be your Lois Lane."

Elyssa elbowed him in the ribs. "Shut it, Shelton."

He paled. "Yes ma'am."

Xanos eyed me up and down. "You seem frightened. Are you afraid of heights?"

I rolled my eyes. "No, but we're all coming so there's no need to fly me there."

She shrugged. "As you wish."

Adam giggled. "That day Justin was amazed to learn that when Xanos was saying as you wish, what she really meant was, I love you."

"I meant nothing of the sort!" Xanos shot back.

I snorted. "I guess you've never seen the Princess Bride?"

Xanos stared blankly at us for a moment. "Which princess bride do you mean, for I have witnessed many over the eons."

"Uh, we can save it for another time." I motioned for her to lead the way and the rest of us followed.

A grassy trail lined with flowers led through the forest. White gravel trails branched off, leading to adorable cottages and mushroom houses. There was even something that looked like a gingerbread house further back. But aside from us, there seemed to be no one living in the forest—nothing but birds and a few red squirrels.

"I think I know why Eve isn't anywhere close to finishing Alden." Adam knelt and touched the grass on the trail. "She became so focused on perfecting every last detail that she lost the forest for the trees."

"Eve told me that on Earth evolution drove most of creation."

Xanos looked at the gingerbread cottage and shook her head. "It seems she took Elohim's approach this time, making a finished product rather than letting it grow and improve upon itself."

"Is that how dinosaurs fit into the grand scheme?" Shelton said. "Were there Sirens and Seraphim and all that junk when dinos were around?"

"Not that I know of." Xanos stopped at a fork in the trail and chose the left one. "I believe humanoids came much later. Then again, Eve did not tell me much about the early days of creation."

"It was like watching a massive experiment unfold before their very eyes." Adam sighed dreamily. "What I wouldn't give to see the lab notes on that."

Xanos left the trail and cut through the trees, leading us up a short rise and then down into a shallow valley. Conrad stood outside a cave opening, his expression blank. He blinked as if awaking from a trance.

"Justin and Emily, I figured it out!" He hurried over to us. "Well, the fount told me."

I frowned. "Figured out what?"

Conrad took my hand. "It knows what happened when you touched the primal fount to save Emily."

"Oh." The flame of hope flickered to life in my heart. "Can you fix it?"

"Maybe." He took our hands. "The rest of you have to wait here."

"Conrad Edison, don't you dare run off like that again!" Ambria raised a fist. "I was worried sick."

He looked down. "I'm sorry, Ambria. I simply couldn't resist the voice in my head."

She growled. "You'd better take me with you next time."

"I'll try." Conrad released our hands and headed into the cave. Emily and I exchanged glances, then followed him inside.

We hadn't gone more than a few steps when the ground swallowed us. I suddenly stood on the shore of an azure lake, a scream dying on my lips. Emily stood next to me, her mouth wide in shock.

Conrad was the only one who looked nonplussed. He stepped up to the lake and dipped his hand beneath the water.

"The fount says that since Justin has touched both the infernal and primal fount but was chosen by neither, he corrupted Emily's powers when he touched her." Conrad paused and nodded, as if hearing voices inside his head. "The residual energy from the infernal fount is conflicting with the energy from the primal fount. It will eventually either kill Justin or leave him an empty shell."

My heart froze. "Can't the primal fount fix it? Is there some way to remove the energy from my body?"

Conrad shook his head. "If you had been chosen by either fount, then touching its opposite fount wouldn't have done anything. But you have touched both, uninvited."

"Well, I didn't do it on purpose, okay?" I threw up my hands and sighed. "What about Emily. Can you help her at least?"

He nodded. "Emily, step into the fount."

Emily regarded me sadly for a moment, then stepped into the blue waters. Conrad held her hand and closed his eyes. She shivered and moaned. A nimbus of azure energy surrounded her body. Sweat beaded on her forehead. Orange sparks crackled around the aura, spraying into the lake where they fizzled and died. The sparks grew louder and more violent until with one final snap, crackle, and pop, Emily gasped in relief and sagged.

Conrad released her and offered a smile. "You're fixed."

Emily hesitantly summoned a small orb of golden light in the palm of her hand. She held it there for a few minutes, waiting apprehensively for a malaether eruption. When nothing happened, she grew the orb larger and larger. After a time, she snuffed it and wiped tears from her eyes. "I'm cured!" She hugged Conrad. "Bloody well done."

He returned a wan smile. "I didn't really do anything. The fount just used me to fix you."

"Why can't Justin be repaired in the same way?" Emily put a hand in the fount. "Tell me how to fix him!"

"Will I corrupt Emily if I touch her again?" I said.

Conrad shook his head. "The combination of Eve's magic and your infernal taint caused the corruption in her powers. Simply touching her won't do it again."

Emily growled and splashed the water. "Answer me, you stupid lake!"

"Maybe the crystalis can fix him." Conrad touched the water again. "It's not talking to me anymore."

"Because it did what it needed to do." I shrugged. "Look, it's okay. You and Emily can take it from here. Maybe Emily can continue working on Alden with the crystalis."

Emily paced the shore of the lake. "Everything has an equal but opposite, yes? And where the two meet is neutral—stasis. Just like your Seraphim powers."

I shrugged. "True. Do you think Stasis can help me?"

"Not the Seraphim variety." She held out a hand. "We've got nothing to lose, Justin."

I hesitantly took her hand. "Uh, what do you mean?"

Conrad's eyes flared. "Are you crazy? You both might die."

Emily scowled. "I don't bloody care. I refuse to lose one more person!"

"Hang on." I tried to reclaim my hand, but Emily wrapped me in a hug. A giant bubble of translucent energy formed around the two of us. Emily picked me up and ran against the side of the bubble like a giant hamster ball until we floated out into the primal fount. When we reached the center, she pressed a hand to the bubble and we sank like a rock, falling into the deep blue depths.

I finally freed myself from Emily's hug. "What are you doing?"

"We're going to the source." The determination on her face told me there was no going back. "I won't lose you, Justin. I won't allow Elyssa to endure the pain I felt when I lost Tyler."

"You're crazy!" I managed a faint smile. "That's why I like you."

She wiped fresh tears from her cheeks. "We will never go out with a whimper, Justin, I promise you that."

"Nope, only the biggest bangs possible for our friends." I took her hand and kissed the top of it. "Thanks."

Emily gave a small smile. "You're welcome."

The waters glowed all around us, but despite the light, the only way to tell that we were still sinking was by looking straight up at the distant surface. "What if this goes on for infinity? What if this isn't the way to reach the source?"

Emily shrugged. "Then I have no idea what else to try." She stiffened and blinked. "But Eve knew." She reached out a hand, grasped at nothing, then twisted and pulled.

The fount turned sideways around us, stretching into infinity like a vast blue tunnel, warping, stretching, and undulating. Vertigo twisted my insides as the tunnel folded in upon itself. An instant later, a vast hole of darkness appeared. The bubble bumped against it, slowly pushing into a gelatinous mound of oblivion. Then it swallowed us whole.

Emily pressed a hand to the bubble and the surface glowed brightly. There was nothing to see in any direction—only absolute darkness.

She furrowed her brow and globes of light separated from the bubble and shot in all directions. They shone like stars in the pitch of space before being swallowed by distance.

"How in the hell did you do that?" I touched the bubble as if trying to sense the darkness beyond.

"One of Eve's memories showed me how to reach the node of these founts." Emily bit her lower lip. "There's a whole network of them, but this was the closest."

"Oh," I said slowly. "That was kind of crazy." I looked around us. "This node is where the infernal and primal founts meet?"

She nodded. "This is the node for Alden." She reached out and shook her head. "But the other nodes are impossible to reach from here."

"Why is it black?"

Emily looked as uncertain as I felt. "From what I can dredge up from Eve's memories, the two founts cancel each other out completely here." She put a hand to the bubble and released a glowball into the darkness. It vanished almost instantly.

I whistled. "That can't be good."

She sighed. "Well, if this is going to work, we'll have to go into that nothingness."

"What if it dissolves us to nothing?"

Emily frowned. "I don't get the sense that it will do that. If it works as I think it will, then it should cleanse you of the corruption from the opposing founts."

I gulped. "Well, here goes nothing."

"Yep." She blew out a long breath. "Ready?"

I shook my head vigorously. "Hell no. But let's do it anyway."

Emily gripped my hand and touched the bubble. It flickered away and darkness rushed in to claim us.

30

I might have screamed and soiled my pants, but there was no air in the gelatinous pitch that swallowed us whole. Reflections of me spanned across an infinite distance like a room of mirrors. I opened my mouth in a silent scream, and they all did the same. The reflections collapsed in upon me, replaced by a distant pinpoint of light.

The light grew brighter, a tiny blue-green marble I soon realized was Earth. The negative space filled with more and more Earths. At first, I thought they were merely projections, but then I slowly realized some were different. Some bore hues of brown and black. Others were red as Mars, or completely covered in multi-colored clouds.

Maybe those are the realms? I thought. But unlike the realms, the planets looked virtually identical in size and landmass. The rows upon rows of countless Earths sped past, stopping on a single white sphere. It rapidly grew larger as if I were moving toward it, or it toward me. I reached toward the oncoming sphere, but felt nothing. Then again, I couldn't even see my hand.

I must be imagining this. It isn't real.

I turned my head toward the neighboring world, or at least imagined doing it, and saw a world covered in lush green vegetation and skies streaked with purple clouds. Without a sensation of movement, I sped toward the world, flying through the clouds and over the land. A massive tower rose before me, an upside-down pyramid covered in hexagonal holes.

Bright red insects buzzed around the perimeter. As I drew closer, I realized they were as big as flying horses. I threw up my hands in horror, but my hands weren't there. I was watching this through disembodied eyes, unable to do anything to stop it.

I soared through one of the holes, zipped through a twisting, turning tunnel, and emerged in what looked like the core of a wasp nest. A jade wasp stood on hind legs in the center of a circular dais, surrounded by wasps of varying colors, though none were red. The jade wasp gesticulated with its arms and wings, its mandibles moving as if talking. I'd seen enough strange things that this didn't faze me in the slightest.

Unable to control my movement, I flew straight toward the wasp, stopping just feet away. It abruptly froze and looked straight at me with multi-faceted eyes. A buzzing, clicking language emerged from its mandibles. Somehow, it translated inside my head.

An outsider has found us.

The other wasps buzzed to life, wings beating the air, mandibles clicking.

In an instant, I was back in space, the panorama of worlds hanging before me. I began falling toward another one, this one brown and brackish green veined with gray. The surface of the world was covered in pulsating gray blobs, long tentacles stretching across the cracked earth.

Pale, fleshy creatures with countless eyes and round orifices for mouths bounded across the plains. A lone humanoid figure ran across the world at incredible speeds, barely outpacing the eye creatures. The humanoid's arms and legs were oddly long, almost insect-like, and its head was oval, the eyes larger than a Disney princess's.

One of the eye creatures leapt from a crater. The humanoid's arm morphed into a spike, stabbing into the creature's frontal area. It screeched and went down. The humanoid turned toward me and its large eyes shrank to pinpoints.

It spoke an alien language, but once again, I heard it say, "An outer god? Here?"

The world blinked away, and I was back in the array of worlds. I started to zoom toward another one when the darkness split apart. I fell and landed on something springy. My eyes were open, but I saw nothing. I pressed a hand to my face. I felt pressure, but no sensation, as if something coating me prevented it. I clasped my hands together and felt something rubbery split apart and fall away. Sensation returned to my hands. I reached them toward my face and felt the same gelatinous substance covering it. I worked my fingers into it and peeled it off, grimacing in disgust as I felt it slipping off my eyeballs.

Vision blurry, I made out another figure squirming and working its way free of the goop. I peeled and scraped it off my body, slowly realizing that though my skin looked fine, my clothing was nowhere to be found.

Emily lay gasping on the bottom of the bubble, the black goop cleared down to her waist. Her skin, like mine, was perfectly clean. Once removed, the substance evaporated to nothing. She looked down at her bare breasts and sighed. "Bloody hell. What did we just go through?"

"Did you travel to worlds?" I asked.

She nodded. "Four of them, each one stranger than the last."

"Insects and weird humans with spiky arms?"

Emily shook her head. "No. I saw a world that looked much like Eden, but these strange locust-like creatures with glowing staffs seemed to be in charge. One of them seemed to see me and said something about another world to devour. Then I reset back in space and went to another world."

I already had a theory. "That had to be the multi-verse, right?"

She nodded. "Almost certainly. I believe that dark place is at the very hub of existence."

Emily put a hand to my chest. "The glow is gone from your skin."

I glanced down at her chest, then quickly moved my eyes back up to her eyes. "Uh, yep!"

She rolled her eyes. "Nothing like pair of breasts to control the minds of men."

"That's for sure." I cleared my throat and reached for my demonic powers. I swelled larger, quickly morphing into demonic form. The rest of the goop split apart and fell away, baring everything I had. I covered my crotch with a giant demon hand. "Oops."

"It's quite all right, Justin. All of us have seen you naked at one time or another due to your demonic shifts."

"Yeah, but I'm not exactly an exhibitionist."

Emily chuckled. "Perhaps you should think about becoming one. It might make it easier to do your demon thing."

Keeping my hand over my dong, I shifted back to human form. I reached for my Seraphim powers, but they were still closed off to me. "So, we're both fixed? Can you restore my powers?"

"Not now. I don't want to try anything in this small, enclosed space." Emily thrust a fist forward, twisted it sideways, and we shot from the darkness and back into the azure tunnel of the primal fount. The bubble reached the surface and bobbed gently in the waters.

We walked the bubble to shore and Emily dispelled it.

Conrad stared at Emily's boobs for a moment before blinking out of a trance.

Emily covered her chest. "Good lord, now I'm corrupting minors."

Conrad grinned. "Don't worry, I'm of legal age." His grin faded. "What happened?"

"A lot." I decided to save the story for everyone else. "Can you take us to the others? I'd rather just tell the story once."

He nodded. "Yes, it does get rather tiring repeating the same stories over and over again." Conrad took our hands. We shot upward, straight for the sharp stalactites on the ceiling.

I shouted in alarm. Instead of being gruesomely impaled, we were suddenly back in the cave. Still clutching our hands, Conrad led us out and into the forest where the others waited.

Shelton guffawed the instant he saw us. "Damn, I wasn't expecting a peep show."

Max's mouth dropped open, his eyes locked on Emily. Ambria scowled and pushed his chin up to close his mouth. "Don't look at her like that you bloody animal."

Max looked down. "I'm sorry. I couldn't help myself!"

Conrad regarded us seriously. "Now can you tell me what happened?"

"Justin, to use common vernacular, is hung like a horse," Cinder observed dryly. "Would you agree with that, Elyssa?"

Elyssa's face blushed bright red. "Cinder, I want to smack the shit out of you right now."

Cinder turned to Adam. "Was that a successful attempt to make a Harry joke?"

Adam doubled over laughing. "You nailed it!"

Grimacing, Shelton tossed me his leather duster. "That's not the first time I've let you soil my jacket with your bared junk. You need to get this under control."

Elyssa quirked her lips at Emily. "I'm afraid I don't have a spare jacket."

Adam took off his shirt, revealing a surprisingly lean, muscular frame, though his skin was white as a ghost. He handed it over to Emily. "Maybe this will work."

Her gaze softened and a tear pooled in her eye. She pulled on the shirt. She was much shorter than Adam so it fell well past her waist where the goop was already evaporating.

"Uh, I'm sorry." Adam swallowed uncomfortably. "Did I do something wrong?"

Emily wiped the tear away. "I used to wear Tyler's shirts around the condo without anything on beneath." She sighed. "I told him I'd never wear another man's shirt like that."

"Oh, wow." Adam cleared his throat. "God, I'm sorry."

She touched his hand and smiled. "Adam, it's okay. I'm certain Tyler would agree that this is an appropriate use of a man's shirt. I'm just barely coping with his death right now, so I'm a bit delicate."

"Hey, we understand." Elyssa took Emily's other hand. "We're here for you, okay?"

"We're family." Ambria put a hand on Emily's shoulder. "I'd give you the shirt off my back, but I don't think that would be appropriate."

"Conrad groaned. "Can we please get to the point? Did it work or not?"

I nodded. "I can use my demon powers again and the infection from the two founts seems to be gone."

Emily touched me and closed her eyes. A moment later, I felt the warmth of an old friend return to me. An orb of Brilliance formed in my right hand, and a sphere of Murk in my left.

I teared up with joy. "My precious is back!"

"Hell yeah!" Shelton clapped me on the back.

Adam high-fived me and did a little jig.

Xanos watched quietly from a distance, her expression neutral. I met her gaze. "Does this mean you're along for the ride to the end of the world?"

She nodded. "I don't want this to be the end."

"Me either." I sighed and took a seat on a tree stump. "But even if this universe dies, it seems there are plenty more around out there."

Adam's grin vanished. "What do you mean?"

"We saw the multiverse," Emily said. "And it's terrifying."

Shelton paled. "Huh? What do you mean?"

I told them about our visions of the other worlds and the alien creatures that ruled them. "Right now, there's just a white void where our Earth used to be. I suspect that's the only thing walling off the outside from us."

"Why do you think these people—or whatever they were—could see you?" Adam said. "And how was it possible to understand them?"

"I suspect it has something to do with the source," Conrad said. "The place where the primal and infernal founts meet must be an interdimensional juxtaposition."

"Okay, that settles it." Adam straightened his shoulders. "I want to go there now. I have got to see this for myself."

"I'm afraid there are far more pressing matters to attend to." Emily sighed. "We need to do anything possible to stop the collapse. I'm willing to take the crystalis and use everything I have to stop it."

Elyssa pursed her lips. "Maybe we should talk to Vitania before doing anything rash."

"How would we even reach the fount in Olympus?" Shelton said. "Elohim will throw everything he has against us."

"Why not use the primal fount here?" Adam jabbed a finger toward the cave. "Isn't the primal fount pretty much the same everywhere?"

Conrad shook his head. "When the fount spoke to me, it said the crystalis would need to be used from either the infernal fount in Hell, or the primal fount in Atlantis since both places are original slices of old Earth."

"It told you all that?" Shelton cocked his head. "Did you ask if it could stop the collapse?"

"It shows me visions," Conrad said. "And yes, I asked it. It said it wouldn't intervene in the collapse."

Shelton grunted. "Well, that figures."

"The founts seem to be impartial entities," Cinder said. "Since they exist across all dimensions, picking sides would likely be counterproductive."

"Well, saving a universe from a crazy god isn't really picking sides, is it?" Shelton huffed. "As usual, we've gotta do it ourselves."

"The real question is, does Emily have the raw power to stop it?" Adam tapped a finger on his lips. "I'm concerned that trying to exceed her limitations might burn her out."

"Can I help?" Xanos remained a distance away from everyone, expression tense.

Adam bit his lower lip. "Maybe." He approached the demigoddess, the scanning spell open on his phone.

I reached inside and felt my Apocryphan aura respond to my thoughts. It seemed Emily had enabled it again, though she hadn't given me the speech about using it carefully. Channeling too much of that incredible power would be like a twenty-amp breaker trying to handle a load ten times greater, or something like that. But if I could help slow the collapse even a little bit, then it was worth it.

Adam looked at the numbers on his phone and did a double-take. "Your baseline is about half that of Emily's, but that's still enough to make a difference."

"Half?" Xanos deflated. "At least I am not completely worthless."

He took her hand. "Hey, you're not worthless. Every little bit helps."

Shelton snorted. "Worthless, my ass. You could decimate an army with your pinky finger. I saw it myself."

Elyssa's fists clenched as Shelton's words dug up painful memories of our battle against Xanos and Zon. She just as quickly looked at me and visibly swallowed what she wanted to say. If Xanos could help in the slightest, then we couldn't afford to alienate her now.

I refrained from throwing my hat into the ring for the time being. I would, of course, discuss it with Elyssa, but if I could use my Apocryphan powers to help, it was worth the risk.

Even if it meant dying for the cause.

31

An army of water dragons and Sirens occupied the field when we emerged from the forest. Vitania raised an eyebrow and glided across the ground toward us. "Where did you go?"

"Emily and I are cured." I patted my chest. "I'm fit as a fiddle and ready for action."

She took in my sparse clothing. "Something happened to your uniform in the process?"

Emily stepped next to me. "Vitania, we need to go the primal fount in Atlantis and try to stop the collapse."

Vitania pursed her lips. "Dactia and I discussed many things on our trip to gather the others. We formulated a new theory that might make halting the collapse possible even without a full god to assist."

Emily's mouth dropped open. "Really? How?"

"The immense gravitational attraction between the Abyss and the Anchor Stone will diminish the moment the Abyss is gone." Vitania summoned an illusion displaying the realms with the Abyss disintegrating into chunks. "This means it will take less force to slow the collapse. By additionally dismantling the Anchor Stone, it may be possible to stabilize the realms in place."

Max scratched his head. "I thought the entire purpose of the Anchor Stone was to stabilize the realms."

Vitania nodded. "It put them in a stabilizing orbit to prevent them from drifting so far apart that the quantum tunnels snapped. But if Emily can simply stabilize the realms in the quantum matrix, then they will no longer need the Anchor Stone."

Emily trembled. "You really think it's possible?"

Vitania smiled and squeezed her hand. "Yes, dear. But I will need Xanos to assist our dismantling of the Abyss and the Anchor Stone."

"This is wonderful news!" Ambria hugged Conrad and kissed his cheek. "The day is saved!"

"Uh, not so fast there." Shelton pushed back his wide-brimmed hat. "Elohim's dragon army isn't gonna let us just waltz into the primal fount."

I shrugged. "Why don't we just go to the infernal fount in Hell, then?"

"Conrad's special link to the primal fount will enable him to amplify Emily's powers." Vitania shook her head. "And Emily isn't linked to the infernal fount. I'm afraid only the primal fount will do."

"Then we'll fight our way in." Elyssa pressed her lips into a tight line. "The fae, Seraphim, and Utopians are gathered and ready to fight."

Dactia, who'd apparently heard everything despite being a hundred feet away, shook her head. "The Sirens will not fight."

"If you don't fight, then what god will be left to finish Alden?" Emily waved a hand at the world around her. "Only I might be able to finish what Eve started, but I will fight Elohim to my dying breath to stop the collapse. Help us, Dactia, or enjoy eternity on a half-finished world."

Dactia frowned. "We will simply return to Aquilis if you stop the collapse."

Emily scoffed. "Do you really think Elohim will just leave you be? If we don't soundly defeat his army and fight our way into the fount, he'll just keep on taking over realm after realm, destroying everything until he can start over."

One of Dactia's companions spoke. "Her logic is sound, my queen. Elohim would be an even crueler master of the realms than the Apocryphan."

Dactia regarded her with a frown and remained quiet for so long, I thought she'd gone into a trance. The Siren queen abruptly dismounted her dragon and glided across the field as if floating on water. She looked angry but troubled. "Emily, your logic is, unfortunately, quite sound. But we have not warred with another species in eons. I'm afraid we're out of practice."

"Oh, you'll get into it in no time," I assured her. "Maybe you can sing some epic battle music when the time is right."

Vitania could not repress a smile. "I am so happy to have my sisters by my side again."

Dactia didn't look nearly as pleased. "It is only because we have no other choice."

"About damned time," Shelton muttered.

Vitania took in the hundreds of Sirens and dragons covering the field. "It will take us some time to portal into the Abyss."

"Not with me around." A golden aura streaked with silver surrounded Emily. She waved a hand and a massive breach stretched across the field before us. "It feels wonderful to be able to do that again."

Though most portals were like windows to their destinations, only inky blackness waited within this one. The gravitational fringe of the Abyss made portaling in a rather unpleasant experience.

I steeled myself and walked into the darkness. The moment I touched it, icy fingers clutched my flesh, slowing me until I could hardly move. Inky pitch swallowed me whole. I hung suspended in dark oblivion for a moment then stumbled onto the rocky, barren wasteland of the Abyss.

Shelton came through a moment later. "Gah, I hate that!"

Elyssa appeared next, motioning us forward. "Get moving. We need to make plenty of room for the Sirens."

"They bringing their dragons?" Shelton said.

Elyssa shrugged. "I didn't ask."

Thankfully, the Sirens didn't bring the massive creatures with them. They filed through the portal gracefully, seemingly unaffected by the unpleasant transition between worlds. Vitania, Lumia, and Xanos joined us as we waited for the rest of their numbers to come through. Xanos remained quiet, an apprehensive look on her face.

Adam took out his arcphone and began recording a video of the surrounding area. "Vitania, what happens to the creatures and spirits living in the Abyss when it's destroyed?"

"Spirits and souls will be freed to return to Haedaemos or the afterlife." Vitania looked up the sheer cliff nearby. "The stone crabs and other physical creatures will likely die. I'm afraid they are too dangerous to simply send to another realm."

"Oh, they would wreak chaos with another ecosystem." Lumia shook her head sadly. "I believe the Sirens imported them from one of the realms used to create the Abyss, so perhaps they'll survive to some extent."

"Doubtful." Vitania began walking toward the maze of cliffs in the center of the Abyss. "I'm happy we have Emily's powers back. She will make the tasks of dismantling the Anchor Stone and Abyss much easier."

"Shouldn't we keep her fresh for stopping the collapse?" Shelton said.

"Perhaps, but with Elohim's dragon army between us and the fount, we will need every resource available." Vitania glanced back at the Sirens following behind us. "Our only hope is that Elohim is still too injured and tired from his fight with Eve that he cannot assist the dragon army."

"Which means we need to strike fast and hard." Elyssa bit her bottom lip. "I should go to the Ranch and update my father. We need to be ready to mobilize."

Adam put away his phone. "Emily can open big portals, but how are we going to coordinate armies from three separate realms?"

"I believe the portal generator can achieve that," Cinder said. "If we use a larger piece of aetherite, it can project portals as large as Emily's."

"Oh, yeah." Adam's face brightened. "We just need to get the other armies to Utopia so they can transport with the others."

Elyssa nodded. "Cinder and Adam, you're with me." She turned to Vitania. "Can you open a portal to the Ranch?"

"Of course." The Siren tore open a portal to the front yard of the Templar Compound. "We will see you on Utopia?"

"Uh, but I wanted to see them take apart the Abyss," Adam whined.

"Child, there will be nothing to see unless you observe from the Glimmer." Vitania gave him a stern look. "And even then, it will not be exciting."

Cinder seemed disappointed as well but nodded. "I'm afraid we have more important duties to attend, Adam."

Elyssa kissed my cheek. "Don't do anything stupid, okay?"

I kissed her soft lips. "I'll do my best."

She, Adam, and Cinder stepped through the portal and Vitania closed it behind them.

Shelton rubbed his hands together. "Man, I'm nervous. We're about to fundamentally change the fabric of our universe."

"You are right to be apprehensive," Vitania said. "There may be unintended consequences to our actions today, but I'm afraid we have no choice."

I scoffed. "Considering the bulk of our armies are on Utopia and it's about to be swallowed by the Abyss, I think we ought to hurry things up and not worry so much."

Vitania nodded in agreement. "Quite correct, child."

Xanos trailed behind us, glancing around like a trapped cat. It was a normal response for someone visiting the prison where she'd been trapped thousands of years with a family that despised her.

"I feel kind of sorry for her," Shelton said. "Kind of, anyway. You know Christmas had to suck with a family like hers."

"Yeah." I blew out a breath. "I can't imagine returning here is very pleasant for her."

We eventually reached the sloping crater walls surrounding the infernal fount and climbed up them. The army of Sirens wended through the cliff maze behind us, their numbers trailing into the distance. The portal winked off moments later as the last of them presumably came through. A golden figure rose into the air and streaked toward us shortly after.

Emily alighted next to Vitania, a grin on her face. "I feel positively amazing. I really think we can do this."

Vitania patted her hand. "Then let's get started, dear." She turned to Xanos. "Are you up to the task?"

Xanos clasped her hands nervously. "Yes. The sooner we can get out of here, the better."

Without instruction, Sirens joined hands and formed a circle around the crater. Another group encircled the first circle and so forth until there were four concentric circles around the crater. Low vibrations hummed through the very center of my being. Sonic waves sliced the crater walls off the ground like a giant pimple, sloughing the rubble far away from the circle.

The infernal fount, now revealed, bubbled and churned like lava. Technically, this was the underside of the fount, an inverted extension of Hell. The more I tried to think about how the Sirens managed it, the more I questioned how it was even possible.

Shelton put a hand over his stomach. "Man, these subsonic vibrations are giving me nausea."

Max ran behind a rock and threw up. Ambria began heaving and ran to a neighboring rock. Conrad frowned, seemingly unaware of the Sirens' effect on the others.

The vibrations abruptly stopped. Shelton breathed a sigh of relief, but it was clear that had only been round one as the Sirens tightened their circles, moving closer to the edge of the fount.

Emily looked aghast as Max and Ambria staggered from behind the rocks, their faces green. "You poor dears." She put a hand to Max's head and color returned almost immediately. She did the same for Ambria a moment later.

"What did you do?" Max said.

"I made it so your ear canals won't be disrupted by the Siren

song." She tapped behind her ear. "The vibrations cause disorientation and motion sickness."

"Hey, what about us?" Shelton said. "I could use a little magical
Dramamine!"

"Emily and Xanos, we need you," Vitania called out.

Emily treated Shelton, then flew toward the center of the Siren
circle. A different kind of singing ensued. There were no explosions,
no fireworks, just changes in pitches and vibrations, some of which
even my demonic hearing barely detected. It went on for what felt
like hours. I finally channeled a fluffy cloud of Murk and tied off the
weave so I could take a nap.

"Dude, no fair." Shelton looked enviously at my creation.

I sighed. "If I make you one, then everyone will want one."

"It took you barely five minutes to make that one," Shelton said.

Ambria pushed on the cloud and gasped. "It's so fluffy!"

"That's the point." I sighed. "Fine." Twenty minutes later, everyone
in our group of non-essentials had their very own cloud pad. I finally
settled down on mine when the Sirens went silent. The ground shuddered, the nearby cliffs rumbled, and gravel rained down. The mountains walling in the bowl of the Abyss quaked, massive cracks
running up their sides. Lightning flashed across mountain peaks and
the ground began to shake in earnest.

Shelton bounced around on his cloud bed. "Man, I just laid
down!"

The circles of Sirens broke apart as they stumbled to keep their
feet. I ran toward the fount and was disappointed to discover my
super speed was gone. *So much for a permanent upgrade.* I found
Vitania and Emily at the shores of the fount, neither of them rocking
and rolling like the rest of us.

"What happened?" I shouted above the apocalyptic grind of rock.

"It appears that unmooring the Abyss from this side made it far
more unstable than planned." Vitania didn't look worried. "We
should be able to evacuate in time."

I grimaced. "Should?"

Xanos flew above the fount and fired a thin green beam into the center. The bubbling waters parted, leaving a gateway where they had once been. "It's open!"

Vitania motioned toward the opening. Dactia nodded and jumped inside. The floor of the cavern on the other side was sideways. Gravity seemed to flip the Siren upright and she landed neatly on her feet like a cat. Sirens began filing into the gateway from all sides.

I ran back to Shelton and the others. "It's time to get the Hell out of here."

Shelton groaned. "You've been waiting all your life to say that, haven't you?"

"And I beat you to it!" I flashed a grin. "But really, let's go before this place falls apart."

An orb of sickly yellow flashed past me, followed quickly by several more. Something cold brushed my skin.

Ambria screamed, jumping and twisting around. "I felt like a ghost just ran through me!"

"It probably did," Shelton said. "God only knows how many souls and spirits are trapped here."

Another kind of rumbling caught my ear, and it became clear souls and spirits weren't the only things we needed to worry about. The distant cliffs came alive with movement of the crawling variety as the giant stone crablike monsters there stampeded down the sides and into the bowl toward us. They'd be on us in no time.

"Everyone run!" I shouted.

Shelton was already running. Conrad scooped up Ambria and dashed away at supernatural speed. I motioned to Max. "Hop on, big guy."

He grinned and jumped on my back for a high-speed piggyback ride, and I booked it toward the gateway. We ran past the lines of Sirens and jumped into the hole. My guts twisted as gravity flipped sideways. I should have crashed heavily on my side, but at the last instant, my body reoriented and I landed lightly on my feet.

Groups of Sirens spread out through nearby tunnels to give room to the others coming behind us. Once the rest of my friends were through, I gathered everyone and herded them further back. Despite the very world crumbling around them and the threat of giant stone crabs, most of the Sirens glided through the gateway as if this were just another Tuesday for them.

As the distant rumbling grew closer and closer, Xanos and Emily flew through the gateway. Xanos spun and slashed green energy across the opening. A massive stone claw stabbed through the opening, narrowly missing her. She dodged to the side and fired another beam of energy into the fount.

Fiery water rushed in from both sides, closing the opening. The claw quivered and sank out of sight.

Xanos sighed in relief and landed on the floor next to Vitania. Without instruction, the Sirens once again began forming circles around the fount to finish unmooring the Abyss from this side. Within moments or hours, the Abyss would be no more.

32

It took considerably less time to finish the job of unmooring the Abyss from Hell than I'd thought it would. There were no earthquakes, no explosions, nothing. The Sirens concentrated on the task for about an hour and then just seemed to call it a day. When they began forming ranks once again, I found Vitania.

"Uh, that's it?"

She nodded. "The task is complete. Now we move to the Glimmer."

"Wait!" Apollyon, flanked by several flaming rock demons hurried around a bend in a distant tunnel. "I sensed you here." He stopped before Vitania. "Why come?"

Vitania regarded the demons uneasily. "We are saving lives."

Other nearby Sirens averted their gazes, apparently feeling the effects of Apollyon's painfully beautiful countenance.

He dropped to his knees and clasped his hands in prayer. "Can you kill me?"

"No, Apollyon, I cannot." Vitania approached him and bid him to rise off the floor. "Why do you want to die so badly?"

"I am bad." He glanced at the demons. "I make things bad."

"Your corrupted powers are at fault, not you." Vitania patted him on the arm like a child. "Your father was so intent on physical perfection, that it must have caused an imbalance in your soul."

I switched to demon view and examined Apollyon's aura. Golden hues blended with caustic yellow. A splinter of darkness penetrated the aura all the way to the core. It was there that yellow overpowered the gold.

I glanced at Emily and noticed the same golden aura, but hers was streaked with silvery blue. At one time, her aura had been markedly different, far more blue and silver than golden, while Olivia's had always been orange. The orange came from her alignment with the infernal fount, and Emily's blue from the primal fount. As Emily used her powers more and more, drawing and expending greater energy, her aura had become more like Eve's, perfectly golden.

It seemed she was evolving.

Shelton aimed his phone at Apollyon and frowned. "No way."

I frowned. "No way, what?"

"That doesn't look like a mistake at all." He turned the screen so I could see the readout from Adam's god analyzer spell. "I think Elohim corrupted his son's aura on purpose."

"Are you certain?" Emily stood near Shelton. "Why on Earth would he do that?"

"Because he made a god that far exceeded his expectations." I shook my head. "A god better than him."

"Well, slap my ass and call me Chucky." Shelton whistled. "He couldn't kill him, so he fucked him up."

Emily scowled. "That sounds precisely like something Elohim would do."

Xanos hesitantly stepped closer to us. "Surely Elohim could kill Apollyon if he could kill Eve. I think he intentionally keeps him alive."

Adam nodded. "Agreed. Unless there's such a thing as true, unkillable immortality."

Shelton shrugged. "Apollyon doesn't seem like a bad kid. Why don't we fix him and let him take care of Elohim?"

Emily closed her eyes. She abruptly cried out in terror and stumbled back into Xanos. The purple demigoddess caught Emily, then screamed and jumped back as if she'd just caught a hot potato. That was enough to send the rest of us scrambling away from the pair while the Sirens looked on in bemusement.

Apollyon looked sadly at Emily. "It cannot be fixed."

Eyes wide, Emily shuddered and looked away from him. "Touching it was like inviting pure madness into my mind. It's no bloody wonder you want to die."

Vitania cast a stern look at Emily. "What did you do?"

"There's a splinter of darkness in Apollyon's aura," I said. I wished I could take a picture of it and show them. "Emily tried to pull it out."

"We think Elohim put it there intentionally." Shelton shook his head sadly. "Elohim created perfection and decided he didn't want the competition."

"Apollyon's corruption aura is intentional?" Vitania seemed aghast. "I cannot believe Elohim would do such a thing to his own creation."

"Oh, I can." Emily shuddered and seemed to collect herself. "Just as Eve created the Apocryphan to be inferior to her, so did Elohim create Apollyon."

Shelton snapped his fingers. "What if Elohim wasn't trying to create another god? What if he was trying to create a race of perfect beings and accidentally gave Apollyon god powers?"

"Father said I was an accident," Apollyon said sadly. "He said I would be a model for second creation."

"And there it is." Shelton grunted. "Elohim kept his kid around as a working prototype. Once Eve's creations are wiped out, he'll probably use his genes to create humans two point oh, but without godlike powers."

"Apollyon, how do you endure the madness?" Tears welled in Emily's eyes. "I barely touched it and it's horrific."

Xanos rubbed her arms as if trying to rid herself of goosebumps. "I felt it second-hand from Emily and it shook me to my core."

"Only Elohim or another god could remove it." Vitania gave Emily another stern look. "You are lucky you didn't break yourself, child. How would we stop the collapse without you?"

Emily looked down. "I'm sorry."

Vitania sighed. "You meant well, child. But please, think before you act."

Shelton snickered and looked at me. "That goes for two of you."

"You try help me." Tears trickled down Apollyon's cheeks. "Thank you, goddess."

Emily scoffed. "I'm no goddess, you poor thing. I can't bear the thought of the insanity you've endured for eons."

"It does not always affect me," Apollyon said slowly, making an effort to overcome his speech impediment. "It affects things around me for too long."

"I promise if it is ever within my power, I shall cure you." Emily straightened her shoulders. "But first, we must defeat your father and save existence."

Apollyon sagged. "My father lied. He made me this way. He will not kill me and end my suffering."

The rock demons standing next to Apollyon rested their flaming hands on his shoulders as if offering emotional support. The rest of us looked at each other in wide-eyed astonishment. Some Sirens looked sadly at the broken god, but there was nothing any of us could do.

"Thoughts and prayers," Shelton murmured.

After everything we'd been through in the past hours, I'd forgotten another reason for coming to Hell. "Apollyon, where is Saila? Is she still with Elohim?"

He shook his head. "No, she gone. She made Father angry, so he took her powers. Sent her to other world. I not know where."

"Maybe Emily can restore her powers," Xanos said.

Emily scoffed. "We certainly don't have time to hunt the realms for her, even if I could."

"It is a loss, but not the greatest loss we could have suffered." Vitania pursed her lips. "Emily is the most important factor. I do not think Saila's added power would have increased the odds tremendously."

"Yeah, but it would've been nice." Shelton sighed. "Too bad Elohim's kid can't help us."

Emily shook her head. "His corruption aura might destroy everything, I'm afraid."

"Apollyon, we must take our leave." Vitania approached him despite the demons and put a hand on his chest. "We will help you in any way possible once this is over."

He nodded. "Thank you, good Siren." Apollyon turned and walked away, his demon friends in tow.

Vitania cleared her throat and turned to Dactia. "Off to the Glimmer then."

Dactia nodded. "Lead the way, Vitania."

Vitania seemed to steel herself, then opened a portal leading into the land of eternal twilight. The gateway was smaller since there wasn't much room between the cave walls and the infernal fount. She motioned our group to proceed the Sirens, so we hurried through, emerging atop the parapet of the massive mountain castle the Glimmer Queen called home.

The massive green Anchor Stone hung overhead. Countless orbs hung captive in its gravity, a live-action representation of the realms.

Ivy and Evadora stood at the far end of the spacious roof, oohing and ahhing at explosions in the distant reaches of the realmverse.

Max took out his phone and ran toward them, recording the light show in the distant sky. "Hey, that's the Abyss exploding!"

I ran after him, eager to get a closer look. I reached for my phone and felt instant regret when I remembered Nookli was fried. The Abyss, usually a dark void in the stars now looked like a space battle in an asteroid belt. The void crumbled like a giant cosmic cookie, fragments colliding and exploding, sending a halo of debris in all directions.

"This is so epic," Max breathed. "I never in a million years thought I'd get to see the Abyss, much less watch Sirens destroy it."

Shelton joined us with a grunt. "Nothing like going to new places, meeting new people, and destroying them. We're like Columbus on steroids."

Ambria looked up at the giant green moon. "What happens when they destroy the Anchor Stone? Will the fragments still grant immortality?"

Conrad stood between Ambria and Max, watching the Abyss. "The immortality comes at a cost. It makes you lose all emotion until you care about nothing."

"I'd consider that a gift," Ambria said. "Could you imagine being trapped in the Glimmer for eternity? The constant twilight is already giving me a headache!"

Cora, the Glimmer Queen, rushed onto the parapet. "We are under a full-scale invasion!" She blinked when she saw us and blinked again when her gaze settled on the Sirens flowing through the portal.

"Mummy, the Abyss is blowing up!" Evadora gripped Cora's hand and began dancing in a circle. "Now we get to blow up too!"

Cora stormed over to Vitania. "What is the meaning of this?"

Vitania stiffened. "The preservation of billions of lives depends on demolishing the Anchor Stone."

"What?" Cora's head flicked toward the giant moon and back to Vitania. "The Sirens destroyed my realm to preserve the others, trapping me and my people on islands floating among the stars. Now you've come to say it was all for nothing?"

"What I am saying is that the collapse of the realms will destroy all life if we do not demolish the Anchor Stone." Vitania sighed. "The sacrifice of your realm was the only way to keep the realms from drifting apart. The magical energies imbued in the earth beneath our feet made it uniquely ideal."

Cora's face paled as she watched the seemingly unending march of Sirens through the portal. "This is how it began all those eons ago. An army of Sirens, flanked by Apocryphan overlords marched into our fair lands and made us watch as everything we loved was ground to dust and reconstituted into that monstrosity!" She jabbed a finger at the Anchor Stone.

Shelton snorted. "Kind of looks like a massive ball of Spam."

Ambria glared at him. "Poorly timed attempt at humor as usual."

I repressed a laugh.

"I cannot undo the torment your people endured, Cora." Vitania clasped her hands at her waist. "Our efforts today will demolish the Anchor Stone and its gravitational magic."

"Will the fragments still grant immortality?" Ambria frowned. "Will they drain emotion and allow us to travel to the mirror world?"

Vitania returned the frown. "We did not imbue it with such magic. It may simply be magic endemic to the land itself."

"We had emotion before the Anchor Stone," Cora said. "Whatever you did, corrupted the natural magic of the land."

"In any case, we must do this immediately, Cora." Vitania closed the portal as the last Siren emerged. The surface of the castle roof was at least half a square mile, but it was getting crowded. "At least you will be rid of the monstrosity, as you put it."

Cora sagged. "And my people? Will they remain in eternal slumber?"

"We will find a way to cure them." Vitania shook her head. "Your mirror counterpart used magic unknown to us."

Cora's evil twin from the reflected world had ruled the Glimmer for quite some time, exiling Cora to Eden, and putting the Glimmer folk into a frozen state. We'd never been able to figure out exactly how she'd done it, so the people remained asleep.

"Very well, then." Cora bowed mockingly. "Do your worst."

Vitania went to work right away, her mouth opening inhumanly wide, a chorus of many voices singing in discordant harmony. She craned her neck, looking straight up at the Anchor Stone. The other Sirens joined moments later as if by some secret cue, their heads also raised toward the green moon.

The singing didn't bother me at all, thankfully, but cracks were already forming in the Anchor Stone.

Shelton backed up a step. "We're not about to get rained on by meteors, are we?"

Ambria grimaced. "That would be disastrous!"

Vitania motioned to Xanos and Emily. She must have communicated to them through the song, because they both nodded and unleashed massive beams of energy at the moon. The Anchor Stone shattered in a silent explosion. Fragments streaked downward, sparking as they hit the atmosphere.

From our view atop the highest point of the Glimmer, we watched as the fragments clicked into place against the rough edges of the land islands, like a galactic jigsaw puzzle being assembled by an invisible god.

The falling fragments were just the outer shell of the Anchor Stone, revealing a multicolored layer beneath that looked like dirt and soil. That layer broke apart and fell beneath the horizon, vanishing from view.

The process continued for hours, each layer of the Anchor Stone falling away to reveal different shades of stone, molten rivers of lava, and glowing pools of magical energy. Sweat glistened on the foreheads of Sirens and demigoddesses alike as they worked nonstop to complete the procedure.

Some Sirens collapsed and were ignored by their companions. Vitania and Dactia seemed to be the only ones not bending under the duress. Even Ivy and Evadora tired of prancing around with excitement.

I felt tired and I wasn't even doing anything. I sat down and rubbed the crick forming in my neck, then must have fallen asleep. A chorus of gasps woke me up with a start. I rubbed my eyes and looked up as the final shell peeled away to reveal a glowing core of dark green energy. More Sirens collapsed. Others looked as if they were barely holding onto consciousness. Xanos cried out and dropped to her knees, caressing the blistered flesh of her hands.

"What now?" Emily shouted.

Vitania slashed a hand and the Siren song cut off. As if on cue, more Sirens fell, some to their knees, others flopping unceremoniously on the ground. Vitania held up a hand toward Emily. "It will take care of itself, child. Rest well while you can."

Emily flexed her hands and winced, though the skin didn't look burnt like Xanos's. "What is that thing?"

"A vast gravity well of Apocryphan magic." Vitania massaged her jaw and winced. "It should lose cohesion soon."

Her definition of soon ended up being a good half hour. The surface of the green star flared and bubbled, the eruptions growing in severity until it burst like a bubble filled with smoke. The energy spread out in a sphere, dissipating to nothing. Without the moon, the world went pitch black.

"No!" Cora screamed. "What have you done?"

I cast a dozen orbs of Brilliance into the air to illuminate the area. The shocked faces of my friends surrounded me.

Evadora crouched on all fours and howled like a wolf pup. "I love the dark!"

Ivy, for once, didn't seem to agree. "This is scary." She channeled orbs of light and threw them into the air alongside mine. "How are we supposed to see where the land ends? We'll just fall into outer space!"

Vitania settled onto the ground and sighed in relief. "It took days to create the Anchor Stone, and only eleven hours to destroy it."

"And now there is no light upon the land!" Cora clenched a fist. Black vines sprouted from the stone, thorns lining their sides. "The Sirens have destroyed my world for the last time!"

33

"Oh snap." Shelton backed away from Cora. "I think they finally broke her mind."

"Cora, no!" Emily gripped the Glimmer Queen's wrists and dragged her back. "This had to be done!"

Tears poured down Cora's cheeks. "My world did not deserve this. Release me and let me have my vengeance on the destroyers!" She wrenched her hands free.

Emily, obviously exhausted from hours of channeling, couldn't hold on.

Conrad rushed over to his adoptive mother and took her hands in his. "Mum, please don't."

She looked down at him, eyes wide as if just now remembering he was there. "I cannot let this stand, Conrad." Her shoulders shook with grief. "My people, my world. They are all gone."

"We will find a way to fix the Glimmer, I promise." Conrad hugged her and kissed her cheek. "Please, mum, we need you now more than ever."

Cora slumped against him as if too emotionally exhausted to stand on her own. Conrad wiped away tears of his own, then guided her into the castle. Lumia knelt next to Vitania and kissed her on the cheek, talking quietly to her before helping her rise.

Other Sirens checked on their fallen companions, helping some up, or weeping silently next to others. I approached one such Siren. "What's wrong?"

She looked up at me, her sea-green hair floating about her face. "She has sung her last song."

That was when it hit me. I turned in a circle and counted dozens of unmoving forms. "Oh, god, they're dead?"

"Yes, child." Vitania stood behind me. "We lost many more than this during the building of the Anchor Stone. The strain is simply too much."

"You and everyone else must rest." Lumia took her hand. "Perhaps we can find you a bed in the castle."

"There are none," Ambria said. "This place is huge, but it's empty and dead."

"It's a wonder Cora didn't go mad after all this time." Max sighed. "I'm glad she found Conrad after Naeve exiled her."

"Some of them need healers and I'm certain they all need food." Lumia shook her head. "You did not think this through, did you, dear?"

Vitania smiled. "It has been too long since I led anyone but myself into trouble."

Shelton turned to me. "I'll bet the Templars could help. They're good at all that logistics stuff. "

"Uh, how are we supposed to get there?" I nodded at Emily. "She and Vitania are too worn out to open portals."

Shelton frowned. "Don't you have your Apocryphan powers back?"

I blinked. "Oh, yeah. I'd forgotten about that." I traced the symbols for Eden, empowered them, and slashed open a portal to Cinder's lab. The weight of opening a portal usually felt like a ton of bricks on my brain because the power drain was insane. This time, I hardly felt it, probably because I was unusually well-rested from not having had powers all this time.

Before Shelton, and I stepped through the portal, he took a picture of the roof so I could open another portal back. Then we went into the lab and I closed the portal behind us.

Adam and Cinder looked up from working on the portal generator.

"Dude, how was it?" Adam said.

Shelton waggled a hand. "One percent epic and ninety-nine percent pure boredom."

"You have been gone for hours," Cinder said. "We were concerned something might have happened."

"Oh, it did, but we don't have time to talk about it right now." I tapped the comm badge on my shirt. "Elyssa, we need help."

She replied a moment later. "Justin, where are you?"

"Cinder's lab."

"Tell me what you need."

I told her what we needed while Cinder prepared the portal generator with a larger chunk of aetherite. Twenty minutes later, Templars with food, cushioned sleeping bags, and other supplies were filing through a portal into the Glimmer. Healers helped those who could be helped while others moved the dead to the compound to keep them magically preserved until the Sirens could give them a proper sendoff.

In the meantime, I gave Thomas and Elyssa an update.

After I was finished, Thomas gave me an update on his activities. "An infernus contacted me today at the behest of Kalesh. We are determining how Baal's former network can help us, but it's tricky. Using the noms is a double-edged sword, if we could even convince them to help at all."

"Any little bit helps." I sagged into my chair at the conference table. "I haven't even done anything today and I'm exhausted. I can't imagine how Vitania and the others are feeling."

"Well, the good news is that Utopia is saved." Elyssa projected a video from her phone. "This was taken a few hours ago."

The video panned around a large meadow covered in tents and temporary housing where the Templars had been helping refugees get settled on Utopia. The world abruptly went dark, all except for an eerie purple glow. The image panned upward to reveal a black void eclipsing the sun.

A female spoke. "Johnson, alert headquarters that we need immediate evac. Utopia is in endgame."

Elyssa paused the video. "We had no way to get that many people out in time. Thankfully, Vitania took care of it in time." She switched to another video. People cheered as the dark void hovering over the planet fragmented and exploded, revealing the sun once more.

I made a fist and whooped. "Dude, that was awesome! Can I get that video too?" I reached for Nookli and remembered I'd given her little metal corpse to Adam. "She's dead, Jim."

Elyssa patted my hand. "Babe, we can get you another phone."

"But it won't be Nookli." I imagined caressing her metallic edges and sighed. "No other phone can find Indian restaurants like she can."

Thomas cleared his throat. "I will hold a war council tomorrow to discuss options for Atlantis, but first I need to know this—can Emily do what needs to be done?"

I took a moment before answering. "Emily has grown stronger since the first time I met her. Her aura has gone from silver-blue to gold, which I think means she's inching toward true godhood. Maybe she and Xanos together can halt the collapse, but I don't know for sure. If we don't at least try, the realms will still collide and billions will die. All we did today was prevent the annihilation of all life."

Thomas pursed his lips. "We've gone to war with less hope before. If I'm honest, I don't know how we'll fight a dragon army. The number of battle-ready Mzodi ships stands at little more than a hundred. Arturo's archangels number perhaps two hundred, and that's with new recruits. Standard ground forces won't stand a chance against hordes of drakes, much less thousands of wyverns."

"We lost contact with Atlantis and Olympus," Elyssa said. "We'll be entering blind."

"On the upside, we don't have to go immediately since the immediate danger is over." I tapped a finger on the table. "The Sirens and their water dragons would be a formidable addition to our army."

"There won't even be enough land for our people to stand on if Atlantis is occupied," Thomas said. "This means lycans, vampires, felycans, and our other standard troops won't have a way to participate."

That was an excellent point and one I had no answer to. "Maybe there's a way to portal directly into the primal fount so we can bypass Elohim's army entirely."

"I spoke with Vitania about that option before I came back here." Elyssa blew out a breath. "The only way in is by the quantum tunnel hidden on Olympus. Apparently the gods didn't want anyone to be able to enter any other way."

I grunted. "Then we'll portal straight into the room on the mountain and use the quantum tunnel there."

"We'll give it a shot, but I'd be surprised if Elohim didn't have portal blockers set down everywhere to keep us from doing just that." Elyssa turned off the holographic video. "Let's go to the Glimmer. I need to see how long the Sirens need to recuperate."

"You got it." I slashed open a portal.

Elyssa frowned. "Don't strain yourself, Justin. We could just use the portal generator."

"Actually, it's no strain at all." I shrugged. "I barely even feel the power drain."

"I'm going to evaluate the situation as well." Thomas stepped through the portal and we followed close behind.

We found Vitania resting in a tent. She painted a rather grim picture: two full days of recovery minimum for the Sirens. Emily and Xanos were in no better shape, having expended enough gigawatts to send Marty McFly back to the future at least four times. At least with the logistical expertise of the Templars, everyone was well taken care of.

Thomas went into the castle to look for Cora, though I didn't expect him to get very far with her. Her world had been torn apart by the Sirens eons ago, and their return certainly hadn't done anything to heal those wounds.

"Hey, what's that?" Evadora perched precariously on the parapet walls, apparently unconcerned with the thousand-foot drop to the rocky ground.

I joined her and looked out over the realm. The formerly floating islands were now connected by a messy patchwork of barren earth. Thorny trees and scrub brush clearly demarked the old land from the new. But that wasn't what caught Evadora's attention. I didn't get it right away because I'd seen it so many times. But for this world, it was unheard of.

For the first time in countless eons, a tinge of pink touched the sky. Gasps rose from the few active Sirens. The Templars present didn't grasp the significance because most of them had never been here.

"The sun is rising?" Ambria rushed to our side, Max and Conrad close behind.

"It's amazing." Conrad stared at the yellow orb peeking above the horizon. "I never thought I'd see the day."

"Me either." Max grinned. "It's a miracle!"

Cora rushed to the rooftop moments later, eyes wide. She hugged Evadora and began weeping softly. "May the sun smile down on our broken, battered world and heal it."

"It's a miracle, mummy." Evadora hopped up and down on the narrow wall. "I want to fly up and touch it!"

Max paled as he watched her careless antics. "Evadora, are you sure you never fall?"

"Like this?" Evadora fell backward off the parapet.

Ambria screamed and looked down.

Conrad shook his head. "She's toying with you."

I looked over the side and saw the girl dangling from a window ledge fifty feet down. She grinned and scaled the wall like a mountain goat, leaping up and over to join us.

"I love you, Ambria!" Evadora hugged her, much to the other girl's chagrin. "Your screams are delicious!"

"Certified mental," Max muttered. "That's what living without the sun will do to you."

Conrad grinned. "Well, at least she enjoys life."

Thomas joined us a moment later. "Cora, I've been looking for you."

"I'm aware." The Glimmer Queen's orange hair glinted in the sunlight. "I will offer what little assistance I can, just don't expect me to work alongside the Sirens."

"Do you hear that?" Evadora cocked her ear. "Do you feel it, mummy?" She dashed across the roof to the other side and looked down. "Oh, come look!"

The rest of us hurried across, dodging between slumbering Sirens. Once again, it took a moment for me to register what I was seeing. A crowd of people had formed at the base of the mountain. Cora stepped onto an invisible platform and beckoned the rest of us to join her. We dropped down the side of the mountain fast enough to make my stomach rise into my throat.

The people at the bottom knelt when they saw Cora and I realized who they were—the Glimmer folk, aka the Lyrolai, aka elves. "Holy smokes," I murmured. They really needed to pick a name and stick with it.

"My queen." A tall woman rose and bowed. "What happened to us? I awoke as if from unnatural slumber only to find others also waking near me. It is as if we froze in place."

"It has been too long, Maewyn. My heart sings to hear your words again." Cora embraced her. The other woman's eyes widened, and she seemed unsure what to do or how to respond.

"You've been asleep for decades," Conrad said.

The other elves looked at our group with frowns of confusion.

"Maewyn, please send word for everyone to gather at the castle." Cora sighed. "There is much to discuss."

"It's amazing," Max breathed. "Maeve must have used the Anchor Stone to keep everyone asleep."

Conrad nodded. "I wonder how, exactly."

"No bloody telling." Ambria shook her head. "That woman was pure evil."

Elyssa shuddered. "Everything from the reflected world creeps me out."

I nodded. "And they don't even have goatees."

Elyssa rolled her eyes. "You and your jokes."

"You'd look good with a goatee." I put a finger under her chin. "It'd feel nice and scratchy."

Ambria scoffed. "Men think they're so funny."

"We are funny," Max said. "Maybe you could grow a goatee and a sense of humor."

"How about I grow a fist, Max?" Ambria clenched her hand and held it up threateningly, but a smile crept through her stern look.

Max grinned back.

Conrad, as usual, ignored their banter. "For the first time in a long while, I feel hopeful."

I took a deep breath and nodded. "Yeah, me too."

Thomas walked among the gathering Glimmer folk, talking to some of them as he passed by. I imagined he was evaluating their abilities for his war plans. Unless they all had powers like Cora's, I didn't know how they'd help.

Within the hour, all the Glimmer folk were gathered in place. I didn't take the time for a headcount, but there were only a few hundred of them at the most. I imagined living in a world like the Glimmer didn't exactly encourage reproduction.

Cora told them everything they needed to know to bring them up to speed. Most of them were understandably shocked to learn everything that had happened during their long slumber. They seemed especially surprised to learn Cora had a child. That was when I realized I hadn't seen a single child among them. I wondered if the Glimmer wasn't just mental birth control, but physical as well.

Cora invited Thomas to give a brief speech which, in usual Thomas fashion, he limited to about five minutes. "I've spoken to many of you and believe your talents will be invaluable in our fight against Elohim. Our efforts could be the key to preserving billions of lives. I hope you'll consider joining."

Murmurs of assent rose from the assembly.

"I cannot order you to fight," Cora said. "It is not in our nature to use our talents for harm, but we may have no choice."

An elf in brown clothing raised a fist. "For too long we have survived in a realm that tried to erase our very existence. You have returned the sun and our lives to us. We will fight so all the realms might have a better life."

"Agreed!" a woman shouted.

More and more elves raised their fists in agreement until a great cheer broke out.

Cora smiled at Thomas. "We are the Glimmer folk no longer, but the elves of yore. You will have us by your side."

Thomas put a hand over his chest in the Templar salute. "We are honored. When you are ready, we will take you to Utopia where the rest of our forces have gathered."

"Gather the mithril and our bows," Maewyn shouted. "We defended our Earthly realm from dragons eons ago, and we can do it once again."

Max grinned and clapped his hands. "Can you believe it? Elohim won't know what hit him."

I wished I could share his enthusiasm, but even with the elves, the Sirens, and the rest of our forces on Utopia, this would be the hardest battle of our lives.

34

The next day, the elves gathered an impressive array of ancient weaponry that hearkened me back to my days of being a level twelve woodland elf when I was a LARPer and began handing them out to their hastily assembled army.

I touched one of the polished white bows and marveled at the electric tingle of magic imbued in it. "What's this made of?"

"Silver ore mixed with phoenix ashes and other exotic ingredients," Maewyn said. "We haven't created new weapons in eons since these last practically forever."

Elyssa tested the string of a bow, pulling it easily back and then releasing the tension. "It feels amazing."

Maewyn watched her appreciatively. "You are strong for a human."

Shelton strained to draw a string even an inch. "What the hell? It's like trying to pull a steel cable."

Maewyn notched a single arrow that looked as if it were made from the same ingredients as the bow. She pulled back the string, and let it fly. The arrow whistled out of sight in an instant. A moment later, arrow zipped back and thudded into the stone at our feet, penetrating it as if it were wood.

"Holy shit balls!" Shelton jumped back in surprise. "How'd you do that?"

"I can shoot the eye of a fly from a mile away." Maewyn smiled. "I can make an arrow weave through trees and strike a distant target."

"Magic arrows?" Shelton asked.

"That, and excellent aim." Maewyn watched as other elves handed out bows and silver mithril armor to those who'd volunteered to fight. "We will give the dragons the fight of their lives."

"Until you run out of arrows." Shelton shook his head. "I don't think there are enough arrows in the world to kill all of Elohim's dragons."

"Our arrows are virtually unbreakable." Maewyn took us to down a path to a large blank patch of earth where the Sirens had pieced the Anchor Stone back into the land. It looked terrible, but it made for an excellent shooting range.

Elven archers expertly downed all manner of flying objects that were being hurled by catapults for target practice. Maewyn went to the nearest catapult and gave them instructions. They launched a dozen clay discs at once. The discs spread apart, traveling in arcs away from each other.

Maewyn fired an arrow. It arced gracefully, shattering the first disc, diving to destroy the second, twisting up to strike the third, and continuing until all twelve discs were reduced to fragments. Maewyn signaled again. The catapult rotated as it fired consecutive discs into the air in all directions. Her hand a blur, Maewyn fired arrow after arrow, destroying twenty discs in a matter of seconds.

Elyssa watched her with her mouth hanging open. "Is it weird that I'm really turned on right now?" she whispered in my ear.

I snorted. "That was amazing."

Maewyn smiled at us. "I think our forces will prove quite capable, provided we have somewhere to stand while we fire."

Elyssa cleared her throat. "Are you comfortable riding Mzodi ships?"

"I'm not familiar with them."

"They're like water ships but they fly," Shelton said.

Maewyn's lips curled into a smile. "Sounds perfect."

I nodded. "We also have gepherons and gryphons if flying animals are a better fit."

"We would probably need training for flying beasts." Maewyn shrugged. "Two days should be plenty of time to learn."

Elyssa returned the elf's smile. "We can put you in touch with someone on Utopia to get that started." She motioned toward me. "Can you open a portal?"

I slashed one open to Solan.

It was Maewyn's turn to gasp when she saw the silver towers on the skyline. "You are truly powerful, Justin. Not even Cora can open gateways to other worlds."

Elyssa motioned the elf through the portal alongside her. "Once your forces are ready, we'll move them through a larger portal to this place."

Maewyn stepped through and looked up and around. "What an interesting city." She stared curiously at the carriages roaming the streets. "These vessels move themselves magically?"

Elyssa nodded. "Some do."

Shelton and I followed the pair through the portal and spent the rest of the day shadowing Elyssa as she showed Maewyn around the Utopian encampment and introduced her to various faction leaders.

Eventually, Elyssa and Maewyn took a pair of bat-like gepherons for a spin over the forest, leaving me and Shelton to wait.

Shelton sat down with a groan. "Remind me why I decided to come with you today? Your girlfriend doesn't stop for even a minute, does she?"

Something about that sentence really bugged me, but not in the usual way. "My girlfriend," I murmured.

He raised an eyebrow. "Something wrong?"

I frowned. "Yeah. Kind of?"

His mouth dropped open. "You've outgrown it, haven't you?"

"Outgrown what?"

"Girlfriend." He clapped my shoulder. "Damn, it's about time."

It suddenly occurred to me what he was talking about. "What in the actual hell took me so long to think about this?"

"Dude, we've been going non-stop for years. Elyssa is like a natural extension of your body by now." He snorted. "All you have to do is make it official."

I spotted Elyssa and Maewyn circling above on their gepherons and sighed. "Is marriage still a thing?"

Shelton grunted. "It just felt right to me. Maybe it's old fashioned and doesn't matter, but I wanted it and Bella wanted it." He looked me in the eye. "What do you want?"

The answer was already there. "I want to call Elyssa my wife now and forever more."

He nodded. "Just don't ask me to be your best man."

"Wait, what?"

Shelton laughed. "Just kidding, man. I'm in!"

When Elyssa and Maewyn eventually landed, Elyssa did a double-take when she saw me looking at her. "Justin, what's wrong?"

I couldn't stop grinning like an idiot at my raven-haired beauty. "I just love you is all."

Her eyes flared. "Yeah, do you?"

I walked over and kissed her long and hard. "To the end of the realms and back. Literally."

Elyssa glanced at Shelton then back at me. "What have you two been up to while we were gone? Did you blow up anything? Did you run off to fight the dragon army by yourselves?"

Shelton nodded. "We won. The universe is safe."

Elyssa mocked a sigh of relief. "Awesome! I never graduated nom high school, so I'm going to finally go back for that diploma."

I snorted. "Might as well just get your GED at this point."

She grinned back. "I gotta get into college somehow." Elyssa glanced at Maewyn who was talking to one of the gepheron trainers. "I've got a few things to tie up here, then we need to go back to the Glimmer. Thanks for being my personal chauffeur to the realms today."

"Anything for my hot ninja girlfriend." I kissed her cheek and let her get back to work.

Shelton sighed. "You know, we really don't do much around here, do we? We let Elyssa do all the busy work and then we just do what she says."

I nodded. "That's probably why we're still alive."

He chuckled. "Amen to that."

I spent the next two days ferrying Elyssa around while she coordinated the most massive army we'd ever gathered. The Overworlders —Templars, lycans, felycans, vampires, Daemos, and Arcanes were only a fraction of our forces. Utopians, fae, elves, Seraphim, and Sirens gave us an impressive array of options. The hardest part was figuring out how to make it all work in Atlantis, a realm that was mostly water, against an airborne dragon army.

On the third day, Thomas ended our final meeting in the war room with a grim announcement. "Though the Abyss and Anchor Stone were destroyed, the collapse continues. Dark matter fragments from the destroyed Abyss will collide with Utopia in two days. We cannot wait any longer to attack Olympus."

The other leaders on the council nodded in agreement. Colin McCloud slammed a fist on the table. "The lycans are in."

Saber, the massive man leading the felycans nodded his assent.

Kassallandra stood, her fiery red hair glowing with a life of its own. "The Daemos are ready to fight."

Mom stood next to her. "As are the Seraphim."

"We are tired, but willing and able." Vitania and Dactia rose together. "The Sirens will fight."

Lumia fluttered into the air on gossamer wings. "The fae are with you."

Magus Agula, Citizen Daana, and Scientist Elaine stood together and declared, "Utopia is ready for battle."

Xanos looked nervously at the others but did not rise from her chair. The Overworlders still had not forgiven her for her part in the destruction of our cities, even though they'd accepted that her assistance was necessary. "I am ready to help restore the balance."

"Too bloody late," Colin muttered.

Kassallandra put a hand on his shoulder. "Let us hope not."

Three quick knocks sounded on the door and a Templar stepped inside. "Commander Borathen, we have new arrivals."

Thomas nodded. "Allow them in one at a time."

A Wookie-sized creature covered in thick white hair entered. I flinched at the startled realization that one of the yeti people was right here in our war room.

"Thank you for the warm reception." The yeti female bowed. "I am Quanqua of the Sasquaeen. When we received your message of peace and aid from your ASE device, we could not sit idly by while evil worked to destroy our world. Though our population is small, we pledge ourselves to defeating Elohim and restoring the realms."

I started clapping and the other Overworlders joined. Quanqua looked startled at first, but then seemed to realize all that noise was a positive thing.

Thomas offered her a curt bow. "Welcome, Quanqua." There were no empty seats, so he motioned her toward him. "Please stand by me."

Shelton leaned toward me. "You're saying sending those ASEs to the other realms actually paid off?"

I nodded. "Apparently so."

A second being entered, this one a human-sized snake with arms. Visible alarm rippled across the room, but the creature didn't seem to care. He or she hissed repeatedly. A silver box hanging around the neck began speaking in a robotic female voice. "My name does not translate so I have picked one from the humans. Please call me Karen."

Shelton face-palmed. "They didn't warn her about that name?"

Adam's face turned red as he tried to hold in laughter.

Karen continued speaking. "My world is four days from collision with the matter from the Abyss. We did not even know of other realms until your device educated us. A prophecy on our world told of the end days, warning us that unless we accepted alien help, all would be doomed. Your device was the sign we had been waiting on."

She paused for a moment as if to let that sink in. "We are eager to fight for the salvation of our worlds."

Thomas motioned Karen to his side. "Welcome to the Overworld."

"Dude, this is epic." Adam shook his head in disbelief. "Am I dreaming or are we living the Star Wars dream?"

"More like Star Trek," Shelton hissed back.

Elyssa cast a stern look across the table at them and put a finger to her lips.

The last being to enter nearly gave Adam a nerdgasm. It was one of the humanoid lizard people from a realm we'd encountered during our search for Emily.

Adam squeed softly. "Holy crap, it's one of the baby Godzilla people."

There was no mistaking the similarities, though this fella didn't have spinal ridges.

He spoke slowly in Cyrinthian. "I am Trax of the Thossorians. Our world also faces imminent destruction. We will answer the call to fight by your sides however we can."

Thomas also motioned him over. "Welcome to the Overworld, Trax."

Shelton raised a hand. "Is everything the Overworld now?"

Thomas regarded him silently for a moment. "That is something we're considering. Unless we win the battle tomorrow, however, it will be a moot point."

"Agreed." Elyssa stepped up to the table and projected an image of Atlantis from an arctablet. "We have very little information about enemy deployments. Every ASE we've sent into Atlantis has stopped working shortly after. We have been unable to open portals anywhere within the borders of the pocket realm except for a very small area."

"This is the only place where portals work." She panned the map outward to a small sliver of black rock on the lower right side of the realm. "There is an island in the southeast quadrant bordering right on the Voltis event horizon. We've been able to scout the area and confirm that there is no dragon presence there. The island is nothing more than a mile-long slab of rock, but it will suffice as a staging area to assault Atlantis.

Elyssa dragged the view toward the island where the city of Atlantis stood. "Our first objective is Atlantis. We expect lighter resistance guarding the island since it's not Elohim's primary objective." She panned over further where holographic dragons filled the skies around the monolithic rock of Faux Olympus. "Once we've taken Atlantis, our forces will loop east and engage on the eastern side of Olympus, forcing the enemy to respond."

She highlighted a blip. "Sirens will take a small strike force deep underwater, unseen by Elohim's forces. Once at the base of the mountain, they will fly straight up, hopefully unseen since the battle will be on the other side. They will enter the chamber at the peak and use the quantum tunnel to enter the real Olympus. We don't think Elohim will have any dragons waiting on the real Olympus since the chamber with the secret entrance is too small for wyverns."

"A sound plan as always," Colin said. "We'll win the battle before they even know what you're up to."

Elyssa paused for more questions. Aside from a few comments, no one had any. She turned off the hologram. "I've sent the battle plans to your arc devices. Contact me if anything comes up."

Thomas nodded. "That is all."

The room hummed with multiple conversations as the meeting ended.

We filed outside and went across the hall into a large training room since the corridors were packed with newcomers.

"Dude, that was by far the biggest war council I've ever seen!" Adam stared at the hallway. "Sirens, fae, Seraphim, lizard people, snake people, yetis..." He shivered. "I wish we weren't all about to die tomorrow."

Shelton pursed his lips. "We can't go into battle without having pizza one last time."

"Amen to that," Adam said. "Let's go to Antico's."

"Sounds delightful." Max sidled up next to Shelton. "Is it true Americans like pineapple on their pizza?"

Shelton made a sign of the cross and hissed. "That's devil talk, kid. Never trust a pineapple-pizza person. They'll steal your soul."

"Lucky for you, Shelton, you don't have a soul to steal." Ambria smirked. "I think pineapple on pizza is perfectly acceptable."

Shelton snorted. "Sucks to be you then."

I frowned. "Uh, didn't you order Hawaiian pizza for Bella on pizza-taco night?"

"She's an exception." Shelton flourished his hands down his body. "She obviously has excellent taste in men, at least."

Adam snorted. "Bella must have issues if she likes pineapple pizza and Shelton."

Conrad grimaced. "The thought of tomato sauce and cheese with pineapples is atrocious."

"Oh, it is," Adam said.

Elyssa joined us. "Pizza talk again?"

"Naturally." Adam nodded at me. "Want to portal us to downtown?"

"I'd like to go." Nightliss squeezed into the group. "It's been too long since we've had a family outing."

I put an arm around Nightliss and kissed the top of her head. "I haven't seen you in a while."

She leaned against me. "I have been giving so many blessings lately that I do nothing else but eat and sleep."

"You know, I was thinking about finally taking you up on that offer for a blessing," Shelton said. "You sure it won't mess with my Arcane powers too much?"

Nightliss offered a tired smile. "There's no way to say for sure as it affects everyone with existing powers differently."

Adam clapped Shelton on the back. "At least you'll be able to run without huffing and puffing."

Michael stepped up behind Max, towering over him by a good margin. "Did someone mention pineapple pizza?"

Standing next to him, Phoebe grimaced. "Pineapple on pizza is sacrilege."

Michael shrugged. "I eat what I like."

"And it's nasty," Elyssa said with a grin.

Mom and Dad somehow fit into the circle. Dad rubbed his hands together. "Are the old folks invited?"

"Pizza, pizza!" Ivy and Evadora pushed past Max to squeeze inside the circle. "We want pizza!"

Shelton groaned. "Ain't no way this many people will fit inside Antico's."

Elyssa sighed. "I just finished planning a battle to save the universe. I suppose I could handle logistics for Shelton's pizza party."

Shelton beamed. "We're having a pizza party?"

She nodded. "One last moment of perfection before the end."

He shivered like an overexcited schoolboy. "I'm gonna get Bella. Guess you'd better order Hawaiian pizza for her and the other weirdos."

Adam watched him go. "Sometimes I wonder why we put up with him."

I snorted. "I don't want to be the group's lovable jackass."

"Just a plain old jackass, then?" Elyssa winked and kissed my cheek. "Let's get this party started."

She and I went into an empty conference room. Elyssa made calls to multiple pizza joints then directed a Templar to set up a dining area for the party. Fifteen minutes later, we went aboveground to find the back half of the barn ready to accommodate everyone. And by everyone, that included nearly everyone in the war room, including our new allies.

"We just had a taco and pizza party," Elyssa mused. "I think it must be our way of coping with the apocalypse."

I chuckled. "Wouldn't have it any other way." I tore open two portals at a time to concealed areas near the pizza restaurants, then Elyssa and I dashed through each one and picked up our orders then handed them off to Templars when we returned. The Templar soldiers arranged the pizzas on the tables in perfect order, then took up positions along the back wall, faces stoic and emotionless.

I approached one of them after Elyssa and I picked up the last pizzas. "You really want some of that pizza, don't you?"

She saluted, hand over chest. "Yes, I really do, Commander."

I chuckled. "Tell the others that you're off duty. Welcome to the party."

Her eyes flared gently. "Thank you, sir." Then she and her comrades hurried to get in line behind everyone else.

Shelton entered the barn a moment later and whooped. "Man, this is the biggest pizza party I've ever seen!"

Adam shrugged. "I'm pretty sure the one in Atlantis was the biggest, but whatever." He froze in place for a moment, then abruptly looked away.

I turned and saw his ex, Meghan, arm-in-arm with some guy I didn't recognize. "Oh, man, I'm sorry."

He forced a grin. "Ah, I don't even know why it bothers me. We were a bad match."

Shelton joined us. "Nosti, if there's one thing I love about you, it's that you always end up with women way out of your league and end up in some of the most disastrous relationships I've ever seen."

Adam frowned. "Thanks, I think?"

I noticed another tortured soul standing in a corner and decided to take mercy. "Be right back."

Xanos looked at me uncertainly as I approached. "I am sorry. I should probably not be here."

"You're here, and you're welcome to actually enjoy yourself despite the atrocities you committed."

Her eyes flared. "Why?"

"Because you're doing your best to make things right." I sighed. "Look, you can't un-murder people or wave a magic wand and repair all the damage you did to the Overworld, but you're doing the right thing now, no matter the reasons."

"Perhaps I just want revenge on Elohim for using me." Xanos straightened her shoulders. "Perhaps I want him gone so I can take over the world instead."

"Or maybe, just maybe, your time as a weak mortal made you realize just how fucking awful it is to be helpless in the face of anyone with powers." I crossed my arms and looked her dead in the eyes.

"Maybe there's a new voice inside that devious head of yours telling you to do whatever it takes to get that awful feeling out of your gut. To clean the blood off your stained soul."

"Maybe." She flinched as a tear pooled in her eye. "Perhaps the only thing my siblings and I lacked was a proper perspective." Xanos turned her gaze toward the barn entrance as Emily entered. "I believe it would have made me a better goddess. A better person."

"Or it might have made you like Olivia." I shrugged. "In the end, we're all responsible for our actions. God knows I haven't always made the right choices."

"Templars look at me as if they want to cut off my head." Xanos seemed to swallow a lump in her throat. "I cannot blame them."

I put a hand on her shoulder. "A lot of people here would like to beat the shit out of you, Xanos. Deal with it, or don't. At the very least, eat a slice of pizza and try to enjoy a moment, because some of us aren't coming home tomorrow."

She nodded. "You're right. Perhaps I will try a slice of the pineapple pizza. I've heard it's quite good."

I gagged. "It's certainly the pizza you deserve."

Xanos managed a tiny smile. "Thank you."

She walked to get in line with me and the rest of my friends. Elyssa visible restrained herself from scowling or casting murderous glares at Xanos. Despite the evils she'd wrought on our world, we needed her right now.

I spotted our new allies sitting at a table with Thomas. The yeti leader, Quanqua, was devouring her pizza while the lizard and snake people watched intently. I couldn't tell if they were fascinated or disgusted. A Templar brought them cages with live rabbits inside and it was my turn to recoil when Karen and Trax began swallowing them whole.

Shelton snorted. "Now that ain't something you see every day."

Bella smacked him on the ass. "Harry, mind your own business. You're holding up the line."

Before long, we got our pizza and found a table. My extended family had grown too large to fit but it was damned nice having everyone all in one place.

Conrad, Ambria, and Max sat with my parents, Ivy, and Evadora at a nearby table. Nightliss, Cinder, and the infernus, Issana, sat at another table with several Templars. Cinder still felt the loss of Bliss, but it probably helped him knowing her memories lived on in Nightliss.

I tried not to get too sentimental as I looked around the room. I tried not to think about who might not be with us at the next meal. Would it be me or one of my loved ones?

Elyssa put her hand on mine. "Justin, stop thinking about it and eat your pizza."

I smiled, nodded. "Okay." I ate my pizza, but I couldn't stop thinking about everything that might happen tomorrow.

The party was over around ten since everyone needed to be well-rested for the fight of our lives.

"I need to finalize battle plans with my father." Elyssa kissed my cheek. "I'll see you in a bit."

Shelton patted Bella's backside. "I know a great spot where we can stargaze and make whoopee."

"You're so romantic, dear." Bella hugged me. "Good night, Justin."

"Night, Bella." I munched on a pizza crust and watched them go. Before long, only the Templars cleaning up were left in the barn. I wasn't ready for bed, so I went out of the barn and headed toward the horse pasture so I could sit on the fence and contemplate life.

As I turned the corner around the back of the barn, I nearly ran into a couple making out hot and heavy.

Adam froze. "Uh, Justin, this isn't what it looks like."

The other person turned around and my mouth dropped open. "You're making out with Xanos?"

"H-he was nice to me when I was weak and mortal." Xanos looked away. "He is a good man."

"Yeah, he's a good man and he's—" I clamped my mouth shut before I said something stupid then opened it and finished. "And he's perfectly capable of making his own choices." Then again, Shelton had hit the nail on the head when it came to Adam's love life. He was batting so far out of his league that I had nothing to compare it to.

"Is it wrong for me to like her?" Adam said. "She's a lot nicer now."

I shrugged. "Maybe she's not the Apocryphan she used to be." I patted his shoulder. "Have fun, kids." I left them and jogged to the horse pasture which, as it turned out, was a mistake because in my haste I stepped in a pile of manure.

A horse neighed, probably laughing at my misfortune.

I climbed onto the fence and sat down. I could have portaled anywhere in the world, but there was just something about this place that calmed my soul. Probably because it was the closest place I had to home. The Mansion near Arcane University had been that place for a while, but it hadn't been quite the same since Daelissa destroyed it, forcing us to move to a replica underground.

Now that the replica and the mansion above it had been destroyed, we were rebuilding yet again. Provided we survived tomorrow, maybe it would become our home again, or maybe it wouldn't. I had no idea.

I heard footsteps and turned to see who was coming. Nightliss smiled and climbed up next to me on the fencepost. "I knew I would find you here, Justin."

I chuckled. "Something about fighting supernatural wars just makes me want to sit on a fence."

She leaned her head on my shoulder. "This will be a battle unlike anything we've fought before."

"The only reason we stand a chance is that Elohim is still hopefully injured from his fight against Eve. Otherwise, I think we're screwed."

"Yes, you are probably right." Nightliss sighed. "But at least we tried our best."

I just hoped our best was good enough, or the billions of humans on Eden would never see the end coming.

I switched subjects. "Did you see Xanos and Adam?"

She smiled and nodded. "I think Xanos will enjoy herself."

I nearly fell off the fencepost in surprise. "Wait—no. Really?" My brain refused to make the connection, but I'd already glimpsed it. "Have you and Adam..." I couldn't finish the sentence.

"Adam and I saw each other for a while." Nightliss smiled softly. "He is handsome and quite gifted in certain areas."

I felt a little light-headed. "Wow. How in the hell does he do it?"

"Do what?" she asked innocently.

"Our resident nerd went from dating Meghan to the legendary Nightliss and now he's with Xanos!" I threw up my hands. "Who's next, Eve?" I grimaced immediately, having momentarily forgotten she was dead.

Nightliss patted my hand. "Adam is a good man, but he spends far too much time in his own little world to nurture a relationship. I knew it would not last, but I enjoyed it while I could."

I sighed and put an arm on her shoulder. "Well, you're a grown-ass Seraphim, so you know what's best for you."

"Not really." She laughed. "And that is what I love about life."

I sighed again but a little louder. "Too bad Elohim thinks he knows what's best for everyone." Anger and frustration filled me. Tomorrow we'd throw thousands of lives against an army of mindless beasts while their masters, Elohim and Drakara, sat back and watched us die. My emotions morphed to rage.

"We had no idea what's waiting in Atlantis or on Faux Olympus." I shook my head. "We need to know, because knowing is more than half the battle."

"Yes, but the ASEs die quickly once they near Atlantis." Nightliss shrugged. "I'm certain Elyssa will send scouts ahead of the army tomorrow."

"There must be better way." I hopped down and began scribing symbols in the air. "We don't know anything about what's waiting for us."

"Justin, perhaps you shouldn't do anything rash." Nightliss jumped down next to me. "Elyssa will not be happy."

"I'm just going to poke around a bit. Don't worry." I concentrated on an image and opened a portal. An island illuminated by bright moonlight spread out before me on the other side. It was little more than a long plateau of rock so close to the edge of Voltis that Elohim's portal blockers didn't work there.

Nightliss gripped my arm. "Justin, don't go."

"I just want a peek." I stepped through, summoned my Apocryphan powers, and took to the skies. Green energy glowed around me, lighting me up like a beacon in the night sky. I channeled an illusion to mask it or else this would be a very short trip.

I soon encountered the first signs of the dragon invasion. Massive pedestals with molten wreckage atop them were all that was left of the turrets the Atlanteans had installed to protect their borders. They obviously hadn't done much good in the end.

I sensed a faint vibration as I flew within view of one. My comm badge crackled and sparked. I tugged it off my uniform and examined it. It was completely shorted out which was strange since it used arcnology to function. Even the massive malaether wave that had killed Nookli hadn't put in a dent in the hardened enchantments protecting this device.

Something told me the faint vibrations I felt had something to do with it.

My demon vision revealed ghostly ripples emanating from the husk of the destroyed turret. I silently flew around the large metallic shell and discovered the source: a brown reptile curled up inside, seemingly asleep. It more closely resembled a stegosaurus than a dragon. Energy waves emanated from metallic spikes along the creature's head and back. It had no wings which meant it must have been airlifted here by other dragons.

Even my dulled wits had no trouble putting two and two together. That creature was able to short out military-grade arcnology. It was no wonder the ASEs kept dying. But that wasn't even the worst of it. The Mzodi ships, flying brooms, Templar platforms, and most of our equipment relied on arcnology to function.

Half our fleet would fall from the sky the moment they flew within range of the electrosaur. I mentally high-fived myself for coining the name even as I despised the reptilian bastards it represented. I flew to neighboring turrets and discovered electrosaurs nesting in them as well. The EMP waves blanketed the perimeter. There was no way our vessels could fly high enough to avoid them.

The electrosaurs appeared to be heavily armored with thick, bony plates. They might be hard to kill with weapons, but their armor was also their weakness. If I spawned into demon form and rolled them out of the turret shells and into the ocean, they'd probably sink like rocks.

I resisted the temptation and thought it through. If wyverns patrolled this area, they'd quickly discover the missing electrosaurs and know an attack was imminent. Surprise wouldn't be a huge advantage, but we needed every little advantage we could get.

I patted myself on the back for not acting impetuously even though this entire exercise was an impetuous decision, and flew onward to Atlantis. The island was completely dark, no street lights, nothing shining from buildings. There wasn't a soul to be seen as I flew over the streets, only the slumbering forms of drakes around the harbor and an occasional wyvern.

Aside from copious amounts of dragon shit, the buildings looked undamaged and I saw no signs of bloodshed. Either Adonis had peacefully given up the city, or the people had evacuated in time.

I headed north toward Olympus. About a mile out, I spotted hundreds of platforms floating on the ocean, each of them bearing countless wyverns. I dodged around a patrol and Faux Olympus finally came into sight.

My mouth dropped open at what I saw. The plan was already a bust.

35

I hovered in place, unable to conceive the power it had taken to make our plans moot. Everything hinged on drawing the dragon forces to the eastern side of Faux Olympus so Vitania and a small group could travel underwater, then covertly fly unseen up the western side of the mountain to the chamber at the peak.

Once in the chamber, Vitania would open the hidden gateway and we'd be scot free to do our business in the primal fount. Drakara or Elohim had apparently foreseen such a plot and obliterated the entire top quarter of Faux Olympus. Where the chamber had once been was nothing but open air.

Another mountain had seemingly grown not far from Olympus, craggy black peaks glistening in the moonlight. But this was no mountain—it was the back of Drakara, the mother of dragons, her ridges jutting from the ocean.

I turned tail and headed back to the small island in the southeast so I could open a portal and go home. Elyssa was going to be pissed about my little stunt, but this new information was critical. The plan to fight our way to the mountain and insert a team wasn't going to work anymore because the quantum tunnel to the realm Olympus was somewhere up in the air.

Even with camouflage, it would be nearly impossible to reach the area and find the quantum tunnel before dragons blasted us from the sky. To make matters worse, Drakara was sitting right next to it.

Moments later, I reached the island. I landed and slashed open a portal back to the ranch. Once through, I closed it.

Nightliss breathed a sigh of relief and hugged me. "You were gone for so long!"

"It didn't seem like that long." I reached for Nookli and remembered once again she was gone, her lifeless husk sitting on Adam's workbench. Even if she'd been functional before this side mission, the electrosaur waves would have killed her. "We've got some serious problems and I need to tell Elyssa right away."

We went back to the main house and found Elyssa and her family in the den.

Her mother Leia looked up from an arctablet. "Justin, you look worried."

Elyssa looked from me to Nightliss and back to me. "Justin, what did you do?"

I cleared my throat nervously. "So, this might sound really stupid, but you'll be happy I did it."

Elyssa rose to her feet. "Nightliss, did he leap without looking?"

"I'm afraid so." Nightliss sighed. "I tried to stop him."

Thomas regarded me icily. "I hope nothing happened that will compromise our plans."

"Oh, our plans are compromised big time." I held up a hand to ward off further questions and told them what I'd found. "There's no way we're getting to the quantum tunnel to Olympus unseen. Unless we defeat the entire dragon army, I don't know how we'll pull this off."

"We need to take out every last one of those electrosaurs." Michael grunted. "If they hide one of those in the middle of an attack wave, it could take out a fleet of Mzodi ships."

"They don't have wings," I said. "And they look too big for a single wyvern to lift, so they'd probably be easily visible."

Phoebe pursed her lips. "They might have them on those floating platforms around Olympus. At least we know what disabled our ASEs."

Thomas nodded. "We might have to delay another day to think this through."

"We've got three realms just a couple of days away from collision with the dark matter from the Abyss," Elyssa said. "We can't afford to delay."

Phoebe took out an arctablet and projected the current battle plans. "Come on, sis. Let's work our magic."

Elyssa looked at me and shook her head. "Justin, I don't know what I'm going to do with you. That was reckless and foolish."

"On the other hand, he might have saved us from immediate defeat." Nightliss shrugged. "We would have no chance without this information."

"True," Thomas said. "Let's find out how to use it."

"Well, I'm gonna go to bed then." I was too hyped up to be tired, but watching them plot battle plans was the last thing I wanted to do. I had one more stop to make.

"Good night, Justin." Nightliss kissed my cheek then took a seat next to Elyssa.

I kissed Elyssa and headed outside toward the barn. I went around to the back and opened another portal, this time to El Dorado. I stepped through and into the vast cave where Altash and Lulu had once lived. We'd encountered Lulu on Seraphina just before we'd made our way back to Eden and this was the only place I might have a chance to contact them again.

"Altash!" I shouted. "Lulu! We need your help!"

My voice echoed through the darkness. I cast balls of light overhead and headed across the cave to the tunnels bored by earth dragons. I wandered through the tunnels for over an hour, shouting their names and hoping for some response. But it was hopeless. They were no longer there. For all I knew, they were on Seraphina.

A pair of red orbs glowed in the distance of the current tunnel, growing larger and closer at incredible speed. I cast a light, revealing a dark blue earth dragon about the size of a bus. It was small by Altash's standards, but plenty big enough to eat a man whole.

The scars on the scaly hide immediately told me who it was. "Slitheren, is that you?"

Yes. His slithery voice sounded in my head and it was a whole lot quieter than Altash's, thankfully.

"Boy, am I glad to see you." I looked him over. "You've really grown."

It has been years since our last encounter. What brings you to my domain?

Oh, I had plenty of stories to tell him, but there simply wasn't time for it. I had one thing I needed to know. "Where are Altash and Lulu? A final battle is coming, and we need all the help we can get."

They travel the realms gathering forces to fight Drakara.

"Can you contact them?"

He regarded me with his parietal eyes. *Why do you sound so urgent?*

"Because we're attacking Drakara's forces tomorrow and we need all the help we can get." I tried to keep my voice a bit calmer, but it wasn't easy. "We have a chance to stop the collapse, but we have to reach the primal fount on Olympus. Elohim is doing everything in his power to stop us."

Then I will do my best to find them quickly.

"How?" I threw up my hands. "If they're travelling through other realms, they won't be easy to find."

I am old enough to make portals now. He opened his mouth and a gout of energy burst from the glowing maw, tearing a hole in the quantum fabric. The world on the other side was a wasteland of ash. Gray smoke billowed from a volcano in the distance. The reek of brimstone tickled my nose. It was close to the sulfurous odor of Hell and Haedaemos, but different in some way. *That is Draxadis, the realm of dragons. It was once beautiful, but Drakara's insatiable desire to create an army of pure dragons overcrowded it. Drakes and wyverns depleted the supply of food and burned forests to blackened earth.*

"I recently met the original mother of dragons." I peered through the gateway for a better look at the wasteland. "Why did Altash never tell me about the drygon?"

Probably because he considered it unimportant. Slitheren arched as if shrugging. *He is not the best at communicating.*

"That's for damned sure." I pulled my head back from the portal. "Why did you show me Draxadis?"

So you would understand what Drakara's forces are capable of. If they leveled an entire world, then your army does not have much of a chance.

I nodded. "It's not the first time we've faced insurmountable odds and mounted them."

Slitheren tilted his head slightly. *I will depart immediately and search for them. Where can we find you if I am successful?*

"Either Utopia or Atlantis." I gave him the quantum symbols for the precise coordinates. "Good luck."

He slithered through the portal and it closed behind him.

It was literally the longest conversation I'd ever had with an earth dragon, or at least it felt that way. I wondered what allies Altash was searching for. Were there more earth dragons, or was he expanding his criteria, drafting beings from other races as well? We were going to need every ounce of firepower to win tomorrow's battle.

I portaled back to the Ranch and went back to the horse pasture so I could think long and hard about anything and everything that could possibly go wrong. Max's traitorous father and brother had tried to blow up our war council just before we fought Xanos and it had nearly ended the Overworld. We couldn't afford another last-minute betrayal this time.

It seemed unlikely Xanos would plot against us since Elohim would never allow her to join his side. With Olivia and Cain dead and his infernus network out of his control, Elohim had few human resources left to him. I also doubted he'd try an all-out dragon attack on Eden. Keeping the mortals in the dark about the supernatural was to everyone's benefit.

Am I missing anything, Kalesh?

He responded a few seconds later. *Sorry, I am very busy. No I don't think we are missing anything. I am working on a backup plan with the infernus, though.*

Good. I have a feeling we'll need all the backup plans we can muster.

Tomorrow could be the end of us all.

THERE WAS HARDLY a soul to be seen in the compound the next morning. The Templars had portaled to Utopia overnight, leaving only a skeleton crew behind. Shelton and Bella were already eating in the cafeteria when I arrived.

He grunted when he saw me. "Did the war start without us?"

I shook my head. "The battle was planned on Utopian Eastern time, and its' not morning there yet."

"How confusing." Bella paused eating. "What time is it in Atlantis right now?"

"Atlantis is minus four GMT, so the attack won't happen until early afternoon their time." I reached for Nookli and sighed when I once again remembered she was dead.

Shelton eyes settled on something behind me and flared. "Jesus Henrietta Christopher on a three-legged mule in a shrimp factory. You've got to be kidding me."

I spun and saw Adam and Xanos entering the cafeteria, hand-in-hand. "I know he's headed for terrible heartbreak, but he's the kind of guy who gives hope to all nerds in the world."

"Adam has always dated stunning women." Bella flashed a smile at him. "I'm happy for him."

"This takes dating out of your league to a whole new level." Shelton stood and gave Adam a pointed look. "Did you drug her?"

Xanos frowned. "No, I went willingly with him."

Shelton rolled his eyes. "It was a joke."

"Oh." Xanos nodded. "I never understood human humor very well, but that is because I lived most of my life aloof. I did not stoop to forming bonds with other beings because I was so focused on proving my superiority."

"She's been alone most of her life." Adam kissed her hand. "This is kind of new for her."

Bella's mouth dropped open. "Xanos, you've never been with a male being?"

"I have been with Seraphim and tridents, but humans were repugnant to me." She gave Adam an adoring look. "I did not realize how well endowed—"

"Enough!" Shelton held up his hands in surrender. "Can we eat and go fight dragons? Because I don't want to hear another word about what happened between you two."

Adam snorted. "I'll text you some pics later."

"No!" Shelton held up a fist. "Your new girlfriend might be a demigoddess, but I will strike your ass down if I get a single dick pic."

"Ah, this is quite unexpected." Cinder appeared behind Adam. "It is a good thing Eve shrank Xanos, or your physiology would have been most awkward."

I snorted. "I mean, not if Adam is well endowed."

"Yeah, her boobs were bigger than my head last time." Shelton flinched as if realizing he was going back into territory he'd just walled off. "Never mind."

Cinder pulled a slim wooden box from his pocket and handed it to me. "Justin, I hope you will feel more comfortable going into battle with an old friend."

I looked at the box and frowned. "An old friend? What do you mean?"

"Open it and see."

I undid the clasp on the side of the box and flipped it open. I gasped. "Is it really her?" I slid out the contents and found the familiar battle scars on the back. "Is she alive?"

Cinder nodded. "Yes, she is."

I tapped the side and Nookli blinked to life. "Nookli!" I kissed her screen and hugged her. "It really is you!"

"Hello, Justin. There is an Indian restaurant three miles from here." The map app appeared and plotted a course. "Marvin T. Jenkins from Yelp recommends the extra spicy rabbit."

"Yes!" I held her aloft and twirled. "After this war, we're eating Indian food!"

Shelton grimaced. "Ain't no power on earth that'll make me follow Nookli's eating recommendations."

I turned to Cinder and hugged him. "Thanks so much."

He hugged me awkwardly and backed away. "Thankfully, there was just a shorted-out connection, and nothing was lost."

"I thought for sure the EMP from the malaether had killed her for good."

"I must admit I had another reason for repairing Nookli." Cinder took out his phone and projected a holograph filled with scrolling lines of code and charts. "Your phone's sensors recorded the malaether buildup during Emily and Olivia's fight. Had Conrad been unsuccessful at curing her condition, I believe I could now fashion an aether filter that would have mitigated her problem, provided the power levels remained below a certain threshold."

"Dude, that's awesome." Adam zoomed in on the data. "Would this also counteract interdiction fields better than the pendants we currently use?"

"Interdiction fields operate on a different principle." Cinder turned off the display and tucked his arcphone into a pocket. "They corrupt the malaether which sickens those trying to channel or cast magic."

"Ah, I see." Adam raised an eyebrow. "What does this one do, exactly?"

"This program creates a field that filters malaether, thus preventing a buildup." Cinder shrugged. "I was able to reverse-engineer the problem by first using the code to create a corruption field to simulate Emily's problem. Any magic use within this field would cause a malaether eruption equal to the power used."

Adam nodded. "Brilliant as usual."

"Thank you." Cinder clasped his hands at his waist. "It only took a slight alteration of the code."

"Maybe you should do less talking and more eating." Shelton

dropped back into his chair. "We don't want to be late for the dragon war and all that."

Adam grinned. "Sorry, I wasn't expecting a nerdgasm this early in the morning."

I winked. "Surprised he can have a gasm of any kind after what he and Xanos did last night."

Bella giggled and Adam guffawed.

Xanos looked perplexed. "Humor is a rather weak area for me." She looked at Cinder. "Scientific curiosity and intelligence, however, are of great interest."

"You've come up with some fascinating, though morally questionable devices," Cinder said. "You, Adam, and I could have many interesting conversations."

"Three-way!" I shouted, then ran toward the food counter before Shelton could punch me.

We finished breakfast and I portaled our group of laggards to the staging area on Utopia. My jaw nearly hit the ground when I stepped through the gateway.

A fleet of sleek, black Mzodi sky ships hovered in place before the massive bulk of the *Uorion*, the capital ship of their leader, the Muhala Kajeen. The *Falcheen*, a ship I'd called home for some time, was in the lead with the other battleships.

Rivalling the size of the *Uorion* was a pair of saucer-shaped UFOs that could have been clones of the secret base in Antarctica we'd destroyed during the Crystoid Incident. Dozens of smaller vessels were parked alongside the motherships. Countless other people jetted overhead on silver rocket sticks. Phoebe had been more than successful in getting Science Academy operational and ready for battle.

Shelton and Adam were speechless, probably having simultaneous nerdgasms. Bella gasped and spun in a circle to take it all in. I summoned my Apocryphan powers and jetted straight up for a better look. It was even more amazing to see the diverse array of our forces from altitude.

Yeti with long rifles stood around a fleet of gunmetal-gray rocket sleds. Humanoid bird people with hawk heads and large wings stood nearby in loose formation. They must have been late additions to the party because I hadn't seen them last night. Lizard people rode the backs of pterodactyls while the snake people rode winged anacondas.

The Utopian humans had assembled a massive gryphon and gepheron air force that also included elven archers. Smaller Mzodi ships carried a dozen or so archers each. The Utopian magi, their magic users, weren't among these forces. I spotted them in their distinctive robes among the Mzodi on the larger battleships.

The colorful fae army was like a bright spot in the midst of black and gray uniforms. Not only were their clothes bright and festive, but they rode the backs of the giant bees. Glacia perched on the largest one of all, the queen bee, if I had to guess. I was shocked to see Pyra riding a bee as well and wondered if all the fae would have blood on their hands after this battle.

As I took in the massive array of forces, a familiar face lodged in my vision like a splinter. It seemed we were so desperate we'd drafted another old enemy to fight for us. I zipped down to the transport ship carrying him and scowled at the man who'd nearly ruined Utopia with his dark magic.

Vokan glared at me. "It seems I must not only die this day, but be tormented by seeing the impetuous imp who defeated me at the peak of my power."

I glared back. "Taking people's souls and consuming them for power is bad, mkay?"

"I am a hundred times more powerful than those fools even without the power of my cantraps." He waved contemptuously at the magi on the other ships. "They have even given me my own transport."

Probably because the instant he was identified as the greatest threat, the dragons would focus on him. I didn't tell him that, of course. I wanted him to be brimming with confidence, so I blew even more smoke up his ass. "Vokan, you are the greatest magus of all time and this will be the greatest battle man has ever seen. We've had our differences in the past, but I'm glad you're fighting by our side."

He grunted and looked mollified. "I have bargained for my freedom once we prove victorious. Pray we never meet again after this glorious day."

I forced a grin. "That'll be at the top of my prayer list, believe me."

"Justin, where are you?" Elyssa's voice sounded over my comm badge. "Report to the command center right away."

It seemed my girlfriend was ready to get this war going.

36

I flew through the dizzying array of allies and could not, for the life of me, find the Templar command platform. I spotted Templar patrols among grounded Mzodi ships and flew toward them. In their midst, I saw one of the most glorious sights I'd ever seen.

A massive gray vessel sat in the middle of a group of Mzodi battle-cruisers. It could have easily passed for a Borg cube except for the giant red Templar crosses on the sides. It seemed the Mzodi had given the Templar command platform a massive upgrade. Shelton's design suggestions for the fleet were pretty evident considering that a few vessels resembled Klingon and Starfleet warships as well. I just hoped he wasn't opening us up for copyright infringement lawsuits.

I flew toward the Templar command cube™ and a door with a red Templar cross slid open to admit me. A levitator shaft took me up to the bridge on the third floor. A large hologram in the center of the room displayed three-dimensional map and color-coded blips for every unit in our armada wearing a comm badge.

Templars stationed around the room monitored smaller holograms, relaying commands from faction leaders to the units under their direct control. It was the ultimate setup for a real-time strategy game, not that many of the Templars would even know what that was.

Symbols next to the levitator shaft told me that the level below us was weapons control, and the first floor was cargo space for troop and heavy equipment deployment. It was an impressive setup.

A yeti, lizard man, snake woman, and bird being of unknown gender occupied stations as well, presumably since they could translate orders into their own language. All the other personnel were Templars. I imagined it took a lot of trust for our new allies to accept commands from people they'd only recently met. Then again, maybe the ASEs bearing our message of greeting and desperation had paid off even better than we'd hoped.

Cutsauce trotted over. *I wanted to fight, but they won't give me a flying broom!*

I knelt and scratched his ears. "Can't you morph into human form?"

He growled. *I am still weak from having Saila torn from me. No matter how much I sleep, I feel as if a part of me is gone.*

"Saila's spirit lived inside you and literally mutated you into an Apocryphan pooch." I shook my head. "She was an integral part of what you've become."

I hope that doesn't mean I will go back to being a basic hound.

"I think you'll be fine. You just need time." I rose to my feet. "I've got to go. Keep everyone safe, okay?"

Cutsauce bared his teeth. *No dragon will get past me.*

I repressed a grin and saluted him.

Elyssa, Thomas, Vitania, and other faction leaders sat or stood near the central hologram. I struggled to remember the names of our new allies and failed. Then again, I couldn't even remember what their people called themselves. Thankfully, no one relied on my diplomatic skills.

Elyssa marched over and pulled me aside. "Justin, I don't feel good about this. We had to throw together a plan in light of your new intel and haven't had any time to run it through simulations."

I frowned. "You can usually throw together a plan and have it running smoothly in an hour."

"I don't usually have four new species from alien realms joining at the last minute." She stared out the window at the army. "There's serious lag between the test orders I give and the translations before their troops respond. Those lost seconds could be the difference between life and death."

I nodded and gave it some thought. "How complex are the orders?"

"That depends on how badly the battle plan shits the bed when the fight starts." She pursed her lips. "If things go close to plan, then the orders are straightforward. If things go wrong, then we've got to issue new commands on the fly and have each one translated."

"Use icons, then." I flourished Nookli with a proud grin and ran a search for one of my favorite real-time strategy video games.

Elyssa gasped. "Nookli is alive?"

I held back tears of joy. "Yep, thanks to Cinder."

"Wow, he's a real Miracle Max."

I found what I was looking for and projected a chart of icons for various formations and movements used in the video game. "Instead of sending text commands, you could utilize icons like this, or even a combination of them for more complex movement commands."

Elyssa studied it for a moment and nodded. "It's basically an expanded version of hand signals. I know exactly how to apply this." She copied the images and began tapping on her arcphone. Moments later, she tucked away her phone. "I sent that to the coordinators to finalize the codes. If it works, we might save a lot of lives."

"Or possibly none if the dragons kill us all."

Elyssa sighed. "True. We don't even know the full extent of the dragon forces, but we suspect the odds are at least ten to one."

I gulped. "This is Sparta?"

"Except over two hundred thousand dragons are the ones defending a single objective." Her gaze lost focus. "Justin, this might be the last time we see each other in this life."

A knot caught in my throat. "Don't talk like that. At least if we die, we've got the afterlife."

"For how long?" Elyssa bit her lower lip. "Vitania thinks there's a chance it'll be wiped out or reset when all the realms collide at the zero point."

"Then we'll enjoy whatever time we have left no matter what." I pulled her to me and pressed my lips desperately against hers. We gasped for breath when I finally pulled away. "I can never get enough of you, Elyssa. I love you as much now as I loved you at the start. I refuse to let you be taken from me by a dragon army and their god."

A tear trickled down her cheek. "When you put it like that, how can a girl be afraid of anything?"

I laughed. "You've saved me more times than I've saved you."

She booped my nose. "True. So it's your turn." Elyssa kissed me again. Her hot tears warmed my skin. She pulled away, wiping her face. "Justin, just be careful with your Apocryphan powers. Don't overdo it."

"I won't, babe." I swallowed the lump in my throat. "How much time do we have before launch?"

She checked the time. "Thirty-two minutes."

"Long enough." I slashed open a portal to our bedroom and pulled her through before she could resist, then closed it behind us.

She shoved me on the bed, leapt on me and kissed me until I ran out of breath. We deactivated the Nightingale armor. Elyssa was naked underneath. I wore my favorite banana-shark underwear because I didn't like being commando in anything. She snorted in amusement and yanked them off. "At least you'll die in your favorite underwear."

I nodded. "Elohim can never take that away from me."

We made love, and it was as amazing as the first time we'd done it in a rundown hotel room after battling Vadaemos. We took a quick shower, had a quickie in the shower, then returned to the Templar command cube with two minutes to spare.

Thomas raised an eyebrow when we stepped through the portal. I blushed. Elyssa blushed. The corners of his lips rose in what passed for extreme amusement from him. He left the command table and approached me. "Are you ready, son?"

I was speechless for a moment at this rare moment of familiarity. "I am, sir."

He held out a hand.

I took it, gave it a squeeze and a shake. "Is something wrong, sir?"

"I'm just taking a moment." Thomas released my hand and gave Elyssa a hug. "A moment before the storm that could end everything."

Fear glinted in Elyssa's eyes. "Dad, we can do this."

He nodded and his face became impassive once more. "I know. I'm just following advice someone gave me a long time ago."

I vaguely remembered telling him he should relax and enjoy life a time or two, but I wasn't sure if he was talking about me. "This is the biggest army we've ever assembled. I've never seen so many realms united."

"At least not since the Apocryphan were banished." Thomas returned to the table, once again all business. "Operation Olympus commences now. All units report ready."

The coordinators below relayed the command to all stations. Gray blips on the holographic screen turned green in rapid order.

Thomas tapped the controls on an arctablet. "Portal control prepare for countdown."

"Portal control reports ready, Grand Commander," a voice replied over the central communications console.

Thomas turned to Elyssa. "Commander Borathen, count us down."

Elyssa tapped her arctablet. "Five, four, three, two, one, activate."

The portal generator, a tiny ring on the savannah below, glowed. An instant later, a portal the likes of which I'd never seen ripped open across the horizon, revealing the rocky tableau of the small island south of Atlantis.

"Holy farting fairies," I breathed. "How much aetherite did Cinder load onto that thing?"

"A lot," Elyssa said.

Thomas peered out the main window. "All units, forward."

Mzodi warships took the lead, flanked by the Science Academy motherships, airships, and rocket stick riders. The yeti sleds rose into the air and followed a moment later, along with the bird, lizard and snake people. I really needed to look up their proper names again, because that was a mouthful.

The cube lifted off and shifted forward, keeping us in formation in the center. Despite all the flying units, we had a good number that were ground-based. Those marched through the portal and took positions on the island, installing defenses in case of a retreat.

Sirens on their water dragons glided to our right. Arturo and his archangels rode a special Mzodi ship designed for them and other Seraphim in Daskar flying armor. They numbered in the hundreds, a pitiful amount considering the odds. Other Seraphim rode flying brooms, members of the greatly expanded Skywraiths.

I spotted a few familiar faces among them and flashed back to the bad old days of the war against Daelissa. The odds had been massed against us then too, but this was no ordinary battlefield. We had no firm ground beneath us, only open ocean. The enemy had superior air units and nearly unlimited firepower.

It would almost be a mercy to have to fight Daelissa's goliaths once again.

The archangels shot ahead of the fleet on their mission to disable the electrosaurs. Unless they were dealt with, our fleet would fall apart.

Vitania stepped back from the command table. "I'm ready, Justin."

I cast one last look at Elyssa and nodded. "Let's do this."

Vitania and I climbed a ladder and emerged through the top hatch on the cube. Vitania's water wyvern landed and knelt atop the cube. We climbed on her back and took to the sky. The massive roiling storms of Voltis commanded the southern horizon, curving east and west as far as the eye could see. The vista was broken only by the massive portal and the army flying through it. Vitania guided her mount west, skirting the storm wall, but keeping us well away from the tumultuous winds that could smash us to bits.

The rest of our forces continued northeast, a course that would take them over Atlantis and headlong into the dragon army. I hated watching them go, but this plan had the most chance of success.

Three more water dragons separated from the Siren formation, each one bearing two riders. Dolpha rode with Emily, Narine with Conrad, and Balaena with Xanos. None of our heaviest hitters would be there to fight with the others. Despite the top of Olympus being sheared off, we were going ahead with the covert option, drawing away enemy forces and sneaking through the door while they were away.

Without a visible or audible signal from Vitania, the wyverns dove in unison nearly straight down toward the ocean. Conrad's eyes flared. Emily cried out and gripped Dolpha tighter. Xanos watched grimly, as if resigned to whatever fate awaited.

The water rushed to meet us. I held my breath and prepared for impact, but we dove beneath the surface as easily as traveling through air. My clothes, my hair, everything was wet, but I didn't feel wet at all. I was so surprised I took a breath. Instead of water rushing into my lungs, I inhaled without issue. Bubbles trailed from my lips when I exhaled.

The others looked equally shocked. It was apparently such old hat to the Sirens that they didn't even seem to consider the trauma of tossing land creatures straight into the deep end of the pool.

We continued into the dark depths. The water around us began to glow, lighting the way, though Vitania seemed to automatically know where we were going. We swam through a massive school of fish, alongside massive whale-like creatures, and over a graveyard of ancient ships, probably remnants of the original Atlantis fleet.

We slowed as we reached a series of underwater ravines. Dolpha met Vitania's gaze and nodded. Vitania turned to me. "I will be back." She thrust herself off the dragon and jetted away so fast, I barely had time to register what had happened.

"What is she doing?" I called out. Though I could breathe just fine, my words were somewhat muted as if the water still tried to silence me.

Dolpha turned to me. "Securing a last resort just in case."

"And that would be?"

She shook her head. "We are sworn to secrecy on the matter."

Conrad frowned. "Now is a bad time to be keeping secrets." He turned to the other Sirens, but none broke their silence.

Emily waved her hand in the water, as if trying to understand the paradox of speech and breathing. "What kind of magic allows us to breathe and talk underwater?"

"We are extending our auras to you," Balaena said. "If you were to swim too far away from us, the water pressure would crush you."

"Even her?" Xanos scoffed. "Emily is practically a goddess."

"Oh, it might not kill her, but it would be agonizing," Balaena said in a cheery voice.

"I don't wish to test the theory." Emily shrugged. "I could make another shield bubble anyway."

I felt a bit anxious and sick to my stomach just thinking of the walls of water all around us, so I kept talking to keep my mind off of it. Vitania returned moments later, face impassive, and boarded her dragon.

"Well, were you successful?" I asked.

"We shall see." She turned to the others. "The fleet should be in sight of enemy forces now. By the time we reach our objective, the battle should be underway."

Emily bit her lower lip. "I'm so bloody nervous. How are we to find the exact location of the quantum tunnel without the mountain top to guide us?"

"I have plotted the approximate location," Vitania said. "I make a habit of measuring interesting things, and Olympus is one of them. The hidden tunnel was near the top center. That means I will have about twenty meters of space to search. At most, it will take me one minute per meter."

"If the enemy didn't take the bait, then we've got to hold position for up to twenty minutes?" Xanos shook her head. "Let us hope the ploy worked."

Vitania nodded. Without another word, the dragons shot forward again. The landmass of Atlantis came into view, a dark wall to our right. We circled the island and glided above a sunken city, the other parts of Atlantis that had fallen into the ocean after the Sundering. Crumbling walls and buildings continued for miles until we reached the base of Faux Olympus.

Vitania narrowed her eyes and nodded. "It is time."

The wyverns swooped upward. We burst from the water and into cold air. Vitania leaned against the neck of her mount so I leaned against her as the wind beat at my face. The cliffs of the mountain blurred past beneath our vertical ascent. I turned my head left and right, searching for enemies, but the skies on the northern side of the mountain were clear.

Within seconds, we reached the new summit, the jagged remains of the former peak and continued higher until Vitania slowed her mount to a stop.

Emily thrust out her arms and the air around us shimmered. "I've cloaked us, but I don't know how well it will work against dragon senses."

Already searching for the quantum tunnel, Vitania didn't seem to hear her.

The brilliant flashes of light and explosions on the near horizon drew my attention away. The enemy forces resembled a dark cloud. I couldn't imagine the vast number of drakes and wyverns making up that cloud, but it looked large enough to engulf our entire fleet whole. Drakara was no longer in the ocean near Faux Olympus, nor was she fighting alongside her swarm.

Emily gasped. "Bloody hell. That's not two-hundred thousand dragons. That's nigh on a million!"

Balaena nodded somberly. "It appears we greatly underestimated their numbers."

I hissed. "There's no way we beat a swarm that size."

Emily's eyes flared. "Do you feel that?" She looked up just as a shadow eclipsed the sun.

I looked up, hoping to see it had been a cloud, but it wasn't.

Drakara dove toward us, drakes and wyverns launching from the craggy spines along her back. It was obvious from their perfect aim that they knew we were here despite Emily's cloak.

"How in the hell can they see us?" I thought back to the drygon in Seraphina and realized they'd seen us through the broom camouflage as well.

"Maybe they smell us?" Emily held up her hands helplessly. "I don't know how to mask odors."

"Just imagine another odor and focus on the air molecules around us." I had no idea what I was talking about, but since her powers bordered on the divine, I figured she could probably alter the chemistry of the air just by thinking about it.

Emily closed her eyes and thrust out her hands again. The air rippled and a horrific odor stung my nose. "Bloody hell!"

"Oh, god, what is that odor?" Conrad pulled his shirt over his nose. "It smells like the privy at a petrol station."

"I was nervous!" Emily shouted.

I gagged so hard I nearly threw up. It was like sniffing the bowels of a filthy toilet. The rippling air reached the dragons and they roared their displeasure. Unfortunately, it barely seemed to slow them.

We were out of time.

37

Ignoring the horrific odor, Vitania searched frantically for the quantum tunnel as Drakara and minions bore down upon us. At long last, she plucked the golden strand leading to Olympus, but it was too late to open it. The dragons were here.

The Siren's wyverns dove toward the ocean, enemy wyverns and drakes snapping at our heels. We plummeted beneath the surface. Multiple impacts splashed into the water behind us as the other dragons either tried to follow, or couldn't stop in time.

"Does Drakara have water dragons?" I said.

Vitania shrugged. "I don't know. The Sirens formed a special bond with water wyverns eons ago. Most left Draxadis for Aquilis, since a realm of mostly water was ideal for them."

"Then they can't follow us?"

"Not the ordinary dragons." Vitania's mount leveled off its dive just above the sunken city and continued flying south. "We have no choice but to rejoin the main force and fight."

She was right. Emily and Xanos were our heaviest hitters. Getting us back to the main fleet was our only chance. We couldn't afford to retreat. This was the battle to end all battles—at least for this particular war.

We burst from the ocean moments later right beneath the center of our fleet.

Elyssa's spoke through my comm badge. "Justin, what happened?"

"Drakara ambushed us." I clenched my fists. "She guessed our plans."

She went silent for moment then spoke in a somber tone. "Then we'll fight our way through."

I nodded grimly. "We fight our way through." I turned to Emily and Xanos. "Let's go."

A golden halo of power glowed around Emily. She leapt from the wyvern's back and hovered in place. Xanos joined her. Flying and fighting would probably strain me to the max, but I had no choice.

Conrad's face filled with regret. "I wish I could fly, but I suppose I'll have to requisition a broom."

"I will take you to the command cube," Narine told him.

Vitania gripped my wrist. "It has been an honor knowing you, Justin."

I swallowed the lump forming in my throat as the weight of her words settled on me. "And you as well, Vitania." I leapt into the air, fueled by the dark green power of the Apocryphan, then Emily, Xanos, and I sped toward the frontlines.

The outer fringes of the dragon horde had already reached the motherships and Mzodi sky ships. Energy beams speared from Mzodi ships and into the cloud of drakes and wyverns. Scores of drakes fell burning from the skies. Injured wyverns fell into the sea, their wings punctured and useless. The Mzodi had been fighting dragons for centuries, though never on this scale. Even so, their expertise was paying off.

Small skiffs bearing elves skirted the fringe. Arrows streaked into the swarm, dropping wyverns and drakes alike with arrows protruding from eye sockets. Utopians on gryphons and gepherons brandished laser swords, slashing enemies to pieces while the gryphons used their steel talons to shred drakes who dared come too close.

Fae on their giant bees cast sparkling clouds of pixies dust.

Drakes and wyverns dropped like bricks, apparently unable to fly with the dust on their wings. The giant bees swarmed wyverns, stinging them even through their thick, scaly hides.

Yeti on flying sleds blasted drakes. Archangels, Daskar, and Skywraiths used agility to their advantage, flying circles around wyverns and slashing holes in their wings rather than trying to kill them.

Gryphons screeched in pain as hundreds of drakes swarmed them and tore them to shreds. A yeti roared as the acid from a green dragon melted through his armor and disintegrated his arm. Gepherons fell by the dozens, wings burned off by fire wyverns.

Emily, Xanos, and I unleashed our fury on the drakes, slashing beams of energy into their ranks, clearing a path for our forces to engage the wyverns. The only advantage their numbers held for us was that the wyverns were literally knocking drakes aside with their wings as they fought their way toward our fleet.

A group of wyverns reached one of the Mzodi ships, blasting the deck with fire while a green wyvern bellowed acid on the crew. Mzodi screamed and died. The ship listed sideways, ramming through drakes as it spiraled out of control, then plummeted toward the sea.

A Science Academy mothership exploded as dozens of wyverns tore through the hull. The blast tore through yeti sleds, and burning bodies of allies and enemies tumbled through the air.

Our frontlines were crumbling and there was nothing we could do about it.

We were killing drakes by the dozens and winging nearly as many wyverns, but it just wasn't enough. It would never be enough.

Justin!

I nearly collided with a wyvern as Kalesh shouted in my head. *What is it?*

I've got an idea, but it might get you in trouble.

I dodged a wyvern and slashed off its head with a beam of power. *Do you really think I care about getting in trouble right now? I'm open to anything at this point!*

Great. Can you open a portal for me?

I blasted another wyvern. *Open a portal to where? I'm kind of busy if you hadn't noticed.*

Contact Cinder. Tell him to call my infernus and he will send a picture. Contact symbols flashed into my head.

Cinder had set up the portal generator on the island to the southeast so he could open a portal quickly in case of retreat. I didn't know how Kalesh could help us, but I was willing to try anything at this point. I tapped my comm badge. "Cinder, call this number and do whatever he says." I gave him the symbols.

"At once, Justin," he replied.

Elyssa spoke on my comm. "We're calling for a fighting retreat. We need to keep out of the main swarm and just keep whittling away at them."

"Understood." I looped through the air, blasting more drakes as I went. It was like fighting off a zergling invasion. No matter how many we killed, the supply of enemies seemed infinite.

The fleet reversed course, fleeing while continuing to fire into the enemy ranks. But we had to maintain the speed of our slowest units so no one was left behind. Unfortunately, our slowest units were barely faster than the drakes.

We were going to lose hundreds of people at this rate. *Kalesh, whatever you plan on doing, do it now!*

You ready to rock? Kalesh said.

I growled. *No, I'm ready to cry!*

A massive portal tore open in the ocean beneath us. I didn't comprehend what I was seeing at first until I took a moment to focus. Battleships and aircraft carriers sped through the breach, crashing through waves at top speed. They bore the flags of dozens of countries—the United States, China, Russia, and more. Jets roared to life, taking off in unison from multiple carriers.

My comm badge crackled with static. "USS Nimitz to Overworld control, we are here to assist. Please advise."

Another voice spoke in Russian. Several more in broken English and voices added their support in various languages.

A jet barrel-rolled as it passed beneath us and the comms crackled to life again. "I feel the need. The need for speed!"

A gruff voice replied. "God damn it, Maverick. Rejoin your squadron!"

I couldn't believe my eyes. *Kalesh, how in the hell did you get all these noms?*

Baal's infernus have apparently been priming nom forces for supernatural incursions by creating new covert operations hierarchies in several countries. I'll save the rest for later since you've got your hands full at the moment.

He wasn't wrong. *You did good, bro.*

Thanks, bruh.

Thomas spoke over all comms. "Eden forces, this is Grand Commander Borathen. You are a go."

"Roger that, Overworld control. Nimitz out."

Antiaircraft batteries on the battleships unleashed on the dragon swarm. Jets reached altitude and unloaded barrage after barrage of rockets. Missiles lifted off from a score of cruisers, smoke trails arcing toward the swarm.

"Overworld ships rotate broadsides and open fire!" Elyssa shouted over comms.

The Mzodi ships spun sideways still drifting away from the swarm and pummeled it with lasers. Emily, Xanos, and I added our own firepower, obliterating countless enemies.

The skies rocked with explosions as cruise missiles detonated in the middle of the swarm. Scores of dragons and body parts rained on the ocean below. A flaming jet flew past, spinning out of control. Drakes swarmed other jets, clogging engines with their bodies, and crashing through cockpits. Phase two of the battle was well underway and it wasn't even noontime yet.

Time lost all meaning as we threw everything we had at the endless swarm. I began to tire and it was clear from the faces of Xanos and Emily that they were too. The second mothership fell. The yeti forces now numbered in the dozens instead of the hundreds. Arturo's archangels and Daskar were forced to retreat so they could rest. The nom forces recalled jets to aircraft carriers for refueling and rearming.

We'd put a serious dent in the enemy numbers, but we had no third string reinforcements to help us. A jet collided with a wyvern no more than fifty feet from me and spun out of control, shaking me from my funk. With our front lines buckling, drakes funneled toward the jets, throwing their bodies against them like living weapons. Drakara had more than enough minions to swarm us to death. If she joined the fight, she could crush us in one blow.

It seemed she was too intent on guarding the quantum tunnel to Olympus to join the fight.

"Defensive retreat," Elyssa commanded.

The Sirens formed a line and began singing. Any creatures attacking fell senseless into the ocean. I didn't know if they were dying or just knocked out, but the sonic barrier protected retreating allies. It gave us just enough space for our slowest units to stay ahead of the wyverns.

"Nimitz here. Members of the Eden Fleet are reporting low munitions. We will run out unless resupplied."

"Supply ships are on the way," Cinder said. "ETA thirteen minutes."

Emily, Xanos, and I returned to the top of the command cube, slumping in exhaustion. I'd been using Apocryphan powers, but thankfully wasn't experiencing the usual effects of burnout. Xanos looked pale. Sweat dripped from her face and dragon blood stained her uniform.

"Too many." She slumped onto her side and closed her eyes.

Emily stared at the swarm and groaned. "What I wouldn't give for a bloody hair tie right now. I'm sick of hair flapping in my face."

I tapped my comm badge. "Elyssa, what's the plan?"

"Cinder informed me that nom crews are setting up anti-aircraft batteries on Atlantis." She blew out a breath. "If the dragons follow, at least we'll have a defensive position."

As Atlantis came into view, it became clear we would have no refuge.

Wreckage smoked on the mountain ridgelines. Wyverns swooped back and forth, attacking unseen targets on the ground. There weren't many of them, but more than enough to kill the noms setting up the AA batteries.

"Son of a bitch!" I slammed a fist into my palm. "We're so screwed."

The side of the mountain exploded outward. A massive red muzzle snapped around a wyvern, shook it, then threw it contemptuously aside. A purple dragon shot like a missile straight up, gouts of energy pouring from its maw. Three more wyverns died.

"Altash and Lulu!" I held up a fist and whooped. "It's not over yet."

Elyssa exited the top hatch and crushed me with a hug. "The earth dragons are here."

I nodded. "Maybe, just maybe we have a chance."

The command cube landed on the wharf while the Mzodi ships settled into the water. Thanks to the Siren song, we'd outdistanced the swarm by a fair margin, but the ominous cloud of death was still approaching.

Slitheren emerged from the mountain and slithered down the wharf toward us. I flew down to meet him.

We are here, he said.

"How many?"

Eighty-three. Only four others are close in age and size to Altash.

I pointed to the swarm. "I don't even know how many we've killed, but there are still hundreds of thousands."

Slitheren observed the distant cloud for a moment. *We will defeat them or die trying.*

"Can your kind fly?"

Yes, but we are not as agile as wyverns. His scales shifted and hidden wings unfurled from his back. *We will be stronger on the ground.*

"Unfortunately, they're not going to just give up their biggest advantage." I estimated ten minutes before the swarm reached us. "Without AA batteries, we're sitting ducks."

We saved several noms who were installing defenses. They told us only five units remained. Will that be enough?

I shook my head. "Not even close."

The Eden naval units pulled into dock, their speed aided by water wyverns. Left to their own engines, they would've easily been overtaken and swarmed.

Elyssa emerged from the cube and jogged over to me. "Hey, Justin, fly me down with you next time!"

I blinked. "Oh, shit. I'm in such a daze I didn't even think about it."

"What's the sit-rep?"

I gave her Slitheren's report. "With the bulk of our forces exhausted, I don't know what we're going to do."

A human wearing white Greek robes emerged from a building near the wharf and jogged toward us.

I frowned. "Is that an Atlantean?"

Elyssa peered at him. "Looks like it."

The young man reached us and stopped, gasping for breath. "I have run many miles to deliver a message."

I raised an eyebrow. "Are you Atlantean?"

"Yes." He spoke between breaths. "Adonis says Atlantis will rise to your aid."

"Your people are alive?"

"We have been building tunnels and storing food underground for years." He stretched his arms above his head and took another deep breath. "We have been repairing our weapons and sky chariots, preparing for a war with the dragons, but the dragons destroyed our outer defenses so quickly, we had no choice but to retreat into hiding."

"Smart choice." I waved a hand at our forces. "We don't have much of a chance at winning, but every little bit helps."

A large section of rocky embankment behind one of the government buildings shifted and moved aside. Hundreds of armored Atlanteans riding sky chariots rolled out and onto the road, pulling carts with metal spheroids composed of hexagonal panels. Their only support was a thick metal spool beneath the bottom panel.

I'd never seen them before. "What are those things?"

"They are like generators," he explained. "Our sky chariots deplete their energy quickly, but they only have to fly over one of these to recharge in a few seconds."

"Cool." The Atlanteans' technology was ancient and much different than our usual arcnology, but they'd stopped advancing it after the Sundering separated them from the rest of the realms.

The generators were placed in a wide-open plaza and activated. They hummed to life, rising from their spool pedestals and spinning. Energy crackled dangerously around them, but the Atlanteans didn't seem concerned. A bolt of power struck a sky chariot. The driver pulled on a lever and the vehicle shot into the air. Other chariots drove past the generators and took flight after a charge struck them.

It was nice having more air units, but those sky chariots stood a fart's chance in a hurricane against the swarm. The yeti sky sleds had proven that. The swarm had drawn to a halt nearly a quarter mile off the coast, an ominous cloud ready to rain fire on the land. I suspected Drakara was evaluating our defenses.

Another thought occurred to me. The dragons had been flying non-stop under their own power all this time. Surely they had to be tiring as well, right?

"Slitheren, do you have any idea how long a wyvern can fly before it needs to rest?"

Drakes and wyverns glide, using the winds to keep them aloft without requiring much exertion. They can remain aloft for a day or more without tiring.

Elyssa must have been privy to the conversation as well because she groaned. "A day or more? We'll never catch a break."

"There's only one way to end this." I stared at the dark bulk of Drakara. "We have to take out the queen."

Elyssa shook her head. "Justin, we can't even get close to Drakara. She's the fastest creature out there and the swarm would stop us before we even got close. Besides, how are we supposed to kill a living mountain?"

I bit my bottom lip. "I've got an idea that might help us with the swarm. I'm going to need two rubber bands, a number four ball-bearing, and a spoon."

She huffed. "Hey, MacGyver, in case you hadn't noticed, we don't have time for jokes."

"Take me to the Utopian magi."

Elyssa pointed a finger toward the aircraft carriers and battleships docked on the pier. "Before we jump back into battle, do you mind telling me where that nom fleet came from?"

I smiled sheepishly. "That would be Kalesh's fault."

Her eyebrows rose. "Your demon spirit organized an international armada, convinced noms to go through a portal, and fight dragons alongside a supernatural army?"

My smile turned to a grin. "Wow, it sounds so much better when you put it into words." I cleared my throat. "Apparently, Baal did all the groundwork. His infernus created the international network of covert operatives."

Kalesh chimed in. *Baal's infernus created separate covert entities in various countries. They then created false alien invasions utilizing creatures from other realms. This convinced the covert entities to covertly create an international covert coalition to fight such invasions.*

I scoffed. "If you say covert one more time, I'm gonna dock you style points."

Elyssa frowned. "What's he saying?"

I relayed the info and added more as Kalesh kept talking. "He says that the black operations groups are insulated from most of their governments, but that there's no guarantee someone won't talk. Thankfully, we now control infernus occupying some of the highest seats of power in government so we may be able to keep a lid on it."

Elyssa absorbed the news with a few nods. "Well, if the cat's out of the bag, we'll deal with it later." She turned toward the distant swarm. "One problem at a time."

"So, back to my brilliant idea." I took her hand. "Where are the Utopian magi?"

She pointed toward a group of Mzodi vessels parked atop the pier. "They should be there."

I held up a finger to Slitheren. "We'll be back in a minute. What I have in mind requires your help."

I tapped my comm badge. "Adam, where are you?"

"Manning the portal generator with Cinder," he replied.

"I need your brains front and center."

"You got it."

I sent them a picture of our location and a portal opened a moment later. Cinder, Shelton, and Adam rushed through. "Wait here," I told the group. "I'll be right back." I ran to the ship with the Utopian magi and flew up to the deck.

Vokan sat on the deck of a neighboring ship, a hopeless look on his face. His troubled gaze met mine. For once, there was no pride gleaming behind those eyes. The magi on this ship appeared to be in equally depressed spirits.

I got straight to the point. "I need your help."

Maniacal laughter bubbled from Vokan's mouth. "Our help? We are but babes in a storm of fire and ash. Without my cantraps, I am nothing compared to these beasts."

"If you want a chance at redemption, come with me." I motioned them to follow me. "There's literally no time to argue."

The twenty or so magi rose and followed. Only Vokan remained. "What good can we do against the swarm?"

"Maybe a lot of good." I gave him a hard look. "You're the only one who's worked with tremendous power, so I need your expertise."

He sighed but nodded. "Very well."

I took them back to Slitheren and the others, then told them my plan. "I don't know if it'll work, but I need you to figure it out in, oh, ten minutes."

It was our final chance for a last stand.

38

Sometimes life gives you lemons. Other times, it gives you a million hostile dragons. What do you do when faced with that?

You make dragonade.

In addition to their vast numerical advantage, the dragons were superior air fighters. The only way we stood a chance in hell of making dragonade was to take away as many advantages as possible.

I watched as Adam and Cinder conferred for several seconds. "Can we do it?"

Adam glanced at the swarm, seemed to make a calculation in his head, then nodded. "I don't know, but we'll figure it out somehow."

I took him aside for a moment. "I need one more thing from you." I told him what it was and he frowned. "For what?"

"A hail Mary."

With a flick across the screen of his arcphone, it was done. His brow furrowed. "Justin, it's been fun. I hope you don't die."

"Same here, man. Same here."

Shelton gave me a bear hug then backed off. "Just remember that if the dragons win, there won't be any more tacos."

"We'll win it for the tacos," I said grimly. I kissed Elyssa on the cheek. "Goodbye again." I flew back to the command cube and landed on top. Emily looked a little better rested, but Xanos looked like a crack addict who'd just crawled out of the gutter for another fix.

"I may have overextended myself," Xanos said. "Or perhaps I am not as strong as I once was."

"It's okay. Rest up." I held a hand toward Emily and helped her up. "You and I have a mission."

She blinked. "What is it?"

I told her and she recoiled in horror.

"That's bloody suicide!"

"Yep." I grinned. "But it'll be worth the one-way ticket."

"Does Elyssa know?"

My grin faded. "She knows and she understands."

Emily took my hand and squeezed it. "It would be an honor to die with you."

"Wait!" Xanos held up a hand. "If you and Emily die, who will stop the collapse?"

"It'll all be up to you." I knelt next to her. "But I'm hoping we can still get out of this alive."

Xanos shook her head. "This is happening because of my poor life decisions."

I shrugged. "Shit happens. Let's make some shit of our own happen."

Emily stretched and cracked her knuckles. "I'm ready when you are."

Vitania was resting near her dragon at the far end of the pier, so we flew out to her.

I shook her awake. "We need you to get us to Drakara."

The Siren blinked in confusion. "We can't reach the mountain with her and her minions guarding it."

I nodded. "I know. That' why we're taking her head on."

Vitania scoffed. "You can't be serious."

"Oh, I'm serious as a gas attack."

Emily snorted. "Rather serious, I must say."

I grinned. "As serious as that gas attack Emily unleashed on us earlier."

Vitania narrowed her eyes. "What is your plan of attack?"

I gave her the scoop and let her mull over it for a moment.

She nodded. "It might work. I suppose we have no choice but to try."

"That's the spirit!" It was all I could do to fake some enthusiasm.

Vitania found Dactia and spoke with her for a moment. They pressed the palms of their hands together and nodded in unison.

"Well, at least they're getting along." Emily sighed. "Dactia put me through hell when I tried to reason with her."

"Yeah, she wasn't exactly kind to Vitania either."

Vitania returned to us with Dolpha in tow. "We are ready when you are."

We had to wait until the swarm was nearly to the island before heading to Drakara. I wanted as much distance as possible between them and her. The massive mother of dragons sat in the water between us and Olympus. I couldn't tell if she was floating or if she was just tall enough to stand on the bottom of the ocean.

Fifteen minutes later, the dark cloud was nearly upon us. I peered down the wharf where Adam and the magi stood. Slitheren opened his maw, revealing the glow of concentrated aether inside. Vokan and the others joined hands. Gusts of wind tossed their hair. The ocean water turned choppy as the wind turned gale force, churning into a tornado.

More tornadoes formed, each growing taller as they crossed the distance between the island and the swarm.

Vokan's cantrap of souls had been a super-concentrated source of energy for him. Since we couldn't exactly harvest souls to save lives, I'd found an alternative. Earth dragons were living magical batteries, filled to the brim with aether. The only problem was finding the proper magical interface to allow the magi to operate their weather magic using the power.

As usual, Adam had figured it out, harnessing the Atlantean

recharge stations to the earth dragons. At least, that's what he said he'd do.

Storm clouds formed and brutal winds slammed into the swarm. The dragons fought to fly higher or around the storms, but the storm system had grown too wide. The strong weather wasn't enough to outright kill them, but that wasn't the point of the exercise.

As the dragon swarm fought its way toward shore, drakes and wyverns dropped into the ocean, too tired to fight the winds any longer. By the time the swarm reached the shallower waters near shore, they were showing signs of exhaustion.

Altash and the giant earth dragons opened their massive maws and fired beams of raw aether into the tired enemies. Instead of raining fire, it began to rain ashes.

I nodded at Vitania. "Let's do it."

Emily rode with Vitania and I climbed on the other water wyvern behind Dolpha. The wyverns dove underwater, jetting beneath the flailing, splashing forms of countless drakes and wyverns that had fallen exhausted into the water. We went deeper, the water wyverns thrusting through the water at top speed.

Drakara's legs were submerged, but weren't long enough to touch the bottom of the ocean. She floated on the water, an island unto herself. I couldn't remember if we'd ever tried to measure her, but her wingspan was at least a half mile across. Even Altash looked tiny compared to her and he could swallow a freight train.

I turned to Vitania. "Are we going to have help?"

She nodded.

"Can I please, please, give the command?"

She sighed, releasing a stream of bubbles. "Very well."

"Awesome!" I pointed up. "Let's get her attention."

We burst from the water and soared up along Drakara's exceedingly long neck.

Laughter filled my head. *Insignificant specks. Did you come to attack me?*

We drew level with her head a hundred yards or more above the water, maintaining a distance that might be just out of reach of her jaws. Just one of her teeth was larger than me.

"I'm here to give you a final offer, Drakara." I lifted off from Dolpha's wyvern and hovered in place. "Stop your senseless attacks. Help us stop the collapse of the realms and defeat Elohim."

More laughter. *I will be a god after the collapse. Elohim has promised to let me shape worlds for my people.*

"Does that include the drygon?" I said.

No. They will perish and be forgotten.

I sighed. "So there's absolutely no way I can change your mind?"

I swore an oath to Elohim and I will uphold it. You cannot prevail against me.

I glanced back at the shores of Atlantis where the swarm had significantly thinned thanks to the storms and the attacks from Altash. "We're already prevailing. Soon, you'll have no dragon swarm."

Then I will destroy you myself. Dozens of wyverns launched from the craggy ridges along Drakara's back, flying up to meet us.

"I won't give you the chance." I raised a fist and said something I'd wanted to say all my life. "Release the Kraken!"

There was one creature in the ocean that was nearly as large as Drakara. It had been used and abused by the gods and just wanted to be left alone. But with the fate of the worlds in the balance, it had begrudgingly listened to Vitania and decided to help.

The ocean roiled as if someone had just cut the most monstrous underwater fart of all times. Massive tentacles burst from the water, each one stretching longer than even Drakara's long neck. More of them must have coiled around her legs underwater because the dragon's eyes flared in almost comical surprise as her body was jerked underwater. Another tentacle wrapped around her neck and squeezed.

Drakara's wings flailed as she desperately tried to take off. She roared and unleashed a massive orange beam of pure energy into the water. The ocean boiled. Steam hissed into the air. Though the

Kraken could destroy an armada of ships and destroy entire coastal towns, it was no match for the might of Drakara.

Which was why this was only phase one of the plan.

Emily flew alongside me, shaking her head in wonderment. "One way or the other, I'm going to miss the unholy shit you get us into, Justin."

I laughed. "Yeah, me too." I watched as Drakara boiled more of the ocean to steam with another energy blast. "You ready?"

Emily shook her hands as if warding off anxiety. "No, but let's bloody do it."

We jetted forward. My plan hinged on one critical flaw in Drakara's ultimate dragon design: her size. There was nothing we could throw against her that would even put a dent in her scaly hide, short of nukes. She could have destroyed most of our forces with one of her energy blasts. But the problem with creatures her size boiled down to science.

The amount of energy required to sustain flight was incredible, and the outpouring of power from her energy attacks could probably power a small city for a week. Like many magical creatures, Adam posited that she drew power straight from leylines, but even leylines had limits to what they could provide.

And that was why Drakara preferred to have her minions do the dirty work.

She blasted the ocean with another attack, trying vainly to hit the Kraken, but its bulk remained underwater and out of reach. Drakara roared, raking the ocean with a beam of sizzling energy, but it blinked in and out, sparking as it strained the local leylines to the max.

"That's our cue." I shot toward our goal. Energy requirements weren't the only flaw to Drakara's gargantuan size. We might look like gnats compared to her, but I had something even smaller in mind.

We flew toward her head while she focused on attacking the ocean, and jetted right into her ear. Casting a light ball ahead of me, I felt like Dennis Quaid in *Innerspace* as we navigated down the ear canal. Emily blasted a hole in the ear drum and Drakara bellowed in surprise.

The hole began to heal rapidly, so we flew through and deeper into the ear. Adam had given me a diagram of wyvern anatomy and I used it like a map. I found a spot of soft tissue just outside the cochlea and burrowed a hole through it with a burst of Brilliance.

Drakara screeched and the echoes inside her head nearly deafened me.

Emily and I climbed through the hole, slipping and sliding through blood and other disgusting fluids until we finally reached what might be our final resting place. We barely made it through before the flesh healed shut behind us. I sent the light ball above us, illuminating the wrinkly bottom of Drakara's brain.

"She thinks we're insignificant specks?" I scoffed. "I guess she hasn't heard of brain-eating amoebas."

Emily gawked at it. "Good heavens, that's a massive brain."

She was right—it was huge. We could probably go to town slicing and dicing all day, but Drakara's rapid health regeneration would keep her from suffering critical damage. That was why we had to do it this way.

I activated the program Adam had given me, took a deep breath and nodded at Emily. "I hope this works."

She nodded nervously. "Me too."

We unleashed everything we had into the brain. Meat sizzled and cranial fluid bubbled and boiled. Vitania had given us shells to breathe in the fluid, but there wasn't much oxygen in it to begin with. To make matters worse, Drakara flailed as her body convulsed from the immense brain damage.

The Nightingale armor was the only thing keeping Emily and I from slipping all over the place. But despite the brutal damage done to the brain, the sizzling meat began to heal. I'd never seen such regenerative power, except maybe in a god. I hoped and prayed our gambit worked. Otherwise, we were going to die for nothing.

"Ten more seconds," I hissed between my teeth.

Others might wonder why were we doing this if Drakara could just heal in seconds. After all, we were expending as much energy as possible for seemingly little to no payout. Drakara probably wouldn't suffer any permanent brain damage no matter what we did.

But that wasn't the point.

Why? Because I'd activated Adam's malaether eruption program on a throwaway arcphone before we started blasting. Even now, the negative energy was building to critical levels deep inside Drakara's brain. Emily's malaether eruption in Hell had killed Olivia, so maybe this would do the trick for a giant dragon.

A low hum built in the background, growing louder and louder with each passing moment. I didn't know if ten seconds had passed, but I was about to pass out and my hands were burning. I stopped channeling and jabbed my finger urgently at the soft tissue behind Emily. "Go!"

She blasted a hole in the flesh and we wriggled our way back into the inner ear. Staggering, we tried to make it back past the eardrum, but Drakara's seizures were too violent, rattling us around like dice in a cup. The hum built to a high pitched whine and then went silent for an instant. An explosion rocked the world. Suddenly, I was tumbling head over heels, blinded and barely able to breathe as the wind was knocked from my body.

I lost consciousness for an indeterminable amount of time and then felt my limbs flailing in free air. I smacked into something soft and fleshy and lay stunned for a moment before I was able to move my limbs. I wiped at my face and found massive eyes regarding me.

I was too tired to scream, so I barfed goo and viscera from my mouth and calmly regarded my savior—the Kraken. I looked around and found Drakara's headless body floating on the surface of the ocean. I half expected her to grow another neck and head like a hydra, but it seemed that once her brain was obliterated, her healing couldn't do much to restore it.

Another tentacle brought Emily to join me. Like me, she was covered in blood and brain matter. "Justin, we did it," she said in a weak voice. "Now I just want to sleep forever."

"Me too," I croaked. But there was one more battle to be won first.

Emily stared at Drakara's body. "Good lord, that thing is going to stink up the entire realm."

"I'll take it." I groaned. "That's the least of our worries."

"You said it would just destroy her brain, not blow her head to bits." Emily shook her head. "We're lucky we didn't explode along with it."

I managed a grin. "We almost did."

Vitania and Dolpha guided their dragons over and the Kraken gently deposited us on them. It roared a couple of times, then peaced out, ducking beneath the water.

"The Kraken is impressed with your work," Vitania said matter-of-factly. "He has been distraught at the lack of ships and armadas to destroy since being trapped here and said it was fun fighting a dragon, even if only for a short time."

"I would have though it impossible." Dolpha stared at the crimson waters. "The scavengers will feast for months."

"I'm happy to give him some entertainment." I slumped against Dolpha. "Let's get back to Atlantis." I hoped our defenses had held up in our absence.

It turned out our defenses had been more than adequate to hold off a swarm of exhausted dragons. And once Drakara had died, the remaining wyverns and drakes had fled. It seemed they were done with the battle now that their mother was gone.

Shelton and Adam whooped, fists raised in the air when Dolpha's and Vitania's dragons circled in for a landing.

Emily and I were too tired to celebrate.

Elyssa helped me off the dragon, and Adam helped Emily down.

We'd defeated the mother of dragons, but this was barely the start. "I need to clean up, then we can go to the real Olympus."

It was time to kill a god.

39

I could hardly believe everything we'd been through, from fighting a dragon swarm with the largest supernatural coalition ever seen, to blowing up Drakara's brain with a malaether spell. But we were only halfway through a laundry list that included defeating Elohim and then stopping the realms from collapsing.

Elyssa put her hands on my shoulders. "You can't face Elohim like this!"

"She's right, man." Shelton blew out a breath. "Letting a few realms fall is better than getting killed two minutes after you find Elohim."

I shook my head. "I refuse to let one more realm fall!"

Emily nodded. "I'm with Justin. Just hose us off and get us to the damned mountain."

"I am also with you." Xanos looked moderately better than before, but nowhere near a hundred percent. "Elohim cannot stand against all three of us."

I scoffed. "Oh, he can squash us like bugs. Our only chance is that he's still weakened from his fight with Eve."

"I don't like it," Adam said. "Utopia and the outer realms have another thirty-eight hours, give or take, before the dark matter from the Abyss hits them."

I frowned. "Fine. Wake me up in two hours."

Elyssa, Shelton, and Adam gave me worried looks, but nodded.

I must have slept like a rock because I barely remembered laying down after I took a shower. When I woke up, every bone and muscle in my body ached. In fact, I ached all the way down to my soul. I felt like reheated pizza—way shittier than fresh, but still highly edible. I checked the time and growled. Elyssa had let me sleep for more than four hours.

A look around the room awakened old memories. I was in a bunk in the *Falcheen*. Emily and Xanos snoozed away in neighboring beds. I stretched and decided to give them a few more minutes while I went up to the deck. A fiery redhead smirked at me when I emerged from belowdecks.

"It's good to see you again, Tahlee." I would have hugged her but I felt like keeping my arms.

She nodded. "Once again, you have proven yourself a warrior, Justin Slade. I lost count of the wyverns we slew."

The other crew members glanced at us, but none of them looked familiar. Illaena, the captain, marched over and put a hand on my shoulder. "I miss our days of adventures on the high winds."

I snorted. "Like the time we journeyed through Voltis to find Atlantis and fought a small war to keep Kaelissa from kidnapping Dolpha, Balaena, and Narine?"

Illaena nodded. "The best of times."

Tahlee sighed and wiped away a tear. "Today was yet another legendary battle. May our adventures never end."

"Hear, hear!" the crew cried out.

I cleared my throat. "Well, they're not over yet. I would be honored if you would take me to Olympus so we can breach the gates and kill Elohim."

Tahlee and Illaena saluted. "Our ship is yours, Captain Slade."

"Argh, mateys, flip the jab and hoist the sail."

Illaena rolled her eyes. "Your sense of humor has still not improved."

I grinned and tapped my comm badge. "Elyssa, I love you, but you let me oversleep."

"You needed every minute of it," she replied. "Our forces secured the remains of the mountain while you were asleep. There were still wyverns guarding it, so you would have had to fight your way through them if we hadn't taken care of it."

I sighed. "As usual, you were right, but now I'm ready to go."

"We're ready too." Elyssa's voice came from behind me. I spun and watched as she, Shelton, Adam, and Vitania walked up the ramp and boarded the ship. Conrad, Max, and Ambria hurried up behind them. Elyssa smiled. "We're always ready to come with you."

My mind flashed back to the beginning: me a chubby nerd, and Elyssa the enigmatic goth girl. I choked up. It was hard to believe how long we'd been together. I thought back to my earlier conversation with Shelton and realized it was now or never.

I blew out a breath. "This is stupid."

Elyssa quirked an eyebrow. "What is?"

"This, all of this!" I waved a hand around vaguely. "I don't want you to be my girlfriend anymore."

Her eyes flared with hurt and surprise. "What's that supposed to mean?"

Adam waved a hand across his throat. "Dude, you're delirious. Shut up and go back to bed."

I shook my head. "No." I stormed over to Elyssa and cupped her chin in my hand. "Elyssa Borathen, I don't want you as a girlfriend anymore. I want you to be my wife."

She gasped and tears pooled in her eyes. "You're asking me to marry you?"

I grinned and nodded. "You're my partner in crime, my soul mate, and the only thing in this crazy universe that keeps me alive. Please do me the honor of being my wife."

Elyssa leapt into my arms and kissed me furiously. "As you wish."

Shelton started slow-clapping. "Well played, sir. Well played."

Adam sniffled. "That was so romantic."

Conrad and friends applauded.

Xanos and Emily emerged onto the deck, both of them stretching and yawning. Emily frowned when she saw the commotion. "Did we miss something?"

"Justin asked Elyssa to marry him!" Ambria shouted. "Isn't that sweet?"

Emily swallowed a lump in her throat and managed a smile. "Yes. Congratulations." Then she turned and hurried down the ramp.

"Yikes." Shelton grimaced. "Maybe we ought to tone down the celebrations and give the woman some space to grieve."

Emily walked back up to the deck, wiping at her face. "I'm sorry. There's no time for self-pity."

Elyssa walked over and hugged her. "I'm so sorry, Emily. Maybe once all this is over, Kalesh can find Tyler in Haedaemos."

Emily leaned her face on Elyssa's shoulder and sobbed.

I felt really bad, but Emily was right, we had no more time to waste. There was no crying in baseball, or during Armageddon. I motioned in the general direction of Olympus. "Can we get underway?"

Illaena nodded and gave the command. Tahlee barked the same orders at the top of her lungs, startling Ambria, and nearly deafening us.

I grinned. *Just like the good old days.*

By the time we reached the empty air where the top of the mountain had once been, Emily was once again all business. Vitania guided the ship to the general area and began searching for the quantum tunnel again. It took nearly twenty minutes for her to locate it. She traced the symbols and a portal slashed open to green meadows and golden sunlight.

I turned to Illaena. "We'll be back—hopefully."

The crew stood and saluted us. Tahlee and Illaena joined them. Illaena spoke. "May the winds favor you, Justin Slade."

"And you." I saluted back and then our group entered the portal.

I expected a surprise attack from an angry god, but everything looked as it had been last time. There was one minor difference. A lone figure sat at the edge of the primal fount not far from the massive waterfall.

I put a finger to my lips and like a cartoon character, tip-toed behind a tree and peeked out. The figure was Elohim. I'd already tried breaking his neck in a sneak attack after his battle with Eve, so I knew how futile that was. It was best if we all attacked at once before he even knew we were here.

He rose and turned, a smirk on his face. "I know you're here. Somehow you got through my dragon horde, but you won't get past me."

I clenched a fist and stepped out from behind the tree. "Your dragon horde is decimated and Drakara is dead." I smirked back at him. "Now you're alone against all of us."

Elohim flinched as if struck. "Drakara dead? Impossible!"

I shrugged. "Sorry, but the deed is done." I started ticking names off on my fingers. "Cain, Olivia, and now Drakara. All of your allies are gone, Elohim. Time for you to give up your mad quest and go into retirement."

"If you'd attacked me even two hours ago, you might have had a chance." Crackling power gathered around his fingers. "I have recovered enough strength to destroy you all. Perhaps I'll leave you alive, Justin. Then I will list your dead allies while you weep."

"You're so damned mean!" I growled. "Why do you want to kill everything and everyone just to satisfy your enormous ego? Can't you go build another world somewhere and leave us alone?"

"He's a jealous god." Emily stepped next to me. "Always has been, always will be."

"He's like the kid who has to cheat on tests and still barely passes," Shelton said. "He tried to copy Eve and failed."

Xanos stepped to my other side. "We will stop you, Elohim. Your time is done."

Elohim laughed. "Emily is the closest thing to a threat among you, but she's nothing compared to Eve, much less me."

"Perhaps you're not nearly as recovered as you claim." Emily summoned golden fire of her own. "Let's put it to the test."

His eyes flared when he saw her power. "How did you—" Elohim's eyelids grew heavy and nearly closed. He abruptly shook himself awake and glared at Vitania. "Quiet, witch!" He thrust out his hand and an invisible force knocked the Siren off her feet. His other hand flung crackling energy orbs at us.

I instinctively threw up a shield with Apocryphan power and was amazed when Elohim's attacks splashed off of it. The last time Vitania tried to sing him to sleep, he'd immediately stopped her, but this time she'd nearly knocked him out. That meant Elohim wasn't nearly as recovered as claimed. It meant we might have a chance.

I fired a green beam back at him. He blurred to the side, too quickly for me to hit him. Xanos fired from the other side and caged him in. He leapt in the air, but Emily fired another beam, trapping him in our triangle of death.

Elohim hurled more orbs at us, giving us no choice but to shield ourselves. He dropped to the ground and summoned a massive ball of white fire. I began to have my doubts that I could shield this one.

Conrad tugged my sleeve. "Justin, we need to get next to the fount."

"What good will that do us?" I said.

"I can link us directly to the fount and it might give you enough power to stop him."

I shrugged. "Let's do it."

Elohim hurled his massive fireball. We scattered to the sides as it rolled across the meadow, crushing trees and burning everything in its path.

"It's like god damned Indiana Jones out here!" Shelton shouted as he and the others ran for cover.

I picked up Conrad, then Emily, Xanos, and I sprinted for the fount a few hundred feet from Elohim. The god's eyes glowed white with malice. He thrust out a hand and an invisible force struck my shoulder, nearly causing me to spin out.

"They're invisible shields, Justin." Conrad's words jolted from his mouth with every step.

I switched to demon view as Elohim thrust his hand out again. A ghostly wall formed in front of me. It wasn't moving, but it didn't need to be. If I struck it at this speed, it would knock me out. I dodged out of the way, then zipped aside for the next barrier he summoned.

Confusion and frustration mounted on Elohim's face, as if he couldn't understand how I knew when to dodge. Since he'd never been a Daemos, it was possible he didn't realize what I was doing.

We reached the shore. Conrad leapt off my back and waded into the water. His eyes glowed azure as the pure power of the fount flowed into him. He thrust out his fingers and electricity crackled, jumping into my chest.

I cried out in surprise and pain, and then there was only the power. The power arced through me and into Xanos and Emily. The golden aura around Emily glowed even brighter. For the first time ever, Elohim looked scared.

"You're energized." Conrad bared his teeth. "Go get that bastard."

We sprinted toward Elohim at super speed. Everything seemed to slow to a stop around us. Elohim, however moved only slightly slower than us. I slammed my fist into his stomach. Emily caught him in the groin with a massive knee slam. Xanos kicked his leg out from beneath him. Elohim shouted and fell in slow motion.

I rammed a fist against his back and he slammed into the ground hard enough to leave a crack.

A thick web of golden energy wrapped around Elohim's throat. Xanos threaded green Apocryphan power around Emily's and I joined it with my own. We tightened the noose, drawing it tighter and tighter. Elohim screamed and thrashed, energy building around his body as he fought to shield himself.

A brilliant flash of light blinded me. Scorching heat washed across my body and threw me back. Shelton shouted in alarm somewhere in the distance. I blinked the spots out of my eyes, but I was woozy from the blast. My vision blinked out and back on as I tried to climb to my feet. My skin was blackened and blistered. Xanos and Emily lay on the ground nearby, their skin cracked and bleeding.

I managed to climb to one knee. Looked up, and saw Elohim

sneering malevolently as he stalked my way. He spoke, but the ringing in my ears was too loud to make out most of his words.

Shelton was shouting something over and over. Elohim's gaze found something behind me. His sneer widened and he spread his arms in greeting. I tried to turn and face the doom coming behind me, but I was so dizzy, I fell backward onto my ass.

A muscular figure shoved past me and Elohim's sneer evaporated. The figure wrapped his hand around Elohim's neck and squeezed. Tears pouring from his eyes, Apollyon strangled his creator, screaming, "Why make me bad, Father?"

Face red, eyes bugging, Elohim clenched his teeth and drove a fist into Apollyon's face. Power crackled and hummed as he tried to burn his creation to ash. But his burning white power hit Apollyon's corruption aura, converting from raw energy to thick crimson flesh veined with black. The flesh vines swallowed father and son, casting a foul stench into the air.

Emily yanked me off the ground and helped Xanos up. We watched helplessly, unable to see what was happening as the cancerous mass of flesh continued growing.

"Ungrateful child!" Elohim screamed from within. "You were too perfect! I could not have a god greater than me."

The mass burst like a popped pimple. Rancid smelling fluid sprayed in all directions. I threw up a shield to keep us out of it. Grass wilted and died where the fluid touched. Elohim and Apollyon appeared again, both of them battered and bruised.

Elohim slammed Apollyon to the ground, and threw him toward the primal fount. Before his son could recover, he shoved his face into the azure waters. Apollyon screamed in agony. Black veins criss-crossed over the fount and the ground trembled. Elohim kicked him in the ribs and Apollyon rolled into the waters.

The surface roiled. Black smoke poured into the air as the corrupted god sank.

Conrad shouted in pain and dove from the water back to dry land. "He's corrupting the primal fount! The backlash could destroy everything!"

40

As if we needed one more thing to worry about, it seemed Apollyon's taint was about to destroy the fount and probably all of creation.

Elohim staggered a few feet from the fount and fell to his knees, exhausted from the brawl. Emily raced past him and dove into the water. Black veins grasped at her as she swam toward the pulsating source. I ran to the water's edge and looked down, but she and Apollyon vanished into the depths. The trembling abruptly stopped and the fizzing black water faded and dispersed.

Screaming, Xanos channeled green energy blades on her fists and plunged them into Elohim's chest. His mouth formed a silent O and his eyes went wide. I channeled a blade and slashed at his neck, cutting deep, but not deep enough. Conrad joined us, reaching a hand toward the now-clear waters and drawing power from it. He summoned an azure blade and cleaved Elohim's head cleanly off.

The body fell twitching. Elohim's mouth tried to scream, but there was no air. Power arced between his neck and head, as if it were trying to draw it back together to heal it. Conrad stabbed a needle of power straight through Elohim's brain. The eyes crossed and the mouth fell open. The body continued twitching, so Conrad stabbed the needle through the heart, twisted, and slashed open the body cavity.

He disemboweled Elohim with savage strokes, continuing until the body twitched its last. Xanos and I stared at him in open-mouthed horror and disbelief. Conrad released the power and stared at the blood coating his hands.

"I killed my father, and now I have killed a god." Tears trickled down his cheeks, leaving streaks of blood. "Why me?"

I had no words of comfort for him. The sudden events left me uncharacteristically speechless. So I hugged him. Conrad shook with sobs for a moment, before taking a deep breath and backing away.

"Thank you, Justin."

I managed a smile. "There is nothing wrong with what you did. Elohim had to die."

Xanos looked down at the severed head and laughed. "I pray his spirit saw what he looked like before departing to the afterlife."

The crossed eyes and slack jaw were gruesomely funny. Elohim's body parts began to glow and a sick feeling passed through me. Had we killed him, or was he about to be reincarnated? With a brilliant flash, his body, blood, and entrails incinerated, reduced to sparkling motes drifting on the breeze.

A translucent bubble bobbed to the surface of the fount with Emily and Apollyon inside. The demigoddess cradled the god in her arms as she hamster-balled the bubble over to us. The bubble popped and she stepped ashore.

She looked around in alarm. "Where is Elohim?"

"Dead." I told her what had happened.

Tears trailed down her cheeks. "It's over?"

"I guess so." I shook my head. "Except for the part where we stop the collapse." I looked at the burden in her arms. "What happened to Apollyon?" I realized his beauty no longer hurt me to look at it.

Emily lay him on the ground. "I took him to the nothingness at the nexus of the founts. I thought it might cure his corruption but it killed him." She put a finger to his neck. "I don't understand."

I examined the body with demon vision. The aura remained, but the splinter and soul were gone. I frowned. "How is it possible that his soul is gone, but his power remains?"

Emily shrugged. "I don't know." She reached out as if grasping something. "I can't remove it. I think Elohim created the body with the powers and only inserted a soul into it later, but it's far beyond my understanding. Somehow, the body is still alive, but it won't be that way for long."

"And we're running short on gods to ask." I sighed.

"Holy farting fairies, that was epic." Shelton strolled over with the rest of the group close behind.

"Conrad, you did it!" Ambria wrapped her arms around him. "Are you okay, darling?"

His entire body seemed to relax. "I'll be fine, love."

Max grinned at me. "I don't even know what happened, but I thought for sure we'd lost when Elohim threw you, Emily, and Xanos away like rag dolls."

"You and me both." I shook my head. "Where the hell did Apollyon come from, anyway?"

"A gaggle of manikin demons flew him through the portal." Shelton threw up his hands. "I didn't even know what was going on until it was too late."

I spotted the short winged creatures on their knees, wailing at the sight of their fallen god. It was mind-twisting to watch demons mourn the very being who'd unintentionally twisted them into these monstrosities.

Emily sat on the grass and took a deep breath. "I'm too tired. I don't think I can do this."

Xanos leaned heavily on Adam for support. "We fought a dragon swarm and Elohim. I don't know how we can stop the collapse without resting again."

"We have to try, right?" I tried to summon some energy, but my brain felt like melting butter. "Maybe just a short nap will help."

Emily squeezed her eyes shut. "Just a short nap."

Elyssa took my hand and led me to a tree. She sat down beneath it and had me lay my head in her lap. "I promise I'll wake you up in an hour."

I kissed her hand. "We did it, babe. We killed Elohim."

"Are you angling for a lollipop, big boy?"

I snorted. "That's exactly the reward I want."

She smoothed my hair back. "Shut up and rest, okay? We don't have much time before the dark matter reaches Utopia."

I nodded somberly, closed my eyes, and entered a state of restful meditation.

"Justin." A hand prodded me. "Justin, wake up."

I opened my eyes and saw a blue-skinned version of me looking down. "Dude, I'm trying to rest so I can save the world."

Kalesh rolled his eyes. "I wouldn't have woken you if it wasn't important." He motioned toward the window. "I think I found something that might solve our problems, but encountered a problem."

I frowned. "What the hell did you find?"

"Not so much a what, but a who."

My interest was piqued. "Okay, show me." I got up and stretched. "By the way, that nom naval fleet was epic."

Kalesh shrugged. "It wasn't as much of a challenge getting them as I thought it would be."

"Well, let's hope it doesn't come back to bite us in the ass—provided we save the day here."

He nodded. "We'll deal with one universe-ending problem at a time."

I snorted. "What's the problem we need to solve?"

Kalesh stepped out of the window and crossed over the astral divide between my world and Haedaemos. My astral form followed him through the window on the other side. I emerged in Juranthemon instead of his room since that was his last location. Unity and much of the city center was nothing but white space, consumed by the collapse. Oblivion had nearly reached the palace.

"My god, half the city is gone."

Kalesh nodded. "Hopefully my idea is enough to stop it." He led me into a room.

I stopped and stared in confusion at the person standing there. "How in the hell is this supposed to help?"

The other person grinned. "Let me explain. No, there is too much. Let me sum up."

"You're quoting Princess Bride to me when the world is about to end?" I threw up my hands. "The apple doesn't fall far from the tree, does it?"

Another grin. "Nope."

They explained the idea to me and I realized it really was our last best chance. There was only one person who could help us overcome our issue, and I just knew they'd be delighted to help.

I went back to my imaginary apartment and woke myself up in the real world. I leapt up, shocking Elyssa from a light nap and ran over to our salvation. I put a hand on Emily's shoulder and shook it. "Wake up. I need your help."

Blinking blearily, she pushed up. "Why in the bloody hell did you wake me? I had to get Vitania to sing me to sleep because my mind was too restless."

"We're too tired to stop the collapse, Emily. By the time we're rested, Utopia and three other worlds will have collided with the dark matter from the Abyss."

Emily scowled. "You woke me just to tell me that? What in the hell is wrong with you?"

"Kalesh came up with an idea that might work, but we need your help." I told her what we needed and her mouth fell open.

"Yes, at once!" All signs of exhaustion fell away and she ran toward the still form lying on the ground where she'd left it. Emily put her fingers to Apollyon's neck and sighed with relief. "There's still a pulse, but it's weak."

I gripped her hand. "Let's do it."

She nodded and closed her eyes. "I'm ready."

I found Kalesh through the window of my soul. *We're ready.*

Hope this works.

It's got to. I reached through the window and pulled on another hand, drawing the spirit through.

Emily's grip tightened as she found the new presence in my body. Memories that weren't my own flashed through my head as I allowed a demon to possess my body. I felt like a voyeur watching years' worth of private moments that I never should have been privy to.

Amusement rippled through the demon at my reaction. *Bet you never picture Emily doing that, did you?*

Someone might wonder how a demon had such memories of Emily. That was because this was no ordinary demon. It was Grimsvokull, also known as Tyler Rock.

Tyler, are you purposefully letting me see your and Emily's live-action porno memories?

He chuckled inside my head. *Nope, it's purely unintentional. Just enjoy the show while it lasts.*

Elyssa is going to kill me!

He chuckled again.

A long time ago in a city far, far away, Grimsvokull had found new life by possessing a man just as the man's soul left the body. That perfect timing and the synergy of a jade spirit with human form had allowed him to live as the human, Tyler Rock. Kalesh figured that if it had worked with an empty human body, it might just work with an empty god body.

There was just one catch. Since Apollyon's soul was long gone, there was no soul for the spirit to bond to as there had been with Tyler's body.

We were hoping Emily could handle that part.

Judging from the way her face screwed up in concentration, things weren't going easily or well. A terrible pain abruptly passed through my entire being. I screamed in blinding agony and consciousness blinked off. It could have only been for an instant, but it felt like a small eternity.

Apollyon's body convulsed and screamed like a man being burned alive. Playback of the life and times of Tyler and Emily vanished from my mind. But the pain was still there, like a cut in the very fabric of my being.

"Emily!" Apollyon looked up into her eyes and shivered.

Her eyes flared. "Tyler?"

He tenderly touched her cheek. "Yes, baby, it's me."

"Tyler!" She released my hand and pulled him in for a passionate kiss.

I vaguely noticed the rest of the group had gathered around us, completely confused as to what in the hell we were up to. I pushed to my feet and winced at the awful pain in my abdomen. It didn't feel like a flesh wound, but something even deeper. To make matters worse, I had a really awkward boner, thanks to all the mind porn.

I gripped her shoulder. "Emily, what did you do to me?"

She blinked as if startled from a dream. "I'm terribly sorry, Justin. To make it work, I need a soul, so I took a part of yours and bound it to Apollyon. It was enough to anchor Tyler's spirit there."

"Why not use your soul?" I said.

"Because yours is strong enough to handle the damage and knows how to bond with a demon spirit." Emily touched my hand. "It will heal quickly, I promise."

"I hope so, because it hurts like a bitch." I looked at Apollyon's former body. "I guess you're Tyler now? Or do we need to start calling you Apollyon?"

"Tyler," he said firmly. Gone was Apollyon's meek and anguished voice. He sounded nearly identical to Tyler in his old body. He stood straight, shoulders back. He looked like a completely different person. "I can feel the powers, but I don't know what to do with them."

"You can bolster Emily and allow her to do what needs to be done," Vitania said. "We must hurry while there's still time."

Tyler grimaced sheepishly. "Uh, explain how to bolster someone, please."

Vitania instructed him, showing him how to do what needed to be done over the course of the next several minutes. When they were ready, Emily and Tyler stepped into the primal fount. Without the corruption aura, there was no reaction to his presence.

"Conrad must be the conduit," Vitania said. "His symbiotic relationship with the fount will help."

"Whoa, this is so weird." Tyler held an orb of golden power in one hand while gently poking it with the fingers of his other hand. "Does this mean Emily can't kick my ass anymore?"

Emily punched his shoulder. "Don't count on it, Mr. Rock."

A smoldering smirk crossed his face. Despite his beautiful new face, it looked exactly like the same smirk I'd seen in his memories before he tore off Emily's clothes and did some pretty creative things with her.

"Tyler, you're smoldering. You need to stop it and concentrate on saving the universe."

He touched his face. "I'm smoldering? I didn't mean to." He cleared his throat. "I suppose the fun stuff can wait." He winked at me. "You know what I'm talking about, right?"

Elyssa frowned at me. "What does he mean by that?"

"Uh, let's talk about that later." I put my arm around her shoulder. "I'm going to enjoy sitting back and watching someone else save the universe for once."

Tyler put a hand on Emily's back. Golden power suffused her aura, bolstering her strength.

Vitania gave her the crystalis. "Tap into it gradually, child. You are not a full god and it might burn you out."

"Wasn't Apollyon a full god?" Adam said. "Maybe he should hold it."

"Tyler doesn't know how to use it," Vitania said.

Adam pushed a finger up his nose despite having no glasses. "Yes, but Tyler can be the circuit breaker, so to speak, while Emily draws the power through him."

Vitania pursed her lips and seemed to think about it. "Perhaps you're right. You are quite intelligent for a human."

"You've told me that before," he said with a grin. "I appreciate it."

Vitania smiled at him.

Shelton groaned. "Hot damn, he's seducing Vitania now. How in the hell does he do that?"

Xanos smiled gently. "By being intelligent and kind."

Shelton rolled his eyes.

Emily handed Tyler the crystalis. "Let's see how this goes."

He cradled it in the palm of his hand. "I just hold it?"

She nodded and closed her eyes. A pinpoint of light brightened in the center of the crystalis.

Tyler flinched, but held onto it.

Emily drew in a breath and the world around us warped as if drawing a breath of its own

"Oh, my." She smiled. "Tyler, you're thinking naughty thoughts."

Shelton groaned. "Hey, if you're not careful, you're going to cause an interdimensional trans-species orgy to break out. So concentrate!"

Adam's eyes widened. "Imagine posting that video on Pornhub."

Emily's face grew serious. "You're right. It's just hard to concentrate with so much power."

"Ground yourself to my voice." Vitania touched her shoulder. "Draw upon the power slowly. Allow the realms to appear before you."

Emily nodded. "I see them."

"Find the quantum tunnels binding them together."

"I see them. The realm are balls of yarn, their strands tangled with all the other realms." Emily gritted her teeth. "It's overwhelming me!" Her eyes opened and she gasped. "I can't do it!"

She fell to her knees, body sagging in defeat.

41

Vitania took Emily's hand and lifted her to her feet. "You can do it, dear. Let the feelings wash over you. Give yourself time to adjust."

Emily shook her head. "I didn't know which way was up or down, left or right. My anxiety overwhelmed me."

"Yes, child. That's because you're tinkering with our entire realm-verse." Vitania tightened the grip on her hand. "Now, close your eyes and just do it."

Emily looked ashamed. "Yes, Vitania." She closed her eyes and shuddered. "I see everything and it hurts so much."

"Take a moment," Vitania said. "Let your mind adjust to the magnitude."

Moaning, body twitching in pain, Emily kept her eyes closed.

"I'm here with you, babe," Tyler said. "I will always be with you."

Emily seemed to relax slightly and nodded. "It's not so bad now."

"Good, child, good." Vitania paused another moment before continuing. "Now reach out and gently touch the dark matter encroaching on Utopia. Stop its momentum."

Emily didn't move her hands, but her brow furrowed in concentration. "They're too heavy. I can't stop them."

"Draw upon the crystalis, child. Use its power to aid you."

Emily jaw tightened. "Yes, it's working. It's working!"

"Whoa, I see it too." Tyler looked around, but his open eyes weren't looking at us. He apparently saw what Emily did.

Vitania patted her hand. "Is Utopia safe?"

Emily scowled. "I moved the dark matter further out, but it won't stay in place. It keeps moving inward no matter what I do."

"Push it harder. Give it momentum in the opposite direction."

"Okay." Her face went through varying degrees of concentration. "They move away for a moment, but then start falling back inward. Something is pulling on the strings."

Vitania sighed. "It seems the gravity of Juranthemon is constant. There is no way to stop it unless the assembled pieces are broken apart again."

I shook my head. "You can't do that. If you do, Apollyon's body becomes the Beast again, doesn't it?"

Vitania frowned. "With Elohim dead and Apollyon's body no longer encumbered by corruption, I don't know what would happen."

Tyler's eyes widened. "I just now imagined us breaking Juranthemon apart and had a vision. With the primary pieces missing, it would create a paradox that slowly ripples across our universe, killing entire worlds."

Shelton grimaced. "Uh, okay, not an option."

Adam nodded. "That makes sense. It would cause a tear in the time-space continuum. The only option is to figure out how to negate the gravity from Juranthemon."

Emily shook her head. "The gravity isn't very strong, but it's relentless. The moment I release any of the pieces, they begin to fall inward again."

"After entering the new data, the simulations don't look promising." Adam tapped on his phone screen. "Even if we relocate the dark matter elsewhere, the realms still fall inward and collide."

Emily opened her eyes. "There's only one thing left to do."

Vitania raised an eyebrow. "What do you mean, child?"

Emily closed her eyes and went silent.

"Child, what are you doing?" Vitania gripped her arm. "Answer me."

Tyler frowned. "You sure about this, Em?"

Emily nodded. "Yes. It's the only thing that makes sense."

Conrad also seemed locked in the same vision with them. "Do it, Emily."

Ambria's eyes flared. "If Conrad thinks it's okay, then do it."

The mountain began to quake. Everyone struggled to stay upright as the very fabric of the universe seemed to come apart around us.

Vitania's eyes grew wide. "Child, you're using too much power!"

Tyler's body glowed bright. His teeth clenched in concentration. "I've got you, Em!"

The ground shook and reality flickered between a white void and Olympus. The roar of the quaking earth grew deafening. The world blinked away, leaving nothing but darkness and silence and just as quickly blinked back. It repeated in rapid succession, and then, darkness.

Elyssa's hand was no longer there. I flailed in the nothingness, straining my lungs to shout, but there was no air, no sounds, only oblivion.

Darkness flickered.

I stood on a vast desert plain. Elyssa, Shelton, and the others looked around in confusion. Emily, Tyler, Conrad, and Vitania were missing.

Shelton spoke. "What in the actual f—"

Reality blinked away, casting me into oblivion once more. Before I could try to shout in surprise, Olympus flickered back into being. I stumbled into Elyssa and we tumbled to the ground.

"—uck! Shelton shouted.

Emily toppled over, splashing facedown into the fount. Tyler picked her up, worry pinching his brow. Conrad looked tired, but satisfied. Vitania stepped out of the azure waters, face pale, body trembling.

I pushed to my feet. "Vitania, what did she do?"

The Siren pinched the bridge of her nose and closed her eyes.

I gripped her shoulders. "What did she do, Vitania?"

She smiled gently. "I only know what she tried to do."

Shelton looked from the unconscious Emily to Vitania. "And that is?"

"She sped up the collapse, allowing to disparate realms to crash together into one Earth again. In the interim, I believe she moved all living beings into limbo so they would survive."

"She juggled beings from hundreds of realms, keeping them just a heartbeat away from death as their realm smashed back to the origin." Tyler looked as proud as a new father. "That's not all she did. Turn around." He stood and pointed behind us.

I rotated and my mouth dropped open. The entire world seemed to spread out beneath our perch on Olympus. "What in the hell?"

"She put Earth back together again, sort of." He shook his head. "All the realms are gone, and all the organisms and plant life from every realm except for Eden are now on Alden."

Adam shook his head like a wet dog. "The crystalis gave her the power to move entire worlds at once?"

"Well, yeah." Tyler grinned. "That crystalis is the most potent power-up in the universe."

"Uh, so she moved all of life on Eden back to Earth after it recombined?" I said.

Tyler nodded. "She tossed everything and everyone in Atlantis into oblivion just to make sure no one died."

"She did all that in under a minute?" Shelton frowned. "How in the hell?"

Tyler waggled a hand. "Uh, this might seem weird, but she's been at this for weeks. You spent most of your time in a dream state."

We all looked at each other in confusion. "Weeks?"

He nodded. "She worked nonstop. If she'd taken even a small break, entire civilizations might have gone extinct."

Shelton slapped his forehead. "Man, Alden must be one hot mess with so many races shoved together. Why in the hell did she give Eden a pass?"

"Because evolution in the others realms diverged wildly and she wanted Earth to be as close to the original possible." Tyler shrugged. "She's probably biased toward humans if you ask me."

Shelton snorted. "Thank god for that."

"Alden will need a lot of work with so many incompatible biomes in close proximity." Tyler pursed his lips. "It's a huge mess."

"What about the Utopian humans?" I asked.

"They're on Alden too." He pointed toward a sparkling coastal city in the distance. "Our forces, however, are still in and around Atlantis."

Elyssa dropped to her haunches, staring out at the new world in disbelief. "Eden is Earth again."

I began to sing, "A whole new world. A new fantastic point of view."

Shelton clamped a hand over my mouth. "Don't ruin the moment, Justin. That's my job."

Adam stared in awe from Emily to the earthly vista below. "Is there anything she can't do?"

Tyler smirked. "The crystalis is used up. She's back to being a plain old demigoddess."

"Yeah, but you're in Apollyon's body," Adam said. "You're a god."

He shrugged. "Sort of. Using myself as a conduit is one thing, but I have no idea how Apollyon's powers work. It'll be a major learning process."

"Is Juranthemon back?" I asked.

He waggled a hand. "It had to come back to complete the collapse, but she was able to move it to Alden." He grinned. "She left one chunk of it on purpose."

"What about Haedaemos?"

"Emily couldn't figure out how to give spirit beings physical bodies, so she preserved it."

"There's no way the noms won't notice all the changes. Atlantis is back. Olympus is real." I shook my head. "And why'd she leave a chunk of Juranthemon behind?"

Tyler grinned again. "Just a reminder to certain people."

I didn't know what he meant, but in the grand scheme of things, it wasn't that important.

"Emily put protections around Atlantis and Olympus," Tyler said. "Noms will unconsciously avoid the area and it'll show up as ocean to satellites. So it's not as bad as you think."

"How in the hell can you hide this much land?" Shelton shook his head. "The noms are gonna start asking questions and there ain't much we can do to stop it."

"No, but we'll have time to bring them around," Elyssa said. "Hopefully."

Tyler shrugged. "It's better than annihilation."

Shelton raised a hand. "Amen to that!"

"I want to explore!" Xanos took Adam's hand. "Come with me?"

He nodded. "Sure—" before he could finish, she wrapped an arm around his waist and they flew into the clouds.

Shelton snorted. "Adam really bit off more than he can chew this time."

I sat down against a tree and pulled Elyssa closer to me. "I'm both delighted and terrified about what comes next. It'll be more challenging than ever."

She nodded. "Probably. But at least now we have that chance."

"There's just one other issue." Tyler set Emily gently on the ground and kissed her forehead. "Just before she finished, I saw something—a tear in the darkness. There was something cold and alien watching from the other side."

"We are back in the multiverse now," Vitania said softly. "The outsiders have been waiting and watching."

Shelton face-palmed. "Christ almighty! Can we get five minutes of peace around here?"

"They may mean us no ill will." Vitania shrugged. "But we will have to be vigilant. The Overworld will take on a far more literal meaning now."

"Just wait until the noms figure out where Alden is." Tyler chuckled. "They are going to freak out."

Elyssa's eyes flared. "Where is it?"

"On the other side of the sun from Earth." He guffawed. "They won't even know it's there unless a space probe thingy picks it up."

Ambria raised her eyebrows and turned to Conrad. "Why did you let Emily do all this? We would have been perfectly happy keeping the realms!"

Conrad shook his head. "The realms wouldn't stay in place. We needed a permanent solution." A dreamy smile came over his face. "It was amazing to watch."

Max patted his friend on the back. "You did a fine job, Conrad. I wish I could've watched her juggle worlds."

Shelton clapped his hands and rubbed them together. "Well, I'm starving, and we need to make damned sure pizza, tacos, and burgers weren't fundamentally altered with everything else. So, who's in?"

"Me!" Max thrust a hand into the air.

Tyler grinned. "I could totally use a taco right now."

Elyssa smiled. "I'd love a taco and a huge margarita."

"Me too." I hopped up. "Where do you want to go? The sky's the limit."

Elyssa shrugged. "There's a good place in Toco Hills not far from the Ranch."

I tapped my com badge and told Adam where we were going. "Meet us there later if you're not too busy."

"We'll be there!" Adam said. "We'll grab Cinder on the way."

I chuckled as I imagined Xanos cradling Adam and Cinder in each arm in flight.

"I need to debrief my father first," Elyssa said.

I opened a portal back to Atlantis. The city looked much the same, an island in the ocean. The black spires of the fake Olympus were gone, replaced by the true home of the gods, though it looked much more ordinary from ground level. There was probably some heavy duty god magic hiding its true nature even though it was now part of the Earth realm.

The Eden forces—or were they Earth forces now?—were celebrating in full force. Nom sailors and pilots caroused with Atlanteans, vampires, fae, and too many other races to count. It was so surreal, I caught myself stopping and staring in disbelief more than once.

Elyssa spoke briefly with Thomas, but he was already knee-deep in meetings with Overworld leaders and the infernus who'd orchestrated the nom help. They were probably trying to mitigate the spread of information as best they could before allowing the nom vessels to leave.

She emerged from the administration building, took my hand and led me back to our friends. "Let's get out of here."

I opened a portal and took our crew back to the Ranch. We parted ways to shower off since most of us smelled like yesterday's seafood dinner. As for myself, I was still covered in Drakara's brains and the odor was starting to make me queasy.

We met in the underground parking deck a little later. I requisitioned a sprinter van since I wanted nothing to do with magic for at least an hour. Elyssa, Shelton, Bella, Max, Ambria, Conrad, and Tyler piled inside.

"You certainly can't go in looking so bloody perfect," Ambria said to Tyler. She fashioned an illusion to make him look moderately less attractive. "At least you're not so beautiful it hurts anymore."

"I think that was Apollyon's corruption aura," Tyler said. "Because now I'm ruggedly handsome and not beautiful."

Ambria snorted. "I'm sorry, but even in your old body you were a beautiful man. There's nothing wrong with that."

"Emily might still like you," Conrad said with a grin.

I flinched. "Holy crap. Did I just hear Conrad crack a joke?"

"He needs practice," Shelton said. "But it wasn't bad."

Ambria kissed Conrad's cheek. "He's got a great sense of humor when he's not out slaying gods."

Shelton barked a laugh. "He's a good kid."

It was three in the afternoon when we reached our destination. The waiter didn't seem sure about seating so many people since plague restrictions were still in effect, but the restaurant was mostly empty so the manager gave us a pass. Xanos, Adam, and Cinder showed up not long after. The wait staff were completely enamored with Xanos's purple skin and exotic eyes, but thankfully thought it was cosplay and not real.

Once our margaritas arrived, Shelton filled a glass and raised it.

"Seems like just yesterday I was toasting the end of the Second Seraphim War, but we spent the interim fighting for our lives in Seraphina and barely had enough time to wipe our asses when we got back to Eden before Xanos here threw us for a loop."

Xanos looked down, ashamed. "I was a fool and readily admit it. I can never bring back all the lives lost in my terrible war."

"Well, you helped us save billions of lives, so that counts for something," Elyssa said. "It's not my place to forgive you, but so long as you don't ever try world domination again, then you're okay in my book."

Xanos nodded. "Thank you."

Adam patted her shoulder. "That's the power of friendship."

Shelton cleared his throat. "As I was saying, here's to friends and to at least an hour of peace so we can eat our goddamned tacos."

I raised my glass. "Amen!"

Tyler raised his. "Cheers!"

A couple of nearby patrons and waiters watched us curiously, probably wondering if any of us were in our right minds or maybe just role playing. I couldn't believe Emily had so smoothly recombined Earth that many noms still didn't realize what had happened.

It was the best of times. It was the worst of times. But most importantly, it was taco time. We spent hours telling and retelling stories, reliving memories, and simply enjoying life.

I caught the closed captions from a newscast on a television mounted on the wall nearby. The United Nations was apparently calling an emergency meeting to talk about something they were calling the Blip. I motioned toward the manager and asked him to turn up the volume so we could hear it.

He found the controller and obliged.

"They're calling it the Blip," the newscaster said. "Nearly everyone, including this news anchor, experienced a collective blip of darkness and unconsciousness. Amazingly, there were no major accidents or deaths reported." He continued speaking, switching to a reporter at the White House that was waiting on the President to speak.

Shelton groaned. "Well, at least we gave them something to freak out about."

"While we're waiting on the President, there are other developments in Portugal." The newscast switched to a view of giant statues. "The strange buildings and structures that had been appearing out of thin air on the coast apparently vanished during the blip, leaving behind only these massive statues. For more on the story, here's our local reporter, Carol Baskin."

A middle-aged woman appeared on the screen. "Thanks, Joe. As you know, scientists have been absolutely baffled by the appearance and now disappearance of the structures most locals claim were placed here by aliens. Now there are these statues, and at their base, a small plaque reading, and I quote, 'The gods are dead. We are the only ones responsible for our collective destiny."

Carol nodded solemnly. "If aliens placed these here, then maybe they're trying to tell us something, Joe."

The view switched back to the newscaster. "An interesting warning indeed, Carol. Do the local authorities believe this might be a prank?"

Carol stared at the massive statues and then back to Joe in disbelief. "It would take a monumental effort to build the original structures, remove them, and replace them with statues in such a short amount of time." She waved a hand at them. "They are intricate works of art despite their size."

The statues did indeed look almost alive. Emily had done almost too good a job. As the camera panned, I noticed one statue apart from the others, kneeling not standing.

Xanos gasped. "That is me."

Adam grimaced and nodded. "I guess Emily wanted a constant reminder for you too."

Xanos gulped. "Message received."

Shelton sighed. "Well, it was nice while it lasted. Guess the Custodians are going to have their hands full."

Elyssa nodded. "It's better this than extinction. The Overworld of old is gone and there's no telling what lies ahead, but as long as we're alive, I think anything is possible."

Shelton grinned. "Careful, you're starting to sound like Justin."

Elyssa hugged my arm. "Are you ready for another adventure?"

I gently stroked her cheek with the back of my other hand. "Life is always an adventure with you."

I didn't know what this new world held in store for us, but one thing was certain—it would be anything but boring.

ABOUT THE AUTHOR

John Corwin is the bestselling author of the Overworld Chronicles. He enjoys long walks on the beach and is a firm believer in puppies and kittens.

After years of getting into trouble thanks to his overactive imagination, John abandoned his male modeling career to write books.

He resides in Atlanta.

Connect with John Corwin online:
Facebook: https://www.facebook.com/groups/overworldconclave
Website: http://www.johncorwin.net
Twitter: http://twitter.com/#!/John_Corwin

www.ingramcontent.com/pod-product-compliance
Lightning Source LLC
Chambersburg PA
CBHW021129260626
47169CB00005B/1517